A Journey to My Life

A novel

Rhonda Mumby

Copyright © 2024 by Rhonda Mumby

All rights reserved.

No part of this publication may be reproduced, distributed, or transmitted in any form or by any means, including photocopying, recording, or other electronic or mechanical methods, without the prior written permission of the publisher, except as permitted by U.S. copyright law. For permission requests, contact Rhonda Mumby by email at booksbyrvm@gmail.com.

ISBN 979-8-9911979-0-8 (Hardcover Edition)

ISBN 979-8-9911979-1-5 (Paperback Edition)

ISBN 979-8-9911979-2-2 (eBook Edition)

The story, all names, characters, and incidents portrayed in this production are fictitious. No identification with actual persons (living or deceased), places, buildings, and products is intended or should be inferred.

Book Cover by Rhonda Mumby.

First edition 2024

For RVM,
and other indie authors,
who never gave up on the dream.
You're doing it, kid!

Contents

The Playlist	VII
1. My So-Called Life	1
2. Who Let Me Drink?	9
3. An Attack of Electricity in the Mystery Section	20
4. Hey, Ground, You Can Swallow Me Now	26
5. I Don't Know Why I Try	31
6. Don't Stop Believin'	44
7. Let the Sunshine In	54
8. Emotional Whiplash, Is That a Thing?	66
9. A Tour of More Than the City	74
10. Let It Be Me	87
11. One Too Many Surprises	100
12. An Unwanted Shove Down Memory Lane	111
13. Did I Ever Really Know You?	121
14. No Turning Back	138
15. Can Love Be Enough?	149

16.	Sometimes, Love Just Ain't Enough	156
17.	Excuse Me? I'd Like to Get Off This Ride Now.	171
18.	Our New Normal	182
19.	Luck of the Irish?	196
20.	Are We Out of the Woods Yet?	207
21.	I Don't Want to Be in the Woods Anymore	219
22.	You Are the Best Thing	227
23.	My Life, My Love, My Everything	241
24.	I'll Follow You Into the Dark	254
25.	But I Need You to Stay with Me in the Light	268
26.	Echo	284
27.	After the Storm	295
28.	Wait. What?	306
29.	W.T.F.	312
30.	Mommie Dearest	322
31.	Tropical Depression Victoria	336
32.	I Don't Apologize (for Once)	350
33.	Who's Crashing?	357
34.	I Love You More. Always.	363
35.	Just When You Think Your Journey Is Over . . .	367
Epilogue		377
Acknowledgements		381

The Playlist

Page to start song: Artist – Song

   P. 4: The Bravery – "Believe"

   P. 10: Usher – "Numb"

   P. 13: Damien Rice – "Volcano"

   P. 18: Greg Laswell – "Comes and Goes (In Waves)"

   P. 22: Taylor Swift (feat. Ed Sheeran) – "Everything Has Changed"

   P. 27: Band of Horses – "The Funeral"

   P. 40: A Fine Frenzy – "Almost Lover"

   P. 44: Sia – "Breathe Me"

   P. 50: Dave Matthews Band – "Crush"

   P. 62: OneRepublic – "Feel Again"

   P. 78: Taylor Swift – "State of Grace (Taylor's Version)"

   P. 84: Paramore – "The Only Exception"

   P. 93: Ingrid Michaelson – "Can't Help Falling in Love (Live at Daytrotter)"

   P. 97: Ray LaMontagne – "Let It Be Me"

   P. 101: Sara Bareilles – "In Your Eyes (Live)"

   P. 107: Jason Walker – "Down"

   P. 117: Erin McCarley – "Gotta Figure This Out"

   P. 121: Helen Jane Long – "Turn Away"

   P. 129: Sia – "I'm in Here (Acoustic Version)"

   P. 132: Helen Jane Long – "Through the Dark"

P. 135: Evanescence – "My Immortal"
P. 140: Christina Perri – "Arms"
P. 160: Faith Hill – "Holly Jolly Christmas"
P. 171: Helen Jane Long – "Eclipse"
P. 179: Mat Kearney – "Won't Back Down"
P. 182: Matt Nathanson – "Bulletproof Weeks"
P. 196: Dave Matthews Band – "Where Are You Going"
P. 199: OneRepublic – "If I Lose Myself"
P. 207: The Civil Wars – "C'est La Mort"
P. 215: *Smash* Cast (feat. Katharine McPhee) – "Run"
P. 219: Radical Face – "Welcome Home, Son"
P. 221: Israel Kamakawiwo'ole – "Somewhere Over the Rainbow"
P. 231: Ray LaMontagne – "You Are the Best Thing"
P. 238: Mat Kearney – "All I Need"
P. 248: Christina Perri – "Penguin"
P. 251: Lykke Li – "Tonight"
P. 258: Counting Crows – "Colorblind"
P. 263: Lifehouse – "Storm"
P. 267: Death Cab for Cutie – "I Will Follow You into the Dark"
P. 281: Sia – "My Love"
P. 284: Helen Jane Long – "Echo"
P. 287: Solomon Burke – "Cry to Me (Single Version)"
P. 290: Jason Walker – "Echo"
P. 292: Helen Jane Long – "Stars"
P. 300: Mumford & Sons – "After the Storm"
P. 306: Ray LaMontagne – "A Falling Through"
P. 319: Christina Perri – "Here Comes the Sun"
P. 338: Johnny Mathis – "We Need a Little Christmas"
P. 350: Jimmy Eat World – "Hear You Me"
P. 353: Otherwise – "I Don't Apologize (1000 Pictures)"
P. 359: Live – "Lightning Crashes"
P. 364: Greg Laswell – "This Woman's Work"
P. 379: Charlene Soraia – "Wherever You Will Go"

Chapter One

My So-Called Life

DARKNESS SHADES MY periphery so that a singular focus demands my attention: a pair of matching mahogany boxes on display at the front of the room, an oddly incandescent light shining on both. I seem to float up the narrow aisle toward them, and as I near the substantial boxes, I realize what they are—my breath catches in my throat and my hand flies up, pressing into my chest to still my suddenly pounding heart.

I'm frozen at the end of the aisle, planted to the ground like a great oak, yet fearful I'll tumble backward as the dizziness consumes me and gravity pulls at my heavy limbs. My heart refuses to calm under my ice-cold hand. I look down, wondering if I can mentally force the erratic beating under control, but I find myself instead wondering where this black satin blouse came from—I don't even own a shirt like this. And this long, wispy black skirt that hovers just above a pair of shiny black boots with heels higher than anything I'd ever wear? *Emory*, I think. *I must have borrowed these clothes from Emory.* That makes more sense.

The pieces begin to click together in my mind: the black attire, the long aisle with rows of white chairs on either side, the sorrowful dirge playing from an organ somewhere unseen. The boxes: coffins. Tears threaten as realization dawns on me, but I don't cry. Struggling, I lift my heavy feet and shuffle to the first seat in the left-hand row of chairs. My body is on autopilot. I'm unable to make myself do anything other than what it tells me to do.

I look down at my hands. Suddenly, a paper appears, resting on my palms. A memorial card with the names Richard Templeton and Victoria Templeton in scrolling font. The date of the service catches my attention: December 13, 2008.

But that can't be right. Isn't it only August?

And then I'm inundated with sympathizers, one after another after another.

"You poor dear, let us know if you need anything. Anything at all," my neighbor consoles.

"So sorry for your loss."

"They will be missed."

I dutifully squeeze each hand that is shoved into mine, accepting every embrace placed around my shoulders. Glancing around the now crowded room, I wonder who all these people are. My neighbor I recognized, my physical education teacher from elementary school, the parents of a boyfriend I had sophomore year in high school. I crane my neck to locate Emory or Val; surely they are here somewhere to support me, comfort me.

"Abby, I'm so sorry. I can't believe this has happened." My best friend from high school scoops me into a tight embrace. I think of how good it is to see her—it's been . . . over three years?

"Thank you, Grace," I murmur and lean back to get a better look at her, only to see that her face has changed into someone I don't recognize. Startled, I push away and into the seat next to me. But the stranger is not alarmed or even offended; she merely straightens and walks away as another person reaches out to take my hand and offer condolences. I jerk my hand back, struggling to come up with some excuse to escape these strangers, then proceed to leap up and push past the stifling crowd that has filled the room. Confusion swarms around me, quickly followed by agitation as I realize I am lost among these people. I cannot find my way to an exit, or even to a familiar face who can explain what's going on here. I search frantically for Emory or Val, or Grace, or even my old neighbor. Someone, anyone I recognize.

I don't understand why all these people are here. They have no reason to be here, right? I don't know them. They didn't know them, did they? My parents?

I spin around, desperately scanning the faces surrounding me, hoping for someone familiar. Relief washes over me as everyone seems to fade away, disappearing as quickly as they appeared, until the room is empty once again. I halt my searching, confronted with the real reason I am here. My breath is stolen; my hands begin to tremble. The temperature plummets thirty degrees and now I'm shivering, cold to the bone. Standing mere inches from the coffins now, opened for viewing as they were not before, I notice the sprays of bloodred roses and snow-white baby's breath spilling across the deep mahogany. The darkness wraps around me, and a shudder racks my bones.

"HURRY UP, EMORY! We're going to be late!" I yell as I pull my hair into a ponytail. Checking my reflection in the mirror, I note how it's getting too long again, and I haven't had the money to go to the salon. I rub the bags under my eyes. The nightmares have been sapping my energy, making it hard to get a good night's rest. They're happening more frequently than ever—two, three times this week alone. I dab a bit of concealer under each eye to try to hide the evidence.

The clock on my nightstand shows five minutes have passed since the last time I looked at it, and I fear Emory is no more ready than she was five minutes ago. The stale mood plaguing me is briefly pushed aside by an adrenaline spike of stress. It's the first time in three days that I've felt anything other than numbness or despondency. Even as my pulse quickens in reaction to the stress Emory is causing, I realize I'm a bit relieved. Sometimes, when theses "moods" persist, I'm afraid I'll forget how to feel anything altogether.

"I'm trying to find a clean shirt," Emory's muffled voice calls from her room across our small apartment.

I roll my eyes. She hates to do laundry and therefore never has anything clean when she wants—or in this case *needs*—it. By twenty-two, you'd think she'd get the whole wash-my-clothes-so-they-are-clean-when-I-need-them thing figured out. Lucky for her, we work at the same place. I yank a spare shirt off a hanger in my closet and dash across the apartment.

"Here. Take one of mine." I toss it at her.

"Oh, thank God, Abby! You're a lifesaver!"

"I'm always saving *yours* anyway," I chuckle despite the situation.

She pulls on the Hooligan's Bar and Grill standard-issue polo, fluffs her golden-blond hair, and appraises her reflection in the mirror. My jealousy of her hair surfaces again; it's so much prettier than my own dirty-blond color. "I'm ready . . . oh, wait!"

"What now?" I ask incredulously.

"I need lip gloss!" Emory digs in her vanity drawer, oblivious to the frustration plastered across my face.

"Really, Ems! Come *on*!" I fold my arms across my chest and lean against the doorframe, knowing full well it could take another five minutes for her to find the right shade of gloss.

"Ready," she finally says and smacks her lips together, giving herself one last look in the mirror.

Well, that only took two minutes. Good. I point to the vanity after she turns and smiles at me. "Don't forget your hair tie."

"Oh, right!" She twirls around to grab it and then we're off. I glance at my watch as we run out the door. Five minutes late. We can make that up if we hurry.

About once a week we play out a similar scene. Emory's gotten better lately about prioritizing, but tonight she has this whole party she's been planning, and that threw her out of any sense of time. She spent most of the day running errands and setting up the apartment. I don't dare say a thing to her about how much stress she is causing because I know she'll blame me since I didn't help much with the prep. I'm just not enthused about having another party at our place. The last one ended in our apartment almost catching fire.

We run to the subway and sprint once we get off, so we manage to clock in as Jeff is starting his Teambuilding Speech for the night shift. I wouldn't have minded if we had missed it, although Jeff would have noticed we weren't here. A middle-aged single man with hair a little too long for his age and jeans with a little too much design on the butt pockets, he's made Hooligan's the pride of his life. He acts like a big brother, both as a boss and on a personal basis. But he can also get moody, especially when corporate comes down on him for poor store performance or a customer complaint. Then we have to tiptoe around for a few days or risk being in the line of fire.

I try my best to pay attention to his instructions as he rambles on about tonight's special and what rewards are being handed out to who sells the most of said special, but I find myself falling back into the fog that comforts me on a daily basis.

"Another uplifting pep rally," Dylan leans in toward Emory and mumbles as the group disperses and we head out front. "If you servers could get your act together and impress Jeff for a change, we bartenders wouldn't have to sit through those ridiculous team meetings," he chides.

"Aww, poor Dylan," she teases. "It's so hard being a big bad bartender, huh?"

"Yeah, yeah—make fun of us now," he says, nudging her arm. "But you wait till I talk to Jay and Donovan. Good luck gettin' your drink orders filled tonight, girlie!" He chuckles as he strides away.

Emory smiles after him and shakes her head.

"Your flirting is getting *so* old!"

"What—?" Her eyes snap to me.

"Oh, come on, Ems. It's so obvious you two have a thing for each other! Did you invite him to the party?"

"Um, no. I didn't. I can't decide if I can get past the redhead thing." She wrinkles her nose.

"The redhead thing?" I furrow my brow.

"Yeah. I mean, he's so cute, right? But I've just never liked red hair on a guy. It bothers me for some reason." She shrugs her shoulder.

"Silly reason not to give somebody a chance."

"Yeah, maybe you're right." Emory looks in Dylan's direction again. He catches her gaze and smiles.

"Uh-huh," I huff, shoving a handful of straws into my apron.

"Hey, Emory, Abby, see you at the party tonight, right?" a voice calls out, interrupting our conversation.

I look over toward the bar again. Donovan has a huge, excited grin on his face as he leans over it.

"You won't invite Dylan, but you invited *Donovan*?" I demand.

"Yeah, I felt bad for him," she answers defensively. "Kimber was asking me about it and he overheard. He kept hinting around, trying to get me to invite him.

I'm sorry! It won't be so bad, right? I know he's got a crush on you and all, but maybe he won't even show up."

I shake my head, disappointed in my friend. Donovan not show to what might be a huge event that's talked about for weeks to come? Who is she kidding? The guy waits outside video game stores for stupid stuff like *Aliens vs. Mafia* to be released at midnight. You can tell from his goofy face that this is a big deal for him. My heart sinks.

"Whatever, Ems. I have tables waiting." I wave my hand dismissively and go to work.

AT MY MEAL break, I sit in the stockroom at our tiny break table like usual and read my book. Right now, I'm working through *A Tale of Two Cities*. I'd started reading it during my freshman year at NYU, but I just couldn't get into it. Too much else going on then. I'm more than halfway through it now, determined to finish it this time for sure.

Emory catches me at the end of my break as I head to the front. I tuck my paperback into the left pocket of my apron.

"So, I mentioned to Dylan about the party," she gushes, "and at first he thought he had something going on tonight, but then I flashed my sad eyes and pouted." She gives me a sample of her sad-eyes-and-pouting look. "He caved! Said he could figure something out!" Emory flutters back to the stockroom, clearly very excited. I smile to myself as I walk out to check on my tables. Sometimes, you just have to give people a little push.

"Welcome to Hooligan's, home of the famous double-decker burgers!" I plaster my I-love-my-job smile across my face. "Our special tonight is the Sourdough Supreme and a draft beer of your choice for only $14.95. Enjoy a real San Francisco-style sandwich with our famous double-decker, one-hundred-percent Angus beef burger, Swiss and cheddar cheeses, and our special sauce. We have over fifty great beer choices on tap to suit any taste. What can I start you with?"

The two middle-aged gentlemen at table fourteen stare at me in amazement. I note their sharp sport coats with crisp button-up shirts; from their posture and demeanor, I feel certain this is the first bar and grill they have ever set foot in.

"Wow," says the one with salt-and-pepper hair, wearing a gray jacket.

"I'd say," comments the other one with dark brown hair, graying temples, and a navy jacket with a bright plaid shirt. "Are you required to memorize all that?"

"Well, we have to memorize the basics," I explain. "But they do allow us a little freestyle in the delivery."

"Very impressive delivery," Gray Coat says with a complimentary nod. "Tell me, young miss, what sandwich do *you* recommend? We've never been to Hooligan's before tonight. Thought we'd try something new." He gestures across the table to his friend.

"Yes, I would have been more than happy to have kept our reservations at Samurai NYC, but Geoffrey here thinks we should be adventurous. It's our fifteenth anniversary, which I guess is Burgers and Beer," he responds sarcastically.

Geoffrey shoots a warning glance across the table then looks back to me, awaiting my recommendation.

"Well, happy anniversary to you both!" I congratulate them, unfazed. "Umm, I would recommend the Angus Prime Double-Decker if you'd like a nice thick and juicy burger loaded with pepper jack cheese, tomato, lettuce, pickle, and steak sauce. Or, if you're looking for a spicy kick that lingers in your mouth long after it's gone, try the Chipotle Chaser Burger. That comes with fiery-hot breaded onion rings."

"I think I'll go with the second one. I could go for a little spice this evening." Gray Coat raises his eyebrow at Navy Jacket, who softens a bit.

"I shall have the Sourdough Special—no draft beer, though. I only drink imported and bottled. I'll take a Stella."

I laugh to myself as I turn to leave the table and enter the order. Occasionally, there are those customers that actually made this job interesting. I think this may be one of those interesting couples.

The night is so busy it flies by, and before I know it my shift is over. I checked on table fourteen a couple times and they seemed content. They lingered a bit longer than most customers, I assumed because they were taking in the atmosphere of very new surroundings. Both really enjoyed their burgers, though they seemed surprised by that. They were going to a comedy club after dinner, which neither had been to before either. I applauded them for their efforts to try new things and told them I hoped they enjoyed this experience enough to come back again.

Navy Jacket had noticed my book in my apron, and when I brought their check, he struck up a conversation with me about the lack of truly original bookstores nowadays. When he asked me where I shopped for books, I was ashamed to admit I had bought this one at a Big Books chain store with horrible artificial lighting and elevator music. He told me that if I was willing to be adventurous I should check out a small store called Food for Thought on 42nd Street; he thought I might find it appealing. I assured him I would and thanked him for the recommendation. I knew I would be sharing stories with my co-workers about my interesting table fourteen customers, but little did I know that these two men would become an important part of the fabric of my life in the not-so-distant future.

Chapter Two

Who Let Me Drink?

TEN O'CLOCK ARRIVES, and it's time to clean up and clock out. I find myself moving slowly, so dreading this party. I just want to go home and not have a bunch of people crammed in my apartment. I don't want to make conversation, I don't want to play drinking games, I don't want any of it.

"Let's go, let's go!" Emory practically rips my arm off as she throws her apron down and drags me out the backdoor.

We rush home almost as quickly as we had rushed to work earlier that day, Emory gabbing the whole time about party set up and who's going to be there. Our roommate, Val, hopefully has a good start on everything, but she can't always be relied upon when out shopping. She tends to easily lose track of time when shopping is involved. Luckily for us, we find that Val came through and most of the setup is done, music blaring as we bustle through the door of our apartment.

"Hurry up, you two! Get changed. People will be here any minute," she hollers over the music.

"Valencia! My hero!" Emory runs over and gives her a big hug. "The place looks fabulous. You did great."

"I know, right? Now get changed. Then you can help me get the rest of the bar set up."

In less than five minutes for me, ten for Emory, we're changed, makeup freshened, hair brushed out. I fill the kitchen sink with bottles of beer and ice while Val and Emory put together an elaborate display of various hard liquor bottles and fruity mixes on the counter beside me.

I'll admit, I'm starting to get a little excited about the party now. The apartment does look very festive, and we're already having a good time setting it up. It would be nice to fill my night with something other than the nagging loneliness that has become my companion so often lately. Truthfully, I don't have the money to go out like Val and Emory do, so much of the time I stay at home reading while they go out on the town. I feel an immediate lift in my mood once we pour ourselves the first drinks of the night.

"Templeton Rye and Pepsi," Val hands me a luau-themed plastic glass with little white flowers ringing the top. "I splurged on this just for you, Abby."

"Splurged for me?" I ask doubtfully as I sip my drink. I wave my hand at the bottles lined up on the counter next to us. "I doubt my bottle of Templeton was as expensive as some of these other ones."

"True, girl," she laughs. "Gotta have the good stuff if you're gonna have a good party, right Ems?"

"You know it!" Emory tips her glass into Val's. "Cheers!"

Val—being the loaded one of our crew—and Emory had been the ones to shop for the alcohol yesterday. A few hundred dollars spent on a party is no big deal to her. I, on the other hand, had no extra money to offer, so I prepared all the snacks and finger foods. Which worked out well because neither Val nor Emory has the patience to plan and prepare food for a party.

I sip on my drink and do a few rearrangements of the platters and bowls. "Thank you, though, for getting my Templeton." I had first tried Templeton Rye whiskey because it had my last name, Templeton, and because it's bottled in my home state of Iowa. It became my favorite for mixed drinks because of the flavor. The girls make fun of me because they prefer fruity drinks and margaritas. But I don't care—if I'm going to drink, I'm going to drink what I like!

Mere minutes later, people begin to arrive. By midnight, the party is in full swing. In addition to our co-workers, a bunch of Val's college buddies show up. It gets very crowded in the apartment. And very loud.

Dylan shows up with Jay and Donovan in tow. I notice with satisfaction that Emory barely leaves Dylan's side once he enters the apartment. They look like they are really vibing.

"You guys put together a great party!" Kimber hollers at me over the blaring music.

"Oh, not really me—mostly Emory and Val. But thanks."

"Oh! Donovan alert!" Kimber nods her head in the direction behind me. Then she whirls around and disappears into a group across the room.

Too late for me. I glance back and in one stride he's beside me. I turn and take a long drink, making a mental note to thank Kimber later for ditching me like this. Maybe I can pretend that I haven't seen him.

"Hey, Abby. Great party."

Nope.

"Uh, thanks." I only half-turn toward him so I won't seem interested. I search across the apartment for Emory or Val; surely they would help me escape.

"Sooo . . . work go okay tonight?"

"Yep," I say, my tone clipped. I take another long drink.

"Make a lot of tips?"

I shrug. "I did okay."

"Me, too. I was really working the ladies tonight. One gave me a twenty-dollar tip and her number." He stares at me—waiting for me to be impressed, I'm sure.

"Wow, Donovan, lucky you," I say in mock awe. I take another gulp. My drink is gone.

"Well, I mean, she was, like, fifty or something, so you know . . . not like I'd really call her or anything," he rambles. He notices me looking into the bottom of my empty cup. "Need another drink?"

"Yeah. Thanks, Donovan." I pass my glass, still not making eye contact. If I'm going to have to deal with him, I'm going to need a lot more alcohol.

"Hey," I grab his arm before he gets too far. "Templeton Rye and Pepsi—make sure—and ice."

"Whiskey?" He seems surprised. "My girl knows how to party!"

"Just no fruity crap!" I call after him.

I look around for Emory again. No sign of her or Dylan. I search for Val. She's wrapped around a guy I have never seen before on the couch sucking face. Obviously, she will be of no help to me. I think about darting to my room—there's no one else out here I really want to strike up a conversation with—but I won't be able to sleep with the loud music. I won't be able to get into *A Tale of Two Cities* either. So I'll no doubt end up lying in bed trying to fight off the familiar loneliness that has become my constant companion over the past few months.

Ever since I had to leave NYU, I've felt like I'm spiraling away from civilization into a deep black chasm that's pulled me in with enveloping arms. True, Emory dropped out of school too—failed out really. But she acted like it was no big deal. Me, on the other hand, I felt like a huge failure; I let the depression drag me under. Only Emory and Val have been able to pull me to the surface occasionally. And they have almost been successful again tonight. Well, for a little bit they have . . .

"Here you go, milady." Donovan holds out my drink and bows deeply.

What a dork.

"Thanks," I say flatly. I try to keep my body angled away from him. I wish he would take the hint and go bother someone else. Surely there is someone here who might be interested in Donovan. Someone other than *me*.

But he doesn't seem to be interested in talking to anyone else. To my chagrin, he really doesn't notice that I barely acknowledge his presence. There he stands, going on and on about his brother who went to college and how he should have gone to college. Then it's his comic book collection and all the places he's traveled to collect them, which leads into his stamp collection, which he quit adding to when he was in high school, but it is still really valuable.

I suck down the refill he gave me and reach over the island counter to grab a bottle of beer chilling in the sink. I twist off the top, put it between my thumb and middle finger, and snap it into the crowd. Take that, all you jerks who won't save me from this hell.

"Hey!" a girl yells, looking around to see where the offending object that hit her came from. I grin as I take a swig.

I was hoping that eventually the alcohol would help me drown out Donovan's babbling. But it hasn't so far. I glance over at him as he's flapping his yapper about work. I think about just walking away.

Then I really look at him. Maybe for the first time really study him. He has this naïve expression on his face, like he has absolutely no idea how annoying he is. Like he lives in his own world of collections and comic books and how cool it is he gets to be a bartender and have ladies hit on him, even if most of them are old enough to be his mother. Poor guy's probably never given much of a chance most of the time. And it's not like he's unattractive. Just *sooo* irritating. That's the thing that fools you about Donovan. He is decent-looking, normal-seeming, but once you get to know him, he annoys the crap out of you.

He finally takes a break from talking and gets us both refills. I wasn't done with my beer yet, but when he said he was getting another drink, I shoved my empty plastic cup into his hand.

When he returns, he is uncharacteristically quiet for a minute. I glance at him to see what the deal is: He's looking at my hair. I had taken it out of the ponytail as soon as we'd gotten home from work. It falls well past my shoulders now, and there's a slight wave from my shower earlier today. He picks up a lock and examines it intently. I briefly think about smacking his hand, but the alcohol is making me very calm and relaxed. I merely look at him with a raised eyebrow.

"Your hair is the color of honey mustard." He smiles at me like he's gotten a quiz show question correct.

I extricate my hair from his hand. "Really," I say. "Honey mustard."

"I love honey mustard. On my sandwiches, on a salad, even on my French fries. It's the perfect condiment."

I exhale forcefully and question why I can't just walk away from him. He'd get over it, right?

I finally catch sight of Emory. She and Dylan are holding hands, making their way over to our makeshift bar. As he makes their drinks, she looks over at me. Her eyes widen when she notices Donovan. She gestures with her index finger from her chest to me to see if I want her to come save me. Surprising myself, I wave her off. It's no longer painful to stand here and listen to him. It's actually kind of amusing. And I don't want to pull her away from Dylan when it looks like they're having a good time.

"You sure?" she mouths. I nod and raise my plastic glass to her. She raises hers in return. *Cheers.*

It's after three when I realize most of the party guests have gone. Donovan and I have somehow made our way over to the empty couch. Amazingly, the drunker he gets, the funnier he gets. Or maybe it's the drunker I get, the funnier he gets. Either way, he is making me laugh hysterically.

One of his high school stories has me on a roll, my side hurting from all the laughter. Something about water balloons full of grape jelly and pickle relish and the last day of school his junior year. A group of them had attacked the football cheerleading squad during tryouts for the following year.

When I finally calm down, I lift my cup for another sip. Hmm . . . empty. I stare at it in confusion. Wasn't it full just a minute ago? I let my head fall back on the couch, exhausted from all that laughing. I look over at Donovan and start giggling again. He smiles at me. Then he leans forward and puts one hand on my leg. I stare at his hand, thinking I should pull it up and toss it off me. But I don't. When I glance back up, his face is over mine. Everything is moving in slow motion. I shouldn't have had so much to drink. It's catching up to me.

Wow. He has some beautiful green eyes. I blink hard and try to focus on those eyes. I've never noticed them before. And long, thick lashes.

And then he presses his lips to mine. Surprisingly soft lips. He moves his hand up to my cheek. This is when I should push him away—tell him I don't think so. But his kiss isn't as awkward as I thought it would be. I let him separate my lips with his tongue. And things start to get blurry. I let my eyes fall shut.

THE NEXT MORNING, my head is pounding, sunlight streaming into my room at full force. It hurts to open my eyes. I flop my arm over my face to block the offending light. My mouth is so dry my tongue is sticking to the roof.

I groan as I lift my head and turn to see what time it is. 7:30. Really? Couldn't I at least sleep in? It's Sunday—no work today. I sigh as I fall back onto my pillow, then wince. Even my pillow hurts my head. I try to remember exactly what happened last night and when I went to bed . . . party. That's right. I struggle to count how many drinks I consumed. I can't be sure, but I know I haven't drank like that in a long time.

Suddenly, I hear a sound and nearly jump out of my skin. *Ouch* . . . more head pain. I turn my head to the left slowly and gingerly. My breath catches.

Donovan! He is snoring *in my bed*! How did this happen? My head hurts so bad I can't even think. *Seriously?!*

I throw off the covers and hastily grab my clothes from the night before piled next to the bed, nearly faceplanting as I get a horrendous head rush. I drop my jeans so I can throw my hand to the ground to catch myself, briefly thinking of dropping down and crawling out of the room army-style.

Slow down, he's still snoring. I glance over to see that, despite the roaring in my brain, Donovan remains unmoving. I take a deep breath and pull myself up on the bed as carefully as I can. I have to get out of here without waking him.

I don't believe this. I seriously do not believe this. *What have I done?*

Stealthily, I pull my pants and shirt on and tiptoe around the bed to my drawers and closet, gathering up a clean outfit. I cringe as I shut the closet door, unable to keep it silent. I glance back at Donovan as I quietly hurry to the door—my escape. I don't dare breathe as I turn the knob. I open the door just far enough to squeeze through, then lightly shut the door and rush to the bathroom, still holding my breath.

Once I am safely on the other side of the bathroom door, I exhale and give myself a few minutes to try to reconstruct last night. Bits and pieces come back to me. An apartment full of people I didn't know, my rude friends who stranded me with Chatty Charlie all night long, a small fight between Val's college friends that got broken up quickly, Emory and Dylan being inseparable, kissing Donovan.

Ick. Kissing Donovan. I shudder at the memory. I need to brush my teeth. I stop my mind from putting the pieces together right there, and block the rest out for now. I don't want to deal with all of that yet.

Clean teeth and a shower do a world of good for my body and mind, waking me up completely. I peek around the bathroom door before I emerge, scanning for signs that Donovan has awakened. My pulse slows as I realize the apartment is quiet, so I cautiously make my way down the hallway to the living room. My bedroom door is still closed, so that's a good sign.

I survey the rest of the room, bottles and cans strewn everywhere. Cigarette butts in ashtrays and stale beer scent the air. The potted tree in the corner lies on its side, soil spilling over the carpet. Jay is stretched across the couch, face-down, his long legs hanging over the side. I mentally note that Dylan must have stayed with Emory last night. He was Jay and Donovan's ride. All the food bowls on the counter are empty—except for the veggie tray. Something orange is crushed into the carpet in front of the counter.

My headache is down to a mild throbbing, but my stomach is now unsettled thanks to the smell of the apartment. I need some breakfast. And I need to get out of here.

Heading to the diner up the block, my stomach growls angrily at me as I think of the breakfast platter I'm craving. I cowardly think if I eat slowly enough, Donovan will be gone by the time I get back. I absolutely cannot deal with him today.

And I do eat slowly, but just to be on the safe side, I decide to take a long walk after breakfast. The fresh air and distractions of the streets and shops keep my mind off last night.

When I return to the apartment late morning, I'm deeply relieved to find the boys are gone. Emory and Val are vacuuming and mopping, and the place smells so much better.

"There you are, Abby!" Emory pauses and shuts off the vacuum. "We thought you had run away."

I catch the look they exchange. They know what I don't want to tell them, which is good, because I never want to say the words out loud.

"Abby," Val prods, "so, um, how did your evening turn out?"

I stare at her, my jaw clenches. "It was fine. I drank too much. You know." I try to find something to do to help clean, and I quickly change the subject to Emory. "So, Ems, Dylan was pretty into you last night, huh?"

"Omigod, yeah!" she gushes. "He was so easy to talk to and we have so much in common. Turns out we went to the same high school, but he was a junior when I was a freshman, so we never met. Different circles of friends, you know. And his uncle is my parents' CPA. How crazy is that? And . . . he is *such* a good kisser!"

"Dylan's uncle or Dylan?" I tease.

"*Dylan*, Abby! Duh!"

Emory chatters on about what she now knows about Dylan and about their hookup. My plan worked. The only thing more important to her than finding out the details of my night is being able to tell us about the details of hers. Relieved, I continue picking up bottles, wrappers, and food crumbs until all is spotless before sneaking off to my bedroom for a much-needed nap.

The girls leave me alone for as long as they can stand, I assume, which is only a couple of hours. A soft knock on my door disturbs my slumber.

"Abby?" Val peeks her head in. "Emory and I are going shopping, and we want you to come with us."

I squint at her and sigh. I hate shopping.

"Val, I don't have any money to go shopping." This is true. I only have the eighty bucks to my name that I earned in tips, and I really don't want to waste it on clothes.

"My treat. That shirt you wore last night was totally not party-worthy, and if I had known that you didn't have any decent clothes, I would have taken you shopping beforehand. Come on. Emory and I thought it would be cool to find something coordinating that we all can wear at the next party."

"Next party?" I groan. Please, no.

"Yes, next party. Now let's go. You're not getting out of this." In a matter of seconds, Val throws open the door, tosses her long braids over her shoulder, strides purposefully across my room, and yanks me from my bed. The lengths to which these girls will go to try to get information out of me. I mean, really! This is going to be a very unpleasant afternoon trying to dodge and deflect their inquiries.

And I try really hard. I dodge the topic as long as I can, but they are so darn persistent. By the third store, I'm caving. By the fourth store, they know all the gory details—at least all the ones I can remember.

They play the roles of The Good Friends by being equally supportive yet disappointed in my lapse in sexual judgment. Of course, there is the tentative question of, "Do you really like him though?" I quickly assure them that I am just as nauseated by the thought of Donovan as any other female who has the displeasure of knowing him. It was a moment of weakness, and I'd had a lot to drink. I'm sure never going to tell them that for a brief moment I found him attractive and fun to talk to. I'm pretty sure they'll think I'm crazy. I'm pretty sure *I* think I'm crazy.

So in a tactical move, I switch the conversation to Emory and Dylan, which gets the heat off me. Emory has nothing to be ashamed of, as I do. She begins to reanalyze their conversations for us. She thinks their relationship might really go somewhere, and I was so right that she just needed to give him a chance. She tells me she is so glad she did.

ON MONDAY, VAL skips class to hang out with us again. She uses the excuse that she "is just so stressed out" this semester and needs a little break. Which is weird, because the semester just began.

Emory and I both have Sundays and Mondays off from Hooligan's, and Val is Emory's best friend, so I think Val gets jealous at times that we might be doing cool stuff without her. She might be surprised to find out she never misses out on anything special.

But with the three of us together and a full day ahead, we head upstate and check out the local vineyards. We stop at a few places on the Shawangunk Wine Trail. I've never been much of a fan of wine, but the trip opens my eyes to a whole new world. I had no idea there were so many varieties of wine. Val's family are connoisseurs of sorts, so she acts as our tour guide, making sure we sample unique flavors. She knows a lot, for which I'm glad, because I surely would have looked like an idiot without someone guiding me along.

We each find a favorite and buy a bottle before starting our trip back home, stopping at a bistro-style restaurant on the way. It's a quaint little place in a small town that obviously draws in a lot of tourists to its several restaurants and shops. Feeling confident and adventurous from our day in the vineyards, we each order a glass of wine from the menu. We critique our choices to show off what we've learned today. It's fun. I honestly have a good time. Val and Ems manage to keep my spirits up and my mind from dwelling on my faux pas with Donovan.

And now I am flat broke and glad that tomorrow is a workday so I can earn more tips.

We get home later than expected, and I find I'm quite tired for not really doing anything but riding in Val's car and sampling wine all day. But the girls are still on the go and want to put in a movie and pop popcorn. I'm already yawning, so I excuse myself and crawl into my jammies.

I thought I'd crash out. But now that the day is over and I'm lying in bed, I can't drift off to sleep. That familiar loneliness creeps into my room, which is mildly irritating. I've just spent the past two days with people who are as close to me as I've ever had, and yet I still feel alone.

What is wrong with me that I feel this emptiness? My friends are right outside my door, but the distance between us feels so much farther. I should be reveling in the joy I felt hanging out with them all day.

But I can't.

I just feel sad that the day is over. Tomorrow will be back to work and back to the mundane. My throat starts to ache as my chest constricts. The more I struggle to concentrate on the fun we've had this weekend, the more removed from it all I become. And now I have shame to add to the mix as the thoughts of what I've done with Donovan rush into my mind and push away the last bits of joy.

My eyes betray me as tears roll from the corners. I pull my pillow from behind my head and push it down over my face. I scream out all the air in my lungs.

Chapter Three

An Attack of Electricity in the Mystery Section

On Tuesday, I wake to my alarm beeping, not feeling the veil of depression I dreaded, but not feeling . . . well, not really feeling anything. I finished my book last night when I just couldn't get to sleep. (The rest of *A Tale of Two Cities* did little to improve my mood.) So, I have nothing to read. There's nothing I feel like getting out of bed and doing, either.

I eat a bowl of cereal and decide to shower. I spend extra time in the shower, enjoying the warm water on my back and shoulders, trying to think of something to do today until my shift starts at two.

At ten o'clock, when I'm fully dressed and ready to do *something*, I peek my head into Emory's room and find her still sound asleep. Val leaves by 7:30 on Tuesdays and Thursdays because her first class starts at eight. So that leaves me wondering, as I pace around the apartment, if I should hang around and pretend to watch TV or go somewhere.

I look over at the few dishes on the kitchen counter and tackle those, clean the kitchen, tidy the living room. After all that, I still feel like I need to *do* something.

Then I remember the bookstore Navy Sport Coat told me about the other night at Hooligan's. I do need another book. And I probably have time before work. It's six, maybe seven blocks from here. A walk in the sunshine might lift my spirits and help break me out of this funk.

I decide to check the place out. I've always been game for stores that are original or eclectic. I am definitely not either of those things, but I do appreciate people and places that are.

Knowing I spent a lot of money yesterday, I check my purse before I take off. A folded ten and ones after ones after ones. Can't tell I'm a waitress. I count thirty dollars and some change in quarters. That should be plenty to get a book or two if I find some on clearance.

"See you in a bit, Ems," I call as I head for the door. "*Please* be ready on time today!"

"I will! I promise!" floats out from her bedroom. Shaking my head and chuckling, I head out the door. I have my doubts.

I hurry down the stairs and out into the bright sunshine. I have plenty of time, but I'm strangely excited to get there and see what treasures might await. Since it's not a chain store, I wonder if it will have some old or rare books.

I nearly walk past the store, not because I'm not paying attention, but because it is so unimposing. Not plain but understated. The name "Food for Thought" is scrolled in elegant lettering on the window, but other than that it looks like any other building on the block. There are a few bookstands in the windows displaying various genres. Peering past them into the store itself, I notice it looks like an eatery with tables of one or two patrons and the occasional group. Some appear to be looking at menus. Others are reading or discussing what they are reading. Behind the tables and all the way to the back of the store stretch rows of tall shelves filled with books. A handful of people are milling around perusing the shelves. I am intrigued.

I enter and notice a long counter to my left with boxed sets, collector's editions, and special archives behind it. A dark-haired man of maybe thirty runs the cash register at the front. He looks like the bookworm type—dark-rimmed glasses, flannel shirt, carpenter khakis, scruffy chin. I think, *Maybe he's trying to grow a goatee?*

I glance over at the tables and booths to my right. A few spots are open, but I am more interested in checking out the selection this trip.

The rows of bookshelves are separated down the middle of the store by a wide walkway. A couple of beanbag chairs and a small children's table are at the back of the store where two little girls are engrossed in fairytale books. I turn to the shelves on the right side first. Not looking for romance right now. No erotic romance. No teen paranormal romance. No westerns. No memoirs. I wander up and down the rows until I find a section that interests me: mystery. I'm in the mood for a good, fully engrossing whodunit to take me far away from my bland reality.

A warm, friendly voice drifts over and catches my attention. I glance distractedly over at the tables. One of the employees is giving his spiel on how everything works to a new patron. I half-listen so as to know exactly what those menu papers are for and why people sit there to be waited on as if ordering food. Unlike the cashier at the front counter, this guy certainly does not look like a literary nerd. He doesn't really look like he belongs in a bookstore, let alone working in one. His sandy-blond hair is short on the sides but long on top, so his wavy locks keep falling into his eyes. Occasionally, he runs his hand through it, as if by habit, to clear his forehead. He looks athletic and tall. Though I am barely paying attention to his words, he speaks to the patron in a genuine tone, like he actually *likes* working in a bookstore. Like he might actually *enjoy* helping people find a great book to read.

As he looks up in my direction, I realize too late that I'm staring. I can't look away, though. His features are chiseled, and his eyes are as warm and friendly as his voice. He smiles widely at me. A nice smile . . .

I get hold of myself and quickly turn to the books on the shelf in front of me. Feeling my cheeks burning bright crimson with embarrassment, I force myself to pay attention to the titles on the spines and covers, but a nagging voice in my head tells me to look for him again: *Just see what he's doing.* I ignore it and pick up a book that looks interesting. I flip it over to read the teaser on the back cover.

Only a moment passes, and I feel someone next to me. I don't dare look. What if it's him? But that's stupid, there are lots of people in the store. It could be anybody. I steal a furtive glance to the side. It *is* him! My stomach flip-flops. I glance again. He's looking at the shelf a mere foot away from me. I feel an odd electricity charging the air all around; I can't believe he's so close, running his index finger along the book spines.

"Ah. Here it is," he says to himself as he extracts a book. Then he turns to me, and I hastily look back at the book in my hand, hoping he hasn't caught me looking at him.

"I wouldn't recommend that one," he offers after a brief moment. "It's too easy to figure out the ending. Not enough suspense." He pauses thoughtfully. "Have you read Carson Ripley's new thriller?"

I blink, surprised. He's talking to me! Then I focus on his eyes—beautiful blue eyes, like the clear unending sky on a summer day. Standing this close, he isn't as tall as I'd thought, not much taller than I am. His shoulders are broad. His lips are full. He has a light dusting of freckles on his nose. Then, embarrassed, I realize he's still waiting for me to answer his question.

"Um, no." I blush again and glance down, hoping to hide it. He must think I'm an idiot.

But he smiles that wide smile at me, showing his perfectly straight, perfectly white teeth. "You'll like it. It's a real page-turner. It's up toward the front of the store with the new releases. Let me know if you need help finding it."

He pauses a beat, then raises the book in his hand and aims it toward the tables behind me as if reminding himself what direction he needs to go. He walks past, brushing my shoulder as he goes. All the electricity in the air centers sharply on that spot as if transferring from him to me and leaves my shoulder tingling. I stop breathing for a second, shocked at the exchange, wondering what it means. I recover my senses and spin around to watch him stride away. I let my gaze follow him—no fear of him catching me watching with his back toward me. My eyes slide from his broad shoulders, down his dark shirt just tight enough for me to make out his shoulder blades underneath it and come to an abrupt halt at his butt. A sexy one, I must say, in khakis that fit snuggly enough for me to feel myself about to drool down my chin.

He returns to the table at the front of the store, hands the man the book he retrieved, and talks with him for a minute. Then as he starts to turn, I quickly look at the bookshelf. I don't want to chance him seeing me stalking him with my eyes. Casually, I place the book in my hands back on the shelf.

I walk slowly along, glancing thoughtfully at the bookshelves as I go. I have to be covert. I round the corner and make my way to the front, stopping occasionally to pull a book out and pretend to read the front or back cover. And each time I return a book to the shelf, I look toward the front of the store to see if I can catch another glimpse of him. Once—no. Twice—no. The third time I pause longer with my hand still on the spine of a book in case I have to pull it off the shelf in a hurry. He is talking to Book Nerd at the cash register now. They converse easily and even laugh a couple times, like maybe they're friends as well as co-workers.

The conversation is broken off by an elderly woman asking questions about a handful of books. My Cutie turns his full attention to her and listens. I am amazed at how he acts like he genuinely cares—not like some places you go where the employees really don't know anything about what they're selling and don't really care if you shop there or not. I wonder if this guy climbs trees for stranded cats, too.

Finally, I've made my way up to the new releases display. I am curious about the book he mentioned . . . Carson Ripley? I've heard that name before but have never read any of his books. This one is hard to miss with a bright red, glossy jacket and the title *At Journey's End* in large yellow font. I pick up the book and turn it over, wondering if it is as good as Cutie says.

Alone in a world against her, Samene must prove her innocence to escape capture and death. Her only hope is the dark stranger who seems to know her every move—or is he orchestrating her every move? Samene's journey is fraught with deceit and danger as she tries to navigate across the globe to find the truth that will save her life. Will all the pieces fall into place before time runs out?
"An instant bestseller. Carson Ripley's most thrilling work yet." – *Literary Magazine*
"I couldn't put the book down! The surprise ending left me chilled." – *Ralph Holmes, New York Today*

Hmm . . . you have my attention, Mr. Ripley.

I glance up once more for Cutie but don't see him. Oh well. Time to buy my book and head out; I still have to get ready for work this afternoon.

"Did you find everything okay?" Book Nerd asks as I set the book on the counter.

"Yeah, thanks."

"*At Journey's End*," he appraises my selection while ringing it up. "I hear it's a good one."

"Yeah. Your . . . floor person—" I look over my shoulder one last time for Cutie "—suggested it."

"Ethan did, huh? He's a real Carson Ripley fan. Like head of the fan club. Literally. You read much of his work?" Book Nerd has my book already bagged and is leaning forward on the counter.

"Ah . . . no, don't think so," I mumble, distracted. *Ethan* . . . that's a nice name. Yes, he looks like an Ethan.

"Well, like I said, good choice. That'll be $26.70." He grins, still leaning forward on his palms.

I pull out my ten and stack of ones. I hand him the ten and count out seventeen ones. Good, I still have three left—I'm not completely broke. When I look up and hand Book Nerd the ones, I realize he's staring at me, one eyebrow raised.

"I'm a waitress," I explain quickly, annoyed.

He mouths, *Oh*, and I'm sure he thinks, *Yeah right. Only strippers carry so many singles.*

"Well, we can always use ones around here." He smiles. His sincerity makes me feel less affronted.

"Thirty cents is your change. Thanks for shopping at Food for Thought." He says it like he's trying out a new catchphrase. It makes me wonder how many times he has to say that in a day. I guess I'd get creative, too.

As I leave the store, I look over one last time at the tables where Cutie, I mean *Ethan*, has reappeared and is helping a customer. His gaze locks with mine and he smiles that wide, dreamy smile. He's caught me looking at him again! I can't help but answer with my own embarrassed grin.

Once safely outside the store, I glance back in the window to sneak one more peek at Ethan. Then I tuck my chin down and smile to myself, butterflies in my stomach. When was the last time a guy made me feel this giddy? I can't even remember.

Chapter Four

Hey, Ground, You Can Swallow Me Now

"Hey, Abby."

Crap. Donovan.

"Hey," I say and act like I'm having a tough time getting my apron tied. I really don't want to get drawn into a conversation with him.

"You need some help with that?"

He gets too close to me, and I panic. I quickly knot the ties as I take a step back. "No! No. There—I've got it."

"No book tonight, huh?" He points to my empty left apron pocket.

"Not tonight. The book I'm reading's too big to fit into my pocket." I shrug past as carefully as I can so as not to touch him. I hurry over to clock in and start for the dining area. Unfortunately, he's right on my heels.

I roll my eyes at Emory as I enter the bar area. She takes my hint and stops rolling silverware into napkins.

"Hey, Donovan," she calls. "Jeff wants some help unloading the truck." She nods her head toward the back of the restaurant.

"Uh, I'm kinda busy right now. Hey, Abby, I wanted to talk to you a sec—"

"Well, Jeff said to send you, specifically," she interrupts, "and he's in a pretty bad mood already, so . . ." Emory raises her eyebrows and makes an it's-your-ass-not-mine face.

I begin helping Emory with the silverware, trying to keep my back angled toward Donovan, but I allow a quick glance to see if her intervention has worked. A look of worry crosses his face briefly, then he sets his jaw and takes one more step toward me. I focus on rolling silverware like it is the most important job I have ever done in my life. A second later I hear him sigh and walk away.

I exhale loudly, fully understanding the bullet I've just dodged. "Thank you *so* much, Ems."

"No prob." She leans on her elbows on the bar. "Sooo . . . you haven't talked with him about the other night yet, huh?" She smirks at me.

"Not yet. Seriously, Ems, this is going to kill me. I *cannot stand* the guy. Why, *why* was I so stupid?!" I throw my head back, hoping for the answer to be written on the ceiling above. Nothing.

"Chillax. Blame it on the beer goggles," she says. "Everybody's had that moment one time or other, Abby, where they've done something they really regret." She pauses for a moment. "You just have to let him down easy. And hope he takes the hint. You remember that Trey guy from our first college party, right?"

"The guy you went home with because you said, and I quote, 'He's the best kisser ever.' What ever happened with him?"

"Yeah, that guy. That was severe beer goggles and a major lack of judgment on my part. I woke up the next morning and quickly learned just what a dork he was. Remember, he followed me around campus for two weeks?"

"Mm-hmm. You kept saying you were going to get rid of him, but he was always still there."

"Yeah, well. I finally got up the nerve to break his heart. See, I was the best thing that had ever happened to him, but I had to convince him there were so many better and hotter chicks out there just waiting for him to ask them out. I told him I wasn't good enough for him and that he had serious game." She laughs conspiratorially, "And then I told him I heard Jessica Sparrs had a huge crush on him, so we couldn't be together because I treasured her friendship too much to hurt her. Told him he needed to go ask her out."

"And that worked?"

"Like a charm."

My stomach knots at the thought of having a conversation with Donovan, let alone trying to come up with some elaborate ruse to make him back off without hurting his feelings. I am not looking forward to that conversation. Nor am I looking forward to trying to avoid him all night. It will be difficult in such a small restaurant on a Tuesday night when business is usually slower.

The thing that really gets me is that I don't do this kind of thing. I've never slept with just anybody. I don't let alcohol cloud my judgment, and I sure don't let it get me carried away with someone I would never, *ever* have sexual relations with at any other time! I mean, yeah, I was feeling really lonely and had been for a while. And he was at my side the whole night, a little less annoying than usual. I guess I just looked at him and thought, *What the hell? He could be the best lover in the world, and I would never know it.* I had talked myself into how his messy hairstyle wasn't so bad, and his green eyes were kind of attractive, and he wasn't bad-looking. He kind of smelled nice, too.

Flash forward to the morning-after regret. Well, he definitely was *not* the best lover in the world—far from it. And he snored! Add to that the fact that he really liked me, and I had a recipe for disaster.

Now I have to let him down easy. I curse myself for being so weak.

The rest of the night drags on as I try to avoid Donovan as much as possible, going to Dylan and Jay to get my drink orders filled, not that that's much better. Every time I come up to the bar with a drink order, they smirk at me. Sometimes I even get a full toothy smile and a wink. Yes, they know my dirty little secret. I know I can trust Emory not to blab to anyone else here about what happened, but what about these two? I don't know them well enough to trust them. But even if they keep it as their inside joke to make fun of me (which is fine, whatever) Donovan could very well be telling everyone about his score and that we're dating now. Argh! This night cannot get over fast enough.

Occasionally, I catch a glimpse of him staring at me. I can tell he wants to come over and talk. I don't think he's smart enough to figure out I'm making wide circles around the bar to the other guys for my drinks. Even though it is slow in the restaurant, it's pretty packed in the bar area—some baseball game on the big screens or something—so that keeps the bartenders busy and keeps him away from me.

I don't take any of my breaks—I'm so worried he'll take his break too and come find me. I can't have The Talk with him until I have my speech ready. I don't want to come off as an absolute bitch because, annoying as he is, I really don't want to hurt him. He's not a *bad* guy . . . just not a guy I want to spend any real amount of time with.

When it's finally time to clock out and go home, Donovan is waiting for me by the laundry bin where I have to throw my apron. I briefly consider begging Jeff to let me out the front door, but that would only delay the inevitable. I need to get this over with.

"Um . . . I'll wait for you outside." Emory nudges my arm, then hands me her apron and takes off.

Dread fills my insides. I think I might get sick right here and now. I take a deep breath, trying to muster my nerve. *Get ahold of yourself, Abby. You can do this. It's just a conversation.* About a night I never want to remember. I suck in another breath and propel myself forward.

"Hey, Abby," Donovan says excitedly, like he's waited *all* night to talk to me.

"Hey, Donovan." I don't look up at him as I take off my apron and toss it and Emory's into the laundry bin. "Umm . . . can we talk for a minute?" I gesture over to the stock racks.

"Yeah. A-actually, Abby, I was wondering if you wanted to maybe get a drink or something, maybe," the words fumble out of his mouth as he follows me across the room. I turn to see him assessing me, his green eyes full of expectation. He smiles a goofy, lopsided grin. "We had such a good time the other night, I thought maybe we could hook up again."

Ick. Ick. Ick. I cringe at his words, my stomach crawling up into my throat. I gulp hard to try to force it back down.

"You know, Donovan," I begin slowly, my jaw tight, still not sure of what I'm going to say. My eyes shift to the right, searching for some inspiration to appear on the wall. I chew on my lip and settle on the old standby: "You're a great guy and everything, but, you know, I'm just not ready for a relationship right now."

I flash my best apologetic eyes and feign sincerity.

"Oh." He looks confused, then a little disappointed, but his eyes brighten a second later. "*Oh,* that's okay, Abby." Now I'm confused. "We can still go out and have a good time. Have sex, no strings kind of thing. We know we have the chemistry, am I right?" He does this weird little dance thing that, combined with the words I'm hearing, is really grossing me out. This guy is delusional. I realize that subtle isn't working; time to drop the hammer.

"Well, actually. . ." Suddenly, inspiration hits me. "I don't think the spark was there—at least, not for me. I couldn't live with myself if I led you on when I really didn't feel anything romantic. And, you know, you're too good of a friend for me to be so careless with your feelings. You'll find someone special out there, Donovan, I know it. Someone much better than me who can love you in the way you deserve to be loved."

I smile at him, reaching up to squeeze his shoulder for good measure. I can see he's mulling over what I've said.

"You really think so?" He looks doubtful.

"Of course! Of course I do. You're smart, you're goofy—I mean, funny. You're *sooo* funny, Donovan. And you've got those killer green eyes!" That one isn't a lie at least.

His expression slowly changes. A huge wave of relief rushes over me. He's buying it.

"You're right." He nods. "Hey, thanks, Abby. You still want to get those drinks? Maybe help me scout some good chicks?"

I'm caught off guard by his remark and can't help smiling back at his expectant grin. Who is this guy?

"Thanks for the offer, but I've got to get going. Good luck to you, though," I call over my shoulder. I hurry out the door as fast as I can, a new buoyancy in my step with this awful ordeal dealt with and behind me.

"Well, how'd it go?" Emory demands as I come bounding up to her.

I fill her in on the way home. She can't believe how smooth I was either, how I managed to build him up and make him excited to move on. Maybe I should counsel people on Morning-After Letdown Explanations. There might be a real market there . . .

Chapter Five

I Don't Know Why I Try

I BREEZE THROUGH the Carson Ripley novel over the next week and have one chapter to go by Sunday night. Cutie Ethan was right; it is an excellent read. Very thrilling. Normally, I don't read books this fast, even though this is a page-turner. But I feel a need to get back to the bookstore and see him again. Maybe even work up the courage to have a conversation. My curiosity about this guy is raging. I can't stop thinking about him and that smile. And those blue eyes.

So, once I finish the book, I figure I can go and thank him for the recommendation. Tell him my favorite parts and ask which parts are his favorites. We can compare notes about who we each thought the murderer was and if we changed our minds at all before the ending. We'll have a nice long discussion, which of course will lead to other topics of conversation, so I can find out much more about him. My hopes are soaring as I imagine it.

Unless...

What if he doesn't even remember me? What if he'd talked to me just like he does all the other customers? What if he's the kind of genuine guy who comes across like he's interested in someone (me, in this instance) in a plain, normal conversation? What if he flirts with all the ladies to get more book sales? Maybe he gets paid on commission and figured out the best way to get sales is to flirt with the women. Who knows? Maybe he flirts with men, too. Then I would be making a complete fool out of myself with Cutie by trying to get him to ask me out.

Unfortunately for me, I'm already halfway to the store on Monday afternoon before this realization hits. And now I'm second-guessing my decision. Doubt takes my thoughts hostage, and the high I was gliding on comes crashing down to the concrete below my feet. I stop walking for a moment to pull my thoughts into something coherent. Seriously, I couldn't have really imagined his enthusiasm toward me, right? I try to recall the conversations I'd seen him in with the other patrons in the store that day. Our conversation, brief as it was, had been different, right? It *had* been a bit special . . . right?

Butterflies overtake my stomach as my excitement to see Ethan morphs into nervousness about the reaction, if any, I'll get from him if I try to strike up my planned conversation.

"Move it, girl! This is a sidewalk!" a man snarls at me as he pushes past.

I lose my balance and catch myself on another younger man's arm. He looks angrily at me and acts as if he's going to shake me off to the ground, but his face softens once he realizes I'm just a klutzy girl not meaning anything malicious by grabbing him.

"Sorry!" I blush as I struggle to right myself.

"Uh, yeah," he mumbles, eyeing me suspiciously as he uses his arm to push me upright, then turns back toward his friend and continues to walk.

Okay, decision time, I think as I gather my bearings. I have to either keep moving forward or turn around and go home. I really do need a new book. I can go and check out the new releases for something that looks interesting. Or I can grab *Pride and Prejudice*, which I've always wanted to read. I'll play it cool and look for a sign of acknowledgment from Ethan. No expectations. No delusions of blossoming romance. If there's a lack of interest from him, I'll just chalk it up to my overactive imagination and excessive loneliness and move on. Who cares that I have spent every day since meeting him lusting over the possibilities, barely able to finish the last book before rushing back to the store?

Okay, so whatever reaction I get from him, I will respond accordingly. I square my shoulders and continue on with my altered plan, working out the details and possible lines of conversation in my mind so he won't catch me off guard, no matter his reaction.

I push through the door and casually glance around the store, as nonchalant as I can muster. No one is on the floor or behind the register as far as I can tell. It doesn't appear very busy. A brief moment of bravery pushes me over to the tables rather than the new releases. I have to talk to this guy, and sitting at a table to be waited on is a surefire way to do that. Right away, I'll at least know if he recognizes me.

I sit at a table near the wall so I can watch the store, but it's also by a window so I can look distractedly outside if need be. I pick up the "menu" from the table and glance over it. It's made of thick tan parchment paper. Old-world-style bold font. It gives me the feeling I'm reading a menu from a fancy restaurant. I browse through the sections: new releases, fiction, nonfiction, autobiography, biography, self-help, young adult, and educational. Each section has the top-five sellers of the week, as well as West's Choice and Ethan's Choice. There's even a cute kids' menu on the back with listings of children's books. After each book title is the name of the author, the publishing company, a brief synopsis, and the price. This is the easy way to shop for books. I am impressed.

"Welcome to Food for Thought. My name is Kate, and I'll be your book server today. Can I get you anything?"

I look up, my brow raised in confusion.

"Or . . . do you need a minute?" The unfamiliar woman smiles. She has long black hair that shimmers in the light, with soft, motherly eyes and a kind smile. Her fashion sense is definitely artsy and eccentric—I admire the gauzy teal blouse she's wearing and note the multiple bangle bracelets on either wrist.

"Um, yeah," I recover. "I guess I do need a minute still."

"No problem. Our special today is buy one book and get the second at half-price." She speaks as if we've been in conversation all afternoon. One thing I really do like about this store is how laid back the employees seem. It's refreshing.

"I'll just give you a couple more minutes, then I'll be back."

"Thanks." I watch as she leaves, rather than look at the menu. While she seems like a nice enough woman, she is not the person I had hoped would wait on me today. I search around for a sight of my Ethan. Maybe he's helping other customers; maybe he's on break. I notice scruffy Book Nerd in his flannel-shirt-and-khakis uniform is back at his usual post behind the front counter.

Before long, the female book server is walking toward me again. I realize I haven't even looked at the menu since she left the first time.

"Did you decide on one, hon?" she asks sweetly.

"Um . . . actually, can I take a look at a couple of books? I can't decide." I scan the new releases quickly.

"Sure thing. No problem." She waits patiently.

"Let's see . . . um . . . *Cold Feet* looks interesting, and um . . . Ethan's Choice, *Lies Become Truth*, looks good."

"Both excellent choices," she confirms. "I'll grab those and give you some time to decide which you prefer—or maybe you'll want both." She smiles, and I lock eyes with her for a second before she leaves the table. I notice again how her warm hazel eyes flecked with gold are very comforting—like they see everything about you and accept you regardless. She seems like an old soul. I can't help but like her.

I scan the store again while I wait for her to return with the books. Still no Ethan.

The woman, Kate, brings the books and leaves me alone for a while to make my decision. I do end up liking both books once I've read a few pages of each. And they are BOGO, so I have no qualms about buying both. Kate returns to check on me after about fifteen minutes, so I inform her that I will take both. She smiles at me like she knew I would and lets me know I can just ask if I need anything else.

I use the distraction from the books to take one more sweep of the store for Ethan. Disappointed, I resign myself to the fact that he must not be working today. I let the nervous butterflies finally rest in my stomach and tell myself I'll have to table my hopes of a conversation with him for another day.

I direct my attention back to *Lies Become Truth*, wanting a thorough escape from this reality for a bit. I get through the first two chapters before my stomach tells me it's time to go find something to eat. I gather up the books and head to the counter to pay.

Scruffy Book Nerd, who I have by now figured out is West from "West's Choice," is manning the register still. He has the same amount of barely there goatee on his chin that he had a week ago.

"*Cold Feet* and *Lies Become Truth*—excellent choices," he says approvingly.

"I'll bet you say that to everybody," I tease.

He looks at me, shocked, for a moment. "Well, yeah, I probably do," he concedes. "But it's important to make sure every customer feels confident about their purchase. Helps eliminate buyer's remorse," he says matter-of-factly.

"I see," I laugh. "Gotta keep the customers happy to keep the boss happy, huh?" This is a concept I understand well.

I again hand over a stack of ones along with my ten and five for payment. He stops short as he takes them, then gives me a knowing look out of the corner of his eye as he counts them into the till. "I know you." He nods. "Miss I'm-a-Waitress." He raises his voice an octave, mocking me. "Sure, sure." Then he lowers his voice and narrows his eyes, "Your mother know you're a 'waitress'?" He uses air quotes as if it's a dirty word.

I am taken aback.

A wide grin breaks across his face, and I realize he's joking. I relax. This guy is a weird one all right. Weird, but funny. I laugh in spite of myself.

"Thank you, sir," I say, smiling as I shake my head and pick up my books.

"Sir's my father. I'm West." He holds out his hand.

I look at it for a second, briefly thinking about dissing him, but I like his humor, so I shake hands.

"Nice to meet you, West."

"Would you like a bag for your books, Miss . . . ?"

"Abby."

"Miss Abby."

"Please." I hand the books over, and he places them in a paper bag with handles. "Thank you," I say as I take the bag.

"Hurry back, Abby, and thank *you* for shopping at Food for Thought!"

I return his smile as I turn to go. I hear him say to the next customer, "*Baby on the Way* and *How to Babyproof Your Home*—excellent choices!"

BY THE NEXT Monday, I have read *Lies Become Truth* and am almost done with *Cold Feet*. I only have three chapters left. I could finish that in the next couple of days, I reason, so I should make another trip to the bookstore.

To be honest, I'm impatient to see Ethan. It was all I could do to stay away from the store this past week.

But I am disappointed. Again. Kate and West are running the store. I still find myself spending a couple of hours at Food for Thought in spite of the heavy disappointment. I love the atmosphere and the personalities that fill the space. It has its own vibe. No super-chain cookie-cutter business here. And though I've only been here three times, it's like West is my buddy already. I've even learned his last name (Christiansen), and I got a little wave from him as I entered the store today. Kate even seems to remember me. Or maybe she is just really good at faking familiarity—sometimes you learn that in the service industry. People like to go where people know their names . . . or at least pretend they do.

Kate (whose last name I learn is Saunders) stops by my table a couple of times and chats. She tells me she thought I was an aspiring editor or fledgling author-type by my aura. I tell her I'm flattered, but in truth I'm a college dropout and now a waitress at Hooligan's Bar and Grill. I was a literature major, though, if that counts for anything. I learn she is an artist—photography and painting mostly. She helps out at the store a couple days a week and when needed. I tell her she looks like the artist type. We laugh. It's nice getting to know somebody other than my roommates and co-workers. But the store gets busier, so Kate has to cut our conversation short.

I direct my attention to the book I've selected this time: *Pride and Prejudice*, the one I'd thought about getting last time. I have trouble getting into it though. I keep wondering about Ethan. Are there parallels between this book and our encounter? Feelings that I thought might be between us that weren't actually there? And now I wonder if he quit, found a job somewhere else. Am I never to see him again? I feel a little bit depressed at that thought. I can always ask Kate or West what happened to my Cutie. I'm sure they'd tell me. But I don't want to let on to anybody that I have a crush on him. That is my secret.

I fight through two and a half chapters before I decide I have to get out of here. My mood has shifted, and I want to get home and see if Emory and Val are there. Maybe they can help me forget about the lurking loneliness for a bit.

I HAVE *COLD Feet* and *Pride and Prejudice* finished by Friday night. Saturday morning, technically. I stayed up after work until three in the morning to finish *Pride and Prejudice*. It was getting to the really good parts, and I wanted to see how Elizabeth and Mr. Darcy fared. One nice thing about staying up so late to finish reading: I'm too tired to have any of those pesky nightmares.

On Saturday, when I finally get out of bed, I decide I need a nice compact paperback that I can fit into my apron pocket. I nearly ruined *Cold Feet* at work. I'd set it up on a shelf in the stockroom after my break, and Donovan (bless his goofy heart) tripped while carrying a large glass jar of pickles to the kitchen. The jar shattered, leaving a pool of pickles and juice on the floor. He'd fallen onto the shelf when he tripped, which knocked my book down into the pickle puddle. At least he told me right away, so I could get the book wiped off and somewhat salvaged. It was still readable, but it smelled like pickles (which I hate), so that made me rush through the last few chapters even quicker.

Now, as I enter Food for Thought, I make my way to a table as I have the last couple of times I've visited. I know Kate will have some good suggestions for me. I've given up on the idea of ever seeing Ethan here again. Well, maybe there is the off chance that he still likes to come here and buy books. But I'm no longer going to hold my breath that I'll run into him. I spent the last week letting my crush dissipate and conjuring up a whole awful personality full of flaws that I can think of as the real Ethan. I am over him. I realize it was silly to even think there might have been something there.

I browse the menu as I wait for Kate, debating on a romance or a biography of Marilyn Monroe—that sounds intriguing. Of course, the one I choose will be entirely dependent upon it coming in paperback form, the most important on my list of criteria for this trip. I glance up, wondering what is taking her so long. And then I see.

My heart stops.

Ethan. He's holding Kate's hand, looking into her eyes, laughing. They're both laughing. Boy, are they having a grand old time. She lays a big one-armed hug on him. They continue laughing. Then she plants a big kiss on his lips. My jaw clenches, but I force myself to relax and look away. What do I care? I don't like him anyway. Not anymore. I do feel a little betrayed by Kate, though, for some weird reason.

I shake my head to clear it, breathe out hard. This turn of events is definitely unexpected. But what am I feeling all crazy for? *I don't like him.* I. Don't. Like. Him. Not anymore, I remind myself.

I look back at the menu, hoping Kate, not Ethan, will hurry up and come over so I can get my book and get out of here. This is suddenly the last place I want to be. I think about just getting up and going over to the shelves myself to avoid them both. I glance up, unable to stop myself. Kate and Ethan are talking; she looks over at me and smiles. Then Ethan looks over at me and his brow furrows. I plant my eyes on the menu as quickly as possible. Are they talking about me? Why would they be talking about me? Are they making fun of me, knowing I had a stupid crush on him? Of course, Kate is probably laughing at me. I am nowhere near as good-looking as she is, so why should I expect her handsome boyfriend to ever have any kind of feelings for me? My face is burning with embarrassment. Again, I think about just getting up and leaving.

But it's too late. A shadow falls on my menu; I slowly lift my gaze. Crap. It's Ethan. He's all smiley, too. That warm and wide smile that got me all goofy and worked up before. For a split second I am transported to that first time we met when I looked into his electric blue eyes.

"Welcome back to Food for Thought. What can I get you today?" Still smiling.

"Um, I haven't, ah, decided," I stutter. Great, now I can't talk either.

"How did you like *At Journey's End*?"

I'm taken aback. He *does* remember me. And this is exactly the opening I would have hoped for to get my previously planned conversation going with him.

"It's my favorite Carson Ripley novel to date," he continues when I don't answer. "Very sophisticated. I'm curious about what you thought of the ending?"

I am still too stunned to answer. Finally, I manage to recover, those few seconds feeling like an eternity. "Um, yeah—the ending was a real shocker. I've gotten pretty good at predicting storylines, but this one actually threw me," I reply softly.

"I know, right?" And then he stuns me even further by pulling out the chair and sitting across from me. My eyes dart around the store for Kate. Is this normal employee behavior? I am totally thrown off by this guy. "It's genius how he plays on the title *At Journey's End*, and when she seems to reach the end of her journey and finds her freedom, Samene realizes a new journey has begun. I mean, it's a reality of life, right? Just when you think your journey has ended you see it's a gateway to the next journey in your life. A different journey." He continues, obviously not noticing my confusion at his behavior, "I heard a rumor Ripley may have a sequel in the works. I can see how he's set it up for that. A story that good you have to capitalize on, right? And the characters have such strong, unique personalities. I was really impressed with it."

"West was right," I kind of chuckle when the shock fades.

He blinks at me. "Right about what?" A half-smile pulls at the corner of his mouth, clearly interested in what West might be right about.

"You're, like, the leader of the Carson Ripley fan club. Tell me," I say as I lean across the table, "do you write him letters and kiss his picture every night before bed?"

His smile drops. "I could kill West." He glares over his shoulder at Book Nerd standing behind the register, who grins impishly and waves, a claim of guilt. Does he know what he's guilty of? I'm amused to see that he looks like he's used to it. Ethan turns to me, defeated.

"Here I'm trying to impress a girl, and West has to ruin it." He looks down at his hands.

I sit back, gaping at him. What? Impress a girl? Okay, now I really am confused. I quickly look around to see if Kate might be anywhere nearby. What kind of jerk flirts in front of his own girlfriend?

"Did I—say something wrong?"

Of course you said something wrong, I scream in my head. I frown. "Well, I'm really just looking for a small paperback. I was hoping Kate might have some good suggestions," I say curtly, actually a bit harsher than I meant for it to come out. I crane my neck to look past him. She must have gone on break or something. Thus, allowing Casanova here unhampered flirtations with the lady patrons.

His expression changes, telling me he takes the hint. Good.

"I'll, um . . . I'll go grab a couple." He gets up, too slowly for my liking, and disappears into the bookshelves.

Unbelievable! There is a reason I haven't run into him before now. I thank my lucky stars I had a chance to see the real Ethan before I made a fool of myself, blathering my eternal affection!

While he's gone Kate returns to the front. My eyes drop to my menu, guilt creeping up my insides. Does she know what kind of guy her boyfriend is? I've really started to like her and don't want to see her hurt. My stomach turns.

"Hey, Abby."

My head snaps up at the sound of her voice. A weight pushes down on my chest, making it hard to breathe. Do I tell her what happened just now?

"Ethan getting your book for you?" There is that kind smile and those friendly eyes. The flames of guilt burn higher around me.

"Uh, yeah." My eyes dart to the back of the store where I'd last seen him, and I ramble nervously. "I just need a paperback. I didn't know a good one. He's getting one, I guess. So . . ."

She smiles like she doesn't even notice I'm being a total freak, resting her hand on my shoulder. I think I might cry, so worried I may unintentionally hurt someone as kindhearted as Kate.

"Did, ah, Ethan talk to you yet?"

"Talk to me? About what?" My voice is high and tight. I even *sound* guilty.

She leans forward and whispers by my ear, "I thought maybe he was going to ask you out."

My eyes grow huge. I stop breathing. She caught us—she caught *him*, I correct myself. I'm not doing anything wrong here. I'm not the one coming on to him. At least I don't think I was. My mind is racing. How can I smooth this over? She must think terrible things of me!

Suddenly, she straightens. "Here he comes."

She doesn't leave, though. And Ethan seems distracted when he stops beside her with two books in hand. He doesn't look at either of us. Kate is watching him like she's expecting . . . something. I feel hot with embarrassment and anger.

"So, here's a timeless romance full of misunderstandings and miscommunications and the heroine has to overcome tragic circumstances to find her happy ending." He flops the book in front of me. "And this one's a political thriller set in the late 1980s. No romance but lots of blood and carnage and twists and turns." He flops the other book on top of the first one.

I have no idea how to handle this truly awkward situation. I study the books in front of me, then look up. Kate is watching Ethan in confusion. Ethan is staring at the table.

I clear my throat before I speak. "I'll, um, take the political thriller. Not in the mood for any romance right now." I glare at him until he looks at me. Hopefully I made myself clear. I take the book and feign interest in the back cover. In reality, I am dying to get out of here.

"Ethan," Kate says sternly, "I thought you had something you were going to ask Abby?"

My eyes widen with fear. This is a nightmare unfolding. She's going to try to pull it out of him in front of me.

"Uh, yeah," he mumbles. He looks straight into her eyes. "I already asked her about her take on the Ripley novel." Then he turns and stalks off. He runs his hands through his hair, not in the habitual way I had seen before.

Kate sighs. I train my eyes on her, trying to appraise her emotions. What is she thinking? Is she mad at me? What should I say to her—anything?

"I'm sorry, Abby." She shakes her head.

Wait. What? Why is *she* apologizing to *me*?

"I must have scared him off. I should have stayed away." Kate looks over to where he is standing at the new releases, straightening the display.

Oooo-kay? Maybe they have an open relationship? This afternoon has really gone sideways. I feel like my head is going to explode with all the drama, and I need to get out of here. I look out the window at my safe haven outside of this store.

"Kate, I'm so sorry," I blurt. "I didn't know. I didn't encourage him." I can't leave on bad terms. I already thought of her as a friend. Regretfully, I realize we could have been great friends. Too bad Ethan had to ruin it.

"Know what? What are you talking about?" She slides into the same chair across from me that Ethan had occupied minutes before.

I watch her for a long moment. Is she really going to make me say it? She mirrors my gaze. Clearly, she is.

"I didn't know." I swallow. "Honestly, I didn't know that you were Ethan's girlfriend. I never would have liked him if I had known—"

She holds up her hand. "Whoa—what?" She shakes her head. "Ethan's *girlfriend*? What kind of conversation did you two have?"

"Well, it's not what he said. I mean, I saw you two earlier. I thought—you kissed—you had your arm around him." I gesture toward the front counter where I had seen these things. I look at her, awaiting confirmation, but I know what I saw.

"Omigod!" Her hand flies to her mouth. "Oh, my God! Oh, honey—!" She clasps both of my hands in hers. Why is she trying to soothe *me*? I expected anger and shouting, emotions she has every right to express.

"Abby, I was happy to see him!" She registers my blank stare and continues. "Ethan's like my brother. I've known him forever. I was gone for a few weeks visiting family, then he was gone for a couple weeks trekking across Europe—we hadn't seen each other for two months!"

I am still staring at her, trying to make sense of everything. She continues, "Actually, West and I have been together for five years now. I'm West's girlfriend, not Ethan's!

"The way he acted when he saw you, I asked him what the deal was," she continues. "I thought he was going to ask you out on a date from the way he talked. You're the girl he met right before he left, and he was hoping to see you again."

Things are clicking now. My face is once again ablaze. I was so off-base—and now so embarrassed! This nightmare couldn't get any worse!

Kate searches my face, trying to figure out what to say to bring me back to reality no doubt. I place my hand on my forehead, trying to settle my thoughts and focus. When I look at her comforting face, I am washed with relief. I haven't hurt this kind woman after all. And she is not dating Ethan. And Ethan... *wanted to ask me out?*

I shake my head. I had deconstructed the demigod-like persona that was my Cutie in my head over the past week, and today, I buried any remnants of the crush I'd had on him. What am I to think of him now?

What does he think of me now?

I absolutely have to get out of here. It's getting hard to breathe. I am such a fool.

"Um, actually, Kate, I've got to get to work." I stand and rush toward the door, my escape.

"Abby, your book!" she calls after me.

I don't care anymore about the book. I need air. My lungs are aching for fresh air.

I pull on the heavy door, almost knocking over a woman as she tries to enter. But I don't look back. "Sorry!" I mutter as I take off. After a few steps I start to run. I run for maybe four blocks before I stop to walk. My sides burn and my chest heaves. I am still gasping for air.

Chapter Six

Don't Stop Believin'

I PRETTY MUCH barricade myself in my room for the next two days. Emory figures out quickly that something has upset me on Saturday night as I struggle to get through the shift. She tries talking to me a few times, but I admit I'm downright rude to her. I feel bad about it later, but I'm just so confused and emotionally unsettled. I don't want to make small talk. I don't want to hear about Dylan's plans for them on their day off. And I sure don't want to answer any questions about what's wrong with me.

I hadn't even said anything about Ethan to Emory or Val yet. I mean, why would I? He's just a guy I met at a bookstore. That I happened to develop a crush on. That I then proceeded to lose all chance of having any kind of relationship with. That I made an absolute fool of myself in front of.

Val attempts to lure me out of my room once with shopping and a trip to the spa. She still doesn't recognize shopping is her thing, not mine. I don't have any extra cash for that stuff anyway. I roll onto my side away from her and burrow more deeply under my covers.

Emory pops her head in after her date with Dylan on Sunday night; she takes the hint real quick that I don't want to hear about it. I'm curled up on my bed in the same pajamas from the night before, listening to some good feel-sorry-for-myself music on my iPod—Sia's "Breathe Me" at the moment. I haven't brushed my hair, or my teeth, or even bothered to shower today.

I don't feel like it on Monday either. Thankfully, my roommates leave me alone. I'm sure by now they think I'm mad at them for something. I'm too dejected to worry about it though.

On Tuesday, I finally drag myself out of bed to shower and brush my teeth right before work. Emory gives me plenty of space and is even ready and waiting before it's time for us to leave. I am the one who almost makes us late this time. As I rush around the apartment, I notice that she only talks to me if I ask her a direct question. Probably mad at me for all the silent treatment I've doled out.

Honestly, I just don't have the energy to care or to pretend all is great in Abby's World. I feel myself slipping further into the familiar depression that seems to so easily take up residence in my mind. I have no desire to even read. No interest in talking with anyone. I definitely don't want to explore my emotions with my friends, as I know they'll make me do if I mention what happened. I feel numb. It's comforting actually. Safe. Easy.

On Wednesday morning, the iciness from Val and Ems is palpable in the apartment when I emerge from my room. They stop mid-conversation and regard me coolly. I grab a bowl from the cupboard and pour myself some Frosty Crisps. I'm not really hungry, but I haven't eaten much the past few days. It's probably a good idea to stave off malnutrition. I still have to work, pay bills. As I pour the milk, I feel their eyes boring into me. What should I say? What words would make me not come off as a psychotic, delusional drama queen? I really don't think they will understand, and I don't want to give up my stronghold on the numbness that's keeping me from feeling the sadness about where I am in my life: A twenty-two-year-old college dropout, waitressing, yet broke all the time, no love in her life, with a couple of friends who would probably prefer she move out and take her sour disposition with her. The easier option is to keep it all shoved down inside.

I plop down at the table with my bowl and spoon, still not meeting their stares. I have no idea how to put all of this into words. I start with, "So, I guess . . . I owe you guys an apology."

I look up to see the glares have morphed into interest, a raised eyebrow, a tilted chin. How much should I tell them?

The silence is deafening. I clear my throat. It feels bone-dry all of a sudden. "So . . . I'm sorry for acting like such a jerk wagon the past few days." Patting my cereal down into the milk as I continue gives me something to focus on other than their intimidating faces. "I don't know what's gotten into me. I just—I just don't feel like myself . . . anymore."

Finally, the Cold War ends. "What happened to you, Abby? Saturday morning you're fine and dandy, and Saturday night—," Emory pauses to snap her fingers, "you're Super Bitch."

"We started thinking *we* did something wrong," Val interjects. "*Did* we do something wrong? Cause you gotta be straight with us. We don't know if you don't tell us."

I shake my head fervently. "No, no. It's not you guys, honest. And I'm truly sorry if I made you think it was. I'm just going through something." I glance out the window to avoid their interrogating stares. Tears sting behind my eyelids, and I want to keep it together. I haven't cried over this whole situation, and I won't start now.

"You can talk to us about anything. You know that, Abs." Emory softens and reaches over, squeezing my arm.

"I know," I say softly. When I regain control of my emotions, I look back at them. "And I appreciate you guys. I do. I just need to sort through some things, I guess. I feel like I'm an emotional mess right now, and I don't like it. I don't know how to deal with it." I try to smile for reassurance, but they still appear worried. "And I promise I'll stop alienating you both. I'll be a more pleasant person again."

"We just hate to see you like this," Val says gently. "It's no fun when you're all sad and moody."

"Well, I won't be anymore. How's that?" I put on my best fake smile, the kind I plaster on my face at work all the time for customers. Maybe if I can convince them, I can convince myself.

Later that day, as we lounge on the couches and flip through Val's new fashion magazines, I ask Emory about her date with Dylan. That melts the residual frost like a fireball shooting down from the sky. She must have been dying to tell me the details, since she spends half an hour gushing over how Dylan treated her and where they went and how she felt. She thinks this could be the real deal. I remind her that this was only, what, their fourth date? I also remind her of when she solemnly swore she would not rush into another relationship after the last one ended in disaster. And the one before that. And the one before that. All of these in less than a year's time. Emory has a bad habit of sprinting through the first stages of a relationship only to have the guy slam it to a screeching halt when he finds himself overcommitting and overwhelmed. She doesn't recognize it until it's too late. So, Val and I have promised that the next time we will rein her in whenever necessary. I ask her if it is necessary.

"Oh, Abby! Don't be ridiculous! Do I sound like I'm getting carried away?"

"Maybe not yet . . . but I'll be monitoring the situation," I warn, only partly joking.

"Good! That's what I'm counting on you for!" She points her finger at me, then hugs herself and sings, "I'm just so happy right now."

I laugh at her giddiness. I realize it feels good to be back in the civilized world. A world of conversation and interaction. With the sunshine breaking through the clouds, the gloomy haze isn't so oppressive. I start to feel a little less hopeless, a little more like myself.

"I am very happy for you, Ems," I say as I check the time on my phone. "Oh! We have to start getting ready for work. I don't want to be late."

"I'm on it!" She tosses the magazine onto the coffee table between us and runs off to her room.

I head to my room and begin my ritual of grabbing blue jeans from my drawer, boots from my shoe rack, and a shirt from my—crap! I was so intent on disappearing into my bed this weekend I haven't done a single load of laundry. I look over at my hamper, overflowing to the floor with dirty clothes. No way to salvage a shirt out of there. I resign myself to trekking across the apartment.

"Ems?"

"Yeah? What's up?" She twists a hair tie at the bottom of her golden French braid and turns from the mirror.

"Um . . . so . . . how much do you love me?"

"What'd you do?" she demands.

"Do you happen to have a clean shirt I can borrow?" I ask sheepishly. I know her answer will probably be no—this is Emory we're talking about here—but I hope anyway.

"The Always Prepared One asks *me* for a clean shirt?" she chides.

"I know, I know! Please? I didn't do any laundry yet." I lace my fingers under my chin, begging. I know it will make her feel superior for once if she can come to my rescue.

She keeps me in suspense while she digs around in her closet. Then finally, she produces a shirt. "You so owe me!"

"Totally!" I sigh with relief. Grabbing the shirt from her, I hurry to finish getting ready. The shirt-borrowing is bad enough; she'll never let me live it down if I am the reason we are late to work.

THE NIGHT IS unusually quiet at Hooligan's. Jeff sends Kimber home at seven. I'm relieved he didn't pick me—although he's made it clear he is disappointed in my lackluster attitude last night. I need the money, so I go overboard tonight to prove my value.

I notice Emory chatting up Dylan several times between orders. I sure hope he is the real deal. He seems like a decent guy, but guys can fool you. Woo you into contentment, then lull you into complacency, then abandon you when they're through with you. And manage to make you feel like it's all your fault that it fell apart.

A weird thought pops into my head out of nowhere. I wonder what my dad is up to these days. I realize I haven't seen him since . . . my high school graduation? He never came to visit me at college—said New York was too big; he'd never set foot in a city this size. And I never had the extra cash to buy a plane ticket to Cedar Rapids.

I sigh as I think about the last time I saw him. One of the very few times I have seen him sober. Like clean and sober, not just sober for the day because he had to be. He'd looked good, very put-together with his suit jacket and dress slacks. He'd even worn a tie. I remember being a little surprised at how happy I was to see him . . . and relieved. It had been a long time coming. I think I was as proud of him getting sober as he had been of me for graduating high school.

He'd probably be disappointed in me for not finishing college. He didn't even know I quit school. But I feel sure he'd like Hooligan's. The restaurant and its double-decker burgers are right up his alley.

"Excuse me, miss?"

"Yes?"

A woman at table nine has her arm outstretched. "Can we get our check, please?" She looks exasperated. Her twin preadolescent boys are throwing French fries at each other across the table and howling with laughter.

"I'll be right back with it," I assure her.

I walk up to the register at the bar and print out the tab for table nine. "Hey, Ems?" I call over to where she is talking with Dylan, leaning over the bar as they make eyes at each other.

"Yeah?" She barely peels her eyes away from him. I almost laugh.

"Um, I'm getting table nine's ticket out. Mom's ready to get the brats outta here!"

"Oh, gosh!" She glances over at them, panic registering on her face.

"No, no. Don't worry about it. I've got it." I wave my hand and grin, so she knows it is really no big deal.

"Thanks, Abby! I owe you!"

"Well, I owed you, remember?" I point to her shirt that I'm wearing. "Now we're even."

Table nine taken care of, the mom smiles gratefully as I set the check on the table.

"I just seated a gentleman at table fifteen," one of the hostesses, Tasha, says in passing. She spins around and looks at me conspiratorially. "He asked to sit in 'Abby's section.'"

I'm confused. Who would ask to sit in "Abby's section"? Who even knows there's an "Abby's section"? I walk around the corner to the booth, ready to give my spiel, but I stop short, mouth open. I can't force a single sound out. I think about turning and darting back to the kitchen, but that would make me look even more foolish to this man than I already do.

He looks up from his menu. "Abby?"

Too late to run now. I force myself to speak around the blockage in my throat: "Welcome to Hooligan's, home of the famous double-decker burger. Would you like to try our new Sourdough Supreme—?" Then I lose it. My mind goes blank. I futilely search for the words to finish the special, but I have nothing. My face burns with embarrassment.

"Um . . . Abby?" Ethan's voice is almost amused at my floundering, but still . . . sympathetic? "You forgot your book the other day. When you didn't come back to the store, I thought I'd better bring it to you." He produces the light blue paperback I'd selected on Saturday.

Ugh. Saturday.

It seems like he wants to smile—his sparkling eyes are smiling, but maybe he's afraid I'll go all psycho on his ass again. I finally come to my senses. "Um, it's not my book, actually. I never paid for it."

"*I* did." This time his mouth smiles, too. That wide, sexy smile. My heart skips a beat.

"Wha—why did you do that?"

"Well, I know that you wanted this one. So . . ." Ethan looks down at the book. I realize he's fidgeting with it, flipping the pages with his thumb.

"Okay, look." When his eyes meet mine, I can see a blush color his cheeks. "Here's the deal, Abby. I'm not really good at this, you know. I had worked up all my courage to ask you out the other day. Kate and West had said that you'd been coming in regularly, and I thought maybe there had been a—I don't know—a spark or something there that first day we met." He searches my eyes, looking for something, maybe a sign that I'd felt it, too. I don't know if there's anything there but sheer surprise, but he continues nonetheless. "You intrigued me." His gaze drops away from mine. "But you kind of blew my whole plan out of the water. Then you tore out of there like a whirlwind."

Ethan shakes his head, then looks at me again with questioning eyes, "I thought maybe I was way off-base thinking there might have been a connection there . . ."

He waits for me to respond. I still can't make my voice work. Even if I could, I'm sure the only sounds that would escape would be blathering nonsense.

Inhaling deeply, he continues, "So it took me a few days to decide, the hell with it, I'm asking her anyway—I'm asking you anyway . . . do you, ah, want to go out with me sometime?"

He stops flipping the pages of the book and slides it over to the edge of the table, a peace offering. A new start.

Gingerly, I reach for the book, trying to make my eyes focus on the title in big block letters across the front. I realize the butterflies are back fluttering around in my stomach. I can't help but smile at him in all his handsomeness. "I have to be upfront with you about something. You see, I have episodes of psychotic behavior."

"Really. Well, that's perfect then, because I only date psychotic women. I have a history of it."

I forget the buzz of the restaurant around me, lost in Ethan's blue eyes. I never could have dreamed my night would turn out like this. I start thinking I'm dreaming the perfectness of the moment . . . until Jeff breaks into my euphoria.

"Ahem," his voice booms from the bar.

I look over apologetically, then morph back into a Hooligan's server—home of the famous double-decker burgers! "Sorry, Ethan, I've got to get back to work." I point my pen behind my shoulder at Jeff. "Can I get you something to eat? My treat, for the book."

"The book is a gift," he points out. "Just bring me whatever you would recommend. *I'll* buy my dinner."

"You trust a psychotic woman to recommend food?"

"I do," he laughs. "By the way, we've never been formally introduced." He holds out his hand. "I'm Ethan Lansing."

"Abby Templeton." I shake his hand. He has a nice, strong grip. My heart leaps in my chest as electricity charges through my body. Point of origin: Ethan's touch.

"Nice to meet you, Abby."

I nod and leave to place his order. Then I have to hurry and check in with my tables. I have no idea how long I've actually been engaged with Ethan. Time seems to stop around him.

Table eleven is mad at me for taking so long with the check, but I can't stop smiling. Table thirteen tells me I forgot their ketchup. I apologize but keep smiling.

"Abby, what's gotten in to you?" Emory questions at the register as she elbows my side. "And who is that guy you were talking to forever over there?"

"That," I murmur, "is Ethan. We're going on a date."

"Stop it!" She slaps my arm. I mock injury. "What, he just asked you out on a date? Do you even know this guy?"

I hold up the book from my apron as explanation.

"What? *Scandal and Sacrifice*?" She looks at me, puzzled.

"He works at the bookstore I always go to. He just gave me this book."

"Ohhhh." She has a moment of understanding, then confusion clouds her face again. "Why this book? Weird."

I laugh. "I'll tell you all about it later. I've got to get to my tables. They're already upset with me."

"Order up, Abby! Let's go!" Jeff is clearly not happy with me either. He probably wishes he'd sent me home instead of Kimber. But I don't care. Nothing can crush my high now. I float through the rest of the night.

By the time I take Ethan his check, the restaurant has calmed down, so I can spend an extra minute or two without Jeff coming down on me. "So, what did you think of my selections?"

"Perfect. Sweet and tangy honey barbeque? Just what I would have chosen. And the pale ale was a nice complement." There is that smile that makes my heartbeat quicken.

"You're just saying that." I smile back.

"I'm serious. Really," he insists. His smile drops and his eyebrows shoot up. He appears nervous all of a sudden. "So, ah, about that date?"

"Oh. Yeah. Um, what day are you thinking?" I want to squeal with delight—he really does want to go out on a date! It takes a mountain of effort to remain composed.

"Are you free Saturday? There's a great band playing in Central Park."

"Actually, the only days I have off are Sundays and Mondays."

"Oh, um . . . well, I work this Sunday. My only day off right now is Saturday."

My heart sinks. Maybe this isn't going to work after all. He puts his thumb and finger to his lower lip, contemplating. "Well, I tell you what." He looks up hopefully. "I really want to see you, but I don't think West can find somebody to work for me this Sunday. How do you feel about hanging around the store for a bit with me? Not much of a first date, but it'll give me time to work on West."

He wants to see me—how can I refuse? "Yeah, sure. Here," I scribble my number on his receipt. "Give me a call?"

"I will." There's that smile again. And there go the butterflies.

"All right." I try to control my grin. *Not too eager, Abby. Don't let him see the power he has over you.* "I've got to go now. And thanks for the book," I add as I turn toward the kitchen, walking as quickly but calmly as I can. I push through the door and hold myself against the wall, trying not to scream. Emory bursts through the door after me. She squeals and pounds her feet, shaking me back and forth.

"O-M-G, Abby! He's totally hot!"

"I know, right?" My cheeks hurt already from smiling.

"You have *a lot* to explain to me and Val tonight!"

Chapter Seven

Let the Sunshine In

Between our work schedules, Ethan and I barely get to talk before our date on Sunday. He used his breaks on Thursday and Friday to call me before I had to head off to work. He wanted to eat at Hooligan's both nights, but I told him not to. I'm already on thin ice with Jeff, and I can't afford to lose my job. He said he understood, but both times I smiled at the distinct sound of disappointment I heard come across the line. That made the butterflies kick up their dance.

Saturday finally arrives, and I start to worry because Ethan hasn't called before I have to leave for work. I try to reason that something has come up and he's probably really busy. It is his day off, after all. I mean, it couldn't be because he's changing his mind . . .

I have a hard time concentrating at work, trying not to think of all the things that could have gone wrong, of all the things I could have said in our phone conversations that might have made him change his mind about me.

Jeff shoots me a warning look once when I mess up a customer's order. I apologize profusely to both him and the customer, hoping that is enough to save my job. Although I'm really starting to doubt it. I went over and above on Thursday and Friday to save face. I really don't want to fall backward after the strides I've made in Jeff's good graces.

At the end of the night though, as Emory and I make our way to the back, Jeff is standing in the hallway to the stockroom, leaning against the wall, arms crossed. "Abby, you got a minute?" He jerks his head toward his office.

"Um, yeah." I glance nervously at Emory. She gives my hand a supportive squeeze before taking my apron. He turns and strides into his office. I take a deep breath to prepare myself before following; I know what's coming.

He closes the office door as he motions to the chair in front of his desk. Jeff's a manager who spends most of his time out in the restaurant, monitoring his staff or chatting up the customers, so you only sat in this chair in his office when you were hired . . . or fired.

I slump down in the chair, bracing for the worst. At first, I stare at the nameplate on his desk: JEFF TRAINOR, MANAGER. Eventually, I lower my eyes to focus on the fringe of the tears in my jeans, picking at the frays. When the silence becomes unbearable, I lift my gaze to see him sitting there, hands interlaced, his forefingers pointed together at his lips. There's something in his eyes I can't quite recognize. We've all seen his anger, his happiness, his freaked-out excitement. This look is different.

"Abby," he says, finally breaking the silence, "you've worked here for almost four years now, right? And when you came to me last November and asked if I could put you on full-time hours, I gladly did that. Do you know why?" He pauses, but I realize he's not expecting an answer. "Because you were one of the best damn servers I had out there." He points out the door toward the dining room. "I was happy you wanted to be a full-timer. Sad for you that the college thing didn't work out, but hey, I understand that kind of thing happens." He shrugs, then folds his hands across his stomach, leaning back in his chair.

I know I should be begging for my job right now, arguing all my good points. But I can't say anything. I feel . . . defeated. I chew on my lip. Another long, silent moment passes. I wish he'd just get on with it.

"Abby," Jeff continues, leaning forward to splay his hands on his desk, "what's going on with you lately? You're walking around like a sad sack half the time, messing up orders, forgetting about customers. Then you're busting butt, my best server of the night . . ." He shakes his head and lifts his fingers up off the desk. "I never know which version of you is gonna show up to work each night."

He pauses, staring at the door for a long time. When he finally brings his eyes to mine, I see something in his face that really hurts me, like a disappointed father when his child does something he never thought she'd do. He relaxes into his chair and folds his hands in his lap. Here it comes. I hold my breath.

"I don't know what to do with you." He shrugs. "Do you . . . have anything you want to say?" He waits, eyebrows raised.

"Jeff . . ." I have to clear my throat. "I know I've had a bad week, and I'm sorry. I'm really sorry." I plaster on my best apology face as I lean forward in my chair. I mean, really sincere. Because I do feel bad that I've put him in this position. It's my fault, and I know it. But I'm not sure if I care to keep my job anymore or lose it. I can't afford *not* to keep it though.

"Abby, I need some assurance that this isn't going to keep happening."

"I *need* this job, Jeff," I plead, but he sits unconvinced. "I like this job, and I love the people I work with. And you're a *great* boss," I throw in for extra points. "I've been trying to get through this funk. I've been working on it. I promise when I come back on Tuesday, you'll see the old Abby, ready to go." I feel a bit of relief when I see his face soften while he ponders my appeal.

"So . . . this 'funk' has nothing to do with anything work-related, does it?" he asks pointedly.

I'm confused.

"Donovan thought maybe you were upset he broke up with you."

"What?! Donovan said *what*?" My eyes bug out of their sockets. My mouth drops to the floor. *Seriously?*

"When I asked him if he had any idea why you were so distracted, he said you two kind of had a thing going, but he told you it wasn't going to work out," Jeff says in a way that sounds more like a question than an answer.

I shake my head, disbelieving. I'm furious, but I have to laugh. Only Donovan could come up with something like that. Paint himself the picture of a heartbreaker. "No, no," I choke out after I quit laughing. "It's *not* Donovan, I can assure you."

His expression relaxes and he chuckles, too. "Okay, good. I didn't think so, but I had to check. Sorry, kiddo."

"Jeff, I promise you, no more Bad Abby." I smile, still shaking my head and thinking about what an irritating goof Donovan is.

"Great! That's great to hear. You know I think a lot of you. You're a wonderful employee." He stands and motions to the door. I follow him, surprised by how relieved I am that the meeting turned out this way. I guess I'm more attached to this place than I'd realized. I mean, these people are the closest thing to family I have right now.

Jeff pats me on the back, then squeezes my shoulders in a paternal fashion as he opens the door.

"Thanks, Jeff. I really appreciate it." And I mean it. I guess he is the closest thing to a father figure I have right now, too.

"See you Tuesday, kiddo."

I nod and hurry out, finding Emory and Dylan waiting. Well, actually, they are in a full make-out session, leaning up against the side of the building. Clearly, they got bored waiting. I roll my eyes. "Ahem."

"Oh! Abby!" Emory startles and pushes Dylan away. I arch my eyebrow at them. "What happened? What did Jeff say?"

"No big deal." I shrug as we start to walk to the subway. "I just have to step it up."

"Whew! I was so worried you were going to get fired. Dylan didn't think so." She nudges him with her elbow and gives him a gushy smile and goo-goo eyes. He smirks and pulls her into his side. They really make me want to puke sometimes.

"Get this, Donovan told Jeff he thought my problem was because he dumped me!" I laugh again at the absurdity of it. "Can you believe it?"

"What? No way!" Dylan hoots.

"You're kidding!"

"I knew that kid was delusional, but wow." Dylan is still laughing, shaking his head. "I'm gonna give him so much crap!"

"Oh, don't, Dylan! Poor guy. I don't think he can help the way he is."

"You're way too nice, Abby." Emory turns and walks backward, facing us. "But then, you *do* know him much better than we do!"

I reach out to smack her shoulder, but she skips and spins around Dylan before I can reach her.

"Nice, Emory, real nice. Are you ever going to let me live that down?"

"She may," Dylan chimes in, "but I won't."

He's close enough. I nail him in the shoulder with a closed fist.

"Ow! Hey!" he bellows. "But seriously, you can't blame the kid for bragging, can you? When Jay found out, he was so jealous. He thinks you're hot."

"Oh, please!" I say, exasperated. Can we stop the Pick-on-Abby Hour?

"I'm not kidding," he swears, wide-eyed.

"You don't give yourself enough credit," Emory reproves.

I shake my head, dismissing them. "Well, if Donovan told Jeff and you and Jay, who else has he bragged to? Are people talking about me behind my back?"

"I don't think so, Abs. I haven't heard anything," she reassures me.

"Nobody would take him seriously anyway. Jay and I had a hard time believing him, and we were there the next morning."

I frown at Dylan's knowing smirk.

"But, if it will make you feel better, I'll tell him to keep his mouth shut about it or I have orders from my girlfriend, Abby's best friend, to beat him into silence." The smile on his face tells me he rather likes the idea of putting the hurt on Donovan.

"Thanks, Dylan. I appreciate you looking out for me."

The vibration of my cell phone in my pocket stops my breathing. Could it be Ethan? Maybe he didn't forget about me after all? I pull it out, excitement dancing through me as I see a familiar number. "Hey!"

"Hey, Abby!" No, he hadn't forgotten about me. I can tell by his tone. He's as happy to hear my voice as I am to hear his. "Sorry I didn't call earlier—things were crazy at the store today, so West called me in to help out."

I close my eyes and sigh. *Way to overreact, Abby.* "I figured. No big deal."

"You're not still at work, are you?"

"No. Walking home with Emory and Dylan."

"Good. So . . . you're still coming tomorrow, right?" He sounds a little worried that I might not be. I like that.

"Of course. What time?"

"We open at ten, but I wouldn't mind it if you came a little early. We could hang out before the place gets crazy. Actually, can I pick you up? We can walk to the store together. You don't live that far, do you?"

He wants to pick me up! What a gentleman. "No, sure. I'm not far."

I fill him in on the details of how to get to my apartment. I glance over at Emory smiling at me.

"All right. I think I've got it. If not, I'll call." He pauses. "Hey, Abby?"

"Hmm?"

"I can't wait to see you again."

"Me, too." *My sentiments exactly.*

"Good night, Abby."

"Good night."

I slip my phone into my pocket, goofy grin plastered across my face. My spirits have just shot up, up, and to the moon.

"Val is going to scream when she finds out she'll get to meet Ethan!" Emory dances around and grabs my arm. "What time is he coming over?"

"Nine-ish." She almost knocks me down with all the arm-yanking. I stumble and try to keep upright. She may be more excited than I am to see him. "No interrogations though! I don't want him scared off. I hardly know him yet."

"Sure, of course," she assures me.

❊

"OH, HEY, ABS," Val calls as I walk into the kitchen to grab a granola bar the next morning. She's painting her toenails on the couch. For whatever reason, she got up early, showered, started a load of laundry, and cleaned the bathroom. This is so not like her, especially on a Sunday.

"Yeah?"

"Your mom called yesterday. Said she'd been trying to call your cell phone for a few days. Thought maybe you'd lost it or something. I told her you might have, so I'd tell you she called."

I groan as I drop onto the couch beside her, peeling the wrapper on my breakfast. "Well, thanks for covering for me. Did she say what she wanted?"

"Nope. She just *really* wants you to call her. Asked me, like, three times if I 'would be sure to tell you.'" Val does an impression of my mother's condescending voice that is pretty spot-on. I chuckle around a bite of granola.

"All right. I'll call her later. I've got to start getting ready. Ethan's coming in about an hour. Did Emory tell you?"

"Yeah, she did! I've got my list of questions ready to go."

"No! No questions, please! I'm begging you!"

"Don't worry about it," she laughs at my freakout. "We'll just be carefully observant. You can bet I'm gonna be checking this guy out. Gotta make sure he's worth all the hassle you've gone through because of him."

I roll my eyes but keep my mouth shut. I think my "hassle" had less to do with anything he's done and more to do with my own stupidity and snap judgments.

"Where is Ems?" I look around. "Her door's open."

"She's walking Dylan downstairs." It's Val's turn to roll her eyes.

"I see." We both snicker. "You know, I don't have any complaints about the guy ... yet."

"Me neither." Val fans her toes. "He seems genuine. And Emory seems to be taking things much slower this time. I hope she doesn't mess this one up."

"I know. She hasn't been this happy in a long time."

The front door opens, cutting our conversation short.

"Hey, what's up, guys?" Emory sings.

"I was just headed to the shower." I jump up, toss my granola wrapper in the trash, and give Emory a quick high-five as I pass her to get to my room.

"You'd better hurry! You have less than an hour."

"I know! I know! You're making me nervous—now stop!" I scold as I walk past her again with my clothes and towels in my arms.

I'm ready in no time, but then the girls have to put in their two cents on my hair and outfit. As a result, I change tops three times and shoes twice. Val thinks my hair should be sophisticated and pulled back from my face. Emory thinks I should go with tousled, sexy curls. In the end, I trust my own instincts and use the blow dryer and paddle brush for a straight, sleek style. Simple, easy. I don't want to go overboard—I mean, it's a date at a bookstore. I rub my fingers back and forth in my bangs to give them a little lift and scrutinize my reflection.

The buzzer rings and I panic, realizing I'm not ready to see Ethan yet. I want to see him, yes, but I am not *ready* to see him. The butterflies are bouncing around in my stomach, and I need time to rein them in. My hands are shaking as I struggle to get my eyeliner on without making a huge, jagged line across my face.

"Abby, you want me to buzz him in?" Emory hollers.

"Uh, yeah, thanks." I press my hands down on the counter for a second and take a deep breath. Then another deep breath. *Calm down, silly.* I hear Emory talking to Ethan over the speaker and buzzing him in. The fact that he is on his way up the stairs only makes me more nervous. I hear the apartment door open. I realize I haven't moved since I heard the buzzer.

"Ethan's out here," Emory calls.

"Um, I'll be right there!"

Somehow, I manage to get my nerves under control and finish my eyeliner. I have to get out there before Emory and Val start giving him the third degree. I toss my makeup into my designated drawer and give myself a once-over. Smooth my hair with my hands, then fluff it, then smooth it again. *Okay. Good enough.*

All my nervousness dissipates as I walk out to the living room and see Ethan smiling. At me. His smile has an amazing calming effect.

"Hey, Abs, Ethan grew up here in the city," Val says.

"Yeah, and he went to NYU, too," Emory adds. "And he's an only child, like you."

"Really? Did you guys get through all your twenty questions?" I shoot a glare at Emory. She knows better! She smiles innocently in return. "So, you've met Valencia Preston and Emory James, my roommates and former friends." I smile slyly at their glares. "Let's go." I nod toward the door.

"Oh, that's harsh, Abby," Val takes mock offense. "Don't worry, Ethan." She turns to face him. "She's not usually this mean. Just to small children and puppies."

He laughs as he stands. "Nice to meet you both. We should really get going though."

He walks to the door and holds it open for me. I look back at my so-called friends sitting on the couch. "I'll deal with you two later," I scold. They grin childishly at me.

Outside, the sun is bright and the sky is clear. A beautiful, mid-September day, still very warm, but not baking hot.

"So how far are you from here?" I ask casually.

"West 57th Street, in the Metropolitan Tower. Just a quick subway ride and a short walk."

"I'm on your way to work then?"

"Yes, you are." I love the way he smiles at me.

We are quiet for a minute as we walk. It doesn't feel uncomfortable, though, quite the opposite.

"I was curious about something," I wonder aloud. "How did you know where to find me?"

"You gave me directions to your place, remember?"

"No, I mean the other night," I correct. "How did you know there was an 'Abby's section' at Hooligan's?"

"Oh, well," he kind of chuckles. "Kate told me where you worked. Said I'd better go find you because she was sick and tired of seeing me watch out the window for you. Her words," he adds.

I nod my head once. I guess I owe it to Kate, then, for pushing him along. I sure wouldn't have gone back there. Not without knowing how he really felt about me. I had no desire to add insult to injury.

"Well, I'm glad you did. And thanks again for the book. I'm halfway through it. It's a good thriller. I really have to pay attention to what's being said and what's not being said. Normally, I would've had the book finished within a week, but I'm getting sidetracked this weekend," I tease.

"Well, far be it from me to keep you from a good book," he plays along. "Or perhaps you'll find my company a million times more interesting than any book," he adds archly.

"I'm sure I will."

We walk a bit in contented silence. To my surprise, he laces his fingers between mine in a natural movement. My heart jumps. It's been a long time since I've held anybody's hand. I'd forgotten how nice it is, the closeness I feel.

"I talked with West yesterday, and the good news is I can get my day off switched from Saturday to Sunday. So next week we can actually spend one whole day together."

"You'll have to think up a real date idea then."

"Yes, I will. You like tattoos and motorcycles?"

"What?"

"The Tattoo and Motorcycle Festival is next weekend. Or maybe the Burlesque Festival?" The look I shoot him answers his question. "Never fear, I'll think of something."

When we reach the store, he unlocks the door. He grabs my hand and pulls me in behind him, turns on the lights, and locks the door again from the inside.

"Wow, we beat West here." He checks his watch. "It's 9:30. Plenty of time. Let's have a seat." He motions toward two stools behind the front counter.

"So have you always wanted to work in a bookstore with Mr. Christiansen?" I ask as we sit. I'm curious as to how he ended up here and not in a more glamorous profession.

"Ah, no. I always wanted to be an astronaut, but alas, that never worked out. My mom wanted me to be a lawyer. My dad didn't really care what I did with my life as long as I wasn't a deadbeat," he jokes.

"You went to NYU, though? Did you graduate?"

"Yeah. I graduated from law school. Tried the whole lawyer thing out for a year or two. But I couldn't kid myself—I only did it for my mom. Hated it actually. I wasn't cut out to be a lawyer."

"Was your mom upset that you gave it up?"

"No." He looks down. Something changes in his expression, darkens. It is a quiet moment before he speaks again. "She couldn't be upset. My parents died when I was twenty. Car wreck."

Instinctively, I reach over and clasp his hand with my own. My heart constricts as I think of the pain he must have felt. I want to tell him how sorry I am for his loss, but he continues, apparently not wanting to dwell on this part of his story.

"I went on with my pre-law studies, got my degree, thinking the most important thing was making my mom proud. I knew she'd be looking down on me, and I didn't want to let her down. But in the end, I realized I *was* letting her down. She wouldn't be happy if she knew I wasn't happy. And I was miserable." He gazes into my eyes, his own eyes misty. He pauses, maybe trying to compose himself.

"And then I ran across West, who was an old buddy of mine from high school. He was opening a bookstore, and he suckered me into his grand scheme." He smiles as he motions around the room.

"Excuse me, I seem to remember a much more excited Ethan at the idea of my grand scheme," I hear West behind me. I was so into Ethan's story that I hadn't heard him come in.

"Yeah, yeah. It's about time you got here. Thought I was going to have to open the place without you," he chides.

"Hey, Abby. How's my favorite customer this morning?" West's in his usual attire: flannel over a dark blue shirt and khakis.

"I'll bet you say that to every customer, West." When he looks at me with a hurt expression, I smile. "I'm good. How are you?"

"I. Am. Great. It is going to be a great day!" he exclaims as he turns on the register.

"Is he always this cheerful?" I ask Ethan.

"Most of the time. You get used to it."

"Hey—life is good, people!" West calls as he flips the sign on the door from Closed to Open. "And now for the onslaught of New York City readers!" He swings the door open. "I proclaim this store—open!" he yells out into the street.

❦

BUSINESS IS STEADY, so Ethan only has a few minutes here and there to chat. I try to pass the time by flipping through magazines while he's busy. Honestly, it does little to hold my attention. I find myself wishing we had some real time to talk. I feel like he's opened up on some pretty important life events, and I want to find out more about these things that shaped the person he is today. But I still enjoy watching him work, watching him interact with people. He is such a genuine soul, an unexpected ray of sunshine breaking through my gray clouds.

At two o'clock, he asks if I want to run up the block with him to the sandwich shop and get us all something to eat. I am happy to go. In truth, I'm starving, but I didn't want to leave Ethan, so I'd suffered in silence.

In no time we are back at the store, sandwiches in hand. West is nice enough to let us go to the breakroom and eat first. I still don't get to ask Ethan the questions I want to. We're too busy trying to eat so he can let West have his break. So, we stick to small talk for now. Not that I mind. Anything Ethan has to say is interesting to me. He has an old soul, and he seems very comfortable in his skin, very confident in his life choices. I envy that. I feel like I'm still trying to find my place in the world, like I don't know what I want to be when I grow up. Definitely not a Hooligan's server.

At six, I decide I'd better go. Ethan is obviously spending more time with me than he should be. A couple of customers have gotten annoyed waiting for him to help them. I figure I'd better call my mom too, before she sends a search party to New York.

We say our goodbyes, and he promises to call after he gets off work at nine. He wishes I wasn't walking home alone, which makes me smile, but I remind him that I know the way. I've walked home from the store before.

I float all the way to my apartment. It was a perfect first date. The only thing that could have made it better would have been a kiss to end the day. I close my eyes and shudder at the thought. Ooh, I cannot wait for that kiss . . .

Chapter Eight

Emotional Whiplash, Is That a Thing?

WHEN I WALK through the front door of the apartment, Emory and Val are ready to pounce. Of course they want to know every detail.

"But first," Val says, holding up her hand, "*please* call your mother. She called *again*. I think she thinks you've died and we're not telling her. She was downright rude this time!"

"Sorry, Val. I'll call her right now. Then, I'll dish." I head for my room, searching my mother's number on the way. I shut my door. No doubt she will be mad, and I'd rather deal with her in private.

"Hey, Mom?"

"Abigail Templeton. It is about time you called me!"

I cringe. Yep, she's mad. "Yeah, I'm really sorry, I, ah . . . I lost my phone for a while." Tiny fib, harmless really.

"Didn't your roommates tell you I called? I've called the landline three times now."

"Yes, Mother. Val told me you called when I got off work last night. I meant to call you earlier today, but I got busy."

"Well, I have been worried sick these last two days, not knowing if something had happened to you! You know I can't just hop in a car and drive over there. It's not like you're across town!"

I flop down on my bed, wondering how long this tirade will last. I'm not sure why she feels the need to throw such a guilt trip on me. I highly doubt she spent more than two seconds being worried. It is rare for anything to take my mother's thoughts off herself.

"You need to be a little more responsible, Abigail. It is a good thing you found that phone. How much would that have cost if you'd had to replace it? You know you'll be graduating from college soon, and you'll be out there in the real world with real responsibilities. You need to start acting like a grownup. Are those two roommates of yours still throwing parties all the time?"

"No, Mother. We don't throw parties anymore." Another tiny lie—we don't throw parties *all the time* anymore. I feel a headache coming on. My mother still doesn't know that I dropped out of school last year. I couldn't bring myself to tell her. I was afraid of just this sort of reaction—multiplied by a thousand.

"Well, good. Your studies should be the most important thing. This is your last year, you know. You need to make it count."

I squeeze my eyes shut tight, thinking maybe that will stop the thudding in my brain, but no such luck. "So, um, did you need to tell me something? Is that why you're so mad I didn't call you sooner?" I try to fake concern so maybe she'll get on a different track. Off my irresponsibility and off school.

"Oh, yes, I do need to talk with you about something. Janice and Caroline are planning a girls' trip to New York for the weekend to see a Broadway show and go shopping. They've invited me to come along." In typical fashion, she flips her mood like a switch. I've never known another person who could be full tilt on destruction in one breath and spin around to rainbows and butterflies in the next as quickly and seamlessly as my mother.

"That sounds like fun." I hope my engineered enthusiasm isn't obvious.

"Yes, it will be. We are heading out Friday afternoon from the Quad Cities airport. We'll be landing Friday evening, but Janice has already made dinner reservations for us, so I won't be able to see you until Saturday morning. I thought we could have brunch and catch up for a bit. The girls will be shopping until afternoon, and then we have another dinner reservation before the show. We head out on Sunday morning, so I won't be able to see you before we go. So, can you find a place for us to have brunch on Saturday morning?"

"Saturday morning? *This* Saturday morning?" It's hard to comprehend all that she is rattling on about with this headache.

"Yes. Saturday morning. You don't have plans, do you?" The familiar annoyance colors her tone.

"Um . . . no. No plans. I'll make the reservation. I can't pick you up from the airport Friday since I'm working, but do you need me to drop you off Sunday?" I immediately regret the words after they escape my mouth.

"No. Janice has a shuttle lined up for us. She really has a packed itinerary while we are there. She frowned upon my separation from them on our shopping day, but I put my foot down. I said, 'I never get to see my daughter as it is. She would not forgive me if I was in New York City and didn't see her.' So, she gave up on trying to change my mind. I assured her I would have plenty of time to shop with them in the afternoon."

A long pause elapses before I realize I'd tuned her out. I was lingering on the thought that I really wouldn't mind if she let Janice change her plans and she decided to stick with them rather than see me. "Ah, okay. So, I'll see you Saturday then. Have a safe flight."

"Okay, Abigail, I will call your phone Friday night to let you know we have made it to the hotel. I'll leave the address, so you'll know where to pick me up in the morning. All right. Love you."

It's funny to me how she can say those two words with none of the emotion you would expect to hear, like it's just another sentence in her string of rambling. "Love you, too." Of course, it's also funny how I can match her lack of emotion.

I drop my phone next to me and fall backward onto my bed. I just want curl up under my covers and sleep my headache away. I glance at the clock on my nightstand. It isn't even seven o'clock. And Emory and Val are probably hovering outside my door, waiting on the details of my day with Ethan that I promised them. I turn my head and gaze at my closed door. I shut my eyes. I could fall asleep if I lie really still for a few minutes.

Then the image of Ethan enters my thoughts. I see him standing before me, the setting sun turning his face golden-red. We are standing in front of my apartment, at the bottom of the stairs. He holds my hands in his. His blue eyes sparkle, staring so deeply inside me—all my thoughts, all my desires. He leans in ever so slowly. My breath catches as I wait for his lips to touch mine.

"Abby! Abby, you done in there?" Emory hollers.

"Get out here, girl!" Val demands.

I sigh and reluctantly pull myself off the bed. Surprisingly, my headache is fading.

"THIS IS A nice restaurant, Abigail," my mother says, appraising the dining room.

"Thank you. Val's parents brought us here a couple months back for her birthday. I thought you might like it." I knew she would like it. Victoria Templeton likes anything that is high-class and expensive. I note the new diamond necklace and tennis bracelet she's sporting as we survey our menus. I'm not quite sure how she manages it on an English teacher's salary. Granted, she's been a teacher for almost thirty years, and she tutors in the evenings to supplement her income. But I never felt like we lived the kind of life she presented with her jewelry and hobbies.

In fact, I'd worked part-time and summers since I was fifteen to be able to afford prom dresses, athletic shoes for sports, or going out with friends. My mother made it sound like the child support she'd gotten from Dad every month was barely enough to cover my clothes, schoolbooks, and lunch ticket, so I never dared to ask for money for anything. And when it came time for college, I never even thought of asking for financial help from my parents.

I remember saving all summer one year to pay for my senior pictures, but Dad had shocked the hell out of me when he'd offered to pay for them. I guess it made him feel like he was contributing to my life, making up for not being around. If I'd had the nerve, I'd have told him paying for pictures and making it to a couple of my games didn't really count for much. Popping into my life when it was convenient for him just wasn't enough.

I'm not sure if my dad had always been a deadbeat type, living his life inside a bottle, or if being married to my mother made him that way. I can't imagine her ever being attracted to him; she's had such vehement loathing for him for as long as I can recall. And he wasn't around enough for me to learn his side of the story, so I guess my picture of my father is pretty tainted. I blame him as much as I blame her though. He had every opportunity to show up in my life, to let me know who he really was if he'd wanted to. I mean, we'd lived in the same city. Cedar Rapids wasn't *that* big.

The waiter finally arrives to take our orders. I know my mother won't pay for my meal—won't even offer—and truthfully, I'm afraid she'll find a way to get me to pay the whole tab, so I order the cheapest thing on the menu.

"So, Abigail," Mother says in a monotone as she hands her menu off to the waiter, "tell me how school is going. What classes are you taking this year? You should be into some interesting literature and composition classes this far into your major."

Ack. The dreaded topic so soon into our brunch. I'd hoped we could get through most, if not all, of this morning without that. I'd run through my responses repeatedly this week, bouncing back and forth between spilling my guts and keeping the charade going just a little bit longer. I briefly think this might be the best time to break it to her. She'll never make an embarrassing scene in a fancy restaurant. On the other hand, a few strategically placed white lies and I could breeze through this conversation and worry about telling her the truth when she is five states away again.

I open my mouth to begin my fabrication then clamp it shut. Who am I kidding? I should just rip off the bandage. Get the initial pain and torture out of the way, face my mother's reaction, and deal with the anger and disappointment she will spew at me.

I drag in a deep breath and clench the arms of my chair with my hands, bracing myself for the fallout. "About that . . . there's something I need to tell you." I glance up at her expectant face. I take another deep breath and sigh as I try to think of the best way to break the news.

"What is it, Abigail?" She is vaguely concerned now.

Rip the bandage. "So, I'm not . . . actually . . . enrolled in school this year." I wait for the anger. But she sits, eyelids fluttering.

"I'm sorry, what?" She has that smile you smile when what you've heard is not at all what you were expecting. And when she recovers: "You're taking a year off? Is that what you're saying?"

"No."

"You only have one year left, Abigail. This is a poor, poor choice. You need to finish what you have started. You may not go back if you take time off now."

"I couldn't afford tuition anymore. I had to leave school," I say quietly.

"You couldn't afford tuition anymore? Abigail, what have you been doing with your money?" There's the anger. "I told you it was not wise to move off campus and live with those girls. I told you it would be too expensive." She cuts herself off, but I'm pretty sure she wants to keep going. She is seething, but just loud enough for me to hear, darting her eyes to the side, making sure no one else has picked up on her agitation.

She's not wrong. She did say those things. But after Emory moved off campus with Val, as soon as Val's parents had gotten her the apartment, she began trying to convince me to move in with them. And I missed having her just a floor away from me in the dorm. We hung out all the time before she moved. Not having any siblings growing up, I thought about how great it would be to have two girls just like sisters to hang out with, stay up late and gossip with. So at the break between semesters in my sophomore year, I moved in with them.

My share of the rent was steep: $1,700 a month. But I foolishly thought I could handle it and still pay my way through school. I picked up more shifts at Hooligan's. But the extra work took away from my time to study, and I found myself pulling less-than-stellar grades. Embarrassing grades in a couple classes. The snowball kept growing as I slid farther and farther down the slope, engulfing me as it rolled over a steep cliff, out of control. I was barely making enough money to pay my way; I was failing out of school. I couldn't keep it all up anymore, so I dropped college and focused on making a living.

But the last thing I'm going to do at this moment is concede she was right.

"Mother."

"Abigail, why didn't you call me? I could have figured something out. I could have taken out a loan to help."

"*Mom.*"

"Did you call your father? *He* could have helped. It's about time he stepped up to help you."

"Mother! Please!" I plead through clenched teeth. Of course she would drag my father into this.

She pauses her tirade and composes herself. Sitting upright in her chair, she glances around once again to be sure no one has seen her misbehavior, then the prim and proper mask washes over her face. The redness of anger subsides to pale disdain. Her eyes bore into me. I begin to think that her words were better than this silent assault.

"I—I didn't want to burden you two. I thought, I don't know, if I took some time off, I could work and save some money. Then I could re-enroll." I truly did think that at the time. Now, it seems like a distant promise. I don't think it's attainable anymore—too much time has passed without any progress toward my goal. More time than I am going to let on to my mother. She now knows I've dropped out; she doesn't need to know how long ago. "I'm sorry. I should have told you sooner," I say softly.

"Yes, you should have. Do you know I have been bragging you up to my friends? Telling them about my daughter, going to graduate from NYU with an English degree, planning to be a professor or a writer? How embarrassing that I must tell them it's been an elaborate ruse on your part! Did you not think of how this would affect me?"

I'm stunned. Her venom shoots painfully through my body. Of course this would be about how *my* failure is affecting *her* image. I should have known better than to expect any sympathy or understanding from her.

"I'm sorry," I murmur, looking down at the napkin I've been twisting in my hands under the table.

"Clearly, you know I am disappointed," she continues, controlling her voice. "I expect you to call your father and tell him. I hear he's on the wagon again, longer this time than the last. He may be able to help." She says the last sentence with no hint of hope. Then immediately, her expression clears. She places her napkin in her lap and smooths it. Pats her hands on the front and sides of her blond hair, making sure no plastered curl has fallen out of place. She clears her throat and meets my eyes, a slight smile forming on her lips. "Do you like my hair? I had it colored last week. Can you tell?"

Switch flipped.

The rest of brunch is mundane compared to how it started, thankfully. She asks polite questions about my work and my roommates, feigning interest. She goes on and on about the things she has done with Janice and Caroline—wine tasting, French cuisine cooking classes, pottery classes. They've started a book club that meets monthly, alternating in each member's home. Of course, no one has a decorating sense like she has, she's noted, and Janice agrees.

I am exhausted by the time I arrive back home. I slump on the couch and turn on the TV; it's just noise, something to drown out my own thoughts, to keep me from dwelling on the conversation with my mother. She's crazy if she thinks I'll call my father. I've never had the nerve to ask my dad for money. And I don't care if he ever finds out that I've left NYU. I'm not worried about him being disappointed in me, don't care if he is. There is no fiber of my being that could muster the courage to ask that man for anything. I've faced more than a lifetime's worth of rejection from him already.

It's not long before Emory and Val come bursting through the door from a morning of shopping. They show off their bargains, then we settle on a movie on the women's channel and veg for a while before Emory and I have to get ready for work. I'm actually glad I have work to keep my mind busy tonight.

Ethan calls right before I have to leave, which brightens my mood immensely. I've said nothing to my mother about him yet. Somehow, I worry if I tell her, a black cloud will form over us and ruin our relationship before it has a chance to really begin. If I can keep him to myself for a while longer, it will grow and flourish and be strong enough to stand against her doubts and scrutiny.

Ethan promises me he has our date for tomorrow all planned out. He is certain I'll be impressed. I attempt to pull clues from him about our plans, but he refuses. He wants everything to be a surprise. His excitement makes me even more excited to see him. It carries me through the night as if my visit with my mother is just a distant memory with no lingering sting.

Chapter Nine

A Tour of More Than the City

Ethan arrives at nine o'clock again this Sunday. "Why so early?" I'd questioned him when he told me what time on our Saturday phone call. His answer: "Because I don't want to waste any of the one day we have to spend together. We have to make it count."

That made me melt.

This week is a little cooler than the last; the autumn changes are subtle in the air. The sky is overcast, but the day is still so bright. Having Ethan walking next to me makes everything better. He grabs my hand right away, and we stroll along as if we've known each other forever. There is something so right about this man. He makes me feel like everything is going to be okay for once in my life. The loneliness and sadness that have been my constant companions are now replaced with feelings I've never felt before. I can't even describe them—happiness, of course, and hopefulness, and something else . . .

We talk as we walk, about anything, about everything. It's all so easy with him. We catch the subway to the Chelsea Market area, where we spend some time checking out the shops. Then back to the subway to Tribeca, where we emerge to walk again, soaking up the little bits of sunlight that break through the clouds. Before I know it, we're at the water's edge. I gaze across the expanse of dark blue water leading my eyes to the Jersey shoreline. Ellis Island is to the left, and just beyond the Statue of Liberty is guarding the harbor.

"It's so majestic. I haven't been on this side of the island for so long. I'd forgotten how awesome the Statue of Liberty is." I breathe in the fresh air from the breeze off the ocean.

"Have you been to Staten Island?"

"Oh, yeah, that was one of the first places I went when I moved here. Emory and I spent the first few weekends of our freshman year exploring the city. Like from dawn till dusk exploring. She knows so many local treasures and was dying to show them all to me." I turn my attention from the view back to Ethan. "How about you?"

"I've been a few times. Field trips, official tour guide for visiting friends." He smiles that glorious smile.

"I'll bet you're a great tour guide. Are you going to guide me around today?"

"Well, I have some ideas," he muses. "Tell me, have you ever been on a boat tour around Long Island?"

"You know, in the four years I've lived here, I never have."

"Great. We'll start there. I've actually never done that either."

The boat ride is fantastic (not so much for the tour, but because Ethan sits so close, his arms wrapped around me). The breeze on the water is cooler than I had expected, making me shiver. But I am thankful for that when he notices and pulls me into his body, so close I can nestle my head into his neck. It's our first really close contact, and it makes my heart race. We are quiet for much of the ride, taking in the sights, enjoying each other's presence.

After the tour around the island, we ride the subway to Grand Central Station, then walk again, hand in hand, at a leisurely pace. We have all day to be together, no need to rush. We eventually arrive at Central Park. The sun is peeking out from the clouds now, warming the day. The park is full of walkers, bikers, rollerbladers, and tourists, all trying to enjoy the last warm days before the fall weather sets in. The trees are still lush and green but for a few leaves here and there, yellow or red ones floating to the ground.

"Are you hungry?" Ethan motions to a hot dog cart a little way up the sidewalk. I nod. I hadn't realized I was until he said something.

We order and find a bench to sit and eat, watching the tourists explore around Belvedere Castle. Noticing a large family with all ages of children makes me tentatively ask, "So, do you have family nearby?" I want to know everything about him, but I hope this question doesn't open any old wounds since I already know the story of his parents.

"I have an uncle on my father's side here in Manhattan. And an aunt and her family on my mother's side upstate. I was never close to my cousins, and they're spread across the country now. My uncle never married. He's had a companion living with him for . . . maybe fifteen years now? I never saw much of him growing up. My dad had a problem accepting Uncle Geoff's life choices. Once my grandmother, Susan, passed away, the holiday get-togethers stopped completely." He shrugs as he gazes across the park. "I saw Uncle Geoff at my parents' funeral for the first time in about eight years. I could tell my dad's death hit him hard. I think he thought there would always be time to get my dad to come around.

"I made a point to get his number . . . I wanted to keep in touch," Ethan continues. "He was the last link to my dad's family I knew about, and I didn't want to lose that. So, I call him a couple times a month. I stop over when I can. To me, there's no excuse—he's right in my back yard."

I watch Ethan's eyes, crinkled up at the corners as he stares at the castle ahead. I want to reach up and run my fingers along his cheek, cup his chin in my hand, and turn his face toward me so I can see exactly what he's feeling in those eyes. But I'm afraid it's too early for that intimate contact. Instead, I knot my fingers together and simply respond, "That's great, Ethan, that you've opened the door again. It's so easy to lose touch nowadays if you don't try." I know that all too well.

"I do resent that my dad's prejudices kept Uncle Geoff out of our lives. He's a great guy. Traveled the world for years. He has so many fascinating stories. But I feel like I'm making up for a little of that now. And your family's your family." As he returns his gaze to me, he continues fervently, "With all their faults and baggage—you can't shut them out because they don't live their lives the way you think they should. You can't project your assumptions onto them, to make them be what you think they should be, and then turn away when they don't measure up." He shakes his head, a fierce look in his blue eyes. "It doesn't work that way."

I could argue that point, but I'm not going to. I don't want Ethan to know what a messed-up family I come from. What if he derides me for not forgiving and forgetting and having my own happy family reunion with my dad? It isn't the same in my case, though. It's not like my dad is just gay and I have to accept it. I don't think that would be a problem. It's not a matter of *who* my dad is, but *what* he did . . . does. You can't excuse so many years of making alcohol the most important thing in your life—I don't care what anybody says.

"I'm sorry," he softens. "I'm going on and on over here. I want to know about you, Abby."

I laugh him off, trying to disguise my inner struggle. "I'm not nearly as interesting as you, I promise."

"Tell me who Abby Templeton is. I want to know." He looks at me intently.

I flounder. Who is Abby? Abby is . . . what? I cannot think of one interesting thing I can tell him about myself.

"Well . . . I'm a twenty-two-year-old Capricorn who enjoys reading and long walks. I was born and raised in Cedar Rapids, Iowa," I start as if I'm a contestant on *Wheel of Fortune* telling Pat Sajak something about myself. Then the funny wears off as I realize Ethan has really opened up to me today; he deserves the same. I sigh, "I thought my big break was when I was accepted to NYU. I moved out here with delusions of grandeur." I throw my arms out to my sides and look up at the trees sprawling out above us, driving home my point. "But alas," I sigh again. Turning serious, I let a touch of sarcasm color my tone. "My college career ended much too soon. And now I'm a server at Hooligan's Bar and Grill, touting the deliciousness of the famous double-decker burger!"

"They *are* delicious," Ethan affirms, nodding, a smile breaking across his face.

"That's me in a nutshell." I shrug and flash him a goofy grin. What else is there to tell? *Before I met you, I was a horribly lonely and depressed person contemplating my place in this world?* Yeah—no.

This time he laughs. "I love a woman who can make me laugh!"

"Shoot! I was trying to keep my sense of humor a secret. Now I have to break up with you." I grimace. He laughs harder, which makes me giggle, too.

"But seriously," he says as we recover, his hands clasping on top of mine. I feel that electric charge travel up my arms. "What made you decide to come to NYU?"

I feel as though he can see inside my soul as his touch burns into my hands. His sky-blue eyes make me fear I will have an impossible time trying to keep my past hidden from him for long. "Ah, I guess I had this vision of me on my own in New York, discovering myself. Maybe writing the next Great American Novel. You know . . . that kind of thing." I pause for a moment, thinking that is enough about me for now, but something about Ethan's calm expression and interested gaze makes me feel like maybe I can open up to him, like maybe he won't judge me.

"My plan was to major in English and literature and eventually become a writer, maybe a professor. I loved reading growing up—still do, as you know. And I've always felt like I could do that. I could write." I shrug and look down, immediately embarrassed that I've shared something so personal.

When I glance back at him, I realize he's watching me, curiosity burning in his eyes. "So, what changed for you?"

I inhale deeply, trying to quantify what has changed. "There was the obvious issue—I couldn't afford tuition. My mom blames the poor choices I made moving off campus and wasting my money . . . and that may have been part of it. I hadn't fully realized all the expenses that go along with renting an apartment, like paying utilities and buying groceries. But looking back on it now, if I had wanted to—I mean *really* wanted to stay in school—I could have found a way. I could have picked up more shifts and still handled my class load. I think college was lacking what I was really looking for. It wasn't the miracle solution I had thought it would be. It was just another place—granted a much different place than Iowa—and I was just another person." I shake my head and bite my lip, letting the words resonate in my ears. I peek over at him from the corner of my eye. "Wow, Ethan, you're making me admit things I never fully allowed myself to own up to before."

"Is that a bad thing?"

"No . . . I suppose it's quite the opposite."

I pause for a moment, then try to lighten the mood again. "So, there you go—not so much that I couldn't afford college as I was disgruntled and disillusioned with the expectations I'd placed on my enrollment that never materialized. I just didn't want to admit it to myself, so I hid behind the false truth that allowed me to not face my real issues."

"Spoken like a true writer. You're off to a great start," he teases.

It's my turn to laugh now. "I'm not as lucky as you to have figured out what I want out of life."

"Well, it wasn't so easy for me, Abby. I made it clear through law school and paid the bill on top of it before I discovered my true passion. And you're still so young. You have a lot of life ahead of you." He smiles his brilliant smile, sending shockwaves racing through me. "Tell me, why don't you start writing? Have you given it a shot?"

"Ah—you know—I don't know." I look away, trying to find some type of distraction. "Hey, I could really use some water. Are you thirsty? Let's walk over and get a bottle."

He seems content to drop that line of questioning for now, and I manage to get him talking about himself again as we walk, finding out his favorite color is blue, like mine. His favorite football team: the Jets. His favorite book: *Treasure Island*—he read it as a kid and always loved it for the pirates and the adventure. His favorite season is autumn because he loves the colors of the leaves, the excitement of the impending holidays, and the start of football season.

Hours fly by with us just talking, just hanging out, but it's never boring. It's as if we're two lost souls who have finally found one another. We walk over to Strawberry Fields, then make our way over to the carousel. I've never been on the carousel, so he says we must take a ride. Part of the tour.

"Oh, I've got a question for you," I begin as we ride around in a circle perched atop our chosen horses. "What would you do with your life if you were a millionaire? A multimillionaire. I'm talking *really* rich. If you could do anything you wanted?"

"Wow. There's a loaded question, huh?"

I laugh. "I'm being serious, Ethan. I think you can tell a lot about a person by what they would do if they were rich. Would they be generous? Would they be selfish? Would having all that money change them?"

"You know, money never really meant much to me," he says quietly. "Family is so much more important."

I feel the weight of his seriousness.

"But as a multimillionaire, I wouldn't change a thing. I love what I do. What about you?"

"Hmm . . . I think I would go to Disney World!" I joke.

"Really? That's all you've got?"

"I've never been," I justify. "No, if I'm being really honest, I'm not sure what I would do. I mean, I know I would want to give money to organizations and charities I believe can use it, but beyond that . . . I really don't know what I would *do*." I gaze off in the distance at the slowly spinning New York skyline as I wonder. "I guess you'd have to help me figure it out." I smile at Ethan and wink. How's that for being presumptuous?

The corners of his mouth turn up as he reaches over and takes my hand. I lean my head against the pole and let my eyes lock contentedly with his. He mirrors my pose. We stay like that for some time, until he lifts his head and glances at his watch. He seems disappointed when he realizes we've got to dismount our horses and head to the restaurant to make our reservation. When I chance asking what kind of restaurant, I'm a little surprised that he divulges the information: Italian, his favorite. I tell him he's lucky it's my favorite too, or he would have been in for a miserable dining experience. He laughs. I'm relieved he thinks I'm funny.

We continue our conversation through dinner, and when it lags, I never feel the typical awkwardness of what to say next. I've never been out with a guy I didn't feel like I *had* to talk with, however ridiculous the topic. And believe me, I've brought up some ridiculous topics in the past (which breakfast cereal should never be served to children and why, the importance of filling out the FAFSA form correctly the first time to get the most student aid, how I feel about fingernail polish that doesn't stay on more than two days—I could go on and on). And I don't think I've ever had such deep and thoughtful conversations with a guy before. I've never felt like anyone gets me like Ethan does. It's as if he's pulling information out of me effortlessly. Information I have never intended to share with anyone. Especially not so early in a relationship. I've always believed that the less someone knows about you, the more protected you are. They can't hurt you if they don't know how to.

And then he catches me off guard when he really cuts to the chase. "So, tell me, Abby, how did I get so lucky to find someone as funny and smart and beautiful as you who doesn't already have a boyfriend?"

My eyebrows shoot up and I nearly choke on my fettuccine. I wipe my mouth with my napkin and use the extra moment to try to figure out the shortest answer that won't invite more questions about my past romantic life.

"You think I'm beautiful?" I try to deflect.

"Gorgeous," he states matter-of-factly. "And don't forget smart. And funny."

I flush crimson. My heart flutters. He thinks I'm gorgeous. And smart. And funny.

"I mean, you must have men lined up on your doorstep," he continues, and I drop my gaze away from the directness of his stare. Actually, I can think of only one man who might be lined up on my doorstep, and I vehemently hope I have him turned around and headed the other direction. How do I explain to Ethan that my parents have me so ruined on love that I have had very few *actual* relationships? This conversation could turn awkward fast.

I bite my lip trying to think of the shortest and sweetest way to discuss this topic. "I'm not a serial dater or anything like that." That's good. Doesn't give too much away. "I've had a couple serious relationships, but I don't jump into relationships lightly. There has to be something very powerful in the attraction for me to take a chance on a guy. I'm kind of picky, I guess you could say."

"Picky, huh?" His mouth twists into a crooked smile. "I guess I should take that as a compliment then. There must be something powerfully attractive about me if you're willing to spend your time with me."

I grin and gaze across the table at him from under my eyelashes. Man does he look handsome when he's being cocky.

"So what about you?" I toss back at him. I'm dying to take the focus off me and use this opportunity to find out about his romantic past. "I can't believe someone as smart and funny and handsome as you doesn't have girls falling all over him all the time."

"You would think I would, wouldn't you?" he teases. "In all honesty, though, I've been out of the dating scene for a while. I needed a break after my last relationship."

Oh. My interest is piqued. I try to nonchalantly take a sip of my wine to hide the obvious curiosity I must have plastered all over my face. Ethan pauses and sips his own drink. When it feels like he might be stopping the story there, I lead him along a bit. "So, pretty bad, huh?" I try for a little disinterest in my tone. I don't want him to get offended thinking I'm prying. I feel like my raised eyebrows are about to make contact with my hairline though.

He places his glass on the table and runs his finger across his mouth. Then he softly clears his throat before making eye contact with me again. He seems to be having some type of internal conflict. I answer my own question: *Pretty bad then.*

"Um, no, I guess," he starts. My brows knit together as I see the uncertainty in his expression. *He has secrets, too?* "Well, actually," he continues, reaching out to adjust his silverware. He inhales deeply and sets his jaw, a decision made. He returns his blue eyes to my wide, wondering gaze. "I was engaged, Abby, for about a year, to a girl I met in college and dated for quite a while."

Whoa. Not what I expected at all.

I watch him from the corner of my eye as I grab my glass again. I take a swig of my white wine as I let the full weight of his confession sink in: He was engaged.

As if he senses my burning curiosity, he divulges more: "We met at law school, actually. She came from money, so I learned quickly that she expected the finer things in life. And I loved to provide what I could for her. I loved to make her happy. We dated for a couple years before I proposed. But looking back on it now, I realize I always felt pressure from her to keep moving the relationship forward, to get married as soon as possible. She started planning the wedding before we even graduated, started making appointments with realtors to view condos and homes, even planning the number of kids we would have and the schools they would attend. She was very much concerned about the social circle around her and making sure her future would keep her in the society pages, you know?

"One day, I realized I had started doing whatever I could to slow the wedding planning down—I skipped appointments with the wedding planner, dodged out of viewings with the realtor. I started hyperventilating at our appointment to pick out the invitations." He lets out an uncharacteristically bitter laugh. "That's when I knew—I mean, she was all about spend, spend, spend. How big could we get the wedding, how large of a place could we live in, how many rich fake friends could we fit into our circle? I didn't even recognize the person I had fallen in love with anymore. I started to have nightmares about our future selves."

Ethan pauses, his gaze drifting left, as if remembering a scene from his past. I am completely entranced by his revelation.

"So, I suggested we skip the big wedding and elope. I told her this wasn't me—this over-the-top, exaggerated display of wealth. Told her I loved her and the pressure she was putting on us to be the perfect couple was too much for me. I just wanted a simple wedding and a simple life together."

"I can't imagine she took that very well."

He chuckles without humor. "No, she did not. It turns out the appearance of wealth and the façade of the perfect family with a perfect life were so much more important to her. And I no longer fit into her perfect picture."

My heart hurts at the pain that flashes across his face. In the brief second that passes, I consider reaching across the table to take his hand in mine, but he suddenly jerks back in his chair, squares his shoulders, and sniffs defiantly. "She was gone as fast as she'd appeared three years earlier." He shakes his head. "Amazing, really, how quickly she took off."

"Oh, Ethan, that's terrible. I'm—"

He raises his hand and shakes his head again, cutting me off. "You don't need to say it. I've realized that I am so much better off without her. Really. It took a while. I was hurt, really hurt. I felt used for a long time. But . . ." His face warms and he gives me his sexy, crooked smile. "I believe every relationship helps you grow. Whether it's a successful one or a failed one, you learn something about yourself. You become stronger, better. She helped me open my eyes and really look at people and the motivations behind their actions. She made me wiser. So, if I ever see her again, I can thank her for that."

"Wow. I must say that is very mature of you." I grin wickedly. "If a guy broke off an engagement with me like that, I'd probably key his car and spread nasty rumors about him."

"Oh, believe me," he says before taking another drink, relief apparent on his face for sharing this big piece of his past with me, "it took quite a while for me to get to this Zen place."

I giggle at his confession, and he grins in return. Her loss is definitely my gain. Still, it's difficult for me to picture an Ethan who is at the beck and call of a pampered rich girl. I just can't see it in the man I have known so far.

AFTER DINNER AND a lot more conversation, we walk back to Central Park for an outdoor concert. A new band, one I haven't heard of before. We find a spot on a hill near a large tree to sit. I quickly discover the band is a good mix of blues and Southern rock. I really like their sound. Ethan tells me he's seen them perform before and likes them, so he's glad I do as well.

The coolness of the evening allows me to snuggle close again. I breathe in his scent, a musky, bold fragrance that suits him well. I feel the definition of his chest muscles through his shirt as he pulls me in and wraps his arms around me. A hot blush creeps up my cheeks as I think about how his chest would look without his shirt. I settle in and try to keep my focus on the band. I'm almost sad when the concert ends, and I feel him lean away from me. I want this night to go on forever.

"That was great! Even better than the last time I saw them." Ethan stands and reaches out his hand to help me up. I briefly think about yanking him back down with me as I put my hand in his. The fear that he might get mad at me for pulling him over makes me reconsider. I guess I don't know him well enough to know what his reaction would be to something like that. Maybe one day soon I will.

"Yes, it was fantastic," I agree. "I wonder if they have a CD?"

"I'm pretty sure they do. Let's check it out." He nods toward the merchandise tables.

We walk to where a couple of young kids with long hair wearing band t-shirts and stocking caps are hawking merchandise. As we stroll across the grass among the dispersing crowd, Ethan slips his hand around mine as casually as ever. I love how he does that, and I have to turn my head away to hide the grin on my face.

They do have CDs, so I pick one up. He grabs one, too. "I've got two CDs here," he tells the kid with the longer hair and more shiny metal in his face.

"Oh, no, Ethan, I'll pay for my own," I argue.

"No, you won't. My treat. I insist." He hands over the forty dollars before I can even get my purse open.

"Thank you. Really." It's a good thing it's dark so he can't see the deep blush I feel burning up my cheeks. He's already given me way too many things. The book, the boat tour, dinner, this CD. I really don't deserve it all.

"My pleasure." He grabs my hand again as we walk. "I'd better get you home—you're shivering," he notices.

"Oh, I'm fine." I shrug it off. I'm not ready for our time together to end. He pulls me closer and wraps his arms around me. The benefit of being cold.

We walk without talking. I muse again about how nice it is to be able to just *be* with someone. It feels so easy with Ethan.

"Is it too presumptuous of me to make plans for us for next Sunday?"

"Next Sunday?" I'm thrilled that after a whole day of me he still wants to make plans. "I'm free. Sure."

"Good. My uncle has asked me to drop by next weekend. Would you like to join?"

"Oh, Ethan, I don't want to intrude on your family time. You go see your uncle. We can do something another time."

"I'd really like you to come, Abby. And Uncle Geoff loves meeting new people. Or should I say loves having new people to tell all his stories to," he chuckles. "He'll entertain you, and Simon will dote over you."

"Simon?"

"My uncle's companion. I guess you could say he's the . . . home . . . maker. Simon takes great pride in the appearance of the house and in hosting visitors. It'll be great. We'll do lunch with them and have the evening to ourselves." He squeezes me as he smiles. That smile.

"I'm looking forward to it already." I grin in return. To myself, I wonder what it means for us that he wants me to meet his family so soon.

My heart begins to flutter as I realize we're approaching my apartment. I think about the kiss I imagined we'd share, and a wave of warmth sweeps over me in anticipation. Will he try to kiss me? Should I let him kiss me? I will *definitely* let him kiss me if he tries. Will it be as spectacular as I'm hoping it will be?

We pause by the side of the stairs that lead to the entrance of my apartment, and he turns to face me. His hands clasp mine and his thumbs trace gently over my skin, leaving fire trails in their wake. I'm feeling very lightheaded all of a sudden. I mean, I have kissed guys before, no big deal. But I haven't felt this nervous to kiss one since high school.

"So, I guess this is good night." His eyes pierce so deeply into mine that I feel he can see my thoughts. My nervousness escalates. I'm afraid my hands will start sweating, but I don't dare pull them out of his electric grasp.

"Mm-hmm," I manage. I hold my breath, trying to calm myself. His blue eyes are mesmerizing; I can't move my body.

Then it happens. As he leans forward, time slows. I inhale his musky scent as I close my eyes and tip my chin slightly upward. His lips brush mine briefly, then softly, tenderly. My skin ignites when his hand cups my cheek as he deepens the kiss. My legs are about to crumple beneath me. I grab onto the fabric of his shirt with my free hand to steady myself. A shiver explodes up my spine.

The moment seems to last forever, but it ends too quickly. I want to savor his lips on mine. My eyes reluctantly open and are met again with his beautiful blues smiling at me. I bite my lip to keep from showing him a goofy grin. My heart is soaring.

"You're beautiful, Abigail. Thank you for sharing today with me."

"Thank *you*, Ethan," I murmur. I'm certain he can see my scarlet cheeks in the streetlight. How embarrassing.

"I'll talk to you tomorrow." He takes a couple steps backward before letting go of my hand, untangling one finger at a time.

"Okay." I smile as I turn to walk inside on my jelly legs. I sure hope I don't embarrass myself further by tripping up the stairs. I clutch tightly onto the railing for good measure and glance at him one last time before I step through the door. He smiles and gives a little wave. I really think I might burst with happiness.

Racing up to the apartment, I cannot wait to tell the girls all about my fantastic date and my fantastically wonderful Ethan!

Chapter Ten

Let It Be Me

Ethan rings the doorbell to his uncle's home. I peer over at him, wanting to say how nervous I am but feeling silly at the same time. I quickly run my hands through my hair, hoping it looks nice—I used the straightener on it, trying for a sleek look. I clamp my hands together to keep from biting my fingernails. I mean, this moment is the equivalent to meeting his parents, right? As soon as the euphoria from our first kiss wore off, about Tuesday afternoon, the fear of meeting his family began creeping in. What if they don't think I'm his type? What if I make a fool of myself in front of everyone? By Saturday night, my stomach was in such knots I thought about calling Ethan and canceling the whole day.

He reaches over, grabs my left hand in both of his, and rubs it reassuringly. "Nervous?"

I hadn't realized I was wringing my hands. "Yeah. I mean, it's your family. I hope they like me."

"Don't worry. They will." He squeezes my hand. His calm blue eyes have me believing him, and I relax a little. Talk about mood control—those eyes are dangerous!

With Ethan's confidence wrapping itself around me, I take a deep breath and square my shoulders.

The front door swings open.

"Ethan! Good day! Come in, come in!" A deep, elegant, almost singing voice rings out. The man who greets us is of average height, slender, and very poised. His skin is smooth and flawless but for the few lines around his eyes that give away his maturity. I feel terribly underdressed in my sundress and sweater next to his perfectly pressed tan slacks, crisp white button-up, and navy sport coat. He pulls Ethan inside and embraces him with a hearty pat on the back.

"Simon, how are you?" Ethan asks as he steps back to bring me into the foyer with him. Next thing I know I'm swept into a tight hug. I'm caught off guard by the immediate warmth and welcoming.

"And this must be Abigail. I am Simon Cassaday, and it is a genuine pleasure to make your acquaintance. Welcome, my darling! We are so excited to have you as a guest!"

I look backward, wide-eyed, at Ethan as Simon ushers me past a grand open staircase into a large sitting room. He shrugs and quietly chuckles in response.

I marvel at the high ceilings and ornate woodwork. While the outside of the home is relatively unremarkable, the interior is anything but. Paintings cover the walls, statuettes and vases decorate tables and desks, a stately grand piano anchors the corner. The colors and patterns lend a sophisticated character to the room. Imagining all the places they must have traveled to create such a collection, I wonder if the rest of the house has such flair.

Simon walks me to a sumptuously patterned, Victorian-style loveseat and motions for me to sit. Ethan sits beside me and takes my hand in his. "Please, make yourselves at home. I shall return with tea," he says warmly and briskly strides from the room.

"This room is amazing," I breathe, trying to take in all the pieces of artwork.

"Yes, they have amassed quite a collection in their travels. If you give them the chance, they'll tell you stories for hours about each painting or vase. Even the littlest trinket has a story."

"Well, hello, young ones," a gravelly voice travels to us from the entryway.

I assume this is Uncle Geoff, a tall, athletic-looking gentleman with wavy salt-and-pepper hair. Unlike Simon, the lines of age are showing on his face. He is also dressed much more casually, wearing khakis and a patterned polo shirt. We stand as he nears, and I see he has the same calm, sky-blue eyes as Ethan.

Something about him seems familiar, but maybe it's just that he shares similar features.

He shakes Ethan's hand firmly and gives his arm a smack with his other hand. "Ethan, my boy. Good to see you."

"And you, Uncle Geoff." Ethan turns and places his hand on my back, presenting me. "This is Abby."

"Hello." I smile, tentatively holding out my hand. I don't know whether to expect a handshake like Ethan received or another hug like Simon gave.

"Abby! Pleased to meet you!" his gravelly voice booms throughout the room. Uncle Geoff grabs my hand and turns my palm down. He places a kiss near my wrist. "So glad you could join us, dear." While his voice is slightly on the intimidating side, his face is friendly and his eyes are warm, which puts me at ease.

We sit, and uncle and nephew catch up on the events of the past few weeks, including Ethan's trip to Europe, before Simon reemerges with a tray of tea and scones, bustling around and serving each person like a practiced host before sitting and joining the conversation without missing a beat. He throws out comments like, "Tell them about last Wednesday," or "Did you tell them what we did in France last month?" Waiting, with eyebrows raised, for Uncle Geoff to respond.

"No, would you like to tell them, Simon?" he says, which is apparently the green light for Simon to launch into an animated account. His deep voice is so musical it's easy to listen to every little detail without feeling like the story is dragging, as he peppers in funny little tidbits of this person did this and that person said that. He really is a gifted storyteller, pausing only occasionally to ask Uncle Geoff about a detail he can't quite remember or a name he has forgotten. And Uncle Geoff sits sipping his tea, an amused look on his face as he watches Simon. I have an odd feeling that I have met them both, together, before. But then I shrug it off, thinking maybe it's just how comfortable they make me feel.

We've all lost track of time when Simon sits forward, startled. "Oh, dear!" He looks at the grandfather clock beside him. "How rude am I? Here I am going on and on. Let's move to the dining room, shall we?" He stands and claps his hands together, then begins loading the serving tray with cups and saucers. "Or better yet, it's a lovely Sunday afternoon, let's dine out in the garden—Geoffrey, be a dear and show them out to the garden?"

I'm not really sure it's a question, because before Uncle Geoff can answer, Simon has disappeared with the serving tray. We all sit for a moment, watching the door swinging back and forth on its hinges, and let the whirlwind settle.

"Okay, then," Uncle Geoff finally remarks, chortling as he rises to his feet. "Right this way, youngsters."

Ethan scoops my hand into his as we follow his uncle through the impressive home. We pass through a dining room with the largest cherry table I have ever seen and another collection of paintings on the walls. I notice the table has four place settings of ornate china and etched crystal glasses, but we continue. A hallway leads into a solarium lush with small trees and flowering plants. French doors at the side of the solarium open out to the garden.

Outside, rows of meticulously trimmed hedges and beds of roses and daisies and so many varieties of colorful flowers that I can't even name stretch out in all directions. At the center of it all is a large, white, intricately designed pergola over a brick patio. A glass table and white cloth-covered chairs sit under the pergola, also with four place settings of slightly less fancy china already laid out upon it. Simon really is an entertainer, prepared for any situation.

As we sit at the table, Simon appears with a wheeled tray of drinks and appetizers. He serves better than any waiter or waitress I've ever worked with; I marvel at how quickly he's served everyone and is seated across from me, placing his napkin on his lap. I grab my own napkin, hurrying to unfold it as I realize everyone else has already done so.

"So, Abigail, dear," Simon draws my attention. "Might I ask how you met our Ethan here?"

I blush, thinking of the embarrassing chain of events that led up to Ethan asking me out. How can I put this in a way that doesn't make me look like a crazy adolescent?

"Actually, we met at the bookstore," Ethan offers. I shoot him a grateful glance for stepping in. "I noticed her in an aisle one day, looking for a good mystery. I just felt like I had to talk to her." His mouth creeps into a half-smile.

"Yes." I pause and clear my throat. "Ethan recommended an excellent thriller by Carson Ripley, I remember."

"And she bought the book and disappeared so quickly, I didn't get a chance to properly introduce myself. So, I thought I had blown my chance." He chuckles. "I even quizzed West after she left to see if he'd found out her name or any tiny bit of information I could use to find out who she was. But he had nothing.

"Lucky for me, she returned to the store. I'd made West my reconnaissance man, instructed him to get as much information as possible about her if I wasn't there, and then to report back to me." He grins guiltily at me. "A couple more weeks went by when I went on my trip, and I was afraid I really had missed my chance. But then, as fate would have it, there she was, sitting in the store the day I got back."

My cheeks heat again as I remember that day, a day I would much rather forget.

"But fate was unkind to me that day, and I was afraid I would never get to know this beautiful woman." I stare into the endless blue eyes that appear sad for a moment. I had no idea Ethan had felt as strongly about me as I had about him, longing to know the person behind the attraction. I reach over and squeeze his hand reassuringly, the same way he's done for me so many times. "So, I fought back against fate and made my own destiny. I wasn't going to give up that easily." A broad smile returns to his face. "I tracked her down at this restaurant where she works called Hooligan's, and I refused to leave until she agreed to go out on a date with me."

I smile too at that memory. That was a good memory. "How could I say no? Just look at that face." I gesture to his smile. "Well, and he kind of bribed me."

"Bribed you?" Simon exclaims.

I nod solemnly. "With a book. A very good book, I must say."

Simon and Uncle Geoff burst out laughing. Ethan and I join in. What was once a horrifying experience, we could now laugh about. It amazes me that we're now together in spite of our best attempts to trip ourselves up.

"Tell me again, did you say you tracked Abigail to Hooligan's? Is that right?" Simon questions.

"Yes, that's the place."

"Remember, Geoffrey, we had our anniversary dinner there not long ago. Quite good food, actually."

Suddenly, it clicks in my mind why these men are so familiar. They were the immensely entertaining gentlemen from Hooligan's that night!

"That's where I know you from!" I blurt. Recognition dawns on their faces as I look excitedly between the two. "Simon, you're the one who told me about the bookstore!"

"Of course, of course, Abigail—I remember you now!" He claps his hands together happily as if he has solved a puzzle. "You really did make the experience of Hooligan's endearing for me. Truly."

"I had wondered why you looked so familiar." Uncle Geoff smiles. "And how about that, Simon, you can take credit for creating this wonderful sequence of events."

"Well, I do my part."

We all laugh again. I can tell modesty is not Simon's strong suit. He thoroughly enjoys the thought that he played Matchmaker Supreme.

As the afternoon continues, they ask us to stay for dinner as well. I've enjoyed spending time with Ethan's family and jump at the chance to learn more about the people who know him best. And they have a never-ending supply of interesting and hilarious stories. I haven't laughed so much in such a long time. In fact, the only time I feel anxiety arise is when the topic of *my* family comes up. I had feared just such a conversation all day long. What can I say? I'm ashamed of my father and endlessly disappointed in my mother? Those are not the things you tell people you just met. The last thing you want is their pity, or worse, their disapproval.

Luckily, I find a way to skate over the topic. I explain that my father makes cereal in a factory by the Cedar River (which is true—at least, last I knew that was where his temporary laborer job landed him), and my mother teaches English and lit classes at Kennedy High School. Ethan, Uncle Geoff, and Simon are amazed when I tell them you can actually smell Crunch Berries on the breeze on the days that cereal is made. But I run short on what else to say; what else is there to say? I mean, nice things.

Fortunately, that is enough to satisfy them for now, and I transition nicely back to Uncle Geoff to find out more about his profession. I stealthily wipe my sweating hands on my dress once I realize I've made it through those nerve-racking minutes without having to lie. Or divulge any more of the truth . . .

DARKNESS HAS FALLEN upon the city when we finally leave. We walk for a bit, enjoying the fresh smell of the cool evening, Ethan playfully swinging our hands back and forth. "So, I'm dying to know. What do you think of my family?"

"I think . . . they are entirely . . . wonderful. Truly great. Such interesting stories."

"I apologize for not taking you out to that dinner I promised. I hope you aren't upset about that."

"Upset? Oh, no, definitely not. I really am glad we stayed. They made me feel so welcome. I hope they liked me."

"I'm sure they did." He pulls me in and wraps his arm around me. "I know they did."

After a few blocks, I notice the temperature drop as the breeze picks up, and I begin shivering. Ethan rubs my arm attempting to warm me. I should have brought more than a thin sweater. "Let's get you home," he says as he hails a cab.

"Where to?" the cab driver asks in a thick accent.

Ethan pauses for a moment, then says, "146 West 57th Street." He scoots closer, his arms enveloping me. "I guess I should have asked you—do you mind coming over to my place for a bit? There's something I'd like to show you."

Butterflies overtake my insides. His place? We are going to his place? Is it too soon for that? Should I act like it's too soon for that? Because really, I am dying for this man to put his hands all over me. "Uh—no. I mean, yeah, that's fine." I try to act nonchalant.

I finally begin to warm up in his strong embrace. The heat from his cheek on top of my head is satisfying. I'm as excited as I am nervous about going to his apartment.

We ride in silence for several blocks without any pressure to make silly conversation, and I get lost in the sound of the faint rhythm of his heartbeat through his shirt. I close my eyes and try to memorize the feel of his arms wrapped so tightly around me. I force the butterflies to calm down so I can enjoy this moment, focusing on the movement of his soft breathing, trying to match my own with his.

I still can't believe that all of this is real—that *Ethan* is real. So perfect in every way. For the life of me, I don't know what he finds attractive in me. I am so afraid I'll wake up in the morning to find the past few weeks have all been a dream. It doesn't make sense that I should find someone so amazing who shares my same interests and who is just so darn handsome!

The cab slows to a stop; my eyelids flutter open. As Ethan leans forward to pay the driver, I reluctantly let my arm fall from his chest. Then he helps me from the cab like a true gentleman. Looking up at the towering apartment building in front of us, I can't even count the stories up.

"Which floor are you?"

"Right there." He points toward the top of the building. "Seventy-second floor." He rests his hand on my back and ushers me into the lobby. "Not a penthouse, but still a really nice view of the city." I glance at him from the corner of my eye. Is he apologizing for not having a penthouse? Does he think that kind of thing would matter to me?

Our comfortable silence continues in the elevator. I reach my fingertips out to interlace with his. A nervousness grows inside me with each tick of the floor numbers on the display. Ethan starts to talk about what he knows of the history of the Metropolitan Tower and why he likes the building so much and some other stuff, but I have to admit I'm not really hearing any of it. I'm watching his lips, hoping they'll turn toward me for a kiss.

"Here we are. My floor."

"Here we are," I repeat quietly, then swallow. My mouth feels so dry all of a sudden.

As we walk down the hall toward his door, I wonder what's going through his mind. He unlocks the door and reaches in to flick on the light before having me walk in ahead of him. The apartment is a lot larger than I expected. Wonderfully high ceilings and modern architecture are the first things I notice. It's open from the high-end kitchen on the left to the wall of glass windows that extend from one end of the apartment to the other. The lights from the city twinkle all the way across. "Wow," is all I can say.

"Nice view, right?" He smiles.

"Nice view definitely. Nice apartment." I wander past the kitchen and the dining area to the large living room. I note that he has great taste in decorating. Contemporary dark furniture and some very nice antique-looking pieces mixed smartly together. A few large abstract paintings hang around the room with calming blue and green hues, mixed with some white. My eyes drift to the wall of glass, the sparkling lights drawing me to them. "You can see so much of the city from here."

"Yes." He hands me a drink. I take a sip—brandy, maybe? It's good, I note—smooth. "And the sunsets are amazing."

He walks over to a small entertainment system and picks up a remote. The familiar music of Ray LaMontagne fills the apartment. I turn back to the view and enjoy the soulful sounds of Ray while enjoying the beauty of the sparkling city. And then I feel the heat of Ethan's body close by my side. Oh, why does he have to play such a sexy CD after such a perfect day with such a breathtaking view before us? My pulse quickens.

We stand side-by-side, enjoying the view for a few moments. I glance at him from the corner of my eye every so often to see if I can gain a sense of what his intentions are. He gives nothing away.

"Sit with me over here," he finally says, motioning to one of two couches.

I take one more sip of my drink before walking over. I sit at the edge, waiting for him to join me. But he's disappeared. I set my glass down, but then I don't know what to do with my hands. I run my fingers through my hair nervously, then finally clamp my hands together in my lap. I smooth my dress and clasp my hands together once more.

He returns with a leather-bound book in his hand. He wants to show me a book? *That's* what he wants to show me?

"In the spirit of the day," he begins as he sits, "—and thank you, by the way, for spending time with my family—I wanted to introduce you to the rest of my family." Ethan opens up the leather-bound book and slides it onto my lap. It isn't a book after all, but a photo album. Tears spring to my eyes as I realize what he's sharing with me.

"This is my dad and mom at their twenty-fifth wedding anniversary. It's my favorite picture of them. They were so happy, looking forward to another twenty-five years together." His voice softens, saddens. "They died less than a year later."

I instinctively place my hand on his shoulder and rub it comfortingly. I try to read his emotions. He seems in control but stares at the picture of his smiling parents for a moment longer. Then he quickly flips to the next page. "This is me. Learning to walk. Learning to ride a bike." He points to each picture. "Getting my first *really cool* toy for Christmas." He chuckles, his memories affecting him.

He shares several more pages: sporting events, school programs, family vacation shots. In every picture that his mom or dad is in with him, they look so happy. Always smiling or laughing. They must have been great parents. I am immediately jealous. Then a little ticked off. Here, Ethan had such great, supportive, loving parents, and they were taken away so soon. And I'm stuck with real defects for parents, both alive and well. It isn't fair to him. I mean, really: Take my parents—give him his back.

"I wish I could have met them, Ethan. Really, I do. They seem like wonderful people, so happy."

"They were. They were great. But I try to cherish those memories, rather than be angry that they're gone, you know?"

Wow. That is deep. What a positive attitude to have. I think I could learn a lot from him on the power of positivity. His face lights up as he tells stories and shares pictures from a vacation to California. I'm reluctant to take my eyes off him, but I also want to see the pictures from when he was younger. The cute ones when he was little, the awkward ones when he was an adolescent, the handsome ones when he grew into his own. By the time we hit the last page, I feel like I know a whole other side of Ethan. Like I have a real sense of where he came from.

"Thank you for sharing that with me," I say as he places the photo album on the coffee table in front of us.

"No, thank *you* for sharing it with *me*. I really want you to know my family. They are who molded me. And someday . . ." He trails off, looking at me intently. "I'd like to know as much about your family."

A brief wave of panic sweeps over me. If I can at all help it, Ethan will never know my family. I hope I can spare him that. My brain scrambles as I try to come up with a change of subject.

"So, Ethan, how long have you lived here?" I say as I jump up and grab my glass. I'm very thirsty all of a sudden. I have it emptied by the time I reach the window.

"Ah, I've been here about five years now, I guess."

"Five years? Wow! How did you afford this place while you were still in law school?" I glance down at my empty glass.

"It's not that bad." He shrugs. "There are definitely more expensive places in New York. It took me a long time to decorate, though. I have terrible taste, so I finally gave up and hired a professional decorator. Every couple of years she mixes it up, adds new pieces, takes some away. Except for the ones that have been in the family for generations—the secretary desk, the china cabinet over there, the corner table with the old lamp. She works well around them," he says as he joins me. He hands me another drink and takes my empty glass. Relieved for something to help settle my nerves, I take a long drink, again amazed at how the thought of having to talk about my family gives me such anxiety.

My gaze drifts to the china cabinet. "No china?"

"Yes, actually, there is china. Very beautiful, very old, very fragile china. I broke a piece or two when I was packing them up to move, so I left them in the box in the closet. I don't trust my butterfingers." He sticks his hand out in front of him and wiggles his fingers to illustrate his point, almost dropping his glass in the process. I giggle.

"Well, the whole place looks great. I think it showcases your personality," I say as I turn toward the skyline view.

"Thank you," he says as he moves closer and places his hand on the small of my back. I notice he puts his hand there a lot, but it doesn't bother me the way it has in the past, with other boyfriends, one in particular. Usually, I don't like any gesture, physical or verbal, that makes me feel like I'm someone's property. But when Ethan does it, it doesn't feel like a show of "this is mine" or an attempt to control my direction. It just feels like he's trying to be close to me, to be one with me.

We sip our drinks, enjoy the view. A calmness settles over me, Ethan the master of the effect. But then I think I may have gone too fast with that last drink, feeling a bit dizzy. I blink my eyes and try to focus on the twinkling lights of the city, and I lean into him for support. I feel him turn toward me, and I move my head for a better view of his face. Watching the skyline, I hadn't realized that the lights are now very dim in the apartment.

"Abby, I really want to thank you, again, for hanging out with my family today. It means so much to me." He sets his glass on the windowsill, takes my almost-empty glass from my hand, and puts it next to his. He gently places his hands on my shoulders, then runs them down my arms. A shiver shoots up my spine. My heart is pounding in my chest, but my body is relaxed.

I vaguely realize one of my favorite Ray LaMontagne songs, "Let It Be Me," is playing softly, slowly, and I'm mesmerized by those calm blue eyes, silver moonlight reflecting in them like diamonds.

"Dance with me a bit?" he murmurs.

All I can do is nod.

The warmth of his hand burns into my lower back as he pulls me close. I briefly forget what it is we're doing, lost in his scent and his stare, until he lifts my right hand in his and rests them both on his chest. I blink, trying to clear my head and remember that I should put my other hand on his arm. But that's not good enough for me; I slide it up to his shoulder feeling his muscles under my fingertips as I go. A smile dances across his face as he starts to move. I try to follow, hoping I'm keeping up better than I feel. I can't take my eyes off his face, his eyes, his mouth. We dance for the better part of the song before he stops.

Then everything seems to happen in slow motion. Ethan leans in and pulls my face to his, leaving my hand resting on his chest. Our lips unite, and I swear that fireworks explode in the night sky. The touch of his lips on mine makes my body tingle. He kisses me so softly, then more intensely, then softly again. If he didn't have a hold on me, I think I'd melt to the floor. I can't feel my legs anymore. I wrap my hands around him and pull my body against his for support. He responds by kissing me more passionately, quicker and deeper. My body screams out for him.

"Abby . . ." He pauses and whispers in my ear. I don't want him to stop kissing me. "Spend the night with me?"

I pull back and look deeply into those intense blue eyes, the sparkling lights of the city dancing in them. Everything about him is so right, how can I say no? More importantly, I don't *want* to say no. I want to tear his clothes off and enjoy every moment of this night.

"Yes," I breathe, and in less than the second it takes to utter the word, his mouth is on mine again. His kisses—more than the brandy—keep my head spinning.

Somehow, we make our way to the bedroom, a tangle of arms and falling clothes and kisses. And I know this night will be far beyond all my expectations.

Chapter Eleven

One Too Many Surprises

Ethan is waiting for me when I get off work Saturday night, just as I knew he would be. Every time I see him standing there with that smile on his face, I'm caught off guard by the surge of excitement that flies through my body. And I'm certain my responding smile is bigger than his.

"See ya at home later!" Emory says as she and Dylan follow me out the door, hand in hand. I glance over long enough to agree, and in that brief instant I notice her expression seems weird, something in the set of her eyes. I can't place it exactly, and I'm preoccupied with getting into Ethan's arms, so I quickly push the thought aside. I'll talk with her later about what might be going on.

"Hey, you!" I coo as I step into Ethan's embrace.

"Hey yourself." He kisses me on the cheek before allowing me to turn my eyes up to his.

Every Saturday for the past six months he's greeted me this way outside the employee entrance to Hooligan's. Rain, snow, wind—it doesn't matter. It's the official beginning of our weekend together, and he always has something special planned, whether it's lounging at a piano bar, viewing a late-night movie, or just strolling around Times Square, catching up on the events of the week. Always ending up back at his place and spending the next full day glued to each other's side or tangled up in his sheets. As much as I dislike our work schedules being so different, I do enjoy the fact that he makes the little uninterrupted time we spend together so special.

At first, Emory and Val had seemed a little put off by me spending every weekend with him. I felt bad because we no longer had that time to hang out together, like I was betraying our friendship by putting them on the back burner. But in reality, Emory was spending more and more time with Dylan, and Val had started an internship that kept her busy. It didn't take long for our dynamic to adjust. It was as if we were growing up a little more, learning to be independent of one another and moving farther down our own paths. Learning to shift our orbits around our own individualities, while still including those friendships important to us.

"Dylan and Emory must have gotten over their little disagreement," Ethan notes, watching them walk away.

"Yeah, just a little tiff. They're fine." Actually, Emory made it out to be a little argument, but I think it was more than that. Her weeklong cold shoulder finally got to Dylan, and he came crawling back a couple days ago.

"Where to?" I'm ready to shift my thoughts from Emory and Dylan to Ethan and Abby.

"Well . . ." Ethan takes my hand and we start walking. "I was thinking we might just grab sandwiches and stay in tonight." He shoots me a sideways glance, as if trying to gauge my reaction. Surely, he can't be worried that I would be disappointed to stay home rather than go out?

"Okay, sure," I say, looking more closely at him avoiding my gaze.

"Great." He squeezes my hand but keeps his face forward. He's smiling and seems almost excited that I am fine with staying in. *This* makes me a little nervous.

I finally pull my stare away from him and notice we're almost to our favorite sandwich shop. We order our sandwiches to go and continue toward Ethan's apartment. Then he leads us in a different direction, so I begin wondering if he's changed his mind. I think about asking him what he has up his sleeve, but if he's trying to surprise me with something, I don't want to start asking questions and ruin his giddy excitement. It's too cute. So I keep up our conversation about the day's happenings. I tell him about the obnoxious family with four boys who terrorized me for an hour and a half. He tells me about West and Kate's trip to

Chicago last week and the great art finds Kate gushed about bringing back with them.

As we walk, the chill in the night curls around me, making me glad I remembered to grab my jacket this afternoon. As if he's read my mind, Ethan wraps his arm around my waist and pulls me in close.

"How about a ride home?" He motions ahead to a small black open carriage with horses and a driver in tails and a top hat. My mouth drops open as I gasp aloud. Ethan's excited smile has returned, and his eyes are glowing as he watches my expression, appearing very satisfied with the effect the surprise has on me. The driver opens the carriage door as we approach and bows deeply.

"Wow, Ethan! I've never been in a horse-drawn carriage before. This is great!"

"Just one more thing." He reaches into the seat and pulls out a beautiful bouquet of spring flowers. "Here you go, my dear."

"Ooh!" I inhale the sweet fragrance of lilies, daffodils, and roses. "They smell so good. Thank you!"

"Let me help you in." He holds out his hand, my prince in waiting, and I take it as I climb up into the carriage. He follows and pulls me close as he sits next to me. I inhale the luscious scent of the bouquet again.

"I love daffodils. They're so dainty," I giggle as I touch the yellow flower petals, overwhelmed with the romantic gesture. Ethan planned an excellent surprise for sure.

"I'm glad you like it." He squeezes me tightly.

I snuggle into him, my head on his shoulder. As we ride, we talk a little, but mostly we enjoy the sights and being close to one another. Then he lifts my face up to his and brushes his lips tantalizingly across mine before sliding his hand around my neck and taking my breath away with his kiss. A swell of emotion crashes over me. How did I manage to find this sweet man, so thoughtful and perfect? I had thought men like this didn't really exist.

The kiss lingers as we're lost in the romance of the ride. I feel so lucky, and I truly hope he feels the same way. This is a man who could really set my world right. Maybe forever. He is completely unselfish; his biggest concern seems to be my happiness.

Despite the cool night, heat burns inside, a passion rising as our kiss deepens—I hope we're almost to his place, so I can show my appreciation for his thoughtfulness. Ethan pauses kissing me and pulls his face back to meet my gaze. He traces his thumb along my chin.

"I love you," I murmur through my smile and bite my lip as if trying to wake myself from this dream. "This has been amazing."

"I love you more." He kisses me one last time. "I think we're here."

"I don't know whether to be upset the ride is over or happy we're that much closer to your place." I look at him demurely from the corner of my eye.

I think I see a blush color his cheeks . . . and not from the cool evening.

We exit the carriage. I carry my flowers; he carries the sandwiches, though I had completely forgotten about being hungry. I do notice, as we walk through the lobby, that same excitement from earlier bubbling up in his demeanor again. But it doesn't seem to be the same excitement as I'm feeling. As we impatiently wait for the elevator to deliver us to the seventy-second floor, it becomes palpable, like he has another surprise. He becomes fidgety; there's a definite glint in his eyes. I bury my face in my bouquet to keep from letting on that I'm aware of his odd behavior.

It takes forever to traverse the long hallway to his apartment. I want to be inside. Now. To continue what we started on the carriage ride. I nearly release a nervous laugh when his key turns in the lock. I hold my breath as he pushes the door open, ushering me into the apartment. He deposits the sandwiches on the kitchen counter and returns to take the bouquet from me, placing it on the side table. I can wait no longer. I'm bursting at the seams. I grab his face in my hands, lock my lips on his. He's caught off guard, and his keys hit the hardwood floor as he's trying to place them on the table. But I don't care because I'm focused on one thing—him.

Releasing him to slip my jacket off and let it fall to the floor, my palms then navigate swiftly up his chest and under his coat to his shoulders. His hands leave me for only a second as he helps pull it off, then tosses it onto the countertop. He pauses with his arms around my waist, an expression on his face I can't quite read. But then I'm lost in those beautiful, usually calm eyes, now smoldering. I feel so much love for Ethan in this moment—a love I know he echoes. Slowing our pace as we move together, enjoying the intense emotions pulsing through our bodies, fusing into one. He holds me more tenderly, kisses me more softly as he explores my face, my neck with his lips. Oh, those lips. A shiver of excitement races up my spine.

I turn my head to allow him better access, and oddly, something on the kitchen counter grabs my attention. A bright red toaster, just like mine, stands out like a sore thumb among his other black appliances. Did he like mine so much he bought one himself? Weird to be thinking about a stupid toaster at a time like this! I shut out the ridiculous thoughts and return my focus to Ethan. I meet his mouth with my own, hungering for the fiery passion again.

He responds by walking us through the dark apartment without ever removing his lips from mine, the only light shining from the entryway, landing on a stray spot here and there to guide our way. I glance to the left at the old secretary desk and know we'll be in his bedroom in a few more steps. The light reflects, off a familiar picture in a familiar frame atop the desk, catching my eye. But my eyes must be playing tricks on me. I can't believe I'm letting these silly things distract me at a time like this.

Ethan tightens his arms around me, and I'm startled as he lifts me, still kissing, and carries me the last steps into the bedroom. I curl my legs around his waist. He gently places me on the bed, and in the darkness, I hear his shirt come off, then feel his kiss again as he leans into me. In an instant, my shirt is off, his warm hands on my back guiding me to the bed. Fire radiates through my body.

"Ow!" I arch up.

"What? What is it?" he asks breathlessly.

"What *was* that?" I am equally breathless. Reaching behind, I search for the offending object that jabbed into my back. Ethan sweeps his hand around too, but it's useless. It's too dark. I feel his weight lift. A moment later the room floods with light. I clamp my eyes shut; it's one extreme to another. Ethan's hands take mine, and as he pulls me up, I try to open my eyelids. I blink to focus on the bed.

"Is that... *my* alarm clock?"

"Um, yeah. I, ah, guess I forgot to plug it in," he says sheepishly. He walks around the bed and scoops it up.

I watch him set the clock on the nightstand, reach behind the stand distractedly, and plug it in. Then, frowning, I scan the room, my eyes searching, as I wonder how my alarm clock materialized. On his bed. I didn't bring it here.

Realization sneaks in, snaking around the confusion, pushing me toward understanding. Those two pictures on the wall were not there before. They're from my room, my favorite watercolors. The lamp behind my alarm clock, from my grandmother. It's from *my* nightstand by *my* bed. And that is *my* pillow on Ethan's bed. The red toaster in the kitchen—*my* toaster. The familiar picture on the secretary desk—of my dad and me, fishing together on the Cedar River when I was six. That picture has been hidden away in a box for a long time now.

So I know what he's done, but the surprise and enormity of it all is overwhelming. Honestly, I don't really know what to think. I don't know how to process this turn of events.

"I'll set the time on it later, okay, hon?" He looks up at me after he straightens the clock on the nightstand and freezes. I can't even imagine the expression on my face—maybe shock, maybe anger, maybe just a blank stare? He must have been expecting a much different response. Or no response. Maybe he thought it would be no big deal.

He finally speaks, a timid, "Surprise . . . ?"

Suddenly, I'm very cold, all through my body, and very vulnerable standing here, half-naked. Turning away, I grab my shirt and pull it on. Familiar boxes stare at me from atop his dresser, and I cannot help the flash of anger that sweeps over me. The passion from moments ago is long gone, replaced with a much worse feeling.

Ethan hurries to my side, tries wrapping his arms around me, which I would normally welcome. But this time . . . this time I hold my hand out to keep him at a distance, my eyes briefly meeting his before being pulled back toward the boxes.

Now he's the one confused. He doesn't understand my reaction. I mean, how could he? I don't really understand my reaction.

"I thought it would be all romantic and a great surprise. You're always saying how you wish we could spend more time together. And I do, too. We've been together eight months . . . this feels like a natural progression. Right?" He starts out explaining, but it morphs into pleading. I can tell he's waiting for some concession on my part. For any answer that will help him understand what I'm thinking.

But I can't look at him. I can't take my eyes off those boxes, open, rifled through. He's gone through them. He should never have done that. Why would he think it was okay to go through my things? The anger is swirling now with a growing feeling of betrayal. I step toward my boxes, forcing my hands to touch them, to confirm they're real and I'm not just imagining them here. My fingers brush across the open notebook inside the first box.

"Did you . . ." My breath catches. "Did you . . . read these?" I'm not sure if he hears me because I can only whisper. But I don't need him to hear. Don't need him to answer. I already know. I swallow hard as I notice several notebooks are scattered around on the dresser, some wide open.

I become aware of Ethan behind me as he wraps his fingers around my elbow. The gentle tug wanting me to turn around and face him. I won't. I stiffen and stand my ground. Fury is boiling up inside, simmering, about to bubble over. No kiss and make-up will fix this.

"Abby?"

"Did you read them?" I demand, finding my voice.

After an agonizing moment, he finally speaks. "Yeah, I did. Some of them, I mean. They're really good, Abby. They were hard to put down." He runs his hands from my shoulders down my arms, trying to comfort me. My muscles tense in reaction. "I'm so sorry. I never meant to offend you. I didn't realize . . . I'm so, *so* sorry."

He brushes my hair to the side and kisses my neck, then my cheek. I believe he meant no harm but can't shake this feeling of betrayal soaking me head to toe. He read my deepest, most personal writings. He now knows things I'm not sure I want him to know. The rage flares and I whip around to face him. "What gives you the right to go through my personal things? To display my personal photos? To rifle through my *most personal possessions* and read through them—casually—as if you're not invading every last inch of my privacy? I mean, who does that?" I recognize I'm almost shouting, but I can't control it.

"I'm sorry, I didn't realize—"

"No! You didn't. These—stories, these—journals were never meant for anyone else to read. They're not after-dinner reading or coffee table books." I feel awful as I berate Ethan, his expression a mixture of shock and injury. But he *hurt* me. He *betrayed* me. Hot tears spring to my eyes, so furious I'm going to start crying. That angers me even more. I don't want to cry. I want to yell, to scream, to punch my fists into his chest. He needs to know this is a big deal!

"I know. I know." He shakes his head. "I was just unpacking, and they caught my attention. They're papers from college, right? Assignments you kept? I didn't think it would hurt anything if I read them. I mean—they're graded and all—someone else has read them . . ."

As if it should make perfect sense to me.

But it doesn't. I just feel violated. "They were never meant for anyone beyond my professors to read. That's why they were packed away. I should've thrown them out. But I didn't—I couldn't. So there they were, and . . . you couldn't help yourself?" Accusation hangs heavy on my words. I angrily wipe at the stray tear that escaped down my cheek.

"Come here. Let's sit down and talk about this." I can tell he's forcing his voice to be calm as he tries to guide me, but I pull back, crossing my arms in defiance.

"I don't want to talk about it. I really don't. I mean, how do you just completely uproot someone and move all their stuff and take over their life and think that everything is going to be fine and dandy? How did you do all this without me knowing?"

And then I know.

"Emory," I breathe. "Really, you got my roommates convinced of your little plan?"

"Abby, would you listen to yourself?" Ethan's voice is rising. He shrugs on his shirt. "You're sounding paranoid!"

"*I'm* sounding paranoid? Really? I don't think I'm too far off base here. You've made the decision *for* me to move in here. *And* you've already moved me in! Where's *my* vote in all of this?"

"Your vote! What do you mean your vote? I was trying to do a nice, heartfelt gesture for you, and you're going off the deep end!" We are really fighting now. Our first real, big fight. "What's your problem anyway? What's your real problem? You don't want to live here, fine—go! I'm not going to force you to stay somewhere you don't want to be." He holds his hand out toward the door.

"But I don't think that's the problem here, Abby. I think you need to open up to me, and let's talk about the real issues you're having right now."

"I've already told you my issues, Ethan—you're not listening! You don't get it, do you? You have completely violated my trust. I feel like you've taken my voice from me. You're making all the decisions, and you don't see how that's wrong! What you've done is wrong." I clench my jaw so I won't bawl like a baby in front of him. I must show my strength. He doesn't own me. He can't do whatever he wants and expect me to roll over and accept it.

I march over to the dresser. I have to get these pieces of me hidden away, to get them back into the boxes and somewhere Ethan can't touch them. I feel too vulnerable with them sprawled about in the open.

"I'm sorry you feel that way, Abby. Truly, I am." Ethan is quiet now, but with a bitter edge to his tone. "I guess I thought I really knew you. Thought I knew how to make you happy." He lets out an exhausted sigh. "I never meant to hurt you, to make you feel like I was trying to control you." I hear him drop onto the bed. "I just want to make you happy."

Another hot tear falls. Then another. I sniff, struggling to maintain control. My wall of anger is crumbling at his confession. But I'm still so confused by this ambush, by my reaction, by these emotions that have hijacked my reason. I can't free myself of the feelings of betrayal and mistrust. I don't like it, but this whole situation feels wrong.

I throw the last notebook in the box, wipe my eyes, and set my jaw. I pick up the box filled with my notebooks, my memories, my secrets, and turn to face him. He looks defeated, slumped forward on the bed, his elbows propping him up on his knees.

"I don't want to fight with you, Abby. I don't know how many more times I can say I'm sorry." He runs his hand through his hair and settles his gaze on me.

Who knows how long I stand, staring at him, unseeing, cradling my box. I don't know what to say. I don't know how to feel.

So I run. I take my box and rush out of the bedroom before Ethan can stop me. I grab the picture of me and my father from the desk as I fly by and throw it in the box.

"Where are you going?" He's on my heels, but I don't stop. "Abby!"

I swoop down in the foyer, snag my jacket, and throw it on top of the box. "I've got to get out of here," I mutter, not caring whether he hears me. I can't breathe in here anymore. My chest is collapsing in on me.

"Abby! Abby, wait!"

I keep going, out the door and down the hallway. I don't know if he's following me; I'm too focused on finding the exit. My pulse pounds in my ears. I need air. My face is hot, and my fingers ache from squeezing around the box so tightly. Luckily, the elevator is right there when I push the down button. I rush on and pray for the doors to close before I see Ethan. They do.

When the elevator begins its descent, I slump against the corner. Everything around me blurs. I cling to my box, thinking the tighter I hold it, maybe the easier it will be to breathe. I have it safe and sound again. But I still can't get enough air.

Pieces of our argument echo through my head. I hear Ethan yell, *"You're going off the deep end! You need to talk about the real issues you're having right now!"*

I am a block and a half up 57th Street before I realize I'm outside. I don't feel the relief of the fresh air I'm craving so badly. At the end of the block, I round the corner. Throwing my back against the hard brick of the building, I try to remember how to breathe. I mean, if I'm breathing, my chest wouldn't hurt so badly, right? The cool air would be rushing in and calming me, saving me.

I suck in a deep, ragged breath. Still no relief.

My eyes dart around the half-empty street, wondering who else notices that I can't breathe over here. Does anyone know I could drop dead at any second?

No one does. No one takes so much as a second glance my way. Not the couple walking by. Not the group of college kids across the street. Not the homeless guy sitting in front of the store. He doesn't even look at me once.

I realize no one is concerned because I'm *not* dying. Still breathing, even though it doesn't feel like it. I am just a crazy girl on the corner clinging to a box, not an abnormal scene for New York City.

Gradually, my heart slows to a more normal pace and my chest doesn't feel so restricted. I'm aware of the cold now, and I start to shiver. Setting the box down, I pull on my jacket. Better, but not warm enough for the late April night. I pick up my box and begin to walk.

I don't know where I'm going. I seek out the solace of the city, like I used to do when my depression was at its worst and I felt so alone. The lights, the sounds, the activity take my attention away from what I'm feeling, deaden the pain. The gentle, comforting swaying of the subway. The bright chaos of Times Square. These things are my friends.

And you're never alone in New York City.

Chapter Twelve

An Unwanted Shove Down Memory Lane

I'VE LOST ALL track of time. I walked for a while. Rode the subway for a while. Sat on this bench in Grand Central Station for I don't know how long, my box beside me, never taking my hand off it. Pinpricks of numbness attack my toes to the point I think I should uncross my legs or risk permanent damage.

My gaze wanders toward the front entrance. Light blue and purple hues peek in, signaling the coming dawn. I could pull my phone out of my jacket pocket and look at the time, but I don't feel like it. My eyes absently take in the other people moving about Grand Central, then shift to the box by my side. Such a small box, so full of enormous things.

I flip up a flap with the back of my hand. The picture is right there on top. Me with a toothless smile stretched from cheek to cheek. Dad kneeling behind me with a big grin. He holds my old fishing pole in one hand, the other helping me hold up a rope full of fish. I don't remember what kind of fish they are... crappie, maybe? I just remember what a great day it was. We'd spent the whole July day fishing, going from lake to pond to river. He had his favorite spots, showed me them all that summer. I really thought my dad was something great back then.

And he was, I guess. Before the alcohol really took hold. He used to be involved in my life. He used to be around. I'll bet it wasn't two—maybe three years later he started drinking every night. And the fights he and my mother would get into would keep me awake. The verbal onslaughts, a slamming fist on the table, a shattering glass. I was so afraid someone would get hurt.

It dragged on for years. They would split up. Dad would move out, then he'd be back for a while as they tried to work it out. Then he'd split again. When they finally told me they were getting divorced, I was kind of relieved. No more fighting. No more scared, sleepless nights.

But then there was no more Dad either. He fell so far into his disease that I wouldn't see him for months at a time until he'd show up at a basketball game or a track meet, like it was no big deal. Like that was enough to make him a good father.

He took me shopping once my senior year, a gesture to make up for not being around, I'm sure. By midafternoon, I could see his hands shaking when he signed the credit card receipt for the cashier. He was getting fidgety, short-tempered. I decided to cut the day short for his sake, making up an excuse that I had a huge report due. He weakly protested, but I could tell he was relieved. He could get back to drinking.

Our relationship dissolved. He got sober once or twice, but it never lasted. And being sober didn't make him any better at being a dad.

At the urging of my Modern Storytelling professor at NYU, I explored some of the emotions entrenched in my relationship with my dad pretty candidly. Sometimes I got downright mean. Granted, it was all shrouded in a fictional setting with different characters in each story. Anyone who didn't know these things about me wouldn't have known the stories reflected truths in my life. The professor had encouraged us to draw from what we knew, from our own experiences, to create our stories. Said that some of the best works of fiction have been inspired by real people, real situations.

It had been somewhat therapeutic for me to get it all out, too. But I wasn't ready to forgive and forget all that had happened.

I remember the summer after that semester, planning a trip back to Iowa. I'd heard through Grandma Mary that Dad was sober again. This time it had been almost a whole year. I hadn't talked to him since my high school graduation—the last time he'd been sober. I'd wanted to see him, to maybe start the process of healing our broken relationship. The prospect of which was almost overwhelming. I'd saved money for months, purchased a bus ticket, packed my bags. The only thing I hadn't done was call Dad to tell him I was coming. I mean, what if I changed my mind and decided not to go? What if it was just too much?

So I headed to Cedar Rapids without telling anyone. Not even my mother. I didn't want her to know my plans to see Dad. She wouldn't have approved. And she would have made me feel like a real jerk for even wanting to have contact with him. The bus ride was so long and boring. I read a little, listened to music. Mostly, I daydreamed. I thought about how he would look, what I would say, what we would talk about. Always imagining I would tell him exactly how his drinking made me feel growing up. How his absent father routine had affected me. And he would listen and hear me. Say he never realized, that he regretted it all. And he would wrap his arms around me and tell me how very important I am to him. How wrong he had been, how he would make it all up to me. I thought about how we might go fishing like old times. Or maybe bowling. Or see a Kernels game. Dad always did like baseball.

When I arrived at the bus stop, I finally felt like I could call him, see if he could pick me up.

I called. And I called. And I called. I'll bet I called twenty times in those three hours I spent sitting at the bus stop. Then I worried that something bad might have happened. What if he was in the hospital or something? I called Grandma Mary first. No answer. So I called the only other person I knew who would know.

"Hello?"

"Hi. It's Abby."

"Abigail? Hello, dear. How are you doing?"

"Good. Fine. Umm... I just wanted to check in. See how you were doing."

"I am fine. The girls and I are going to a wine tasting tonight, so I am getting ready right now."

"Oh. Sorry. I'll let you go if it's a bad time."

"Why don't I call you later?"

"Uh, yeah. That's fine. Umm, but Mother, I was just wondering..."

"What is it, Abigail? Spit it out. I'm on a schedule, dear."

"Sorry. I was just wondering . . . if you knew if Dad's okay? I mean, I was thinking of calling him, maybe, and was wondering if you might have heard anything."

"Yes, actually." There was a pause. "I did hear something from your grandmother last week." If it was possible, my mother's voice turned even colder when she spoke of my father. "She mentioned he fell off the wagon again. She was quite concerned. She said he had all but disappeared for three weeks straight. I told her I was sorry she had to deal with his situation, but I didn't think he would ever change. Now I've got to go, Abigail. I'll call you later?"

"Uh—yeah. Okay. Bye."

"Goodbye, Abigail."

And that was that. It was nothing new to be disappointed by my dad, but I was crushed. I got on the next bus headed east and made my way back to New York.

I buried all my emotional ties to my dad after that. The stories, my journals, pictures, anything that reminded me of him went in a box and was packed away. This is the first time in a long time these thoughts have surfaced, about how it had affected me.

I tuck the picture into the box and close the flap. I remain on the bench, motionless, for a little while longer, ignoring the prickling sensation moving up my feet. The anger has passed, the betrayal subsided. Now I just feel empty. And tired.

I pull myself up. After a stretch of my neck and my back, I shake out my tingling legs, grab my box, and start walking. Stepping outside into the cold morning, I sigh. I gaze around at the changing sky, my eyelids heavy, the pinks and oranges of dawn becoming more visible. I turn and make my way home.

By the time I reach my apartment, exhaustion is thick in my bones. I turn the key in the door. It feels heavier than normal as I push it open. Maybe I'm just weaker than normal, struggling to even keep my eyes open.

"Abby! Oh my God, girl! You had us so scared!" Val shoots up from the couch.

"Abigail Templeton, where have you been?" Emory demands, sitting up, and I register that she and Dylan must have slept on the couch. He's still sprawled out snoring.

"How did you—?"

"Ethan called. He said you took off. He sounded really worried about you," Val says, concern evident in her voice. "So we were really worried."

"But where have you been? Why didn't you at least call us?" Emory is agitated.

I pull my phone out of my jacket. She's right, I should have called them. I'd forgotten to turn my phone on again after work last night. "I'm sorry, you guys. I'm just really tired right now. I've been up all night and I need my bed." I trudge to my room. "My bed is still here, right?" I ask dryly.

"Yeah, your bed's here," Emory says, confused, as she tries to follow me in. She wants details. But I shoot her a pleading look and she backs off.

"By the way," I yawn, "you are so in trouble."

"What? What do you mean, I'm—"

I shut the door on her. There is my bed. I love my bed. I walk out of my shoes, set my box on my empty nightstand, and curl up on my bare mattress.

CRAZY, VIVID DREAMS plague my sleep. The kind that feel so real while you're in them, but when you wake up, you can only remember bits and pieces. The kind where you think there's something important there, but you just can't get back into the frame of mind from the dream to put your finger on it. At some point, I know I dream that Ethan has come to get me. I hear him talking out in the living room with Val and Emory. I know it's his voice, so I get myself up out of bed. I need to tell him I was wrong, to apologize and beg him to give me another chance. Maybe I can explain about the stories and the picture and my whacked-out overreaction. And he'd forgive me. I know he would. He will understand. Hope fills my heart as I walk to the door. But for some reason, I stop, my hand inches from the doorknob. I press my ear to the door instead.

"I really feel for you, Ethan. I don't know how you put up with her mood swings."

It takes me a second to realize Val is talking about me.

"You need to move on and find a more mature, more stable girl. Abby is definitely not either of those things," Emory adds—and then laughs. She laughs!

Oh, I am furious! I'm about to rip that door open and give those bitches a piece of my mind. My so-called friends! But I am frozen by what I hear next.

"You're right," Ethan says. I hold my breath and bite my lip, pressing my ear as flat as possible to the door. "I can't deal with it. I have to move on from her destructive force. You'll tell her, won't you? I mean, I just don't want to see her again."

"Oh, sure, Ethan. Anything for you, you know. You deserve to be happy."

I jerk back from the door. I shake my head to rid these words from it—I don't want to hear any more. I *have* ruined everything. But I know I can change his mind. I just need to explain. He will listen. I swing open the door and march out to set the record straight. All three of them stop and stare. They stare like condescending royalty eyeing a lowly village thief, waiting for some explanation as to why *I* should be allowed in the grace of *their* presence. It makes me sick to my stomach that I'm being treated this way. I'm not that bad of a person, am I? I know I have my faults, but still . . .

That's the only part of the dream I can pull out of my subconscious. For the life of me, I can't remember what happened next, what I said, or Ethan's response. I just can't remember. That leaves me very perplexed.

I must have had a few unsettling dreams, because when I wake, I don't feel very well-rested. Judging by the angle of the sunlight streaming in, it must be afternoon. I pull my phone out of my jacket pocket to check the time, then decide not to turn it on. No doubt there will be messages beeping at me from Val and Emory. Maybe even from Ethan. I don't want to hear those messages yet. I still need time to clear my head and collect my thoughts. I lay in bed a few more minutes before forcing myself up. I allow a glance at the box on my nightstand that caused all this trouble.

I wrestle out of my jacket and toss it aside. I get up, just like in my dream, and head for my bedroom door. I open it, slightly apprehensive about what might be awaiting me on the other side, half expecting Val, Emory, and Ethan to turn and aim their awful stares at me. But the living room is empty, the apartment silent. I realize I'm fine with that, relieved even.

I plug my phone into the charger on the kitchen counter and decide to take a long, hot shower. But my stomach feels hollow—I need to eat first. There's nothing appetizing in the fridge. Only bran cereal and a box of stuffing in the cupboard. Two cans of peas. I better cut that shower short and go get some food.

The clock on the microwave shows 5:30—I must have slept twelve hours! I shake my head in disbelief. Emotional trauma really takes a lot out of you.

After my shower, I find the nearest eatery, a pizzeria, and grab a slice and scarf it down. I buy a second slice, which I regret by the time I have half of it gone. I throw the rest away.

I remember that I forgot to unplug my phone from the charger when I left the apartment, which is okay, I guess. It needs to charge; it was nearly dead when I shut it off before work yesterday. A clock on the wall of the restaurant informs me it's almost 6:30.

I wonder if Ethan is at home. It's his day off. I decide I should go talk to him. Then promptly decide I shouldn't. The aftereffects of that dream really have me shaken. What if Ethan *does* feel that way? What if he thinks I'm too much of an emotional basket case to tolerate?

My final decision: I will go. I'll try to explain everything. Lay it all out there, why I reacted the way I did, why I came out so strongly against his surprise. Then I'll handle whatever choice he makes about us. No matter how painful.

For the first time, real fear of his reaction settles in. I mean, I ran out on us—just like his former fiancée did. What if I've dredged up all those terrible feelings he felt when she left him, reopened those old wounds? I'm the bad guy here. I could very well have lost him. And I have no one to blame for my irrational behavior but myself.

I stand outside Ethan's building for a long while, watching people go in and out. I guess I hope maybe he'll come bursting through the front door, arms wide open. But he doesn't. Finally, I take a deep breath. I just have to do this.

Unfortunately, by the time the elevator reaches the seventy-second floor, my resolve has dissipated. I'd focused on the numbers climbing higher and higher, afraid that if I let my mind wander I would surely change it. Now, I push myself out of the elevator as the doors open and head down the hall to Ethan's place, keeping the same pace until two doors away, when I stop. Slowly, I walk to his door. I pause one last moment, trying to compose myself, and knock. I hold my breath, waiting for the door to open. And when it does, I'll throw my arms around him and kiss him until he forgives me.

An impatient minute passes. I knock again, louder this time. Maybe he hadn't heard me the first time? Another minute passes. Then two. My heart sinks. I start to knock a third time but stop my hand in midair. I should go. I'm sure he sees me through the peephole and has decided he's not going to talk to me. I'm making a fool of myself now.

But, I remind myself, *Ethan isn't that guy*. He would never run from a situation like I did. He would face it head-on. He would want to hash it out. If he wanted to end it, he would listen to my side, make his decision, and be very straightforward with me. That is his way.

I convince myself he isn't home, that he's running errands or something and will be back. Maybe he's taking a load of my stuff back to my apartment. I slouch down next to his door and wait, propping my elbows on my knees.

Time drags slowly along. I don't know how long I sit here, playing out every possible scenario of our meeting in my mind. Some with good endings, some with bad endings, some with terrible endings. The window at the end of the hallway has darkened when I decide he's not coming back anytime soon. Maybe he's at the bookstore. Maybe he told West and Kate all about my crazy behavior. And now they will hate me, too.

Leaning against the wall for support, I drag myself up. My body has stiffened from sitting so long in one position. I stretch my neck from side to side, rubbing it, before I start toward the elevator.

It doesn't take long for me to get to the store now that I've once again set my resolve. I am going to find Ethan and get this sorted out tonight. When I arrive though, West is locking up, Kate beside him. No sign of Ethan. I run the last half block to reach them before they take off.

"Kate! West!"

"Oh, hey, Abby." Kate's warm smile suggests she knows nothing of the previous night's events. "No plans with Ethan tonight? You two are inseparable on Sundays," she teases.

"Um, no. Actually, I was wondering if either of you have seen him?" Can they hear the desperation in my voice?

"He hasn't been around all day," West says.

"Everything okay?" Kate reaches out for my arm.

I struggle to keep it together. I could break down and cry on her shoulder, tell her everything. She'd understand. She'd make me feel better, tell me everything will be all right. But I don't want to do that. I have to find Ethan. Tonight. I have to fix this. "Uh, yeah." I force a half-hearted smile. "Can you . . ." I swallow hard. "Can you let him know I'm looking for him? If you see him? My phone's . . . charging." I hitch my thumb over my shoulder as if in explanation. "So when I get home, I'll have it. He can call me."

"Home meaning . . .?" West questions.

Crap. They know. He's told them about The Surprise.

"My apartment," I confirm. "So, I'll talk to you later." I turn away before they can see the tears filling my eyes. They know I should be blissful roommates with Ethan by now. What will they think of me when he tells them how I freaked out and ran?

I just want to get home. Maybe Emory is there. I need somebody to talk to, somebody to reassure me that Ethan will forgive me. I know it won't be like my dream. She will support me, like always. Help me figure out what to do.

When I do arrive home, I'm relieved to find her alone, eating ice cream and watching a movie. "Hey, Ems."

"Abby! I'm so glad to see you! Get yourself a bowl and get over here girl! Tell me what the hell happened last night!"

"Oh . . . I really think I ruined it, Ems." I pick up my phone—charge complete. I power it on. "Let me check my phone first and see if there're any messages."

"Oh, hey, speaking of messages, your mom left two messages on the landline for you today. Sounds urgent. You need to call her."

Great. I do not want to talk to my mother at a time like this. But if she called twice in one day—and there are two missed calls from her on my cell—something must be up.

No missed calls from Ethan, I notice.

"Okay." I try to get my head straight. "I'll call my mother quick and then we can get into it." I walk to my room as I dial her number. I never talk to my mother on the phone in front of anyone. It's hard enough trying to get through a conversation, let alone having an audience during it.

"Hey, Mom," I say when she answers. "What's going on?"

"Abigail. It's about time you returned my calls. Do you realize how many times I have called you?"

"Yes, Mother, I'm sorry. My phone was dead, and I wasn't around today," I apologize, like usual.

"Abigail, you need to come home. Immediately."

Chapter Thirteen

Did I Ever Really Know You?

"Another delightful conversation with your mother?" Knowing my mother, Emory is sarcastic.

"Umm. I need to go."

"What? You just got here. You're taking off again?"

"I need to get some clothes. I need my suitcase."

"Abby, what's going on? What did your mom say?"

"My dad died." It comes out emotionless, flat.

"Oh, Abby, I'm so sorry!" Emory rushes over and wraps her arms around me. It is no comfort.

My mind is in a fog. "I need my clothes. My stuff's all at Ethan's?" I ask what I already know to be true. I can't think of what to do. Part of me just wants to slump to the ground and curl in my knees, wait for this storm—now more tortuous than before—to be over.

"Didn't you see the key?"

"What?" I feel a million miles away, and Emory is making no sense.

"The key."

My gaze follows her arm to where she's pointing. On the counter, by the telephone, is a small navy box with a red fabric bow on it. I squint my eyes—are they playing tricks on me? I'm still very confused.

"Ethan brought the key earlier today, while you were still sleeping."

"Ethan was here?"

"He said he planned to give it to you last night, but you left. He wants you to have it."

He wants me to have it? What does that mean? Does he still want me to live with him? Does he want me to get my stuff out while he's gone? I don't have time to sort out the meaning, I have to go. The wake is tomorrow, and the funeral is Tuesday. I need to get on a plane.

"Okay. I'll go get my things . . ." I shake my head to clear it. "Then I've got to go."

"Do you want company to the airport?"

"No. Thanks, though. I'm fine."

Am I fine?

I call a cab on the way to Ethan's to pick me up from there and take me to the airport. I vaguely wonder if he will be there. I can't talk to him about last night now. I have no time.

I get to his apartment in record time. Holding my breath, I slide the key into the lock as discreetly as I can. What will I say? What will he say? My hands are shaking as I dislodge the key and push open the door. But I don't have to worry about explaining anything to him tonight. The apartment is dark. I exhale and almost crumple; the jittery anxiousness I felt all the way over here releases out of my body when I realize, thankfully, I won't have to face Ethan now while I'm trying to deal with the news I received about my father. I grasp the door handle for support and allow my eyes a moment to adjust to the darkness. The sparkling lights of the city shine across the windows at the back. I'm not prepared for the stab of pain that hits me being in his apartment. A place I loved to be, now mixed with regret for my actions and fear that I will never really be welcome here again. I flick on the lights. A bouquet of flowers catches my eye on the counter to my left—my flowers, from last night, now beautifully arranged in a crystal vase. . . waiting patiently for my return? I step over and caress the petals of a daffodil between my fingers as I had done last night. Regret sweeps over me like a hand pushing me down from behind. The backs of my eyes sting with unshed tears. I have no time to fall apart now. I propel myself to the bedroom, hoping I can find everything I need.

My suitcase is in the closet, luckily. Ethan has taken great care in organizing the closet with our clothes. I find everything I need quickly. My dress shoes are even organized. How had he done all of this in such a short time without me knowing?

My phone rings, startling me. "Hello?"

"You called a cab?"

"Yes, I did."

"Waiting out front. Clock's running."

"I'll be right there. Thanks." I dash to the bathroom, grab my toiletries, and throw them into the suitcase. I take one last second to see if there is anything else I might need. I wish I had time to write Ethan a note. I'll have to call him when I land in Iowa. I can figure out what he means with the key then.

A REDEYE GETS me as close as the Quad Cities, then I rent a car to make the hour-and-a-half drive to Cedar Rapids. I guess it's a good thing I got so much sleep during the day; I'm able to make it through the early morning hours alert enough to drive. Thank God for satellite radio to help with that.

It's five a.m. by the time I hit the city limits of Cedar Rapids. It will be another ten minutes before I reach my mother's house. Hard to believe I haven't been back to see her for . . . three years now? Once I escaped the cold, repressive atmosphere she cultivated in that house, and realized the freedoms I could have in my own life, I dreaded returning.

I decide to prolong my absence a little longer as I catch sight of a twenty-four-hour restaurant just off I-380. While waiting for my breakfast, I think about calling Ethan. It's after six already in New York. But I don't know what to say. I really feel like we should talk in person. He can't hang up on me in person. Not that he would ever hang up on me. He is too open-minded and willing to hear any side of any argument. That's the lawyer in him. Or really, that's the kindness in him. I touch my phone to see the time. My eyes are heavy; it's hard to focus. Five . . . twenty-eight. No, twenty-three. I could text him, tell him I'll call him later.

"Here's your omelet, dear. Need anything else?"

"Um, no. I'm good. Thanks." I try to smile, but I'm too tired.

I can only eat half of my omelet and a few bites of my hashbrowns before it becomes too difficult to raise the fork to my mouth. I need a bed more than I need food.

The cool morning air slaps me in the face as I push through the door of the restaurant. It gives me that little jolt of alertness I need to finish my drive. The closer I get to the house, however, the harder it is to keep my eyes focused. I pull into my mother's driveway and heave a long sigh of relief. Which is quickly followed by a wave of dread.

Lights are on in the house. Victoria is awake. I should have expected as much; it is a school day. I briefly think about laying the seat back in the rental car and sleeping in the driveway. It's preferable to an awkward conversation with her. I grab my suitcase then trudge up to the front entry with heavy feet. I dig through my purse for the key as I stand swaying in front of the door.

As if in answer to my unspoken prayer, the latch turns and the door opens. "Abigail, what on earth are you doing? Did you lose your key? You always were losing things. Come inside."

Good to see you, too. "Hi." I step into the entryway. "I know they're in here somewhere. I'm just too tired to search." I force a little laugh to try, ineffectively, to lighten the mood.

"Well, I hope you weren't planning on us having breakfast together this morning, I'm getting ready for work," she states as she walks into the kitchen and grabs her coffee mug. "There is coffee brewed if you would like. You know where the mugs are." She raises her mug toward the cupboards. Of course I know where they are. By the looks of things, my mother has not changed much about this house since my departure.

"That's okay. I just really need some sleep. It's been a long trip."

"Suit yourself. You know where the bedroom is." My mother gives a little wave as she strides out of the kitchen to the hall toward the bathroom. With her other hand, she holds her coffee mug up to her mouth. I assume she's trying to tell me good night or goodbye or something.

I head down the hallway toward the room that used to be my bedroom. That may be the only room in the house she's changed in all these years, wasting no time after I left making my room into a guest bedroom. She even took interior decorating classes to get just the right look: a Tuscan theme, which I'll give her credit, turned out pretty nice. But she must have had her fill of designing after this room because the rest of the house is still late 1980s tan carpets and faux brick paneling. That, or she ran out of money. I lug my suitcase up onto the dresser, and an overwhelming feeling hits me as I glance around my former room. It's almost like she's trying to erase the fact that she has a daughter. Nothing of mine remains in this room—not even a picture or one of my porcelain horse figurines. I remember her telling me at one point that all my stuff was boxed up in the basement if I wanted it, but I never really cared about anything I left behind. So there it stayed. Maybe she's thrown it all away by now. I guess I don't care one way or the other.

"Your grandmother called yesterday, Abigail," my mother calls from the doorway of the bathroom. I step into the hallway to see her molding her hair into place. I pause for a moment and look at her, not really seeing. "She would like you to meet them at the funeral home by ten this morning."

"'Kay." I can barely get my tired voice to work. I mechanically turn and move toward the bed.

"You'll pass along my condolences, please?" It is a statement more than a question.

"Yeah." It's probably too soft for her to hear. I don't care. I fall onto the bed. With my eyes closed, I maneuver my way under the covers and drift swiftly into a deep sleep.

***

AS I ENTER the funeral home, I realize my nightmares have come to life. My father is dead, before his time, and I have to walk up to a casket, view his pale, lifeless body. When I had these dreams in my youth, the funeral home was always so dark, the carpeting and draperies always bloodred. Different from the nightmares of my adulthood, where I'm overwhelmed by people I barely know or know not at all; in the dreams of my childhood, I was the only one who made the long, dreadful walk down the endless aisle to my father's waiting body. I was the only one who even cared to show up. And always, I would get up to the casket, place my hand on the edge, and feel the puckered satin on the inside with my fingertips. My eyes would rest on my father's face, waiting. Waiting for something. Sometimes, I would wait a long time, sometimes only briefly. Then the dream would dissipate, and I never remembered when I awoke if I'd found out what I was waiting for. Was I waiting for him to wake up? Was I waiting for him to tell me why he had chosen the life he did, why he chose it over me? Was I waiting to feel something, like sorrow or forgiveness?

This funeral home is nothing like the one from my dreams. The carpeting is a comforting blue color, the curtains white, the walls a creamy tan. Many tall windows allow light to stream into every corner. This could be any foyer in any large home. It isn't a place you would expect to round a corner and see a dead body in a casket. Instrumental music drifts softly around, somewhat hopeful music, adding to the feeling of comfort and serenity.

A young man stands at the far end of the entryway wearing a navy suit and a gold nametag, but he looks very young to be in the business of interment. At any rate, there are four rooms directly off the entryway, so I guess my best bet is to trust this kid to point me in the right direction.

"Good morning." His voice is smooth, soft. He smiles comfortingly, and his eyes show a maturity beyond his years. "Which family are you with?"

"Um, Templeton."

"Yes," he confirms as if he knew who I was before I even said it. "Right this way, please."

As he leads me down a hallway to a small room, I notice his suit coat is too long for his arms. The length of his fingers is swallowed up by the cuffs, only the tips peeking out. "Here we are." He turns to face me as he holds his arm out at the room I'm to enter. He offers the standard sympathy smile and a nod, definitely well on his way to being a proper funeral director. It's kind of depressing, knowing this young kid is going to be spending his whole life around dead people.

I nod my thanks as I enter the room. I expect to be face-to-face with a casket at the end of a long aisle, but this room is very small. And missing a casket.

"Abby, honey, over here."

I look over to see Grandma Mary holding her arms out to me. A fresh wave of tears bursts from her puffy red eyes as I walk over to embrace her. Her sister, my great-aunt Virginia, is beside her, and my cousins, Jack Jr. and Tom, sit around one of the small tables with their families. Aunt Jeannette, their mother, died when I was young, and our families really didn't keep in touch. I think the last time I saw Jack Jr.—known as just "Junior" back then—and Tom was at Grandma's fiftieth birthday party, so long ago. The boys are older than me by a few years, so we never had any interest in hanging out or playing or whatever kids do at family gatherings. In fact, the only attention Junior or Tom ever showed me was pulling my hair when I walked by or pushing me down and tickle-torturing me until I screamed loud enough to irritate the adults. That would send the boys scrambling off for fear of punishment.

They appear so grown up now, both with pretty wives at their sides. Both with two young children. All girls, which I find quite humorous. Ironic how the two bullies have grown up and now dote over little girls. Junior actually lets his younger daughter hit him on the head over and over again with a plush phone because she giggles at the ringing bell chiming inside the toy.

Of course, they're not sad. How could they be? They barely knew my father and probably have few memories of him. It's nice of them to show up, though. They display the proper amount of mourning one would expect from distant relatives, offering their condolences to me. I graciously accept them, and that is the extent of our conversation.

I make my way back over to Grandma Mary. She looks rough. Great-Aunt Virginia is handing over tissues in a constant stream. I've only seen my Grandma Mary cry like this one other time, when Aunt Jeannette passed. She holds her right hand out to me. It's shaking, not from age but from emotional stress. My heart melts and tears well in my eyes to see her in so much pain. I clasp her hand in both of mine and sit at her side. I don't know what I can say to make her feel better. I want to give her some kind of comfort.

"Abby, baby . . ." She wipes her eyes with a wadded-up tissue. She tries to control the sobs so she can speak. "Abigail, it means so very much to me that you could be here. I know you and your father had some difficulties." She dabs at her eyes again. "But I sure am pleased you are here." She squeezes my hand and looks deep into my eyes. "Your father was always so proud of you. So proud. He may not have shown it, but he sure talked you up to everyone he knew. And he loved you. Remember that."

She looks away, across the room, like she's thinking about my father—maybe about a conversation they had or something he had done. I don't know. But I do know he was a different person around her. Respectful and loving with her whenever she came to the house. If we were at family gatherings, he made time to sit and talk with her. They would reminisce about Grandpa Joe or Aunt Jeannette and him as kids. And he would try to stay in line as long as he could around her, try not to drink too much. He never wanted to disappoint her.

I remember one time long ago when he had way too much to drink at Christmas. He and my mother had been fighting for days. And while they tried to keep up a tolerant, slightly affectionate façade in front of the family, the tension was thick. Dad took to drinking early on and got obnoxious and mean shortly after dinner. There was a big commotion and he wanted to fight somebody. He was getting in everybody's face—Uncle Jack's, Great-Uncle Earnest's, his cousin Paul's. I was frightened by what was happening. My mother hid in the kitchen, pretending to do dishes or something. The other wives held their children out of the way. But Grandma Mary stepped right up to him and grabbed his elbow. I don't know what she said to him in her low, stern voice, but within a minute she had him backed down and apologizing over and over again to her and everyone gathered for ruining Christmas.

Grandma Mary was the only person I knew who could control my father. I used to wish she would come over more often, that way Dad would drink less. But my mother didn't get along with Grandma, so her visits were few and far between. And as my father fell further and further into his disease, Grandma's ability to control his behavior dwindled. He isolated himself from everyone, because if we didn't see him, then we wouldn't know how bad he'd gotten.

Somewhere along the way I reached a point where I really didn't care anymore. Let him do what he wanted, and I'd ignore him as long as he wanted. Problem is, he was my father. And as hard as I tried to shut him out, I couldn't close that door all the way. I left it a tiny crack open. And that's what let him back in every time; that's what got me hurt. Every time. But I didn't have the strength to shut that door completely.

"Good morning." A soft feminine voice draws our attention. "I'd like to discuss the arrangements with you now. Is that all right?"

I notice her eyes are trained on both Grandma Mary and me as she speaks. I hope she doesn't think I will be participating in this part. No way.

"Yes, we're ready, dear," Grandma Mary confirms as she stands to go over to the small table where the woman is placing books and binders out for viewing. She clasps my hand, forcing me to get up and follow her. I'm sure everyone sees my reluctance plastered all over my face, but I'm not about to argue with my grandma, even though I really, really, *really* do not want to have any part in this. I wanted to show up, mourn, and leave. Simple. I certainly am not prepared to make decisions about my father's casket design and plans about his service. Who am I to know what he'd want? I barely knew the guy.

But as usual, I do what is expected of me. I sit next to Grandma Mary and look at all the pages she shows me. I agree with the things she thinks Dad would like. I manage to deflect any questions about what I think he would like. And really, it doesn't take as long as I thought it would. The woman helping us keeps things moving along, looking at her watch occasionally as if maintaining a schedule.

I'm relieved everyone else vacated the room shortly after we started, so I don't have to worry about what they think of my lack of involvement. Jack Jr. and Tom wanted to let the little ones go outside and play. And Great-Aunt Virginia—not having her son, Paul, and his kids around to talk to—went out with them.

The arrangements settled, Grandma decides we should all go eat and catch up, since we never see each other anymore. I try to come up with an excuse to save me from the awkward situation. Plus, I really want to take a nap. I'm still so tired.

But the hurt look on Grandma's face when I try to back out makes me suck it up and agree. It's only lunch. I will survive another hour or two of family time.

Grandma Mary chooses the same restaurant for lunch that I ate at early this morning. Immediately, dread creeps in around me at the thought of a drawn-out meal. Afraid that the same lack of wait staff and slow service awaits us, I find myself wishing for Ethan's presence now more than ever. Luckily, the wait staff is in full force and prompt. Luckily, the awkward silences are few, mostly due to the antics of the youngest generation, behaving as kids do in a restaurant—which is to say not well. Unluckily, everybody seems to focus their questions on me.

"So, how do you like school, Abby? NYU, right?" Tom asks.

"Actually, I'm not attending anymore. It wasn't really my thing, I guess." I frown when I notice the look of disappointment on Grandma's face.

"So, what type of work are you in then? Wall Street? Theater? Fashion?" Tom's wife, Gretchen, asks curiously. She obviously knows very little about New York City. Probably just what she's seen on TV in their small Ohio town, like *Real Housewives of New York City* or *Sex in the City* reruns.

"I'm a waitress." Quiet falls on the group for a long moment.

"Are you seeing anyone?" Grandma asks hopefully.

"Um . . . not really."

Probably not.

"I'll bet there's all sorts of nightlife and things to do in New York. Do you go out a lot?" Gretchen prods. She seems a bit in awe that I am a New Yorker. I notice she watches me a little more than I'm comfortable with. Well, by the end of the meal, at the rate these questions are going, I'm sure she'll be pretty disappointed at how boring a New Yorker I turn out to be.

"I'm more of a homebody. I read a lot." See? Boring.

But that's not the end of the questions. There are a few more that I provide disappointing answers to, so by the time they decide they know enough about me, I thoroughly feel like a real loser. College dropout, waitress, no man, no life.

To top it all off, I get to hear about how great Junior and Tom's jobs and lives and families are. They have proof of how great they're doing—attractive wives and adorable children, expensive cars. At least Gretchen seems to feel better about herself when she realizes she leads a more interesting life in the Midwest than the New Yorker does.

I survive the lunch and family bonding time, awkward and depressing as it was, and we head back to the funeral home to prep for the visitation. As I sit in the family room we gathered in earlier, I begin to feel like I should really make some life changes when I get home to New York. I shouldn't be such a boring person in such a vibrant city. Well, I didn't think I *was* boring when I was with Ethan. He made me not-boring. I really need to see him. I make up my mind that he will be my first stop when I arrive.

"They're ready for us now," Great-Aunt Virginia says softly from the doorway.

We file out of the family room to the room marked with a placard that reads:

RICHARD "RICH" TEMPLETON

VISITATION: APRIL 27, 2009, 1 P.M.

INTERMENT: APRIL 28, 2009, 10:30 A.M.

"*Rich?*" I question half-heartedly.

The procession heads for the chairs at the front by the casket. Suddenly, the anxiety of my nightmares floods over me; my fears come to life. I can't look at the front of the room. I am not ready. Instead, I focus on Grandma Mary. She's sitting alone, dabbing her eyes with crumpled tissues, her chest heaving unevenly. I sit and gently rub her back.

I search for anything to distract my eyes, so I don't have to look at that casket. I watch Grandma's face, lined with age and fraught with sadness. I appraise the flowers at the front of the room on stands and on the floor. A surprising amount—I didn't think that many people cared about my dad. My mother even sent a large bouquet. I see her name and mine scrawled in large black lettering on the equally large sympathy card. Just like my mother to make sure everyone knows which flowers she sent. Make sure everyone comments on how lovely they are and how nice of a gesture it is.

There's a picture of Dad by the lectern. It isn't one I recognize. Maybe it was Grandma Mary's picture? It must be several years old. It's actually a really good picture, one that embodies the way he would have wanted people to remember him, taken outdoors, his eyes kind of squinting in the sunlight. He's dressed sharply, like maybe he was going somewhere important. He has a big smile on his face—the kind I used to see when I was a kid. It's the same smile from my picture of me and him fishing. He looks happy, full of life. It gives me the tiniest swelling of pride, seeing him look so good, so put-together.

"Grandma," I whisper, "is that your picture of Dad?" I nod in its direction.

"Yes, dear." She gazes at the picture for a long moment. Then she pats my knee. "I took that picture on your graduation day. Your father was so proud of you. I had to take a picture. He looked so handsome all dressed up and excited to see you walk across that stage." She attempts a smile, but it looks more like a grimace as she tries to hold back the tears.

My chest tightens and my eyes get wet, but I hold my breath until it passes. My dad was that happy because of me. That really hits me, makes me feel sad I hadn't seen more of him like that. Then I get angry, because for so many years I had tried to reach out to him, I had tried to have a relationship with him. He was the one who didn't care enough to try. He was the one who put alcohol above me. It was his fault I didn't get to have those moments with him.

People are arriving, which I hadn't realized. Quite a few people, actually. A few I know—old neighbors, Dad's friends. Most of them I don't. They file through, pay their respects at the casket, make their way down the line of family members. I have to talk to each one, at a minimum nod at what they say to me. I feel like several of them are sadder than I am. Some sob like it's their own father they've lost.

I start to feel guilty, like I'm not sad enough. I mean, I am sad. I guess. Maybe I'm still numb from the shock. It has been less than twenty-four hours since I found out he died. Maybe I'm not far enough along in the grief process. I decide I have to get away from these sobbing strangers, though, who are making me feel so guilty. I can't stand it.

Sneaking away from the line, I make my way outside for fresh air. To the side of the building is a big white gazebo on a grassy expanse. I head for it. I drop onto the wooden bench and look around at the clear blue sky surrounding the peaked roof. For a moment, I wish I had a cigarette, even though I don't smoke. Or a beer. A beer would be better. A nice, tall, cold bottle of light beer. Or two.

I sigh. Leaning forward, I rub my temples. After a long moment, I lean my head back, letting the warmth of the late-April sun seep deeply into my bones. Letting it bake into my brain and burn up every bad thing holding my mind hostage.

"Abigail!"

My eyes fly open. I squint in the bright sunlight to see Great-Aunt Virginia standing with her hands on her hips by the side door, the one I sneaked out of. She beckons me with an aggressive wave of her hand. Reluctantly, I pull myself up from the bench and head in.

I barely enter the room when I hear Grandma Mary calling my name. "Oh, there she is! Abby! Come over here, honey!" She signals me over. Next to her is a woman I have never seen before and a child, a boy, maybe six or seven. The woman doesn't look very old—not much older than I am. She has a kind of haggard appearance, though. Her hair is brushed but doesn't look very clean. The boy has holes in the knees of his jeans and wears a hooded sweatshirt two sizes too big zipped up halfway over a superhero t-shirt. His hair is buzzed short. I wonder who these people are. Distant relatives? Friends of Grandma's?

As I near, I realize the woman has been crying. Her eyes are puffy, and her nose is red from wiping. I give Grandma Mary a questioning look.

"Abigail, dear," she says, pulling me next to her, "this is Colleen Matson and her son, Bobby."

The woman barely lets Grandma finish the introduction before blurting out, "I am *so* sorry for your loss, Abigail." She reaches out and clasps my hand in a death grip. "Your father was a great man. A great man. He was like a angel from heaven—" she breaks off with a sob. She has a bit of a southern drawl, but she could have been speaking in a whole other language as far as I'm concerned. Her words make no sense to me. But she continues as if I'm fluent in the language she speaks. "We are gonna miss him so dearly. He truly was a light in our lives. When I was in my darkest days with my addiction, he gave me the courage an' the strength to pull through it for my Bobby. He made me go to meetin's when I didn't want to, an' he was always lookin' out for Bobby and me.

"He pushed me to be a better person an' a better mother. He tole me I had to be there for my son. He tole me how he weren't there for his daughter an' how it made him feel an' how he could never forgive hisself for that. An' he didn't want me an' Bobby to go through that same pain.

"He was strong for me when I couldn't be an' he taught me so I could be strong. I wouldn't be here without his angel touch on our lives. I know that. An' Bobby wouldn't be here without his—his—" she breaks off again, sobbing harder this time.

"Oh, there, there, dear," Grandma soothes and hands the woman a tissue. "Colleen, you *are* a strong woman. You are doing so well, young lady." She squeezes her arm. I wish Grandma would take Colleen's arm—her death grip is making my fingers tingle with numbness.

"Rich took real good care of us," the woman continues, trying to compose herself. There is clearly more she wants to unload on me. "He was like a father fer little Bobby here the past couple years." The woman finally releases my numb hand to put her arms around her boy. "Took him fishin', took him to the park, took him anywhere. Rich got him his first pole, ya know. Was always buyin' him things." She smiles ruefully as she continues on and on about "Rich."

Boy, that sounds odd—*Rich*. Actually, it irritates the crap out of me. Nobody ever called my dad *Rich*. At least, I'd never heard it before. The more she says his name, the more it bothers me. And how does this woman know so much about my dad? What—were they together? Did they live together? I steal a look at my grandma to see if she is as put off by this person as I am. Grandma only ever called Dad Richard. Surely it bothers her, too.

But Grandma listens to this woman go on and on about my dad, occasionally dabbing at her eyes, almost like she knows the whole story already. Like this storytelling is merely for *my* benefit. Has she been keeping something from me? *Did* Dad have a relationship I knew nothing about?

"I'm sorry," I finally interrupt—I have to find out. "How did you meet my father?" I try to sound polite, but I think it just comes out rude.

"Oh, um. Me and your dad knowed each other fer years," she goes on, not even phased by my rudeness. "We used to hang around the same crowd, see. An' he got cleaned up an' saw me worse then ever. He stepped in. Did one of those—whattaya call it—a intervention thingy. He helped me get cleaned up, too.

Saved my life really. We sure are gonna miss his visits an' Bobby's fer sure gonna miss those fishin' trips with Rich.

"Meetin's ain't gonna be the same without him. Everybody's said so. At the meetin' last night, I mean. Everybody talked real great about your dad. I wish you coulda heard em. He was a good, good man."

Before I know what's happening, Colleen's arms clamp around my neck. She is a good half-foot shorter than me, so I stand awkwardly bent down in her arm lock. She's sobbing into my shoulder, blubbering incoherently. I don't know how to hug her back. I don't even *know* this woman. I want to push her off of me, but not wanting to make a scene, I give in and kind of put my hands on each shoulder, trying to touch as little of her as possible. She smells of fried food and old grease.

Finally, I can't take it anymore. The confusion and the irritation of what has just occurred boils over. I feel like everyone's eyes are on us; she is creating such a scene. I push on her shoulders and try to back away a bit. After two steps, she finally releases me. She reaches out for another tissue from Grandma Mary. I check the shoulder of my dress for signs of snot. It's wet from her tears. I'm about to excuse myself when I realize she isn't finished with her display yet.

"And if Rich hadn't been there that day, I know my little Bobby wouldn't be here no more." She dabs her eyes. "I feel so bad for him, but he did save my boy. He did." She shakes her head and drops her eyes to the floor. She pulls her boy to her and clenches her hands on his sweatshirt.

"There, there, honey." Grandma reaches for the woman's hand, her voice trembling. "We know."

We know what?

"I just—I just feel so bad fer y'all . . . but that truck sure woulda killed my boy." She starts a fresh wave of tears. "If it weren't fer Rich. He's a angel, straight from God above. Gone back now to be with his Maker," she chokes out.

"There, there," Grandma murmurs again. Then they embrace, both sobbing.

I stand, unable to process all of this. Who is this Rich that she talks so highly of? A good man? A hero? He traded his own life for the life of a little boy? This is not the selfish, alcohol-diseased, vanishing man I had known, had grown up with: Richard. Why did I not know Rich? Why was I stuck with Deadbeat Richard while she got to know Hero Rich? And most of all, why did this boy get the best of my father? The fishing trips and the parks and all that crap? What the hell!

It hits me like a ton of bricks. All the emotion, all the years of anger and disappointment that have built up inside of me, all the frustration and the letdowns. Why were this crackhead and this boy more important to my father than me—his own daughter?

My fists clench and unclench, and my jaw grinds until it hurts. I want to go up and punch my father in the face. I want to beat on his chest. I want to slam the casket closed on his stupid face and knock it to the ground!

What this woman said about my father makes no sense. None.

For the second time, I feel the need to flee the room. What a stupid emotional rollercoaster. It wasn't supposed to be this way. It should have been easy. Come, say goodbye to the father I didn't know, and leave.

I've had enough. I'm at my breaking point. Turning on my heels, I push my way through the crowded room. When did all these people show up? They're all here for my dad?

"So sorry to hear about your father," an older man says, grabbing my elbow as I try to pass. He is scruffy and wearing a striped shirt from the eighties and dress pants that are clearly too small. His hair is greasy and combed over his balding head. "He was a staple at the meetings. He helped a lot of people. A lot. You should be proud."

I try to pull up the corners of my mouth to be polite. I try to say thank you, but it comes out voiceless.

I continue on, maneuvering my way to the door. My chest is tightening again. I can't breathe right. I head for the restroom and lock the door. Turn on the sink and splash water on my face, hoping for some relief from this physical torment.

My chest is heaving now. I hold my breath to get myself under control. But that makes the pain in my chest so much worse. So I let it out—huge, embarrassing, disgusting sobs. The tears fall. I don't stop them or wipe them, I just stand there with my hands gripping the sink, water running, and bawl my eyes out.

Gradually, the pain subsides. The relief I've been longing for follows. My tight muscles relax as a wave of sorrow crashes over me. Sweet release. I don't fight it anymore. I let myself grieve for my father. Who I did love, no matter what.

Who I did have good memories with that could not be taken away from me. Who, despite his many failures, had some successes too, and did, in fact, help many people. I mean, he saved a boy's life. He tried to make up for the wrong he had done my mother and me by helping people he could help. People who really needed him. I couldn't fault him for that.

As I slump to the floor by the bathroom stall, I cry until I can't cry anymore. It's cathartic. I think about my father doing all those good things over the past few years, and my view of him shifts. I start to see him as that man in the picture out front, the way many of those people out there mourning his passing must see him. And that's how I want to remember him.

Eventually, I pull myself together, splash more water on my face, and try to soothe my puffy eyes. I wipe my smudged eyeliner and take one last deep breath, unlock the bathroom door, and walk back into the visitation.

I make my way down the blue-carpeted aisle, past the rows of white chairs, focusing on the dark wood-grained casket at the front, draped with roses and floral spray. I march right up to the open end, no fear of what I might find this time. I stare down at my father's face, creased with age, brown from the sun—he'd spent some time out fishing already this season. He looks so peaceful. I place my hand on top of his folded hands, startled at the coolness. He's dressed in the suit from my graduation day, tie and everything. I touch the lapel, remembering his greeting to me that afternoon after the procession out of the gymnasium, the pride in his voice. I touch his cheek, remembering the happy smile from the days of our fishing excursions. There is no fear in this moment, as in so many of my nightmares. He is at peace. No more struggle with alcoholism, no more pain.

As I gaze down at my father, I feel a peace settle on me as well. I let go of the anger, the jealousy I felt that these strangers had seen a better side of him than I had. I embrace the good.

And I forgive my father for whatever wrongs I held against him, both imagined and real.

Chapter Fourteen

No Turning Back

BY THE TIME the plane lands at LaGuardia Airport, I am completely exhausted. I napped en route but feel no better for it.

I managed to score a flight back home on Tuesday evening, so I didn't have to spend one minute extra with my mother. Victoria, of course, had to show her face at both the funeral and the luncheon. And not for my father, or even my grandma, but just so everyone would know she had been there. She accepted condolences like she was still married to him. After we ate, I'd hoped for some downtime at the house to recharge. I'd wanted to use the landline to try to call Ethan as well. My phone had died, and I'd forgotten my charger at the apartment.

But no such luck. Mother had taken the whole day off from school and wanted to have some "girl time." Like it wasn't bad enough sitting through a funeral all morning, I was forced to sit through two hours of my mother talking about her hobbies, her friends, her plans for the summer break. When she got tired of talking about herself, she switched to talking about me—what I needed to do with my life, what jobs I should go after, how I should go back to school, how she was so disappointed in my choices lately, how I needed to find a rich New York businessman to marry and have children with. If I had children with him, I would fare better in the event of a divorce.

Really? I wondered if she even noticed I had no comments for the gibberish she was spouting.

I was actually thrilled that I had a long drive ahead of me to the Quad Cities and that I had to be at the airport two hours early due to heightened security. I was *happy* to use the excuse that I had to pack and get on the road.

Now, I'm relieved to be home, to have all of this behind me. It has been a tough three days. I realize my stomach is churning as I walk toward baggage claim. Must be hunger—it is pretty late.

But after grabbing a bite to eat, my stomach doesn't feel any better. In fact, it feels worse. As I make my way to a cab, it dawns on me that it isn't hunger making my insides do backflips—it's nerves. I am so nervous to see Ethan again. I haven't talked to him for three days. My phone is dead, so I'll have to track him down. Which is good, because I want to do this in person. But not knowing where he is or if he even wants to see me keeps my stomach in knots.

I hail a cab and throw my bag in on the seat, squinting as I try to read the clock on his dashboard.

"Where to?"

"Um, actually, can you tell me what time it is first?" I ask apologetically, hoping he won't be irritated.

"Time? 9:35. Where to?"

Ethan should be home—I'm going for it. I give the driver his address, and he takes off like a true New York cab driver, driving faster than I want. I need time to rehearse my pleas. I am not quite ready to face him yet. Not ready for the anger or the resentment. What if he isn't willing to forgive me? Especially after three days of no communication?

I try to breathe slowly, to calm myself, but every argument I think of brings to mind an angry response from him. What if I've hurt him too much? Again, my mind returns to the fact that I ran out on him, just as his former fiancée had done. Maybe that's unforgivable. I'm so ashamed of how I must have made him feel.

The taxi comes to an abrupt stop. I rub my sweaty hands on my jeans as I remember the last time I came to his apartment to try to make my apology. I inhale deeply and slowly let the air out, hoping it will calm my pounding heart. The driver stares, annoyed. I pay him and pull my luggage out onto the sidewalk.

Okay. Here we go. No turning back.

I look up, trying to make out Ethan's apartment, wondering if I can tell if his lights are on. No such luck—it's too high up. I stand for a minute telling my feet to move, but they refuse. Heaving another breath and shaking my head to clear out the noise, I reassure myself.

I know what I want now, and I have to go get it.

I hurry to the elevator, getting on just in time before the doors close. It is the longest elevator ride of my life, but I make it. I am outside his door, breathing heavily, my suitcase cockeyed beside me. Now to knock. Why is this part always so hard for me?

Just do it. Just knock.

Finally, I do.

I turn to go, then turn back to the door. My stomach is so upset I think I may puke. Right on Ethan's doorstep. I look down at where it will land if I do.

The door swings open so fast I nearly jump out of my skin. I am face-to-face with him—and my mind is blank. I don't know how to start; I don't know what to say. So much has happened in the past few days. And there he stands, looking at me, hand on the door like he's ready to slam it shut in my face. I muster up all my courage to get everything out before he does just that.

"Um, look, Ethan, I'm . . . not very good at this. I mean, I'm really, *really* sorry for the way I've behaved, and I'm sorry I freaked out on you. I thought I wasn't ready for this, but I realize this is what I want." The words are racing out of me now—I can't stop. Yet I can't pull it together to make convincing arguments like I had planned. I am ruining it, but I continue. "I want to be with you. I want to share my life with you, to let you in. I do love you, and I hope you can forgive me. I'm really—"

He holds up his hand. The nervousness inside changes to fear. He can't forgive me. He is done with me. Staring into those beautiful blue eyes, I feel like crying.

"Abby, what are you doing?"

"Wha—I—"

Suddenly, Ethan reaches out and grabs my arm, pulling me into his embrace. I crumble like a rockslide down a mountain, melting into his body.

"Abby, please, *please* don't apologize. This was all my fault." He squeezes me tighter. The tears begin to fall, and I don't care. "I never should have gone behind your back. I know that. I never should have moved your things. Never should have invaded your privacy. I was so caught up in what I wanted that I didn't even think about how you might react." He pulls away, holding my shoulders with his warm, strong hands. His face is so apologetic, it seems wrong. *I* should be the one apologizing.

"Ethan, no. I overreacted. I was the crazy one."

"Don't say that. I was the crazy one for sneaking around behind your back and not thinking it would upset you. I made excuses for why what I was doing was okay, because I really wanted to surprise you. I should have *known* better." He slides his hands up to my face, wiping the tears from my cheeks with his thumbs.

I open my mouth to argue, but he holds up his hand again.

"You don't get to apologize on this one. It's all me. Clearly there are things we need to discuss, and I'm so happy you've come back so we can do that." His eager face morphs into a pained expression. "When you left, I knew I'd messed up. Big time. I thought I'd give you a little time to be pissed, then I'd catch you off guard and apologize in the biggest, most adorable way, and you'd have to forgive me." He smiles that smile, which makes me smile, relieved. "Then when I came home Sunday night and found the closet open and your suitcase and clothes gone . . ."

He trails off and shakes his head. A pang of guilt seizes me at the thought—I should have left him a note.

It is a long moment before he looks into my eyes again. His are filled with volumes of emotion. When he speaks, it's almost a whisper. "I thought . . . I'd lost you for good."

"Oh, Ethan." A fresh wave of tears springs to my eyes at the sight of him in such agony. He was punishing himself for my reaction.

"That night was absolutely horrible for me. I felt like such an idiot for losing you like that! I spent all night wondering where you had gone to, wondering if I should call you, afraid I might push you further away if I did. I was losing my mind, I tell you!" He is exasperated, reliving the night.

"I wasn't running away from you. You have to listen to me."

"No, no. I know that now." His comforting eyes reassure me. "I finally stopped at your apartment Monday after work, hoping to catch you there. I couldn't take it any longer. But Emory told me about your dad. Oh, God, Abby . . ."

He wraps his arms around me tighter than before. I bury my face in his neck, afraid the mention of my father in the wake of recent unexpected revelations will send me into a bawling fit all over again. He smooths my hair. I want to stay in his arms forever. This is what I had longed for in Iowa, the strength and love only Ethan can provide.

"I feel so terrible that I chased you away, and then you had to deal with your father's death—I should have been there for you. You needed me, and I wasn't there for you. I'm so sorry."

I pull my face up to argue. "Ethan, you cannot apologize for *that*. I won't let you. You had no way of knowing, and it all happened so fast. I had to leave in such a hurry to make my flight. I wanted to tell you. I wish you could have been there, too. But—I just felt like it was something I had to do on my own."

He looks at me doubtfully.

"Really," I assure him. "And as it turns out, I think it was a good thing I went alone." I sigh at the thought of the last two emotional days. "I'll tell you all about it sometime. But right now . . ." I lean in. "All I want is to kiss you."

As if that is the invitation he needed, he grabs me up by the waist and presses his lips to mine. He wastes no time getting us to the bedroom, a familiar path we followed just days before. I have no worries about what I might catch a glimpse of around the apartment or his room this time. I'm ready to live with Ethan, ready to plan a future with him. I don't have to convince myself that I can trust him with my heart. If he can take me back with open arms after all this, I *know* I can trust him.

As he peels off my clothes, the hungry passion returns. I want him so badly, want to feel his body all around me. His kisses, his caresses become more urgent. I hold on to him as I never have before, tighter and tighter. If it were possible, I would pull myself inside his body. I want his warmth and comfort to surround me. The fire inside consumes me. I need him now.

"I love you so much, Abby," he whispers into my ear.

That sends me over the edge.

"BABE! GET OUT here. I've got eggs for you." Ethan's voice sounds so far away. I roll over and snuggle down under the covers. I've slept in this bed many times, but never have I felt such an attachment to it before. It is my bed now—*our* bed—and I want to stay in it forever!

"Come back to bed," I call drowsily. Breakfast smells good, but my delight with this bed is better.

"If you won't come to breakfast, I'll bring it to you," he chirps as he climbs into bed with a steaming plate. He is way too energetic this morning. I pull the covers higher over my head in protest.

"Come on, you! I made this delicious breakfast just for you," he feigns disappointment as he pulls back the covers enough to expose my face.

"But I don't want to get up," I murmur. I have yet to open my eyes to the bright sunlight streaming in. "I like it here."

"I'm so glad that you do," he whispers as he leans down. He nibbles on my ear, then kisses my cheek and trails to my neck.

"Mmm . . . if you keep doing that, I'm *not* getting out of bed."

"Hmm," he chuckles. "Come on. We've got to get you settled in before work."

I groan. I can't win this match. Reluctantly, I sit up and rub my eyes. "Ooh, yummy." Before me he holds out a plate of bacon, toast, scrambled eggs with cheese, and strawberries. "Thank you," I coo. "You take such good care of me." I grab the plate with one hand and his face with the other, planting an appreciative kiss on his lips and gazing into his blue eyes for a moment. True happiness.

"So, you finish that, and I'll hop in the shower. I don't have to be at work until eleven today, so we've got time to get you unpacked and get the rest of your stuff from the apartment."

I look around the bedroom for the first time since our blowup. Half-emptied boxes sit on the floor and the dresser still. My alarm clock is flashing on the nightstand. He hasn't even set the time yet. It's almost as if the past few days haven't happened. If not for the lingering emotional pangs I feel, I would think it was all a bad dream. I could very well be waking up the day after The Surprise, but with the desired aftereffect Ethan had been hoping for all along. Love, happiness, appreciation for one another.

"Are you working tonight?" Ethan calls from the bathroom.

"Ah, yeah," I reply between bites. "I suppose I should call Jeff and let him know I'm back in town." The thought of returning to Hooligan's puts a dark cloud right over my good mood. "I really don't want to. I'm so tired of that place. I need to find a different job. A better job. Waitressing is *not* what I want to do for the rest of my life." The sound of the shower running tells me I am only complaining to myself.

Soon, though. Soon I will start looking for something else.

I finish my breakfast, which is admittedly the best I've ever had—made by Ethan and served in our bed. I load the dishwasher and clean up the kitchen while I wait for my turn in the shower. As I wipe the countertop, I find myself staring around the apartment, appreciating the open kitchen-dining-living area. It really is a rather large apartment by New York standards. And the wall-to-wall windows let in so much light. I gaze around at my things mixed in among Ethan's. My red toaster beside me on the counter. My candle centerpiece on Ethan's mahogany dining table. My favorite blue-and-white-striped throw pillows on his couch. My pictures intermingled with his on the desk. I have always felt so comfortable in Ethan's space. He's always wanted me to feel at home here. And now I truly do.

I see his I ♥ NY coffee mug, half-full, on the counter and think how nice a cup of coffee would be. I pour a cup and make myself comfortable on the window seat, sipping and soaking up the warm sunlight, breathing deeply, enjoying the serenity of the moment. The stress of the last few days has really taken an emotional toll. Spending these precious morning hours with Ethan will do me a world of good.

My packed suitcase catches my eye sitting in the foyer by the door. I place my cup on the window ledge and decide to unpack the contents and put the suitcase in *my* closet. It feels unofficial, like I'm not really moved in, with my suitcase full of my things staring at me.

Back in the bedroom—*our* bedroom—I lug the suitcase up on the bed and unzip it. The first item that greets me is the framed picture of my father. Grandma Mary gave it to me after the funeral. I wouldn't have asked for it, but I am glad she gave it to me. I can't get over how happy he looks in this photo. And knowing it was taken on my graduation day makes it very special. All the good things I remember about my father are in the picture of us fishing when I was a kid. All the good things about him I didn't know—but learned this week—are in this picture. I set the frame on the bed and clean out the rest of the suitcase.

I jump when Ethan's hand wraps around my waist. "Sorry." He rests his chin on my shoulder. "Unpacking for good, I hope?"

"Definitely . . ." I smile. "Definitely."

"That's a great picture of your dad. When was it taken?" he asks as he reaches over and picks up the frame. He flops onto the bed, looking like a total goof with my bright-colored floral towel around his waist and his black socks pulled up on his calves, his damp hair tousled. I grin at the sight.

"Ah, Grandma Mary took that picture of Dad before my graduation."

"Really?"

"Mm-hmm. She liked it so much she had it blown up and framed. She said my dad was so proud of me that day." I bite the inside of my mouth, feeling emotional all of a sudden. My voice becomes small. "It means a lot to me that she let me have it."

Ethan reaches out and gives my hand a squeeze. "So, pretty tough couple days?"

I inhale deeply, not sure how to put it all into words. "Yeah. I mean . . . you think you know someone, and you have all your judgments . . . you know?" I fidget with a blouse from my suitcase. "It's just, I had all these *feelings* about my dad and his alcoholism and his phantom fathering—" I draw in a sharp breath. I thought I was over the crying thing, but it's knocking at my door again.

Ethan pushes the suitcase out of the way and pulls me down beside him. He wraps his arm around me. Immediately, I feel calmer.

"I had always thought the alcohol would kill him. I went to Iowa *believing* that was what had killed him. So I had this vindication for the resentment and the anger I felt toward him all these years. Alcohol had made him leave me for good this time." A tear escapes down my cheek. Ethan reaches over and wipes it away.

I pick up the picture from his lap and stare at my father's smile. "I've never told anybody about this before. Only my family knows what my dad was really like in his disease. It's always been easier to pretend my dad didn't exist than to have to explain him to my friends, you know? Not even Emory knows how I felt about him. I mean, I couldn't even tell *you* about him, Ethan. I felt so guilty for shutting him out, but every time I would let him in, I would be the one who got hurt. Every. Single. Time. I just couldn't deal with him anymore."

The tears come more freely now. I wipe my wrist across my face. Ethan pulls me in tighter. "And then . . . something happened . . . that shattered everything I thought I knew about him." I shake my head, remembering the confusion and disbelief I'd felt when Colleen and her son showed up at the wake, when strangers told me how he'd helped them. "All these people went on and on about what a great man Rich was and how he had helped people with addiction get cleaned up. This woman and her son—a young boy—told me about how he had helped her get sober. And he did all these things with this boy: took him fishing, took him to the park—all the things he should have been doing with me all those years ago. I was furious at first, Ethan. I was so angry that this kid had stolen my dad. He'd done all the things I had longed to do. Why did Dad treat this kid like his own, and he couldn't—" I suck in a ragged breath, not sure I can say what I think. I swallow, determined to get all this out for the final time, to put my anger to rest. "Why couldn't he be a father to me?"

"Abby," Ethan whispers and kisses me on the cheek. "I'm sure your father never meant to hurt you."

"I don't know—no. I'm sure he never *meant* to. But I've felt so abandoned all these years . . ." I clench my jaw. There is no sense feeling sorry for myself. My father is gone; it is over. I forgive him. I have to move on. I have no answers for why he kept the distance between us. I will never know. I do know, however, that he *did* do good things for many people.

I continue, wanting Ethan to understand. "But he did such an amazing thing for this woman and this boy. He helped her turn her life around for her son's sake. Made sure they were taken care of, had been a father figure for this boy, and he *saved his life*. He sacrificed his own life to save this little boy from being hit by a truck, Ethan. My dad did that. My selfish, alcoholic father put another life in front of his own." I trace my father's smile in the picture with my finger. "I can't hate him anymore. He *was* a good man. No matter what I felt before, now all that has changed. And it was so overwhelming, and I wished you were there for me to lean on. But really, I needed to get through it on my own. I needed to forgive and to remember him for the good he had done. He did the best he could, right?"

"I'm sure he did. You can't punish him for the past, but you can't feel guilty for your feelings either. You have every right to your feelings, Abby. No one can deny you that. But the fact that you can put all that aside and see the good? That is monumental. It takes some real maturity. I just wish—I wish I could have been there for you."

I look deep into Ethan's blue eyes. I don't deserve such an amazing man. "You're here for me now. That's what matters."

He leans in and gives me a tender kiss. I rest my head on his shoulder, and a wave of calm passes over me. I told Ethan some of my deepest secrets and feelings, and he listened. And he hasn't passed judgment. In fact, he's made me feel so much better.

"Tell me, why do you put up with my craziness?" I wonder aloud.

"Why do I put up with your craziness?" He repeats, seemingly amused by the question. "Well, it's very simple, Abigail Templeton. Because I know what I want out of life. You see, I've been through a journey already, from losing my parents, to reconnecting with my uncle, to feeling trapped in a career I didn't want, to finding work I truly love to do. I thought I had found a real love once . . . but was forced to reexamine everything I thought about love and relationships when it didn't work out. By the time our paths crossed, I knew exactly what I wanted: to marry someone who is a true partner, to have a family someday, to make that family as happy as I possibly can.

"And then there you were, standing right in front of me. I knew there was something special about you. And I was right." He squeezes me tightly.

"What made me so special?" I ask, doubtful that I am special in any way.

"*You* made you so special, Abby. I hope someday you can look in the mirror and see all the greatness I see in you. Don't ever sell yourself short—you are an amazing, strong, sassy woman!" He ends his exclamation with a passionate kiss that takes my breath away.

"Now. What do you say we finish getting you unpacked and settled in?" He wants to lighten the mood, and I am ready for it.

"Sounds good. If you don't mind, I know exactly where I want to put this picture," I say as I jump up. "On the secretary desk."

"Perfect," he agrees.

Chapter Fifteen

Can Love Be Enough?

AS MUCH AS I dreaded returning to Hooligan's, my friends make it worth it. Emory hugs me three separate times and tells me that if I need a girls' night out, she will ditch Dylan and make it happen. Donovan pulls me aside and tells me he will cancel his date tonight if I need someone to talk to. Even Dylan tells me he's sorry to hear about my dad and he'll make himself scarce if I need to hang out with Ems.

I try to make sure everyone knows how much I appreciate them because I do. I just really hate the stress of eight hours of running tables. Halfway through my shift, I want to run to the stockroom screaming. I have never been so happy for a shift to be over as I am tonight. I make a point to thank Jeff for allowing me the time off and to thank Emory for her support lately. I reassure her that I am fine more than once so she will quit worrying. And I am. I know Ethan will be waiting for me outside like always.

"Hey, you!" My smile feels bigger than my face as I greet him outside the employee entrance.

"Hey yourself." He gives me a big kiss as he embraces me. "What do you want to do? Grab a bite to eat?"

"You know what I want to do? I want to go home. To our place . . ." I smile as I say it. The first time I've said "our place."

"Then that's what we'll do." He smiles back. My favorite smile.

We start off in that direction as we wave goodbye to Emory and Dylan.

"Oh, by the way, West asked me to ask you to come by the store tomorrow before we open."

"West did? Why? What's up?"

"I don't know." Ethan shrugs. "He wouldn't say, really."

I look up at him, but his expression gives nothing away. What could West possibly want to talk to me about, aside from his usual witty banter? Maybe he's planning something for Kate and needs my help.

"What do you say we grab some Chinese takeout on the way home?" Ethan asks as he laces his fingers through mine.

"I'd say let's get on it. I'm hungry!"

"HEY, ABS. HOW'S it going?" West calls as I step into Food for Thought.

"Hey, West. I'm fine."

"Listen, I'm sorry about your dad. You doing okay?"

"Yeah, I'm okay."

"Good, cause I'm not real good at feelings and all. But I could call Kate down here if you need me to. She's much better at the touchy-feely."

"No, I'm good," I chuckle. West can always lighten a mood. I'm grateful for that.

"Okay. Good. So, come over here and have a seat. I've got a hot cup of Joe for you."

"Thanks." I inhale the smell of fresh coffee as I sit. "So . . . what brings us together this fine morning?"

"A woman who gets right down to business. I like it." West pours a lot of sugar in his coffee, then focuses intently on stirring. "So . . ."

"So . . ." I mimic.

"Yes. Okay. So." He finally sets the stir-stick down and makes eye contact with me. And . . . stares . . .

I turn my head and look at him from the corner of my eye. "Sooo . . ."

"Ahh. Yes!" West clasps his hands together and rubs them as if a great thought has just come to him. "Abby, we are really busy right now, and we need another person to help out."

I sip my coffee, waiting for him to finish his thought process. "Oh, you're really busy?" I finally ask when he doesn't continue.

"Yes, we are *really* busy."

"Well, that's great. That you're really busy." I take another sip of coffee wondering why he keeps repeating himself.

"Yes. Yes, it is."

We look at each other for another long moment.

"So, yes. Umm, Abby . . . ?"

"Yes?"

"Abby . . ."

"Yes?" I am starting to get impatient. This doesn't sound like a Kate-related thing like I had thought last night. Honestly, I'm not sure where this conversation is going at all.

"Abby. I was wondering if you would consider helping us out. And working here. Would you?"

I am stunned. Did he really just ask me to work here?

"Well?"

I shake my head to recover my senses. "Are you serious, West? You are asking me to work here? Like a *job*?"

"Well, yeah . . ." He raises his eyebrows and gives me a *no-duh* look. "I would like to hire you. Would you like to be hired?"

"Are you kidding me?"

"Umm. No?"

"Are you kidding me?" My voice jumps an octave.

"Normally, yes, I am. This time, no."

"Wow, West! I would *love* to work here. Are you sure you're serious?" I can't believe this is happening. An awesome job falling right into my lap!

"I thought we covered this part. I am serious. We need help, and before I put a sign in the window, I thought I would offer the job to you."

"I would love to work here! Thank you, West!" I nearly knock over our coffee cups as I throw my arms around him. No more Hooligan's! I don't believe it. Then my high plummets. "Oh . . ."

"What?" West asks, as he straightens his flannel post-hug, his brow creasing.

"Well, I guess I should give Jeff two weeks' notice. To be fair. Is that okay?"

"Oh. Yeah. No problem."

"Great. Wow. Really?"

"Really! What do I need to do to assure you this is real?" He laughs at me.

"Just pinch me, would you?"

He pinches my arm, rather hard. "There you go!"

"Two weeks. Okay. Thank you so much!" I squeeze his hand before I hurry out. He pinched me—it is real!

Oh, I can't wait to tell Jeff tonight. No more waitress, baby! I could do cartwheels down the street!

"SO HOW DID Jeff take it?" Ethan asks as he rubs my arm with his thumb. We lie snuggled in bed, both fully satisfied and relaxed. I turn my head and kiss his shoulder. I feel closer to him than ever. Long gone are the days of loneliness and depression that used to plague me. And good riddance.

"He understood. He's like a dad, you know? He wants what's best for me. Now Emory, on the other hand . . . When I told her, I thought she would start throwing steak knives at me."

"I'd think she'd want what's best for you, too."

"Oh, she does. But she feels like she's lost me, I think. First I move out, then I quit my job. I'll have to make sure to spend some extra time with her."

"You will," Ethan assures me. "Abby . . ." He starts, then pauses like he's not sure what he wants to say. Or maybe he isn't sure I want to hear it. "You know you don't have to work. If you don't want to."

"Not work? What would I do? Be your housemaid?" I giggle.

"Well, no, of course not." He sounds almost offended at my suggestion. I bite my lip to keep from laughing at his reaction.

"Working is all I've known, Ethan. I've always worked one, two, three jobs, as long as I can remember. I've always needed the money."

"But that's just it. You don't need the money now."

I frown. How could I not be self-sufficient? As much as I love and trust him, a small part of me can't let go of the need to prepare myself for the eventuality we won't work out—which means keeping my own income-earning potential. Hmm. Maybe I don't trust him as fully as I thought. Trust is a very hard thing for me.

"I think I'll really like working at the bookstore. Plus, I'll get to see you more often." I lightly kiss his nose. "And seriously, what would I do all day long if I didn't work? I'm afraid I'm not the Susie Homemaker type who can master four-course meals, have them hot and ready for you every day when you arrive home."

"I would never ask you to do that, Abby. I would never expect it. I'm just saying you can do something you really want to do. You could write."

That strikes me. I haven't thought about writing since my last college semester. I've never had the time or the desire to write since I've been out in the real world trying to earn enough money to survive. And now Ethan is telling me we have more than enough money. That is something I can't be sure of. What *exactly* is more than enough money?

I don't express that concern. Instead, I say, "What would I write about? I don't have any inspiration. My life is so perfect right now." I caress his face.

"That's good to know," he teases. "But it wasn't always. You could write about the journey you took to get here."

"I'm pretty sure no one would think my life is at all interesting."

"I do."

"Thanks for the vote of confidence," I chortle.

"I'm serious, you know."

"I know, but I guess I never thought of my life as a journey. My whole life I've felt like I've been running away from the things that aren't working. I ran away from my family, from Iowa, from college, from you. I feel like a coward, really."

"Don't say that because you're not. Not ever," he says sternly. "And I don't think it's running away—I think you're just searching for what works for you.

Even though you ran from me, you came back, which tells me you are a very brave person, to recognize you made a choice you weren't happy with and to fight for what works. Believe me when I tell you, I've never had anything work as well as we do, Abby."

"No, you're right. We do work very well together," I muse. "I think I was just scared of how happy I felt with you. The next step meant I had to let down my walls, to share everything with you, even the bad things, the things I don't want anyone to know. But I underestimated you. I should have known you would accept me as I am, flaws and all."

"Your past makes you who you are, and I love who you are. Don't ever feel ashamed of where you've come from. You're not flawed. You're amazing."

I heave a long, contented sigh and intertwine my fingers with his. "Ethan, you know just what to say to make a girl feel wanted, safe, and special. I've never felt that before. Thank you for that."

"Well. You are special and wanted and safe. And I hope you never feel otherwise."

I angle my face up to him and give him a long kiss. "I love you."

"I love you more."

A different sigh escapes as an unwelcome emotion rolls over me.

"What?" he asks, alarmed.

"It's just—"

"Tell me."

"It's just that—I don't know . . ." I struggle for the right words to express what I'm feeling. "Sometimes I wonder if love is enough, you know?"

"What?"

"What I mean is, my parents obviously loved each other at some point. That's why they got married. People love each other. But things happen. People change. Outside forces can ruin everything. How do you know that love can keep you together?" I feel a tightness in my chest, an anxiety that no matter how much we love each other, something could rip us apart down the road. We could be vulnerable in our relationship, hit a rough patch, and it all could be lost.

"Abby . . ." Ethan pulls me closer and kisses me on the forehead. "Baby, I love you enough for the both of us. And I know you love me. We know it's enough. It will be enough."

I believe him. It will be enough.

Chapter Sixteen

Sometimes, Love Just Ain't Enough

"**A**NOTHER HOLIDAY SEASON almost over, Abby!" Kate breathes as she sinks down on a stool at the counter across from me. She leans forward and props her chin up with her hand. "I have been run ragged between here and my art shows."

"It's been a busy month, hasn't it?" I continue arranging the display of new releases. "I can't believe this is my second holiday season here already. Boy, the time flies by."

"Tell me about it," she agrees.

"So, are you and West joining us for Christmas Eve dinner at Uncle Geoff's house?"

"Wouldn't miss it for the world." Kate sits up, eyes sparkling. "Ethan's uncle and Simon are a hoot. They've got some amazing stories, you know."

"All true, they swear." We chuckle at the thought of Uncle Geoff and Simon's elaborate tales.

I place the last book on the display and look at her. "I'm really glad you two will be joining us this year. Your friendship means a lot to Ethan, and I count myself blessed to be included in your circle. You are true friends, no matter what."

"Aw, Abby-girl!" Kate reaches over and squeezes my hand. "Aren't you a sweet one! You and Ethan are like family to us. You two complete our circle." We smile then laugh at how corny we sound.

"What's going on out here? It ain't quittin' time yet, slackers!" West calls as he emerges from the back.

"Calm down, Westley," Kate scolds. "We're having a little bonding time here."

He rolls his eyes. "This is what I pay you two for?"

She grins and gives him a little shove. "Go lock the door, you! It's close enough to closing time, and I'm done! That had to be a record day for customers, I'm certain."

"I think we had record sales anyway," West comments as he locks the door then flips the sign in the window from Open to Closed. "Hmm, looks like it wants to snow out there. Maybe we'll get a white Christmas this year, ladies."

"Are you going to take me on vacation in January so I can recuperate from all this stress, dear?" Kate asks.

"I would love to, my dear," he replies sweetly as he comes and puts his arm around her shoulders. "You'd best ask your bonding-buddy here if she minds holding down the fort so you can go get your beach tan on."

Kate shifts her hopeful eyes to me. West smiles like he's gotten one over on me. Little does he know that I have no problem staying here and running the store with Ethan if it means some rest and relaxation for my friends. "Absolutely. You'd better start making travel plans."

Kate claps her hands and beams, overjoyed. "We'll start looking at travel packages tonight!"

West's expression falls. "Well, now, hold on there, hon. You'd better clear it with Ethan, too. I don't want him mad at me because you want to go on vacation."

"No, it'll be fine." I wave my hand nonchalantly. "I'm sure Ethan would love to do it. In fact, I'll ask him tonight, just to be sure. Problem solved." I smile sweetly at West.

Kate's face lights up again; West narrows his eyes at me, mock resentment clouding his face. "Let's go, Westley. Hurry and take care of stuff so we can get home!" She pushes him toward the back of the store. She whispers an excited "Thank you" to me before following him.

I shake my head, amused as always by those two. "See you tomorrow," I call after them. I take a moment to gaze around the empty store, adorned in festive holiday decor. Kate let me help her decorate this year, but as usual, all the creativity and design came from her.

It's been more than a year and a half since West offered me a job. Honestly, the best year and a half of my life. I get to see Ethan all the time now that we are scheduled to work together so often. And it's such a different atmosphere to work in than Hooligan's. No stress, other than the busy month or so leading up to Christmas. The customers are always so friendly and interesting. The same people come here again and again, so it's easy to get to know many of them. There is a real small-town feel in this store in the big city. And occasionally, we even have famous authors drop in for book signings. Ethan got to meet Carson Ripley at a signing. He'd been over the moon that West had gotten *the* Carson Ripley to come to our store.

Not only has my work life been positive lately, but Ethan and I are happier than ever, stronger than ever. As I let myself out of Food for Thought and head for home, I think about how, in everything, he puts me first, which is something I have never had before. He takes care of me, even spoils me sometimes. He is always patient; he knows I have things I need to work out for myself.

I opened up more about my family after my father's death, realizing that I needed to share things with Ethan. As hard as it was sometimes, I had to let him know about the things that made me such a crazy person, so he could understand why I didn't like to talk to my mother and why I overreacted at some of his "surprises." For example, I had to explain why I really didn't want to visit Iowa after he "surprised" me with round-trip tickets to go see my mother for Thanksgiving last year.

I like to think I won that battle in the end. After only two days in her house, he fully understood my emotional distress when it came to Victoria, even suggesting we stay in a hotel for the remaining night of our visit. I tortured him by refusing. As much as I wanted to go, he needed to get a real taste of my mother so he wouldn't pull a stunt like that again. But she was more than gracious to Ethan. To her, he's a handsome catch. She flirted constantly. The only flaw she found in him is that he works in a bookstore. *Too bad*, she said. What really got to him, though, was that he had to sit by and listen to her judgmental comments about my choices and my lack of doing anything important with my life. Had to hear every condescending comment she made to me, had to hear stories about my father as she tried to prove how she had been the far superior parent, and had to hear how my lack of ambition was definitely not something I learned from her—more likely due to my father and his "disease."

Now he understands that my feelings about my mother come from a very real place, not from imagined injustices or misunderstandings. He even apologized to me on the flight back home. Three different times! I told him I would only forgive him on the condition that he never, ever "surprise" me with a visit to my mother again, which he quickly promised. So yeah—victory there.

The December evening chill makes me shiver. The bustling streets are a sign that last-minute shoppers are still running around. I wonder if Ethan is one of those shoppers. He planned to finish Christmas shopping today. I glance up at the sky, a dark blanket of gray hovering over the city. West is right—it does look like it could snow. I pull my coat tighter around me as the crisp wind bites.

The subway ride is a nice reprieve from the cold, but I must return to it once again for the last couple blocks. Hurrying through the lobby door, warmth washes over me, causing my frozen face to ache. I blink to adjust my eyes to the difference in temperature. Home at last. My legs are tingling from the cold, so I rush onto the elevator, anxious to get up to Ethan and have him warm me up. When I enter our apartment, I expect to see him reading on the couch or window seat like normal.

"Ethan?" I glance around—no sign of him.

A muffled sound drifts from the bedroom. "Hey, babe! I'll be out in a sec!"

"Oh, okay," I call back. I hang up my coat, watching for him to walk out of the bedroom.

I make a cup of hot cocoa, walk around the breakfast bar, and pull out a chair, still waiting for him to appear. I can just barely see into the bedroom from my vantage point. He's hovering over something on the bed. "Ethan?"

"Yeah?"

"What are you doing in there?" My concern is mixed with a touch of amusement. Mostly, I hope it isn't another "surprise" that will send me into freak-out mode.

"Um, nothing, babe. I'm almost done. I'll be right out—dang it!" He tosses something out of his hand. I giggle at the sight, continue to sip my cocoa, and watch the show. He grumbles another curse or two before stepping back, running his hand through his hair, and putting his hands on his hips. He reaches forward once more, then steps back, then reaches forward again. He finally scoops up the item and turns to find me laughing at him.

"What's so funny?" He smiles, embarrassed.

"Nothing!" I laugh harder and hide my mouth behind my mug. "You're just so cute! Are you wrapping presents?"

"Uh, yeah. But I might be returning them if you keep it up!" he scoffs.

"Aww, don't do that," I beg, trying unsuccessfully to get rid of my smile. I hop up, place the mug on the counter, and try to compose myself. Strolling over to him, I watch as he arranges the present with the others under our tree. When he turns toward me, I pout. "I'm sorry, honey. I'm done making fun."

"You'd better be." He frowns. "I spent a lot of time shopping for you today."

"Oh, come here." I wrap my arms around him, offer him a long, conciliatory kiss. "Just promise me there are no Famous Ethan Surprises under the tree."

"'Famous Ethan Surprises'? Really? You have a phrase for all my failed attempts to make you happy?"

"Maybe I should call them 'Infamous,' because, yes, unfortunately, due to the growing number of them, a descriptive title is necessary," I tease and kiss him again. "But you make me happy each and every day just by being with me. I need no surprises."

"Mmm..." He gives me a gentle squeeze. "Good to know."

"Now, let me have a look at your handiwork." I move past him to the tree, very curious to see what new presents await.

"Just a couple more for you," he answers my unspoken question. "I got Uncle Geoff and Simon taken care of today, too." I survey the awkwardly wrapped presents. A couple have crumpled bows attached with large amounts of tape. "I gave up on the bows after the first couple. Butterfingers, you know."

I laugh at his wiggling fingers. "You did fine. Do I need to buy more tape, though?" I turn to the tree feeling such satisfaction at the beautifully decorated pine and the spread of presents beneath it.

"Nope. We've got plenty. I'll just leave the rest of the wrapping to you." He loops his arm around me from behind and kisses me on the cheek.

"I love our tree. We picked a really good one, didn't we?" The colorful twinkling lights blend in perfectly with the cityscape.

"Yes. And you did a fantastic job decorating it, Abby."

"I think this is going to be my best Christmas ever," I muse.

"Really? You think so?"

I nod, feeling suddenly very emotional. How could it not be? I have a man I love in a way I never thought I could love. I feel a trust with him I never imagined I could have with any man. I have a great job. And I have a new family with Uncle Geoff and Simon, West and Kate. This is definitely going to be my best Christmas ever.

Unbidden, a thought sneaks into my mind: Only one thing has been overshadowing our happiness lately . . .

"WELL, GIRLS, ENJOY your day off. The day after Christmas will be a crazy one at the bookstore, so I want my employees rested and ready to go!" West demands as he hands Kate a glass of eggnog and sits next to her.

"You'd better watch it, Westley! You may be the only one who shows up to work if you keep it up!" she chides.

"I'm sorry! I'm sorry!" He throws his hands up in surrender.

"So, West, did you two decide on where you're vacationing?" Ethan asks.

"After some . . . gentle persuasion, Kate has convinced me to go to Paris, of all places. I wanted the Caribbean cruise, you know. I prefer warm climates, beaches, and all-you-can eat buffets—"

"But I prefer a more original vacation that takes us to inspirational provinces and historic architecture," she interrupts.

"Yeah, she pulled a fast one on me. Persuaded me with promises of romantic rendezvous in the City of Love and fine dining and wine tastings. Then I see her packing a whole suitcase with her cameras and photo equipment!"

"Now, you know I won't be working the whole time we're there. I just *really* want to take advantage of the time to get some photos for my next show."

"You say now . . ." He frowns. "Ethan, if I call collect from the airport, will you promise to come pick me up?"

"You two!" I shake my head. "Maybe you should stay home, and Ethan and I will go on your vacation instead. I'd love to see Paris."

"West's going to have a great time, and he knows it," Kate states. "He's just trying to get over the beach-lust he had when we first started making plans."

"What's better than the beach and tropical climates in January?" he argues.

Kate leans over and whispers something in his ear. An embarrassed smile crosses his face as it turns three shades of red. "Oh, yes. I'd say that's better. Definitely."

"That's what I thought," she says triumphantly. She turns to me. "When we get back, you guys should make travel plans. You deserve a break, too."

I glance over at Ethan, rubbing his chin, contemplating. "Hmm, that does sound like a good idea, Kate. We'd better start talking destinations, Abs, so we don't end up fighting like these two," he jokes.

Simon enters. "Dinner is served." He directs us to the formal dining room.

"Oh, Simon, you've outdone yourself," I comment, gazing at the amazing spread on the table. There is more than enough for the six of us.

"I had an excellent helper this year, my dear. Those culinary lessons Geoffrey attended have made him a world-class chef."

"You're too kind, Simon. In actuality, the lion's share of the feast was created by him." Uncle Geoff holds his hand out to Simon.

"It all looks so delicious, gentlemen," Kate compliments.

"Yeah, you got doggie bags? I'd like to take some of this home with me." West eyes the serving dishes greedily.

Uncle Geoff carves the turkey and Simon serves us. The meal is delicious, the company entertaining. For a third Christmas in a row, I marvel at how I feel the true spirit of the holidays with them.

Before I met Ethan, I dreaded the holidays as time spent alone or forced to see my mother. Neither option desirable. Emory and Val used to invite me to their family events, but it never had the fullness that this group of people gives me. They have accepted me with open arms and treated me with such kindness and love.

Throughout the feast, I notice Ethan seems abnormally quiet, pushing his food around on his plate. As we move to the living room after dinner, I catch sight of his fists clenched on top of the table when he pushes himself up.

"Simon, can I help you in the kitchen?" I ask, with an eye on Ethan as he slowly leaves the table. I know what the answer will be, but I ask anyway.

"Nonsense, child. Please, everyone make yourselves comfortable in the next room. Enjoy some conversation and drinks, and Geoffrey and I will join you shortly."

I step beside Ethan, wrap my hand around his elbow. "Another headache?" I whisper.

"Yeah." The strain in his voice is unmistakable.

"Should we go? We don't have to stay."

"No." He rubs the back of his head. "No, I can get through this."

"Are you sure?"

"Yes. Let's sit down."

I stare after him as he makes his way to the couch. Kate and West are deep in conversation and don't seem to notice Ethan's mood shift. I want to drag him out of here, get him home to lie down. These headaches are coming more frequently and can cripple him for hours at a time.

I first noticed something was wrong a couple months ago. He would snap at me over simple things like leaving a light on or forgetting to grab milk at the store. It felt like he was growing tired of me and trying to find a way to drive me off. After the initial upset, I became defensive and would argue back when he criticized me. I began wondering if I should move out and give him his space.

But then I realized there was more to it. He was eating ibuprofen like candy. His mood could change in the blink of an eye. He was tired often—partly, I think, because of the energy it took to act like everything was okay when it clearly wasn't.

One evening, while eating at our favorite Italian restaurant, he'd been laughing and acting like normal Ethan all evening. Then suddenly a switch flipped. I simply commented that the alfredo sauce wasn't as good as usual, and he snapped at me. Said I was impossible to please. He told me if I disliked it that much we could just go home, using a tone that I'd never heard before. It startled me. I tried to tell him it was fine, that I didn't mean to make him angry. He said he knew we should never have gone out; he couldn't deal with it. I was confused and hurt. People around us were starting to stare. Embarrassed, I turned away from him. I didn't want him to see that he'd made me cry. I wanted to get up and run out. But Ethan realized he was way out of line and fell quiet. He apologized and said he didn't mean to hurt me, that he wasn't feeling well. I told him that if he didn't want to go out, all he had to do was say so. I said I was sorry I had made him so angry—if he didn't want to be with me, he was free to leave. I thought he might start crying then. His face twisted in pain, and he reached out for my hands. He apologized again for his behavior, said he knew he had been very irritable lately and he was trying to keep it under control.

I pressed him to tell me what the problem was. If it was me, he needed to say so. He needn't spare my feelings because it was causing me more pain this way. He finally confessed he'd been having headaches, more like migraines. He'd thought they would go away on their own, but they were getting worse and more frequent. He tried not to let on that he was worried, but I could see it in his eyes. I told him he should see a doctor; his behavior was not normal, and he needed to get checked out. He promised he would. He just wanted to give it a couple more weeks and see if it would pass. He didn't think it was anything for me to worry about. I told him it was too late on that count. He tried to reassure me, and I acted like it would be fine, so he wouldn't feel bad.

But I worry all the time.

He still gets grumpy when a migraine hits, but I've learned to recognize the signs, and I try to make it as easy as possible for him. I diffuse the arguments as soon as he snaps. I tuck him in bed and massage his neck and the base of his head, where the pain seems to originate. And after tonight, I will be calling the doctor for him and making an appointment.

"All right, youngsters, time for gift-giving," Uncle Geoff proclaims as he enters the room.

"Yes. This is my favorite time of the holidays," Simon says, beaming. "I absolutely *love* sharing the gifts we picked out for each of you! And I wrapped them all myself."

"Ethan wrapped ours, too . . . didn't you, dear?" I try to lighten his mood with no success. He sits with his elbow propped on the couch supporting his head with his hand, staring across the room, focused on some invisible object. "Maybe we should just go . . ." I lean in and whisper, brushing his sandy hair off his forehead with my fingertips. His face is stone sober. It worries me. The others seem to pick up on his unusual quiet.

"Ethan, would you like to start us off?" Simon asks.

"Ah—" he has to clear his throat to speak. "Kate, why don't you start?"

"Um, okay. Sure." She smiles but shoots a concerned glance my way.

Simon keeps the ball rolling after Kate with gift presentation and opening. He and Uncle Geoff have picked out a trinket or art piece from their trip to Asia for each one of us. Naturally, a detailed explanation accompanies each gift.

Kate and West open their gift from us and their gifts to each other. Ethan and I selected a unique intertwined copper and stainless steel picture frame that is just their style. I'm thrilled Kate loves it so much. Even West is impressed with it. I glance over at Ethan to see if he feels the same elation I do that the gift we selected together has gone over so well. He isn't smiling, but his eyes meet mine, and I think I see some relief, a lessened pain in them.

West gives Kate a very festive green sweater with matching gloves and hat. He has quite an amusing story about how he came to decide on that gift. She rolls her eyes and says sarcastically, "Another wonderful sweater, West. I'll add to my drawer of wonderful sweaters." Even Ethan chuckles a little at her response.

Kate tracked down an early edition signed copy of West's favorite book, *The Catcher in the Rye*. He just about flips his lid when he opens it and leaps across the loveseat to give her a big sloppy kiss.

Ethan usually gives Uncle Geoff and Simon books for Christmas, which I used to think was kind of cheesy, because how do you know if they'll like the books you pick? How do you know they haven't already read those books? But in the end, we stuck with his tradition—I agreed to get each of them a gourmet cookbook with wine pairing suggestions. Knowing Uncle Geoff was taking culinary classes and Simon was a master in the kitchen, I figured cookbooks would be safe. And they both seem very happy with our selections, which is a relief. I reach over and give Ethan's hand a squeeze and the corners of his mouth lift a bit. That is a good sign.

Simon and Uncle Geoff's gifts to each other are special ornaments they found during the past year that symbolize their favorite event or trip. This is a tradition they started years ago, and I think it's absolutely endearing. Their Christmas tree is a monument to their life together. And either one of them can stand at that tree and tell you the story behind each ornament. It is so touching.

Simon's ornament from Uncle Geoff is a tiny pagoda he found in Hong Kong, handmade and hand-painted. We all laugh when Uncle Geoff unwraps his ornament—a very similar pagoda Simon found in Beijing, also handmade and hand-painted.

"That's so wonderful!" Kate is awestruck. "You both chose the same ornament, the same trip!"

"Talk about being on the same page," Uncle Geoff laughs.

"I tell you, it was the trip of a lifetime, Geoffrey!" Simon exclaims. "We may never have another that will match."

"Oh, how sweet," I murmur.

"Mm-hmm," Ethan agrees.

"All right, youngsters, your turn." Uncle Geoff directs his attention at us.

Ethan has me open the gift from West and Kate. I shake it by my ear first. It's pretty lightweight. "Matching sweaters, West?" I tease. He scowls in return. I rip off the paper and pull the lid off the box.

"Dave Matthews Band tickets!" I smile at Ethan. "In Central Park in May! That's awesome! Thanks, you guys."

"Yeah, I love them. Thanks." Ethan sounds a bit more enthusiastic, which is a relief.

"We've got tickets, too. We can make it a group date," Kate says.

"Oh, definitely. We'd love that," I confirm. When I look over at Ethan, he's holding out a small wrapped gift with a tiny bow in his palm. "Here's another one for you to tear open." There's a twinkle in his eye.

I stare down at the box, small enough to be a ring box, and my heart skips a beat. I glance over at West and Kate for any clue as to what might be in the box. West is a blank page, but Kate has a look of anticipation on her face. Could it really be a ring? I turn my attention back to the little wrapped box, then look at Ethan. He grins. I pick up the delicate box and finger the ribbon, almost afraid to open it. A part of me hopes it isn't a ring. I'm not sure marriage is for me, given my family history. As wonderful as Ethan is, I don't want to ruin everything we have by saddling it with marriage. But a tiny part of me that believes in white knights and fairytale endings hopes it is an engagement ring. I mean, Ethan is *my* White Knight. He has saved me from myself.

I gingerly pull off the tiny silver bow and ribbon, gently tear through the wrapping paper. I hesitate one more second, hold my breath, and lift the lid. The light reflects brilliantly off a sparkling diamond and silver—

Necklace. My first reaction: relief. I let my breath out. I am surprised to find my next reaction is a wave of disappointment. I quickly recover and smile at Ethan. I'm sure no one saw the flicker of letdown on my face. I hope.

"It's beautiful, Ethan." I swallow. "It really is."

"This diamond represents the past. It's what makes us who we are. The next diamond represents our present—us enjoying every moment we have together. The largest diamond is our future. It represents everything wonderful that is to come for you and me, Abby."

"Aww, I love it. Thank you." I grab his chin and pull him in for a kiss. "Here, put it on me." As I turn away from him and hold up my hair, I notice Kate wiping her eyes.

"That's perfect," she sobs.

"Oh, Kate . . ." I give her a sympathetic smile.

"No, no!" She waves her hand. "I'm sorry. I'm just so glad to have you in our lives. All of you. Thank you for allowing us to share the holidays with you. I love you all."

West reaches over and rubs her shoulder. She leans into him and dabs her eyes.

"Well, we thank you all for joining us in our celebration of family and love," Simon announces. I can tell he's a little choked up as well.

"And I hope you all know you are welcome here as family, not only on the holidays, but any time," Uncle Geoff adds.

I look down, admiring my new necklace. They are rather large diamonds. It must have cost Ethan a small fortune. I feel bad now that my gift isn't as grand. I reach over beside me. "We can't forget you, now, can we?"

He smiles that breathtaking smile as he takes the rectangular package from me. My Ethan is back. He tears off the paper. I watch his expression as he lifts the lid off the box. "Oh, wow!" he breathes as he unfolds the tissue paper from the box. "Abby, this is fantastic—wow!"

"What is it? Show us!" Simon prods impatiently.

He lifts out a black picture frame with five different-sized photos in a collage lay-out. A large vertical frame holds his favorite picture of his parents at their anniversary. A smaller square frame holds a picture of him as a kid. Another horizontal frame holds a photo of him at the beach on vacation with his parents. Another square frame has a picture of me as a kid. The final, largest vertical frame has a picture of us.

"I tried to find a frame that would go with any style your decorator uses," I joke.

"Well done, Abigail," Uncle Geoff commends.

"Yes, well done," Ethan agrees and gives me a kiss. "Well done." He places the frame on his lap and examines it more closely.

"Gentlemen," Uncle Geoff intones, standing. "Shall we head to the smoking room for a cigar?"

"Just one," Ethan says as he rises to join them. He bends down and kisses me on the forehead. "I won't be long."

"Ladies, may I freshen up your drinks first?" Simon offers.

"I'm good, thank you," I answer, smiling.

"I'm fine, too. Thank you, Simon," Kate says, then she comes over and sits next to me on the loveseat as the room empties. "Sorry about my bawling fit over there. I guess I'm overly emotional today. I get that way at the holidays."

"Oh, don't worry about it," I say, waving it off.

"I almost thought he was going to propose. I was kind of hoping he would. Time to make this thing official, girl!"

"Oh . . ." I falter. "No. No, I think it's too soon. For that. Don't you? I mean, we've only been together, what, two years? And he's been engaged before, so I'm sure he wants to be sure this time, you know? Probably doesn't want to make the same mistake twice."

That makes sense, right? I feel like I'm rambling.

"There's no mistake about you two, Abby. You are made for each other. And you both seem so happy together. It'll happen soon, I'm sure."

"I don't know. I get so crazy sometimes, you know? I feel like there's a lot of myself I still need to figure out before I subject someone else to all my craziness. I don't want him to get hurt, Kate. I'm afraid I'll hurt him because I'm so afraid to let him all the way in. And I don't know how a good marriage should work. What if I mess it all up?"

I realize I'm playing with the necklace. I examine it closely and focus on the first diamond, our past—the things that make us who we are.

"Abby, you won't hurt Ethan. You love him. If anything, your parents' failure at marriage taught you what *not* to do, and that's a start. I know you have things to work through, but we all do. It's the nature of life. But what good is a life if we can't work through our troubles and our fears with someone who loves us in spite of it all?" She smiles her motherly smile at me. "I believe you and Ethan have that love. You can conquer anything together."

I stare at Kate for a long moment, letting her words penetrate my cloud of doubt. I realize she is right. Ethan and I have something really special. He's seen the worst in me, seen where I come from. He knows all of that, and he loves me anyway. He makes me a better person just by loving me.

"Thank you, Kate," I finally concede. I hug her, squeezing her like the big sister I never had. "You're the best."

"Stop. You're gonna make me cry again," she says as she wipes a tear from her eye. "But . . ." The tone of her voice gives me pause. "I wanted to talk to you about something else while the guys are in the other room." Her expression has changed to one of concern.

I'm immediately alarmed. "What?"

"What's up with Ethan tonight? And not just tonight either, but lately. What's with the mood swings? Everything okay?"

I sigh deeply and shake my head. "I don't know. He's been having these headaches. Sometimes it's so bad he can't function. And he gets really growly when they come on. I'm so worried about him. They're happening more frequently."

"Has he seen a doctor?"

"I can't get him to go. He's afraid it might lead to hospital tests, and you know how he feels about the hospital. Ever since his parents' accident, he won't go near one."

"Well, he's going to have to get over it, Abby. Something's not right. I'd hate to go on this vacation if I know you're going to be left alone at the store . . ."

"No, no. Don't worry about that. I'm talking to him when we get home tonight. If he doesn't schedule an appointment, I'll schedule one for him." The last thing I want is for them to have to cancel their trip. And Ethan would agree. I'll use that as leverage. I'll tell him that *they've* noticed he's not right, and he's got to get checked out to put them at ease so they can go on their vacation.

Yes, a little guilt trip is exactly what I need to push him along.

Chapter Seventeen

Excuse Me? I'd Like to Get Off This Ride Now.

It's only Wednesday, but I can't wait for West and Kate to get home from their trip on Sunday. I pushed them to go. Told them Ethan's appointment had gone well. The doctor believed it was just migraines, but he would write a lab order for blood work to rule out anything else. They had no reason to worry, and I wanted them to enjoy their week in Paris.

But the week hadn't gone well for us so far. Ethan went down yesterday with a migraine that came on about lunchtime. After an hour of watching him struggle, I made him go home to rest. Fortunately, the store wasn't very busy, and I handled it.

Ethan received a call from the doctor on Monday that the results of his blood work were concerning. The doctor recommended a head CT and a visit with a specialist at the hospital. The CT was scheduled for this afternoon, so that's where he is now. I worried I was going to have to close down the store to take him, afraid he would let his apprehension of hospitals get the better of him. He tried to argue it was a waste of time to get the scan; it cost too much and it would just show what the doctor already knew—that it was only migraines. Or it wouldn't provide any information at all, which would lead to even more unnecessary tests. I spent several hours last night pleading with him to confirm he'd go. I could tell he was still nervous about it this morning, so I told him I was taking him. But he swore he would go on his own. He would be okay.

I'm glad I pressured him into making the initial doctor appointment. It had taken almost a week to get in to that doctor, now another week for the CT, and yet another week to get in to the specialist. That's three weeks. If he'd continued to put it off until it got unbearable—I can't imagine the pain he would be in at the rate his migraines are increasing. And I so hate to see him in pain.

Relief rushes through me when Ethan finally walks through the door. He's smiling. I deliver the books to the customer at table three and hurry over to Ethan, wrapping my arms around him. It's more to comfort me than him, I must admit.

"So?" I release him from my embrace, a ball of nerves suddenly taking up residence in my stomach. "Looks like you survived the hospital. How did it go?"

"Yes. It was fine."

"And how are you feeling?"

"I'm fine."

"So . . . did they say anything?"

"No, Abby." Ethan shakes his head. He continues when my brows knit together. "The technician just does the scan. The scan has to be read by the radiologist. I'll probably find out the results from the specialist next week."

"Oh." I'm disappointed at not getting an immediate answer. "Sounds like a lot of people involved for something simple."

He chuckles and squeezes my hand. "Everyone's got a job. Everyone gets paid."

"I guess," I allow grudgingly as I walk over to the register to help a customer.

"I'll check the floor," he volunteers.

"Are you sure? You feel like it?" I quiz him.

"Yep. I'm good."

I smile as I focus on the customer, complete her transaction. "Thank you for shopping at Food for Thought," I say as I put her receipt in the bag and hand it over. I turn my attention to Ethan. He does appear well, smiling at the customers, walking with his normal gait. Maybe today will go unmarred after all.

Amazingly, the day goes by quickly. Business is steady, and Ethan is able to work all day. After we close down the store, we have a nice dinner out to relax. Then we retreat to our bedroom for some much-needed alone time. It feels like my Ethan is back. He says he feels fine, and he shows no signs of worry about the day's test. It's like we're on our own little vacation from the stresses of the past several weeks. I treasure every minute of it.

Thursday and Friday pass without any major issues. Ethan felt a migraine coming on Friday evening, so he went to bed a little early. He took the painkillers the doctor prescribed, and by morning he was better. Saturday was extremely busy at the store. I could see in his eyes that he was still tired from the lack of sleep the night before, but he pushed through the day.

Finally, Sunday arrives with the cold winter sun breaking into our bedroom, waking me earlier than I want. This has been the longest week of my life. West and Kate should be stopping at the store this afternoon, and I'm looking forward to hearing all about their trip. But really, I'm hoping for some relief from the stress of worrying about Ethan and the store by myself. I quickly get ready, pulling my long hair into a ponytail rather than fussing with it. Then I whip up a light breakfast for us.

As Ethan gets ready, I notice how I always feel nervous now, like an overbearing worried parent of a toddler learning to walk—always afraid of a tumble and an injury, watching for signs that Ethan may suddenly take a turn for the worse. So far, he seems fine. We eat and chat while reading sections of the paper.

But as I feared, it is short-lived. We don't even make it out the door when a migraine hits, coming on so fast it frightens me. I literally have the door open, ready to walk out, feeling good about the day ahead of us when I hear his keys clank on the floor behind me. I spin around to see he's dropped down to one knee, his hand with a white-knuckled grip on the edge of the side table.

"My God," he barely utters.

"Ethan!" I drop my coat, inches from where his coat lies, and rush to him, unsure of what to do. Panic takes over, making my hands shake. I've never seen it hit him this hard before. "Do you want your pills?"

"Yeah," he breathes. Pain is evident in his expression. I help him up and over to the couch. "Close the blinds," he says through clenched teeth.

I quickly darken the room then hurry to the bathroom to get his pain pills. The bottle shakes in my hands, rattling the pills inside. I just about throw the thing across the room in frustration when I can't get it open.

Pull yourself together, Abby. He needs you. I take a deep, steadying breath and try to calm myself. It will do neither of us any good for me to freak out right now. After two more attempts, I get the bottle open. I hurry to the kitchen for a glass of water.

"Here you go." I sit beside him on the couch, put two pills in his hand, and help him with the water glass.

"Thanks," he whispers.

"Are you going to be okay? Should we go to the hospital or something?" I'm trying to keep control of my voice, my heart is still racing. I clench my shaking hands together.

"No. I'm fine," he mutters.

"I don't think you *are*, Ethan." I stare at his face, contorted in pain. "This scares me. Are you *sure* you're okay?"

"I'll be fine. Promise." He tries to focus his eyes on mine, then gives up and closes them. "I just need to sleep it off. I'll call you if I need anything. You need to get going."

Doubt fills my mind. I really don't think I should leave him. His voice is so strained when he speaks. What he must be feeling—I can't even imagine.

As if he senses my worry, he presses, "Go. I'll be okay." He opens his eyes once more, squeezes my hand for reassurance. After a long moment, I lean forward and kiss his forehead. I brush my hand through his thick hair a few times before I allow myself to trust his words.

"Okay." I kiss him once more. "*Please* call me if you need me." I pull his phone out of his shirt pocket and set it on the coffee table next to the water.

"I will," he whispers.

"I love you," I say into his hairline as I place one last kiss on his poor aching head.

"I love you more," he mumbles.

I sit, frozen, for several more seconds before I can make myself get up and leave him.

I worry all the way to the store. My stomach is in knots all morning long. I cannot believe he has to wait another four days before he sees the doctor! Why can't they get him in any sooner? Anger boils up inside me. How cruel to let someone go through so much pain when they have the ability to fix it! I vow to go with him to his appointment on Thursday and give that doctor a piece of my mind, scold him for making Ethan wait so many days. Do they have any idea what they're putting him through?

I force myself to concentrate and be pleasant with the customers. One woman gets mad at me because she has to repeat herself three times to get my attention. But I have a hard time feeling guilty. I feel guilty leaving Ethan alone in the state he's in.

Business finally slows around midafternoon. I don't realize I'm staring out the window when a couple stops and waves madly through the glass. I try to focus on them, but they are already coming through the door.

"Hey, Abby-girl!" she exclaims as she bursts into the store.

"Kate!" I dash around the counter to hug her.

"What? Didn't you miss me?" West whines.

"Of course, West," I say after my long hug with Kate. I wonder if they can hear the relief in my voice. "Let me give you a hug, too. Can't have you feeling left out, can we?"

"That's more like it," he says smugly as he squeezes me way too tightly. If I ever wondered what it would have been like to have a brother, I believe West is it—always picking on me, always rough.

"Let's go sit. I have a ton of pictures to show you." Kate pulls me over to the stools at the end of the counter. "West, you'll watch the register, won't you?"

"What? Put to work already?" he complains. "We just got back." He turns to an elderly customer standing by him. "Do you believe this?"

"So, you had a good time, huh?" I ask Kate.

"Oh, Abby, we had the *best* time! It was fantastic! And I got some great shots for my next art show."

We spend quite a while looking through her photos. She tells me the story behind each place they visited. Her art show photos are already separated into a different folder, and she points out the ones she loves, the ones she hates, and the ones she wishes were just a bit better. There are some stunning night shots, black-and-white photos, and sunrise and sunset pictures at the Eiffel Tower. They obviously visited some vineyards as well. And there are lots of photos of the locals.

"These are amazing. I can't wait to see them in the gallery at another Kate Saunders art show."

"Yes! Me too. So, where's Ethan? I need to give him a big thank-you hug for letting us go on this trip." She beams, scanning the store for him. "Time for you guys to start planning your vacation."

"Um. I'm not sure we'll be doing the vacation thing for a while."

"What? Why?" Her eyes snap back to mine.

"Ethan's home on the couch today."

Her face registers immediate concern. "More headaches?"

"It was so bad. I almost freaked. I was really, really worried about him."

"Oh, no. Are they sure it's just migraines? It sounds more serious."

"Actually, Kate," I sigh as I try to decide how much to divulge. I don't want him to be mad at me for sharing too much. But these are our best friends—and business partners. They need to know. "Ethan's blood work came back abnormal. He had a CT scan this week, and he's going to see a specialist on Thursday."

"Oh, Abby," she sighs as she squeezes my hand.

"I just hate that he has to wait so long to see the doctor. He's in a lot of pain during these episodes." My eyes well up as I talk about it, feeling like I can finally release some of what I've been holding inside this week. She wraps me in a long hug. I realize how much I've missed being able to confide in her.

"Call on Monday. Call the office every day this week and see if they have any cancellations. Maybe they can bump Ethan up," she suggests.

"You think so?"

"Yes. Doesn't hurt to try." She smiles reassuringly. "Everything will be fine. You'll see. This will all be water under the bridge soon enough."

I sigh heavily. "I hope so."

"It will. Come on." She hops up and grabs my hand. "Let's help my boyfriend before he throws a fit." She gives me one more squeeze.

I feel better after talking with her. At least I'm able to get through the rest of the afternoon carrying a little less weight. And after Ethan calls me sometime around five o'clock to let me know his headache has passed, I relax for the first time today and let the worry recede for a while.

CALLING THE DOCTOR every day as Kate suggested pays off. There is a cancellation this morning, so he's getting in on Wednesday instead of Thursday. A day earlier is like a month to me. I go with him, as planned, but my desire to chew out the doctor has subsided since the headaches have stayed away for the past couple days. I'm just happy he got through Sunday alive and seemingly no worse for wear.

We wait in the exam room, sitting what feels like miles apart; I'm in a chair against the wall, while Ethan's on the exam table where the nurse took his vitals and asked about his symptoms. A few minutes after she leaves the room, he stares over at me. I realize I'm chewing my nails. It's just so quiet in here, and I am so nervous. He climbs down from the table and comes over to sit beside me, taking my hand from my mouth and holding it in his. I look at him sheepishly. Maybe I'm making *him* nervous.

"What kind of doctor is this again?" The silence is horrible. I need to have some sort of conversation to keep from going insane.

"A neurologist."

"Oh, okay. That makes sense."

Another quiet minute drags by.

"And he's good? At what he does?"

"I'm told he is very good. One of the best."

"Okay. Good. That's good."

A few more torturously long minutes tick by before a knock on the door pierces the silence. My heart jumps to my throat. Here we go.

The door swings open and a short, white-haired man in the typical white lab coat over a button-up shirt and tie walks in. "Good morning. I'm Dr. Wilkes, and you must be Ethan Lansing, correct?" he asks, shaking Ethan's hand.

"Yes. And this is Abby."

"Good morning," he repeats as he shakes my hand. "Are you the wife?"

"Girlfriend," I say with a tight throat, my stomach aching.

"Very good. Well, Ethan, shall we get down to business?" He extends his arm toward the exam table.

The doctor sits at the computer on the other side of the exam room and looks over Ethan's information and vitals briefly, then begins his exam, going through a long list of questions and entering notes on the computer. Then he rises and joins Ethan to perform the physical exam. He never makes any additional comments or expresses any opinions about the exam or about Ethan's responses to the questions, which is almost worse than the silence before. The doctor is here now, but giving no hints as to what is going on with Ethan. When the exam finally concludes, Dr. Wilkes returns to the computer and clicks the mouse a few times. The CT scans flash up on the screen.

"Can you see this okay?" He asks us.

We both reply, "Yes."

"Here are several views of your brain, Ethan. Let's look at this one here." He clicks on one of the images and it fills the screen. "This is a view from the top of your head. Your frontal lobe is here." He uses his pen as a pointer. "And if you look closely here—" he points to the back of Ethan's brain "—you can see a bit of an abnormality. Now, let's take a look at a side view—" he clicks to the view of several scans "—like this one here." He clicks on it to make it full screen. "This is the right side of your brain. Do you see this mass here?"

"Yes," he confirms.

"Well, Ethan, with the results of your blood work, the characteristics of this mass, and the symptoms you manifest, it's clear you have a tumor."

My heart sinks from my throat to my feet.

"Now, we are unable to tell whether it is benign or malignant just by these scans. It is necessary to perform a biopsy of the tumor to determine what types of cells compose the mass."

"Which is the bad kind?" Ethan asks.

"Well, neither one is good in that a mass growing in the body is never a good thing. We use the terms 'benign' for noncancerous and 'malignant' for cancerous. A malignant tumor requires much more attention and treatment to eradicate."

"So how do you do the biopsy? Open up my head?"

"Actually, it's possible to do a stereotactic biopsy, which allows for a very small incision and as little disruption of the brain tissue as possible."

"But won't you need to remove it anyway?" I ask. "Whether it's benign or malignant, it can't stay in there, can it?"

"There are several treatment options available. Medical advances allow for many more possibilities in treatment than there have ever been. It's important to first perform the biopsy to see what we are up against. Then a treatment plan will be designed—which may or may not involve surgery—that best meets your needs, Ethan."

"Okay, so one step at a time, right?"

"Yes, exactly. I recommend you have a biopsy performed by a neuro-oncologist at Memorial Sloan-Kettering Cancer Center. They have state-of-the-art equipment and excellent doctors who handle your condition. I've sent several cases over to Dr. Jackson . . ."

Dr. Wilkes continues talking, but I no longer hear him. A million questions race through my mind. Ethan has cancer? In his brain? Will he be able to survive this? Will he have to go through those awful cancer treatments? Will he get sicker? How will we do this? We have to do this. We have to fix him.

I realize Ethan and Dr. Wilkes are wrapping up, and I try to focus on what they've decided.

"Our office will contact Sloan-Kettering to set up the initial appointment. There will be many tests before the actual biopsy is performed. A full-body scan will be done to rule out cancer in the body. A representative will contact you with your appointment times and expectations for each appointment. You may be able to schedule two or even three tests on the same day to expedite the process. Do you have any questions for me?"

"No, thank you, doctor."

"Thank you," I mutter. For what? For this awful news?

Dr. Wilkes stands and shakes Ethan's hand. "You'll be in good hands." He reaches out his hand to me as well. I absently shake it.

Then we are alone once again in the cold, sterile room. To my chagrin, a tear escapes and rolls down my cheek. I quickly wipe it away, hoping Ethan hasn't seen it. I need to be strong for him. He has a long road ahead. I turn my stare away from the closed door back over to him.

He holds out his hand. Strangely, his face is so calm.

I force my numb legs to move and walk over to him. The tears refuse to stay in as I wrap my arms around his neck. I bite my lip to stop crying, but I can't. I am so afraid of what this tumor means, so afraid I will lose my Ethan.

"Hey, hey . . ." He rubs my back, trying to soothe me. *I should be the one comforting him.* "We're gonna be okay. Everything's going to be all right. You'll see."

We embrace for a long moment as I attempt to pull myself together. I don't understand how he can be so positive at a time like this. I would be freaking out. I *am* freaking out—why isn't he?

"You have to promise me you'll get through this," I whisper.

"We'll get through this, Abby." He creates space between us and looks urgently into my eyes. "I have no intention of going anywhere." He brushes away my tears and lets his hand rest on my cheek. Then he smiles.

His smile is so reassuring, I have to believe him.

THE NEXT FEW weeks are exhausting. Between Ethan's migraines and mood swings and the hours we spend at Sloan-Kettering, waiting for tests and going through tests and speaking with specialists, I can't remember what day of the week it is. He doesn't work much anymore. West hires another person to help out. I'm relieved—it takes some of the pressure off me. I was trying to cover Ethan's shifts as well as my own and still go to all his appointments.

The news goes from bad to worse. While he doesn't have any tumors in the rest of his body, the tumor in his head is a tricky one. It is growing, and it's deep in his brain, so the stereotactic biopsy had been difficult.

The wait for the biopsy results is excruciating. Although we spend as much time at the store as possible to keep from feeling helpless at home, I'm not sure how much it actually helps. I am so tense. I can't laugh at any of West's jokes. Kate tries drawing me into conversations about her upcoming art show and which pictures we think she should use. Ethan tries to remain positive, but there is a time or two I catch him sitting at a table by the window, staring off in the distance. I figure it's best to leave him alone at those times.

And then the news is awful: The tumor is malignant. It will require aggressive treatment. Surgery is not an option due to its location. The treatment will be hard on Ethan's body, and there is a chance he will not survive. Well, as the doctor put it, there is a sixty percent survival rate for a tumor like this. But to me, that is a forty percent chance I will lose him.

He continues to amaze me, though, never flinching at any of the awful things we're told. He never breaks down. He's upbeat and positive (when he's not having an excruciatingly painful migraine, that is) and anxious to get treatment started.

Fortunately, treatment starts immediately. On the upside, his migraines should be less frequent and less painful. On the downside, the radiation treatment could make him sick, could make his hair fall out. Chances are he will get very fatigued within a couple weeks. He could have blurry vision and headaches, too.

He's scheduled for a new radiation treatment called IMRT, which stands for something about intensity and modulating or something like that. It requires five visits per week to the cancer center for six weeks. After that, we check the progress of the treatment and hope for the best. If necessary, we continue with more sessions of IMRT.

I brace myself for the weeks to come. I must figure out how to be the rock Ethan needs me to be. While he's always been the one to take care of me, now I need to take care of him. I know there may be a time on this journey when he can no longer keep up the smiles and the reassurances. I know there may be a time when he starts to question his ability to handle all the doctors and medicines and side effects and sickness. I have to prepare myself for the eventuality that he will break down and want to quit. From everything I have been reading on the internet, this will be the hardest thing he will ever have to fight through. And I have to get him through this.

Or I won't survive.

Chapter Eighteen

Our New Normal

GROANING, I ROLL over and feel for the snooze button on the alarm. I am not ready to get up, but I want to stop the awful blaring before it wakes Ethan. He's been tossing and turning most of the night. When I roll back, I pause a moment and watch him, taking in his peaceful, calm appearance. He is finally getting some good sleep.

I gently trace my fingertips along his bald head. Gone are the luscious, wavy locks. He decided to shave his whole head after he found out they would shave a section to put marks on his skin to direct the radiation treatments. And chances are he would have lost a bunch of it anyway after the treatments started. He didn't want to mess with the *ifs* and *whens*, he'd said. Hard to believe that was four weeks ago already. Three weeks of treatments and three more to go. He dons a green Jets cap most of the time when he's awake, and he has a Jets stocking cap on his nightstand to use if he gets too cold while trying to sleep.

He looks so vulnerable, so worn down lying here. His eyes sunken, his cheek bones more prominent than normal. The nausea he feels after his treatments keeps him from eating like he should. I want to wrap him in my arms, to stay beside him all day long. I want to pepper him with kisses and stroke the sun-burned-looking skin at the back of his head. I want him to feel the love I feel so strongly for him, now more than ever. With our crazy schedule—me working, his treatments—and his not feeling well, I haven't been able to express my love as I so desperately want to lately.

I reluctantly roll over and slide the alarm button off. The last thing I want is for it to start blaring again while I'm in the shower. I stealthily slide out from under the covers and tiptoe to the bathroom. I know I need to hurry if I want to get to the store when Kate does, but the warm water beating rhythmically on my back feels so nice. After an extra minute, I turn off the shower and towel dry.

After my morning routine, I check my reflection, pulling the collar of my white button-up out over my blue sweater and straightening it. Ethan's sweater, actually, and my favorite. I grab my lip gloss and head out the door that leads into the hallway so I don't disturb him.

"Oh!" I jump.

"Morning, beautiful," he greets me from the couch, afghan draped across his lap. He has apparently already gone downstairs to get the paper. I wasn't expecting him to be up yet, let alone make the trek down to the lobby.

"Hey, baby! Up so early?" I breeze over to give him a quick hug, noticing his sunken eyes have a gray hue underneath, and they lack the sparkle that used to dance in the blue irises. As this week progressed, so did the fatigue they warned would come.

"Yeah. I couldn't sleep. And I hate waking up in an empty bed." He grins then pulls me tighter and gives me a gentle kiss. Even his lips feel thinner somehow.

"I sure wish you could get some good sleep. You need your rest right now." I straighten the stocking cap on his head. He usually wears it in the morning—says his head is always cold first thing.

"Yeah, yeah, Mom," he retorts, offended at my concern.

"You haven't seen 'Mom' yet, mister," I playfully scold. "I've got to get going. I'll be helping Kate with inventory this morning, then I'll be back to take you to your session. So, about one o'clock, okay?"

"Yes, Mother!" He grins obstinately at me.

I shoot him a teasing glare then bend over for another kiss. "Last session this week, you know—yay! Halfway done!" I cheer. "Love you."

"Love you more!" he calls after me.

I can't help but smile as I leave the apartment. He truly is a special man. Even going through all this torture to get healthy, he still has a sense of humor. If our situation had been reversed, I'm pretty sure I would have locked myself in the bedroom, shades drawn, and thrown myself a huge pity party. No humor for me—only sarcasm and bitter cracks at cruel Fate. And back into the arms of my former companion, Depression.

But we've fallen into a routine now. Not one without the occasional bumps or stumbles, but definitely not one with the constant threat of a freight-train migraine or the cloud of wondering what this doctor will say or that test will show. No, now we know what we're facing, and we follow the prescribed steps. We're past the really scary part and on to the more manageable routine of treatment and getting him better. Halfway through treatment, and it finally feels like I can see the light at the end of the tunnel—still very distant, but it is there.

Ethan's side effects are met and managed, expected and handled. That wasn't the case at first, however. Just a couple weeks ago, after his first full week of treatment, I fought with myself about how to broach the subject—I felt I should take time off from the store. His treatments hit near a part of his brain that caused nausea and sometimes vomiting right after a session. And not knowing what else he might encounter, I wanted to be there to get him through the uncertainty of what the side effects would do to his body, to be sure he was safe every moment of the day.

I was conflicted knowing with Ethan off work, West and Kate really needed my help. Don't get me wrong, they're really supportive about everything; I just didn't know how to tell them I felt like I should be available for Ethan—wanted to be there every second of this. But then a part of me felt relief that I had a scheduled block of time when I had to be at the store, when I didn't have to worry about what each sigh, every jagged breath, every groan meant. I had a break from watching him toss and turn on the couch, from wondering how much worse he would deteriorate before he would get better.

I tried bringing it up with Ethan last night, sort of as a trial run before asking Kate and West.

"I'm thinking of asking West for some time off," I started delicately, testing the waters.

"What for?" I heard a tinge of resentment coloring his voice. He knew what for.

"Well . . . you know, I really feel like I should be here for you over these next few weeks. You only have three weeks left, but the treatments are really starting to take a toll. I want to be able to help you with whatever you need." I felt like I wasn't finding the right words to make my argument. I mean, what was I going to say? *You look like hell and it's scaring me. I think you need a babysitter.*

"Abby, you know that's not necessary," he said firmly. "Besides, you're needed at the store."

"Yeah, I know," I conceded, not sure where to go next with my argument. I tried good old-fashioned emotional pleas. "It's just—I hate leaving you home alone after these treatments. And you're only halfway through. What if they get harder on you than what you've dealt with so far? The doctor said it would probably hit you hardest starting in the third week." I felt my eyes getting hot with tears as I thought of how awful it would be if the treatments did get harder on him, if his fatigue got so bad it made it too difficult for him to want to fight the cancer.

"I'm fine, honestly," Ethan said, shaking his head definitively. "Don't waste your time worrying about me. I've handled the nausea, and the headaches haven't been anything like they used to be, and I'm just a little tired. This will all be over before you know it. Just a little bump in the road. Right?"

He flashed a reassuring smile, but it failed to exact its usual effect. I dug my teeth into my lip, trying to decide if he was being honest with me. Did I give up, satisfied with his bravado? Or did I continue to plead my case? I went with the latter.

"Babe, I love you," I said, laughing lightly, trying to change my strategy, keeping my voice upbeat. "But it kills me to feel like I'm not able to help you right now."

"Abby, really. I refuse to have you waiting on me hand and foot. I'm not helpless. And you're doing more than enough taking me to these sessions every day, going to all the appointments. You *are* helping." He paused and pointed a finger at me. "No more of this talk, okay? I'm fine, and I'll continue to be fine. West and Kate need you more than I do."

I wilted. "I'm sorry. I just thought—"

"Hey, there's a Will Ferrell SNL marathon on TV tonight. Should we order in?"

And that had been that. He'd effectively shut down the conversation.

But even today, I wonder if I should bring it up with Kate. I feel like I'm abandoning Ethan with every moment I spend at Food for Thought now. Surely she'll understand, and she'll have no problem convincing West. But how to start the conversation? I mull over the possibilities all the way to the store. We're to meet at seven to have enough time to finish the inventory before we open. I grimace as I look inside and see she's beaten me here.

"Hey, you!" I call before I turn to lock the front door again. "You're here early."

"Hey, Abs!" Kate calls back. "Yeah, I got here about an hour ago. I couldn't sleep well knowing the inventory was unfinished. Silly, I know—we have time yet. But all the same..."

I shrug out of my coat and throw it and my purse down behind the counter. "We just have the two rows left?" I question, grabbing my clipboard from yesterday.

"That's it."

"Yeah, no problem. We'll be done in no time." I meet her in the aisle, and I start my count across and half a row behind her. This is a bad time to start a conversation, while we're both trying to count, so I stifle the urge to bring up taking time off as long as I can. But it's tough, and I find myself having to recount several times. As we near the end of the aisle, it's Kate who breaks the silence.

"So, are things getting back to normal, now that you've gotten all the tests and appointments out of the way and are on to a treatment plan?" she asks, trying to sound upbeat, but there is an undercurrent of concern in her voice.

Normal? I ask myself. *What is normal?* I have no idea anymore after the weeks of upheaval and uncertainty. The norm for us is me rushing off to work, rushing home to take him to his sessions, rushing back to work to finish my shifts. And the norm for poor Ethan is exhaustion, sickness, suffering.

I sigh, searching for the words that will allow me to explain it. How much can I tell her? She is my closest friend, and a good friend to Ethan, but I know he'll be furious if he finds out I let Kate in on how hard these treatments have actually been on him. He stopped coming to the store earlier this week when the fatigue really started affecting him. Ethan won't even admit to himself how tough this ordeal has been on his body and spirit. And maybe he needs that delusion to keep himself positive. He tries to be so upbeat and courageous, and I admire him for that—no, I *envy* him for that. I know I could never have the same outlook, having a monster stare you in the face and threaten to end your very existence.

But Ethan stares right back at that monster and refuses to surrender. He is a fighter, through and through.

"Yeah, I guess," I concede. "I mean, not a *good* normal or anything. Not a normal like it was before . . . before all this. Maybe more of a tolerable level of stress in our everyday lives, if there is such a thing. We know our schedule, and we follow the schedule. At least for the next few weeks." I glance over at Kate, who has stopped taking inventory and is now leaning against the bookshelf, her arms folded around her clipboard.

"I don't know how you do it, girl." She shakes her head. "And let me tell you—we absolutely appreciate all you do to help us keep this store going, especially at a time like this. Even hiring Josh has only helped marginally. Learning curve, you know. And I know you'd much rather be at Ethan's side through his treatments, but you've really helped us keep everything running when we needed you most. I don't think we could have handled losing the both of you for so long."

I stare at Kate. I don't know how to respond. *By the way, about that? I need to take the next three weeks off to take care of Ethan. Sorry!*

"You are such a trooper," she continues. "I hope Ethan realizes how lucky he is to have such a selfless, caring woman in his life. You know, the word 'cancer' would scare off many a person in your same position. It says a lot about you, Abby, that you've stepped up like this to help him through such a difficult time," she compliments me sincerely. "I admire you for that."

"I don't know about that, Kate." I shake my head, refusing to take a compliment on my caregiving. It's a given. A necessity. "I love him." I shrug. What else is there to say?

"You'll get through this." She reaches over and squeezes my arm. "Soon it will be over and behind you. And you'll be an even stronger couple for it. You'll appreciate every day you have together. You won't take each other for granted the way West and I do." She smiles, trying to lighten the mood.

I grin appreciatively. Kate is my best friend, aside from Ethan. She has the maturity of age that I need to learn from. She also understands that friendship is always a two-way street. Each person should feel like they can bare their soul, their innermost thoughts, and receive strength and support from the other person. Whether I can rely on Kate to help me get through this is not the question. If I ask, she will probably give me whatever time off I request.

But I don't. Something she said earlier sticks in my mind—they couldn't have handled losing both of us for so long. *Only three more weeks of treatments*, I tell myself. I can handle this. I *will* handle this. I know how to cope with stressful situations—look at my life before meeting Ethan, right? Well, actually, Ethan has taught me how to handle stressful situations even better than I did before knowing him. What I'd thought of as strength before was merely coping. Coping and surviving. He has shown me how to take that and build it into a strength that allows me to not only survive the situation, but to try to overcome it, to become a better person on the other side of it.

I've made up my mind that this "normal" life I'm living can be continued for a few more weeks. And then, hopefully, Ethan and I can return to the old normal. A norm when every day we spent together was happy and carefree. A norm where the biggest thing I worried about was if it would rain and that I'd forgotten an umbrella. The silly worries of the Old Normal. How I long for those.

"Thanks, Kate . . . for your friendship," I say, my voice thick with emotion. My eyes brim with salty tears I don't want to let escape. I quickly clear my throat. "Shall we get this done before customers start arriving?"

"Yes, let's," she agrees, patting my arm. "Last row!"

I HAVE SOME time before work, and Ethan is resting on the couch, so I decide to tidy up the place a bit. Cleaning has been a low priority lately, and the times when I could have run the vacuum or deep-cleaned, he was exhausted and sleeping, so I didn't dare disturb him. Now, I can at least load the dishwasher and put some of these stacks of papers and bills away.

It takes almost no time to load the dishwasher, what with only two of us to dirty dishes and Ethan still not eating very much. The anti-nausea meds his doctor prescribed only marginally help.

I sweep the floor next, deciding to hold off on mopping until I have more time. Maybe tomorrow when I don't have to work, and we only have the treatment session in the afternoon.

Finally, I turn my attention to the growing pile of paperwork on the dining table. We have two spots cleared where we sit to eat, but the rest of the table is covered. I sigh at the thought of going through all those papers but march over and dive in, deciding to create general stacks that I can sort through. I have a stack for newspapers, one for test results and medical letters, and one for other mail and bills.

Concern climbs to the top of my thoughts at how tall the mail and bills stack is getting. Have we really ignored our mail this long? My initial reaction is to stop my chore and start ripping open envelopes. But I push that urge out of my mind. I will get to that in a few minutes. Right now, I want to finish the stacks, to feel like I actually accomplished something today.

Soon enough, more dark mahogany wood is visible, and all the piles are neatly stacked. I scoop up the pile of newspapers and deposit them in the recycling bin. The stack of test results and communications from doctors have been read multiple times, I'm sure, so I carry them over to the secretary desk and add them to Ethan's drawer of medical information.

That leaves the mail. I quickly sort out sales fliers, solicitations, credit card offers. Those go to the recycling bin as well. Next, I separate the household bills from the medical bills, feeling a tinge of anxiety as I realize the stack of hospital bills is higher than the household bills.

Ethan has always been the one to sort mail and pay bills. Unless it has my name on it, which it rarely ever does, he takes care of it. I have never seen so much as an electric bill for this place. I've told him more than once that I would pay my share of the expenses; he should let me know how much I owe each month. His response had always been, "Let me take care of you for a while, Abby. Don't worry about it."

Deep down it bothers me, though. I have always struggled to buy the things I need, and I've never relied on anyone else to pay my way. It's hard to let go of that control without feeling like I owe Ethan, like I am indebted to him.

I guess he will have to relinquish some of that control to me now. None of these bills are late yet, but a couple are very close. I mentally add the totals together and frown at the dollar amount. I didn't realize how much it cost to live in a nice, large apartment in Metropolitan Tower. Ethan must earn more money than I thought. I open most of the household mail before a wave of guilt crashes over me. I glance over at him, lying on the couch facing the windows. Will he be mad at me for opening these? Was that his deal—that he wanted to have control over the money, and so he wanted to be the only one who saw what was spent? Some people are that way.

I remind myself Ethan isn't that type of person. I will have to talk to him, though, about how to pay these. Does he do bill pay online or write out checks? We'll have to take care of some of these in the next day or two to avoid late payment penalties.

I turn my attention to the last stack—the medical bills. The apprehension I felt earlier returns as I reach for the first envelope. We have insurance through a plan the store offers, but I have no idea how much it covers. The first bill for lab work isn't too bad. Co-insurance is fifty dollars. The next one is thicker but has several pages of descriptions of services over three visits. That one causes a lump to form in my throat. Co-insurance and deductible amount: $2,025. That hurts. The next envelope is thin, but the amount due startles me—$3,500. There must be some mistake. I examine the body of the invoice, thinking maybe they haven't submitted it to insurance yet. The procedure is listed, the amount insurance covers is listed, the office visit copay we paid at the appointment is listed—and we still owe that much? I feel my blood pressure rising. I am only halfway through the stack. The next one is again a thick envelope. I reluctantly tear it open and unfold the pages. For the biopsy and hospital room: $8,014.29. I gasp. The lump in my throat becomes a boulder in my stomach. This is crazy. How can they expect anyone to afford this?

I hurry through the rest, afraid of freaking out before I get them all opened. I line up every medical bill and use the calculator function on my phone to add them up: $25,372.16. That can't be right. I add again. $25,372.16.

Oh. My. God. Ethan still has a couple weeks left of treatment. These bills are a few weeks behind since they have to run the procedures through insurance first. I don't remember seeing any bills for the actual radiation sessions in that pile. And he can't work on top of it all. And I don't make near enough to cover this. I feel myself becoming hysterical, on the verge of hyperventilating. My head spins with the thought of how expensive his treatments could be. Surely there is a limit to the amount we have to pay, right? Like an out-of-pocket max or something? I shudder to think of how long it will take us to get this debt paid off. Years, probably.

"What's wrong?"

I jump at the sound of Ethan's voice behind me. I was so absorbed in my panic I didn't hear him walk over. "Ah . . ."

Okay, do I say something or keep it to myself so he doesn't get worked up like I just did? I move my hands over the papers, shuffle them into a stack, try to cover as much as I can. He doesn't need to deal with this on top of everything else.

"What are you doing, Abby? Trying to hide something from me?"

My eyes widen as I look up at him. I shake my head fervently. I don't want to be dishonest with him, that's not it. "No—it's just—" I pull the papers to my chest. I can come up with a little white lie, right? Just to protect him from the shock of what we already owe. "I was just organizing the mail."

"Do you normally gasp and freak out when you organize mail?"

He's smiling. He is amused at my reaction, and that upsets me. Here I am having a stroke, and he thinks it's funny? I guarantee that smile will fall from his face faster than a lead balloon when I show him the $25,372.16 we owe! My eyes narrow; I want to show him now. I want him to see that I am not acting foolishly. This is something to get worked up about!

"Well, I don't normally get to organize the mail, do I? That's something you always do," I point out.

"True. And it's probably a good thing since you get so concerned over a couple of bills." He is teasing, which angers me more.

"A couple of bills?" I blurt out before I can censor my reaction. "A couple of bills! Ethan, we owe $25,000—" I overenunciate the dollar amount "—*in bills*! And that's just the medical bills! Of course I'm concerned. Of course I'm freaking out."

"That much, huh?" He shrugs. "Well, I expected as much. Considering all they've done to me so far."

I am shocked by his reaction—or lack thereof actually. Maybe his treatments are making him lose his mind. Normal brain function could be impaired by the radiation hitting the wrong cells. Maybe he thinks the therapy won't work and he will die and not have to worry about paying anyone. I stare in confusion as he peels my fingers off the stack of bills and begins to review them.

"How are we going to pay these, Ethan?" I demand, hysterics simmering in my voice. "I'll have to get another job. I can pick up some shifts at Hooligan's, I'm sure. Jeff is still manager; he'll schedule me in."

"There's no need for that," he says matter-of-factly.

"Well, how else will we pay for them? You can't work right now, nor do I expect you to. And you still have a couple weeks of treatments left. I can't even fathom how much more we'll have to pay." I feel my voice rising along with my blood pressure.

"We're fine. Don't worry about it," he says in a calm, even tone. He squeezes my hand to reassure me.

I search his blue eyes, trying to understand. I guess having to battle cancer puts things into a new perspective, but I can't see past the looming amount of debt to be as serene as he is. "But I *am* worried about it. Just knowing we owe that much money, Ethan."

"Not we—me." He walks over to where I stacked the household bills, adding them to his pile. "These are my medical bills, Abby, and I don't want you to waste any time worrying about them. Not in the least. It's unnecessary. I'll get the utilities paid tomorrow. I imagine they're almost late. I'm sorry I haven't done a better job of keeping up with these."

"Ethan..." I watch him walk over to the desk and deposit the stack in a drawer, not necessarily feeling any better about the situation. "We're a team, you know.

The good and the bad, the bills and all. I wish you wouldn't shut me out. I feel like I'm not contributing enough, and I don't like it."

"You contribute more than enough, babe. You're working so hard right now and taking care of me at the same time." He rejoins me and pulls me up into an embrace. "You don't give yourself enough credit."

I frown. He gives me way too much credit. Our contributions are very disproportionate in my view. He gives and gives and gives. He takes care of me. He never demands anything in return. I, on the other hand, live in his apartment, never pay for food or rent, and work at a job I am pretty sure he got for me. I would feel much better if he would allow me to start paying rent or help with some of the medical bills. Maybe I should just take some of the bills, the smaller ones at least, and pay them myself...

"Ethan, you can't just put them in a drawer and not face the weight of the situation. It makes me sick to my stomach, like when I was in college and didn't have enough money for tuition. I couldn't handle the thought of taking on all that student loan debt, so I didn't. I left and went to work." I pull back a little so I can look into his eyes. "This is a lot of debt."

"You're not hearing me. It's not a big deal. It will get paid. You don't—you *won't* worry about debt or money, do you hear me? I will take care of it. I will take care of you. This won't hurt us a bit. I can afford it." He kisses my lips, a kiss I return, a bit more relieved and more optimistic than before. I feel my pulse return to normal. The knots in my stomach lessen. I hold on tightly to him. He has a way of making everything better. Always has.

"Okay, if you say so," I mumble into his shoulder, not entirely convinced, but wanting to trust him.

"I do."

✻

"WHAT? WHAT DO you need from me, Ethan?" I ask breathlessly, my cheek pressed to the hard wood of the bathroom door.

Only moments ago, we were sitting at the table enjoying a nice meal of Chinese takeout that we'd grabbed on our way home from Sloan-Kettering. He'd even suggested we break out the fancy china that was packed away in the closet, asking me to do the honors because of his, you know, butterfingers. We'd laughed, feeling a lightness we hadn't in so long.

After today's session, the doctor visited with him about the results of the blood work that was taken the other day. The numbers were within the range of where they should be at this stage in treatment. There were no signs of the radiation negatively affecting other organs, so Ethan wanted to celebrate. This was good news. He suggested Chinese, and I agreed—it had been a long time since we'd gotten takeout.

Now I fear it was the wrong choice.

He turned pale—paler than normal—only five minutes into our meal. Then he raced to the bathroom faster than I'd seen him move in months.

"Abby—go—away!" I hear his broken, muffled voice through the door. "I'm sick. I'll come out—when I can."

"Ethan, honey, can I get you something? Some water?"

No response.

"Anything?" I hear him get sick through the thick wood door. My chest aches. I want to go in there and rub his back, to comfort him. But he locked the door when he ran in there. I rattle the knob helplessly. "Please . . . I want to help you."

"Go back and eat. I'll be fine. Just give me a minute." He sounds exhausted, defeated.

Reluctantly, I release my hold on the doorknob. I turn and glare at the offending meal spread out on the table. How can I sit and eat now? Was it the food that made him ill? I walk over to the table and examine the takeout cartons. We'd eaten some of the same things. I do a quick self-check: I feel fine. No stomach cramps, no nausea. Maybe it's just his entrée.

Or maybe it's the treatment. I sigh then decide to get rid of it all. If it is the food, I don't want it around. And I am sure Ethan wouldn't either. I scrape our plates into the garbage. I shove the napkins and wrappers into the cartons and gather them into my arms. I throw them away with disgust, angry that they ruined our celebration. It's hard to come by things to celebrate these days.

On the other hand, if it is the treatment—well, I'm already mad at that, so what else can I do on that front? He still has one more week to get through.

I look around the apartment helplessly. My eyes are drawn to the bathroom door like a magnet. I want to kick the door in, to be there with him whether he wants me or not. I hate him suffering alone. But I know he's trying to spare me from the worst of the illness, as he has from the start. What he doesn't know is how guilty it makes me feel, standing out here while he suffers alone.

I march to the door and try one more time. "Ethan?"

No response.

After a minute of silence, alarm bells go off. Is he okay? Can he not answer me? What if he needs help? I try to keep my hysteria in check. "Ethan?" I question more urgently. Another long, agonizing minute drags by as I mentally go through the ways I could gain entry into the bathroom if I had to—from picking the lock to throwing the heavy mahogany chair from the dining table against the door and shattering it.

"Ye-yeah," his weak voice cracks through. A surge of relief washes over me, followed quickly by more apprehension. I wait for him to say more.

"Go put the movie in, Abby. I'll be out in a minute." His reassuring tone is forced.

I sigh again, my eyes stinging with tears. I am not a very religious person. We barely went to church when I was young, sometimes on the major religious holidays. I train my eyes upward now, not sure what I'm doing. Pleading, I guess. Asking God to help my Ethan get through this. Asking for strength to be given to him to fight through this. Begging God to bring my old Ethan back to me.

Chapter Nineteen

Luck of the Irish?

"WE LEAVE IN fifteen minutes. Are you ready?" Ethan leans over my shoulders as I sit on the couch. I'm trying to finish the last chapter of the latest Carson Ripley novel *Til Murder Do Us Part*. He bought the book for himself—before Kate had even finished the countertop display, in fact—but I started reading it earlier this week and found it extremely hard to put down.

"Yeah, yeah." I wave my hand dismissively then place my finger along the line I'm reading. Miranda is finding out the truth about her husband, Carl. He is a serial killer living an elaborate lie. Now it appears she may be his next victim!

"Abigail! We've got to go," Ethan calls—I'm not sure how many minutes later—urgently from the bathroom. No doubt admiring his hair in the mirror before we leave. It is finally growing back. Still really short, but no more baldness.

"Okay!" I say, exasperated, as I slide the bookmark in place and set it on the coffee table. "I was at the best part, you know," I scold.

A smile breaks across his face as he walks out of the bathroom. "I can tell you how it ends, if you'd like."

"No! Don't!" I throw my hands over my ears and cringe, even though I'm pretty sure he's joking. He laughs as he removes my hands and wraps them in front of me, leaning over the back of the couch and kissing my cheek. He releases one hand but holds the other as he coaxes me off the couch. I glance at the book one last time. Exciting as it is, it can wait one more day. Tonight—tonight is for us. A much-needed *normal* night. We are going to the Dave Matthews Band concert.

My stomach begins to flutter with anticipation. We haven't gone on a real date since we got the good news in mid-April. All tests were conclusive—no more tumor! The treatments had worked, and the suffering was over. We'd both been giddy with relief that the storm had been weathered. We've lived on a high for the past month and a half. Once Ethan got over the fatigue from the radiation, we spent three Sundays in a row at Uncle Geoff's house, took walks through Central Park again, snuggled on the couch, and made love. All the time.

But we haven't gone on an official date yet.

So tonight, the air is charged with excitement, an unspoken electricity between the two of us. We are living life again, heady with the knowledge that we have beaten this cancer and come out stronger on the other side.

"Are we meeting Kate and West there, or are we picking them up?" I ask before I give Ethan a quick peck on the lips. I linger there, an inch from his face, my fingers intertwined in his short hair. How I missed his thick, wavy locks during the long weeks of his treatments. Soon, his hair will be long again. Ethan wraps his right arm around my waist, pulling me in so tightly I gasp. He presses his lips against mine, kisses me so long I start to think we should skip the concert and instead go into the bedroom. Then he releases my lips, leaving me dizzy, trying to remember how to breathe.

"We're meeting them there," he says, staring deeply into my eyes—I am overjoyed that the sparkle has returned to them—and then he reluctantly continues, "But we've got to get moving, babe."

As thrilled as I am to go out and have a good time with our friends, at a concert that is sure to be amazing, I would be just as happy to spend the night curled up in bed with Ethan. I purse my lips, debating whether I should argue with him about the alternative to our going out. But he loves the Dave Matthews Band and deserves a carefree night out. So, I tuck my passion away for now and let my lust for Ethan smolder until later this evening, when we can be alone again.

"Let's go."

THE CONCERT WAS everything I hoped for. The Dave Matthews Band was spectacular, of course, playing all our favorite songs. The fact that West and Kate were there to share the night with us made it exponentially better. And afterward, we decide to get drinks at our favorite piano bar not far from Central Park. One or two drinks turn into . . . I don't know how many, actually. But we continue the fantastic evening, playing a couple rounds of pool—or rather, the guys do. Kate and I try, but we really aren't much help for either of our teams. Ethan wins one game by sinking the eight ball, and West and Kate win one game because I sink the eight ball in the wrong pocket.

We relax at a corner table and listen to the entertainment of the evening, a very young, talented piano player named Sabian. It's so great, like old times. Laughing, razzing each other, talking about whatever—just hanging out. It's been so long since we've been able to do this, the four of us.

"Okay, you two," Kate interrupts a heated discussion the boys are having on the state of the economic imbalance in America. "We need to know, when are the two of you taking your vacation? You were so gracious to let us take our trip. Now it's your turn."

Ethan and I gaze at each other for a long moment. We've just gotten used to him being healthy and back to work; we haven't thought past the daily routine we now cherish so dearly. A "normal" reminiscent of our lives pre-cancer. We weren't foolish enough to hope for more than the blessing we've already been given.

"Well, Kate . . ." I shrug. "We're just happy to have Ethan in good health." I grin at him and squeeze his hand, my eyes speaking volumes. He smiles knowingly.

"Oh, come on!" she urges. "Unacceptable!" She looks at West, who takes a moment to realize what she wants.

"Ah, yeah. Hey," he stutters, looking at Kate for direction. She raises an eyebrow at him. I have to suppress my laughter. "Yeah, you guys really deserve some time off. Together." He glances back at Kate, hoping that's what she was expecting of him. Approval is clearly written on her face, so he relaxes in his seat, confident in the role he played.

"So, there you go!" Kate directs her attention to us. "West says you're good to go."

I peek at Ethan out of the corner of my eye, wondering what he thinks about us taking some time, truly leaving behind the stresses we've faced for so many months. How healing it would be to celebrate by taking a trip to paradise somewhere. "What do you think?"

"Well, I don't know, Abs. The weather is turning nice here in New York. Where would we go this time of year? Isn't it hurricane season in the Caribbean or earthquake season or something?"

Kate rolls her eyes. "Earthquake season is not a thing, and hurricane season doesn't kick up until August or something like that! You could go on a cruise or visit a private island—just do something!"

"Really?" Ethan raises his eyebrows at West, looking for confirmation. West shrugs, his eyes wide in mock unknowing. They're having fun with Kate's exasperation, egging her on. I want to laugh, but the smack Kate lands on West's arm tells me she is being very serious. I take note and try to rein Ethan in.

"Hmm . . ." I sigh thoughtfully. "I've always wanted to see Ireland. I wonder what it would be like this time of year."

Ethan hoots with laughter at first, and West joins in. The hurt on my face abruptly stops him mid-guffaw. "You're serious?"

"Yeah, I'm serious." My brow creases with my frown. I wonder what is so funny about my suggestion. I've always been intrigued by Ireland—the luscious greenery, the ancient castles, the history. I just never thought I'd have the opportunity to make such a trip.

"Well, sure," Ethan says, unconvinced. "I mean . . . Ireland would be . . . interesting, right?"

I roll my eyes. Okay, so I am stupid. Let's move on.

"Absolutely. I've always wanted to go to Ireland," Kate pipes up to help my cause. "The history, the castles . . . beautiful." I thank her with my eyes. Whether it's stupid or not, she will support me.

"Yeah," Ethan acquiesces before he takes a gulp of beer. And then, possibly buying into the idea, he says, "Yeah! Ireland. I mean—if it's okay with you guys?"

"Yes, of course it is!" Kate exclaims. "Right, West?" I catch her elbowing him in the ribs.

"Yes! Of course," he concedes as he rubs his side. "Just bring me back some Irish whiskey."

"Then it's settled," Kate proclaims as she flags down a waitress. "We need four shots—do you have Irish whiskey?" The waitress nods. "Excellent! Four shots of your finest Irish whiskey, please."

Things get a little patchy for me after that. I remember Kate's toast to us as we down the burning whiskey shots. I'm pretty sure another round of shots followed. I remember stumbling into a cab with Ethan's strong arms around my waist, gloriously happy that he's finally strong enough to carry my weight rather than the other way around. I remember snuggling into his chest on the ride home in the taxi. I remember the sexy smell of my favorite cologne—it has such a power over me.

I remember stumbling into the apartment, I think—no, stumbling into the bedroom. Him helping me out of my clothes, and me giggling uncontrollably.

"Ireland, huh?" he questions right before the most powerful kiss I've ever felt him plant on my lips.

"Um-hmm," I breathe. "I can't wait—"

I'm stifled by another powerful, hungry kiss. Suddenly, I wish I hadn't drunk so much. I hope I can remain in control of my faculties enough to enjoy this. The anticipation rises, expands throughout me.

Any fears that I wouldn't be sober enough to remember the encounter are quickly squelched. He kisses me with an unabashed wanting I haven't experienced in months. His hands move across my body, exploring areas that have gone untouched for so long. My soul delights in the Ethan I have missed so much. Every touch of his fingertips is a needle piercing into my sensitive skin.

We've had sex since the end of his treatments in April, when he got the all-clear from the doctors. Great sex even. Thankful-he-was-alive sex. But none with the reckless abandon, the passion, we feel at this very moment. I cherish every kiss, every touch, every hungry moment. And the climax is like no other, I think, for both of us.

MY LIPS CURL into an involuntary smile as I wake the next morning. I arch my back in a glorious stretch and sigh, seeing the light through my closed eyelids. My left hand falls to the bed, searching for Ethan next to me, not wanting to open my eyes yet. Not wanting the night to be over yet—that magnificent night! I bite my lip hard at the memory of our passionate finish.

I finally force my eyelids open as I realize my searching hand isn't finding him as expected. Turning my head toward the clock on the nightstand, a muted pain radiates through my brain, a result of too many shots last night. It's 8:30. Late for a workday. But it isn't a workday for either of us, so 8:30 isn't bad after a night of celebrating. I push myself up on my elbows, looking over at his side of the bed to ensure I'm not imagining things in my groggy state. No Ethan.

I try to focus on the doorway, blinking a few times. Things are shifting around in ways they shouldn't be. The dull ache in my head grows fiercer, turning into a throbbing from back to front. I rub my forehead with my thumb and fingers, trying to rid myself of the ache and focus on the door.

At that moment, the bathroom door flies open. My head whips to the side, a wave of pain exploding through it. I suck in a breath. Ethan appears to stumble forward, towel wrapped around his waist. I blink again, exhaling slowly, this time trying to focus on him. I let my head fall onto my pillow. It aches less on the pillow. "Hey," I say with a half-smile.

"Hey."

Does he seem preoccupied, or am I just that hungover? Before I can respond, he lays his palm on my hairline and kisses my forehead. His gaze meets mine on the way down to my nose where he leaves another brief kiss, then on to my mouth. I shy away from that one, letting his lips barely touch mine. I'm afraid of what my breath is like this morning. I grin up at him. He lingers above my face. "So, Ireland?" I question, hoping I wasn't imagining the conversation from last night.

"Uh, yeah, I guess. Kate says we can go as soon as we can schedule it." He smiles, which normally sends my stomach into flips. But why does it seem a little insincere this time?

"Or . . . we could go on an Alaskan cruise, or whatever," I offer. "It doesn't have to be Ireland." I try to sort out his expression, which is difficult to do with my head spinning and his face sideways.

"What?" He seems drawn out of a fog, his eyes squinting. "No, no. Ireland will be great. I'll start looking for travel packages this morning. The sooner the better."

Is he trying to convince me, or himself, that this is a good decision? I can't ask because he turns abruptly and strides out of the room, leaving me staring after him, confused. I start to wonder if I imagined the amazing event from last night as well.

"ARE YOU GETTING excited?" Kate asks. "When are you leaving?"

"Totally excited," I sing. "We fly out Wednesday. I can't believe I'll be across the Pond in less than five days!"

Even Ethan seems excited about our trip. After that time a few weeks back, when I couldn't tell if he was happy about our destination, he jumped on board and has actually been the one to make most of the plans.

"I can't believe you two waited so long, to be honest. I thought you would have been off right away. You really deserve it after all you've been through."

Kate is standing opposite from me, setting up a display of self-help books on the front counter. She's been working at it for a while now, the artist in her never quite happy after she arranges and rearranges.

"Well, unlike you world travelers," I chide, "I had to get a passport first. And anyway, Ethan thought it would be best for us to wait until after his checkup."

"Oh, yes. When is that?"

"Monday, I believe."

"Good. So, does he feel pretty good about the appointment? I mean, he seems almost one hundred percent again." She steps back from the display, surveying the setup.

"That looks great, Kate, really," I laugh, holding up my hands and stepping forward to stop her when I realize she is going to redo it.

She grimaces. "I don't think so." She moves two more books and gives up. "It'll do, I guess—sorry. Back to Ethan?"

"Um, yeah, I think he's been doing well. He's been handling most of the prep work for the trip this week and last. I didn't realize there was so much to do, but I guess there is." I shrug. "He's been a little tired lately, but that's probably because he's running around so much. And now that he's working again... I don't know, maybe it was too soon for him to return full time."

"How long did the doctors say the fatigue would last?" Kate wonders.

"They said it could last months," I reason. "But he's seemed so energetic the past couple months, it just feels like he may be sliding backward, you know?"

"I'm sure it's the trip planning added to everything else."

"Yeah, that's probably it." A thought occurs to me. "I hope he isn't regretting our choice of Ireland. I told him we could do anything he wanted. A cruise might have been less stressful to prepare for."

"Oh, I'm pretty sure he's happy with your choice." Kate's eyes are dancing, and a wide smile lifts the corners of her mouth. I narrow my eyes, wondering what's up. "I overheard West and him talking about it last week. He's as excited as you are. The big reason being that it's what you want, and he wants to make you happy. But—" she leans on the counter and drops her voice to an almost inaudible level. I lean in to hear her. "I heard him saying something to West about 'just the right moment' and hoping you would say yes."

Blinking, I try to process what she's said. Did I hear her right? Between the words and the excited expression on her face, I'm pretty sure I did. "You don't think he meant—"

"I'm almost certain!" she bursts out, clasping her hands on mine. Then, lowering her voice and scanning the store behind to see if anyone overheard her outburst, she warns me, "But don't say anything. You don't want to ruin it! If I know Ethan, the proposal will be romantic and amazing. Oh, I wish I could be there!"

My mind starts racing. I'm not sure how I feel about a possible proposal. I think back to Christmastime when, for a brief moment, I thought he *was* going to propose. I had been relieved that the jewelry in the box had been a three-stone necklace, not a ring. I'd told Kate I wasn't sure I was ready for marriage—I felt like

I still had some growing up to do. But now, after all we have been through in the past six months, and thinking that I could have lost him, I have a new perspective. I want to have that bond with Ethan, the one that says, "You're mine forever." We've already proven to one another that we will stand together come hell or high water.

"I'm going to infer by the smile creeping across your face that you have come to like the idea of becoming Mrs. Ethan Lansing?" she prods.

"Yes, Kate. I think we're ready for it—I think *I'm* ready for it." I can't help beaming now, an excited flutter dancing inside me as I think about the potential proposal in beautiful Ireland.

At that moment, I must leave our conversation to ring up a customer at the register. When I finish, I catch Kate trying to rearrange the book display one more time. "Kate! It looks fine. Really!"

She shoots me a guilty look.

"So, what do you think? Do you think we're ready for marriage?" I ask in a hushed tone. West is around here somewhere stocking books on the shelves, and I don't want him overhearing our conversation. If Ethan *is* planning a surprise engagement, I don't want him to find out that the surprise has been foiled.

"Oh, honey, I think you've *been* ready."

I smile again at her reassurance. "Well, what I want to know is how come you and West haven't gotten married yet? You've been together what, seven years now?"

She rolls her eyes. "Yes, over seven years. Time flies, I tell you."

"So . . . ? Haven't you ever hinted to him that you'd like a ring?"

"West's not that kind of guy, you know. He definitely needs prodding and guidance on everything from buying new underwear to planning a vacation, as you've seen. I can't hint hard enough for him to get it." We laugh. "But seriously, I know we'll get married someday, when he's ready to ask. And I'm in no hurry. I'm very happy with our relationship. There's something about being 'boyfriend and girlfriend.' Makes me feel young still."

"You're not old, you know."

"Wait till you hit thirty, girl. That 'old' feeling starts creeping up pretty fast with each additional year."

I have to laugh. Even though Kate has a maturity beyond her years, I can't picture her actually getting old in the literal sense of the word—she is much too vibrant for that.

"Oh, speaking of proposals, I talked to my friend Emory last night on the phone." It had been several weeks since we last talked, so we had a lot to catch up on. I think Ethan was a bit upset at me for spending almost two hours on the phone with her, but she had exciting news to share.

"Oh, I remember Emory . . . and Dylan, right? How are they doing?"

"Great. Dylan just asked her to marry him, like literally just asked her," I giggle, remembering her excited chatter about the ring and how he had gotten the restaurant to place it in her dessert and how everyone in the restaurant had cheered when she'd said yes. "I think she called me right as they were leaving the restaurant."

"Did they set a date?"

"Um, they're looking at some time next year. Maybe even a Christmas wedding. She has a million ideas already, so I'm sure she'll need a few months at least to get her plans condensed enough to start reserving the venue and buying a dress."

"And to think, that could be what you'll be doing as well very soon. You two can compare ideas and colors and dress fabrics."

Kate is getting a little carried away now. I frown. I don't want to think about wedding planning yet—I'm not officially engaged. And honestly, I'm not thrilled about wedding planning at all; it isn't my thing. Maybe I can get Emory to plan mine, too. I'm sure she's got plenty of ideas that she won't end up using on her own. Suddenly, I'm ready to change the subject.

"Hey, I'm going to call Ethan and ask him to get travel shampoo and conditioner while he's out and about. I forgot to pick some up."

"Oh, no problem." Kate seems a little surprised by my abrupt change in conversation. Surely, she knows I'm not the type to get hyped up over wedding planning . . . but maybe *she* is. Maybe her artistic mind is racing with design ideas and centerpieces and floral bouquets and things she would be fantastic at creating. As I walk to the breakroom, I decide I will definitely ask Kate to help plan my wedding.

But first I have to get engaged, I remind myself. A shiver of excitement runs up my spine as I imagine how Ethan will propose. Getting engaged in Ireland—how perfect! I wonder if I can keep the knowledge of the surprise under wraps. I'm afraid once I come face-to-face with him, he'll see it written all over my face. I'll have to practice acting very normal.

As I dig for my cell phone in my purse, I come across a note I'd written for myself last night—birth control pills. That's right, I'm out of pills and can't forget to run to the pharmacy to get my refill picked up before we leave on our trip. Maybe I can talk Ethan into grabbing those for me as well today. I find my phone and press the button to access my screen. It remains black. I sigh as I press the power button—no response. I forgot to charge it after my long conversation with Emory last night.

I head back out to the store, figuring I can borrow West's phone. I mean, these errands aren't extremely important, but I have them on my mind now and I don't want to forget.

I find the aisle where West is stocking shelves, but he's already on his phone, so I turn to find Kate.

"Abby, wait," West calls after me with an intensity I've never before heard from him. "Abby, here—"

I turn around and my confused gaze meets a pale-faced West, hurrying toward me, his phone outstretched. Before I can respond, he's quickly closed the gap between us and thrusts the phone into my hand. Is Ethan on the phone? That's the only thing that makes sense. And if it is Ethan, why is West looking at me like he's just been punched in the gut?

"It's the hospital. They tried to call you first."

Chapter Twenty

Are We Out of the Woods Yet?

NO! NO! NO! My mind screams as I grip the seat of the cab, clawing my fingernails into the vinyl. This can't be happening. We are leaving for Ireland in a few days. We are going to have a wonderful, glorious, much-deserved vacation together! He is going to ask me to marry him. I dig my fingernails into my thighs now, hoping the pain will wake me from this nightmare. It only makes tears spring to my eyes.

"Can you hurry, please?" I desperately plead with the driver. Why is it taking so long? In the dozens of appointments we have gone to in the past months, it's never taken this long to navigate traffic.

I cover my face with my hands, thinking that if I can't see how slowly we are going, I won't hyperventilate. But my chest catches in ragged breaths, my hands quickly becoming wet with the sobs I can no longer hold back.

And the worst feeling of all is not knowing what has happened. The nurse would only tell me there had been an accident. I couldn't get any more information out of her.

I try to compose myself as I dig in my purse for a tissue, feeling slight relief when I wipe my eyes and notice the hospital only a block away. "Stop here! Stop here!"

I throw cash at the driver and dash out of the cab before it comes to a full stop. I can get there quicker on foot than he can in this traffic.

I run faster than I ever have in my life, pushing people out of the way if they don't move fast enough. I don't care that they yell—I have to get to Ethan. I almost hit the glass automatic doors at the entrance of the ER because they don't open fast enough. I run to the nearest desk, not caring who I budge in front of.

"Ethan Lansing. I'm here—for Ethan—Lansing," I choke out breathlessly.

"One moment please," the receptionist drones as if bored. It's all I can do not to yell at her to hurry up. My fingers involuntarily tap loudly on the counter. She pays no attention.

"And you are?" she asks slowly, her eyes half-closed as she stares at me.

"His girlfriend."

"Take the hallway to your right and turn left when you reach the end. Second door on your left."

I take off before she gets it all out. There's no time to waste. I have to find Ethan. I quickly locate the room but pause before I open the door and force myself to take a couple deep breaths. I must prepare myself for what I might walk into. Pushing open the door, I find two young nurses huddled beside him. I can't see past them to tell whether he is okay, so I rush around to the other side of the hospital bed, my heart in my throat. As I round the foot of the bed, my eyes fall on his face, and I am shocked more than anything . . . to see him smiling at me.

"Abby!"

I let his expression register in my racing mind. He is smiling. He's okay. I start to breathe again. "Ethan, thank God! I thought something terrible had happened! They wouldn't tell me anything."

I rush over and grip his hand, squeezing it tightly—yes, this is real. The hysteria that's consumed me since the phone call begins to wane.

"I'm okay," he reassures me.

I glance over at the blond and black-haired nurses. They are busy putting in an IV and setting up some sort of equipment.

"What happened? Why are you here?"

Frustrated, I realize I will be kept in the dark for a while longer because just then another older nurse with the air of someone in charge enters the room.

"All done, ladies? Let's get him moved. There's a room waiting for you, Mr. Lansing." She brushes past me as she takes my spot next to Ethan and raises the side rail on the bed in a sharp motion. She waves over the black-haired nurse, who promptly raises the side rail on her side of the bed. The blond nurse takes charge of the IV stand and equipment as the three usher him out of the room.

I ponder asking the older nurse for information, but she won't quit her animated chatter with him all the way to his fourth-floor room. She seems to be flirting with him. Actually, I notice all three of them seem to be flirting with him, much to my dismay, as they settle him in his room. He's inadvertently encouraging it by continuing unnecessary conversation with them. I stand against the wall and wait for my turn to have my boyfriend's attention.

"Here's your call button should you need anything," the older nurse explains and touches his shoulder. "And a doctor will be up shortly to go over the scans with you, okay?"

I watch the two young nurses leave the room, both glancing back at Ethan as they go, no doubt wondering if he is watching them leave, wondering if they have caught his eye. Funny how none of them have even acknowledged my presence.

"Thank you," Ethan says to the older nurse, shooting me a half-grin as he sees me narrow my eyes.

She smiles at him before following the others out of the room.

I frown as I toss my purse onto the chair next to me and walk over to him. Finally, I can find out what happened. "So, Casanova, are they keeping you? Is that why you get a room?"

He cocks an eyebrow as he reaches out and takes my hand, rubbing it with this thumb. "Ah, I guess so," he says evasively. He grins at me with a nervous twitch at the corner of his mouth.

"What aren't you telling me, Ethan? What happened?" I press. "What are the scans for?"

"Now, don't get worked up." He pats my hand with his free hand.

"I'm past worked up, Ethan. I was freaking out, fearing the worst."

"I know. I'm sorry. I don't really know what happened. One minute I'm standing at the register paying and the next I'm on the floor in blinding pain. I thought my head was splitting in two. Everything went black. I tried to tell them

I'd be okay, but somebody called an ambulance, and they made me lie still until the paramedics arrived. Not that I could have gone anywhere. The headache lasted a good twenty minutes at full force before it subsided to the dull roar I had before."

"Wait a minute—had before?"

"I didn't want to worry you, Abby."

"What do you mean *had before*?" I demand.

"Well, my head started aching again a couple weeks or so ago. I don't remember exactly when. And it wasn't that bad. So, I called Dr. Jackson and met with him a few times to see if he could figure out what was going on."

Anger flashes in my eyes as I realize what he's telling me. All the errands he has been running—yeah, those were doctor appointments. Nothing to do with the trip. And the emotional tailspin I'd just endured could have been avoided!

"You knew this was going to happen?" I accuse. "You didn't tell me what was going on? After everything we've been through?"

"Well, no, I *didn't* know this was going to happen," he says defensively. He reaches his hand up to my arm. I step back and cross my arms in front of my chest. He has no idea how betrayed I feel. "The fact that we have been through so much is why I didn't say anything. I was trying to protect you."

How am I supposed to respond to that? I have a million words racing through my mind, but the anger swelling in my chest keeps me from verbalizing my thoughts. I am afraid I will yell at him, and I don't want to do that. The anger, the betrayal, the disappointment might make me say something I'll regret. And neither one of us needs that right now. I bite the inside of my lip to try to release some of the emotions boiling at the surface.

After a long moment, Ethan speaks again, now emotional himself. "I'm sorry, Abby, that I didn't tell you. I didn't want to worry you. I saw what the waiting and the doctor visits did to you before, and I didn't want to put you through that again." His eyes start to glisten. His hand remains outstretched, now resting on the side rail, waiting for me to come back to him. I continue to glare, unwilling to accept the apology.

"Dr. Jackson was going to develop a treatment plan, if one is possible, and we were to go over it Monday at my next appointment. I would have told you on

Monday, Abby, I swear—" his voice breaks "—once I had all the answers. Don't be mad at me, please."

I soften. He would never deliberately try to hurt me. I know that. Everything he ever does is out of love for me. How awful that he has gone through a repeat of six months ago with the tests and the doctors, but all alone this time.

"I'm not mad at you," I quietly concede, looking down at his open hand. Stepping forward, I cradle his hand in mine and trace the life line on his palm with my finger. I thought a long life line meant you would live a long life. I frown. "I *am* mad that you didn't tell me you were having troubles again, Ethan." I shake my index finger at him. "I can handle it, but you *have* to be honest with me. I've been blindsided by bad things too many times in my life." I shake my head, close my eyes, remember with a pang some of those times.

"I am sorry," he stresses, his voice thick. He grabs the hand that had been tracing his palm and squeezes it tight. My other hand clasps on top of his automatically and squeezes back. Warm tears threaten to spill down my cheeks. It is almost unbearable how familiar a scene this has become: Ethan on a hospital bed, me worried by his side.

I sigh and look away, trying to compose myself. It's too early for tears. My chest aches at the realization that we still need to hear what Dr. Jackson has to say.

The anger remains, gnawing at my aching chest. But not anger at Ethan. I can't be mad at him. It's not his fault. I'm angry with his illness—this cancer—that threatens once again to steal my Ethan from me.

I can't stop it then; the tears silently stream down my face. I turn my head even farther away, so he won't see me crying. Thankfully, a nurse enters with a pitcher of water and a Styrofoam cup and takes his attention.

"Hi, there. I'm Sheryl, and I'll be your nurse this evening."

I try to stealthily wipe my cheeks dry. *Compose yourself, Abby. Ethan needs you to be strong.*

TO MY SURPRISE, Dr. Jackson comes to the hospital late that afternoon. He wants to see the new scans and how Ethan is doing. His concern is that Ethan has experienced such a painful and debilitating headache.

Ethan asks the doctor to bring me up to speed on the appointments I missed, and I listen carefully as I sit on the side of his bed, gripping his hand as if someone might come and take it from me. The doctor explains the symptoms that led to the tests and scans. He explains what the results show: at least one small tumor and another larger one have shown up in different parts of Ethan's brain. Today's scan shows a third very small tumor now present, and the large tumor is rapidly increasing in size.

Dr. Jackson recommends immediate surgery to remove the small tumors and as much of the large tumor as possible. Then he will use a Gamma Knife to dose what can't be removed of the large tumor directly with radiation. But what concerns him most is the appearance of the smaller tumors. It will be impossible to know if they get all of them, as there could be more too small for the scans to detect. So, after surgery the doctor recommends chemotherapy treatments. There are a few types of chemotherapy drugs that could work in this case. But we must be aggressive to try to stop such an aggressive cancer. He will schedule the surgery for first thing Monday morning.

Monday morning. My gaze drifts to Ethan's face. Dr. Jackson's voice fades out of my consciousness as I watch Ethan. His wavy hair is closer to the length it used to be. His blue eyes, once sparkling and alive with the fervor in which he lived his everyday life, are clouded with worry. No trace of that smile that can drive me into a frenzy—no reason to smile now. But there is something there in his face, something that gives me hope. There is a definite set of determination in his jawline, his mouth, the corners of his eyes.

He is ready to fight again.

"HEY, BABE," I greet Ethan as I enter his room. I wonder if he's as nervous as I am for today's surgery. "I brought you some flowers to brighten up the room a bit." I place the vase on the table at the foot of his bed, so he has a good view of them.

"Hey yourself." He gives me an unconvincing grin. I notice the lights are dim.

"You doing okay?" I place my hand gently at the back of his bald head and give him a kiss. Evidently, the nurses have already been in this morning to prep him for surgery. It makes me sad to see his head shaved again—the telltale sign of his compromised body.

"Better now. I had a doozy earlier this morning," he says with a thick tongue. "They have some pretty good drugs here. I went to La-La Land for a while." His goofy smile tells me he is still on his way back from La-La Land. "Down to a very dull roar again."

I don't know how he does it—suffers with a constant ache day after day. And then deals with an enormous amount of pain that I don't think I could ever fathom, attacking him out of the blue. He is stronger than I could ever hope to be. I bend over him and rest my head on his. "I wish I could take away all your pain," I murmur, smoothing his bare skin from his crown down to his cheek over and over. I remain there for a few minutes, concentrating hard, willing that with every stroke of my hand I am pulling the cancer further and further out of his brain.

"Hey," he says so suddenly it startles me. "I'm sorry about Ireland. I'm sorry I'm making you miss that."

Immediately, I'm angry with him. This is *not* his fault. He shouldn't feel guilty. I force my voice to come across upbeat. "Don't be silly, Ethan. We can go another time."

"But I know you were really looking forward to it."

"Stop it. I'll not have you feeling bad about the trip," I demand. "The reason I was looking forward to it so much was that we could be together, carefree and happy." I smile ruefully. "We still have the together part, and we'll have the carefree and happy part again soon. So don't worry about it."

Just then the door opens and a tiny, pixie-like nurse flutters in.

"Good morning!" she sings as she checks his vitals. "How are we doing today? I see they've gotten you all prepped for surgery. That's great."

She barely stops talking to let him answer her question. "Um, yeah. I'm doing fine—"

"That's great!" she sings again. I put my hand over my mouth to stifle a laugh. The way she dances around the room makes me wonder if she is even old enough to be a nurse. She acts more like a child on a playground. "Oh, those are some beautiful flowers!" She flits over and sniffs them. "Did you bring these?" she asks me sweetly.

I can only nod. I still have my fingers clamped over my lips. I quickly look away from her to Ethan so she can't see my eyes laughing. He glares at me.

"That's great!" She floats back up to grab the clipboard from the table by his head. She jots some things down on it. "Okay, mister, someone will be in to check on you in about half an hour, then we will get you right up to the surgical floor, okie dokie?"

"Yes. Thanks." Ethan smiles as she waves and trots out of the room. I smile too, but because I am thoroughly amused by what has just happened.

"What. Was. That?" I giggle. I can't keep it in any longer.

"Abby, quit," he reprimands. "She's really sweet. The nicest nurse I've had so far."

"Yeah, sure she's sweet! That's great!" I mimic the high sing-song tone of Pixie Nurse. But Ethan isn't laughing with me. "Okay. I'm sorry. You like her. For some reason."

"Because she's genuinely nice, Abby." He aims his glare at me again.

"Right. Sorry," I say sheepishly. I hadn't realized he'd formed friendships with the staff, but I guess it makes sense. He is stuck here in pain, and they are always in and out and taking care of him. I'm sure he feels better getting to know the people caring for him. I make note to be more sensitive to that.

"West and Kate come by yet?" I change the subject. "They said they would before they have to open the store."

"Yeah. They stopped in for a few minutes. I was still pretty loopy on the pain meds. West laughed at me a lot. Said I sounded hilarious or something like that." The corners of his mouth lift. "They didn't stay long but said they'd come back after Josh takes over. They want to sit with you during the surgery."

"Good. That's good." I feel immense relief at that. This has all happened so fast, and Uncle Geoff and Simon are still over in Italy on vacation, so it will be nice to have people here to keep me from going insane waiting alone.

And I realize in a very short period of time, he will have his head opened up on an operating table, his life in the hands of surgeons and robotic equipment. I grab his hand in both of mine. I feel the tears spilling over before I can stop them.

"Hey, come here." Ethan pulls me over to him. He wraps his free arm around me and kisses my hair, my cheek. I can't control it now. The fear that has been building up takes over, and sobs rack my body. "Come here, come here," he murmurs as he pulls me into the bed with him. I cling tightly to him, hoping that my embrace will be enough to keep him with me always.

"I don't want to lose you. I'm so afraid I'll lose you," I sob.

"Shh . . . shh." He strokes my hair and kisses my forehead. "You're not going to lose me. I'm not going anywhere."

I want to believe him. So desperately, I want to. I kiss him hard, letting all my anger and my fear control my mouth. If I can show him that I love him more than anyone has ever loved, he can't leave me. I will give him the power to fight and to win. I will give him all of my passion, and he will take it and it will make him stronger—invincible. And we will overcome.

Ethan matches my fervor in his returning kisses, and I know that it is working. He grabs the hem of my shirt and pulls it up over my head. "Ow! Ah!"

"Oh! What? What is it?" I ask breathlessly.

"Damn IV. I've got to be careful," he chuckles. I smile and kiss him again. "We've got about twenty minutes before the next check in," he whispers conspiratorially.

"Perfect," I murmur, working the string of his hospital gown. Fear and anger have been replaced by love. Pure and honest love. For one brief moment, we can forget all about the cancer, the surgery, and the uncertainty ahead.

"HERE. TAKE THIS." Kate hands me another coffee.

"Thanks," I mumble. My mind is preoccupied. The first couple hours of surgery passed quickly. The memories of our taboo tryst in his room kept my worries subdued. But now, time is dragging, the clock on the wall slowing to a crawl. "It's been four hours, right?"

Kate nods before she takes a sip of her coffee.

"I thought they were supposed to be done by now. Shouldn't they be done by now?"

"I'm sure they want to be very thorough, Abby. Don't worry. Remember, if they find more tumors than they saw in the scans, they will remove them as well. There could be some in there they couldn't see until they have him opened up," she reasons.

"Don't say that, please. Puts an awful image in my head." I shudder.

"Sorry. Why don't you go curl up with West over there and rest your eyes? I'll wake you if there's any news." I follow Kate's gaze across the family waiting room to where he is sprawled out over three chairs. It's only two o'clock, but he managed to crash out almost an hour ago. I guess waiting is not his thing. But honestly, it would be nice to be able to sleep away these worrisome hours.

"I'd probably have nightmares, Kate. Then you'd have to explain to the staff why there's a screaming woman in here."

She rubs my back. I lean my head on her shoulder and attempt to focus on something, anything that will release me from this prison of apprehension. I stare down at my coffee. My stomach is in such knots, I don't think I can handle coffee right now. I lean over, set it on the table next to me, curl my knees up to my chin, and cover my face with my hands. I have to remove myself from here.

I force my mind to the place we should have been in two days' time. I picture lush green rolling hills among rocky crags. A towering ancient castle standing proudly over the land. I picture myself at the top of that castle, overlooking the greenery and the deep blue ocean crashing in the distance. So beautiful, majestic. The salty air fills my lungs with each breath. A melodic Celtic song rises all around, filling the space. I look to my left to find Ethan smiling at me. That brilliant, overpowering grin that takes my breath away as he drops down on one knee and holds his hand out to me. I step forward to take his hand, mesmerized by his dancing blue eyes. He reaches into his jacket and pulls out a tiny velvet box. I inhale sharply—this is it! He holds the box out to me and starts to pull up the lid—

"Miss Templeton?"

I start at the sound of Dr. Jackson's voice. I jump up out of the chair. "Yes—" my voice cracks. I glance over to see West awake and Kate sitting next to him. "Yes?" I repeat.

"We have Ethan in recovery now. We were able to remove most of the largest tumor, and the Gamma Knife allowed us to direct radiation on the remaining tumor cells. I believe we were successful with that one. Now, remember there were two smaller tumors we had seen on previous scans. We were able to remove those as well. We used MRI technology during surgery to scan for any other small tumors that we may not have picked up on before. We found one in a difficult spot, so we used the Gamma Knife on that one as well."

"Okay. Okay. So, did you get it all then?" I feel pretty good about it so far. I mean, it sounds like good news.

"I believe we handled all the tumors that we saw. But this cancer is a difficult one. Tumors are springing up rather quickly, so I feel our best bet going forward is to do a course of chemotherapy, as we talked about. It will need to be a strong course to combat this strain. And we will continue to monitor for the occurrence of more growths. We aren't out of the woods yet, but we are on the right path."

I let out a long breath. "Well, thank you, Dr. Jackson. How long until I can see him?"

"It won't be long now. Someone will come get you when he's awake." He pauses, then squeezes my arm. "He did well today."

I nod. It is all I can do. As he leaves, I crumple back onto the chair. I am so weak, my head spinning. *This is good news,* I tell myself. I should be relieved. I should be happy. He made it through the surgery. I feel Kate's arms wrap around me. She's saying something, but it doesn't penetrate the fog that surrounds me.

We aren't out of the woods yet.

Those words echo around in my mind. Over and over. Again and again.

Chapter Twenty-One

I Don't Want to Be in the Woods Anymore

DR. JACKSON HAD understated the part about us not being out of the woods yet. Plain and simple. He should have said we were so deep into the heart of the forest it would take a miracle and a search party to get us out.

Ethan had to wait about a week after the surgery before they felt his body was strong enough to start the chemo treatments. We found out quickly why Dr. Jackson suggested he remain at Sloan-Kettering and move into the treatment ward. They hit him hard with chemo. Treatment almost every day. And it was strong. I was frightened to death the first week; he was sicker than I had ever seen him before, and each day was worse than the previous. Each day his body grew weaker. He couldn't keep down any food (what little he felt like eating).

I feel so helpless. The only thing I can do is be his cheerleader. I told West right away that I'm not going to be able to work until Ethan is back safely at home. There is no way I'm leaving his side now. He understood and quickly hired someone to fill my spot.

I try to keep Ethan stocked with books and newspapers, any distraction as he sits through the IV treatments. I bake him cookies, which I promptly regret after he vomits them up.

At least he's able to wear normal clothes in the treatment ward, bypassing the terrible hospital gowns that scream "I am deathly sick." Every week, I pack a bag of his clothes and my clothes. Every night, I stay in his room on a chair that reclines into a sort of bed. I bring in a few things from home to make his room feel less sterile—a picture of us, the afghan from the couch, his father's bookends to keep his growing collection of books upright on the table in the corner. I go to Food for Thought every other day it seems to get him another book. Sometimes I grab two to lengthen the time between trips. But honestly, it's nice to have a chance to check in with Kate and West and let them know how Ethan is doing. They still try to come by at least twice a week. Uncle Geoff and Simon visit at least twice a week as well. They canceled their upcoming trip to Mumbai to be here for us. Ethan insisted they not do that, but I'm glad they did. It is a nice break from the mundane to have them visit for a couple hours, full of new stories from their trip to Italy. And any chance to get our minds off Ethan's chemo is definitely welcome.

But after five weeks of treatment, it's hard for Ethan to get excited about the visitors. He's exhausted from enduring the chemo. I'm exhausted from worrying. He's lost a lot of weight. I've lost about ten pounds myself. Hospital food is unappealing, and I really don't feel like eating much. Nausea plagues me on some days, and my stomach starts feeling weird, so I try to make a point of eating at least a salad. I bring in a few boxes of granola bars for snacking when I feel the need. Knowing all Ethan is going through, I'm ashamed to admit I'm tired and irritable more often. When Sunday comes around and I have to make my weekly trip home for clean clothes, I tell him I'll be gone a bit longer than my normal couple of hours. Besides washing a load of clothes and getting us caught up on the mail, I want to lie down for a bit in my own bed.

"You okay, babe?" he asks, concerned.

"Yeah. I'm just really tired today. I think a nap will do me worlds of good." I kiss him on the cheek.

"Uncle Geoff and Simon will be disappointed if you're not here when they visit later."

"Give them my love if I'm not back in time." I grab the duffel bag and lug it onto my tired shoulder. "I'll see you in a bit."

"I miss you already." He weakly waves. I can tell he needs a nap, too.

Outside in the sweltering heat of the day, I hail a cab to take me home. It's too hot, and I'm too tired to walk to the subway. I think I even doze for a minute on the ride home. I jerk up when the cab driver blares his horn and yells obscenities at another driver.

Finally in the apartment, I drop the bag in the entryway and throw the keys on the side table. I toss the latest batch of mail onto the stack that has accumulated over the past couple weeks. I really need to get to those . . . later.

I trudge to our bedroom and kick off my shoes. I flop face down on the bed, not even bothering to climb under the covers, then curl up with Ethan's pillow in my arms so I can smell his musky scent. I drift off to sleep.

I wake up sometime later, refreshed but quickly overcome with nausea. My stomach starts cramping. I haven't eaten since the two granola bars I had earlier. I push myself up off the bed and race to the bathroom, where I promptly get sick.

Immediately, I panic. If I'm sick, I can't see Ethan; I can't risk passing it to him. I feel even worse when I realize I may have already infected him!

Hurriedly, I brush my teeth and go out to grab my phone. I need to see if he's okay. I fumble through my purse, afraid for a moment that I've forgotten my cell at the hospital. I heave a heavy sigh of relief when my fingers finally touch it. Dialing the room number, the fingers of my free hand nervously drum on the side table. In case he's sleeping, the room phone will keep ringing until he picks it up.

"Hello?" a weak voice greets me.

"Ethan? How are you doing?" I question. Then I must sit down, as the nausea sweeps over me again. I slide down the wall and pull my knees up to my chest.

"I'm okay. What's the matter? Are *you* okay?"

"No. I don't think so," I sigh. "I just got sick." My voice gets thick with emotion. It kills me that I can't go back and see him tonight.

"Oh no, Abby." The worry in his voice travels across the line.

"But it's no big deal." I don't want him worrying one second about me. He needs to focus on his own health, not mine. "I'll be fine." Or so I think. My stomach is doing flip-flops. "Um, I was hoping I hadn't gotten you sick, too. You haven't been sick, have you?"

"Is that a joke?" he chuckles.

"Haha," I deadpan. "I mean it. I would feel awful if I got you sick on top of everything else."

"I'm no sicker than I was when you left—how's that?"

"That's good, I guess." He must be doing okay if he can joke with me. "Uncle Geoff and Simon still there?"

"Nope. They left a little while ago. They send their love."

I suddenly want to lie down. I'm afraid I'll have to cut the call short. I sprawl out on my side and place my cheek on the cold tile of the entry to the kitchen. "Ethan?"

"Yeah, babe?"

"This means I can't come back to stay with you." My eyes sting with unshed tears.

"I know it does. You can come anyway. I won't tell anybody you're sick."

"Yeah? Well, if Pixie Nurse finds out I infected you with my sickness, I'm sure you'll see a whole different side of her." I try to joke but it comes out flat, weak.

"Probably so." He sounds tired.

"Okay, so I'd better go lie down. I'll call you later."

"You get better."

"Call me if you need anything, okay?"

"I'll be fine. I've got people, you know."

Still joking.

"I know. Love you, Ethan."

"I love you more."

Reluctantly, I press the END button on my phone. The cool tile has made me feel a bit better. I slowly get up and start for the couch but change my mind and decide I'll be better off in my own bed, right next to the bathroom. I curl up under the covers and wait for the worst—chills, headache, more stomach cramps. But they don't come. After a while, I realize the only thing still plaguing me is the nausea. Then my stomach starts growling.

Maybe I should try to eat something, some toast or soup. I make my way to the kitchen and search the cupboards—not very well stocked over the past few weeks. Finally, I find a microwave can of chicken noodle soup.

The soup soothes my nausea. But I don't get too excited. I figure it will come up again soon enough.

I trudge back to bed.

THE FLOOR OF this bathroom is something I've become altogether too familiar with over the past few days. I sit with my back against the vanity drawers, impatiently trying to wait the right number of minutes. How do people do this? It's excruciating. I stare at the gray panel until my eyes blur, waiting for the result.

After three days of being sick off and on, I began to wonder. This wasn't any illness I'd ever had before. No fever, no chills, no body aches. And I only felt sick part of the time; the rest of the time I felt okay.

Then it dawned on me that I was late by over three weeks. I don't know why I hadn't noticed before . . . probably because I've been so worried about Ethan. His health consumes my thoughts. With everything going on, I never made it to the pharmacy to pick up my refill. But maybe I'm just late because I haven't been eating well and my body is starting to freak out. My mind wanders to the last time Ethan and I made love, the morning of his surgery. That was . . . over six weeks ago.

Finally, *finally* I start to see it emerge—a plus sign. I look at the box then at the panel again. No mistaking it—plus means positive.

A million thoughts race through my mind. Surprise. Fear. Joy. Confusion. Amazement. Disbelief. I reread the instructions that came with the test. Ninety-nine percent accurate. I blink, letting this all sink in, wondering . . . now what? Do I tell Ethan? There is still a tiny chance the test is wrong.

Ethan. My eyes well with tears. What will he think? What will he say? I know what he'll say—he'll be ecstatic. It's what he's always wanted. A child, a family. Pain rips through my chest, doubling me over. How unfair is this? He could have a child, but at the rate he's going, he will probably never get to meet this child! Sobs rack my body at the heartbreaking reality. The odds are stacked against us.

And how can I raise a child on my own? I can't. There is no way. I need Ethan now more than ever. I need his strength. His strength gets me through everything.

But it dawns on me as I hold my breath and wipe at my cheeks that maybe this is it—he has been strong, even through this. He is a fighter. Not once giving up on the idea that he can beat this cancer. He is fighting for himself; he is fighting for me. And now he has an even greater reason to fight. Hope begins to swell, calming me. This baby may be just the thing Ethan needs to crush this cancer and come home to us.

"TABITHA, CAN YOU help me out?" I quietly ask Pixie Nurse at the nurses' station the following morning.

"Sure! What do you need? It's so good to see you, by the way. Ethan's so mopey without you." She is way too energetic for first thing in the morning.

I am dying to see him, but I have to be absolutely one-hundred-percent certain this isn't an illness that I'm experiencing. I can't risk exposing him in his compromised state.

"Is there a way I can get some tests done to see if I have the flu or an infection or something? I need to get back in there to see Ethan." I know I can don a gown and face mask and cap and gloves and all the ridiculous gear to try to keep the germs under wraps, but I don't want to take even the slightest risk that he could get infected. The way our luck has been going . . .

"Yes, actually. I can get Dr. Jackson to write up some lab orders. They can screen for the common illnesses going around now."

"That would be awesome," I say, relieved. Then I toss it out there: "And can he add a pregnancy test?"

"Are you serious?" she almost screeches. I glance around quickly as I shush her. Luckily, there is almost no one around this early but staff. "Oooh! That's great! How wonderful for you and Ethan!" she sings in a softer voice as her tiny body bounces up and down like a child. I want to reach over and clamp my hand over her mouth and hold her still. Instead, I squeeze my hands together and will her with my mind and my stare to *calm down*.

"But he doesn't know any of this yet, Tabitha. I only took a home test last night, so I'm not certain. I don't want to say anything until I'm a hundred percent sure."

"Oh, definitely." She nods solemnly. "I won't say a word. And I'll put a rush on those orders."

"Thank you. So much." Admittedly, I can see why Ethan likes her the more I get to know her. She is genuinely nice. And super-energetic, which is a bit irritating to me, but I suppose it is inspiring for the chronically ill to see someone so jovial.

I grab some breakfast while waiting on the lab orders. I've figured out that if I eat something as soon as the nausea starts, I can keep it at bay. However, that is no guarantee I won't toss my cookies later. But at least I feel better for a while longer.

Tabitha has the lab orders waiting for me when I return to the nurses' station. We exchange conspiratorial smiles as I grab them. I head for the lab and nervous flutters overtake my stomach. This is it—the true test.

I must say, I am not prepared for the sight of deep red blood flowing from my arm into tube after tube after tube. I have to look away, so I don't get sick right then and there. I can't remember the last time I've had blood drawn, and the phlebotomist seems to be taking an unnecessarily large amount.

"How long for the results?" I choke out when he wraps a pink bandage with smiley face pattern around my arm.

"There's a rush on it, so about an hour. You can take off the bandage in twenty minutes."

"Okay. Thanks."

An agonizing hour. I slowly walk back to Ethan's wing of the hospital. The nervous flutters haven't left me yet, but I feel less dizzy from the shock of seeing my own blood traveling in such a large quantity from my body. What to do for an hour besides go insane wondering if the home test was right, wondering what I'll say to Ethan, wondering . . . *what if it's negative?*

As I near the familiar family waiting room, I decide to hang out in there for the term. At least there's a TV to distract me. I have to walk past his room to get there, though. The urge is so strong to forego the waiting area and go in to see him that I slow my pace when I am almost at his room. A brief second won't do any harm, right? I stop at his door, and my hand grips the handle. I sigh, warring with myself. It takes all my restraint not to open the door. I shouldn't do it—not until I have the results and know for sure that I'm not contagious with anything.

I uncurl my fingers from the handle and stand there for one more long moment before I reluctantly head over to the waiting room.

It's empty, so I find the TV remote and settle in. I watch a little *Good Morning America* to distract me. The top story seems to be the latest trouble in paradise for Brangelina. Will they split, or will they not?

It couldn't have been an hour when Pixie Nurse comes dancing into the waiting room. "Abby, I've got your results!" she sings.

My heart jumps to my throat, and the nervous flutters go crazy in my stomach.

"Looks like negative on all tests that were run."

Oh. My heart sinks to the floor, disappointment heavy.

"Except—"

And it jumps back up again—she is smiling.

Chapter Twenty-Two

You Are the Best Thing

"THE PREGNANCY TEST. You and Ethan are going to have a baby! Congratulations!" Tabitha starts bouncing up and down like she had earlier this morning. I leap from my chair and find myself bouncing up and down, too. And then I hug her because I am so ecstatic.

After a few joyous moments, bewilderment sinks in. "So now what? What do I do?" I feel utterly clueless. "Do I have to go to a doctor or something?"

"Yes, you do. Here's the name of my OB/GYN. He delivered all three of my children. He's excellent. You should make an appointment soon and take your lab results with you. That way they won't need to order more. And I'll get Dr. Jackson to send a script to the pharmacy here for prenatal vitamins. You need to take those every day for the baby."

I stare at her for a beat. She has three kids? She sure doesn't seem old enough to have three kids. A new respect for her blossoms, knowing she is a mother.

"Thank you, Tabitha. So much." I can't help myself; I hug her again.

"Now go tell him!" She pushes me toward the door.

"I'm going to go in there, plant a big kiss on his lips, and tell him he's going to be a daddy!" I giggle.

"I'll be at the nurses' station if you need anything," she sings as she leaves me.

I exit the waiting room with a renewed purpose. It has been *too* long since I've seen his smiling face and held his hand. And the news I have will make him unbelievably happy—I can't wait!

I practically skip to his room but stop short when I notice the door is ajar. Maybe the doctor is in there and I should wait. There's a gap of a few inches so I can hear the voices trailing out. Ethan is talking . . . and West. I should definitely wait then. I want to tell Ethan alone. It will be our special moment.

As I turn back toward the waiting room, I hear something that glues my feet to the floor.

"I'm trusting you to handle this, West. I'm counting on you."

Handle what?

"You've got all the paperwork in order?" Ethan questions.

"Everything's in order. I've checked twice to be sure." West sounds odd, so serious. What could they be talking about? The store?

"And you'll have to explain everything. It's up to you."

"I'll do it, no worries," West assures him. "I just—I think it should come from you, man, you know?"

"There's too much going on now. I don't want to add this to her plate yet. It's nothing that can't wait until after I . . ."

"Until after you get better, man," West insists. "You're gonna get better. And then you'll be the one discussing it. It really should come from you anyway."

"Miss Templeton, good morning."

I nearly jump out of my skin at the sound of Dr. Jackson's deep voice. I whip around to greet him, blushing from being caught eavesdropping.

"Ah, good morning, Doctor," I stammer. "How are you this morning?"

"I'm well, thank you. I trust Tabitha spoke with you?"

I flush again, embarrassed for some reason to be talking with the doctor about the pregnancy test. Speaking in a hushed tone, I respond, "Yes, she did. And thank you, sir, for your help this morning. I really appreciate it. I was so afraid I had something contagious that would keep me from seeing Ethan, and I miss him so much already. I had to know."

I am babbling. I'm sure the doctor has better things to do than listen to me ramble. I make a conscious effort to shut my mouth.

"Yes, well . . ." He squeezes my arm kindly, then motions to Ethan's door. "Have you been in to see him?"

"No, I was just headed in." Butterflies dance in my stomach as I think about walking through that door and telling Ethan he's going to be a dad.

"Well, then, I shall make my visit with him brief, and he will be all yours," Dr. Jackson says a bit too loudly for my liking—what if they hear us out here and think I was hovering outside listening? Well, I was, but still—I don't want them thinking that. He pushes the door open wide and I follow him, sheepishly, trying to gauge the atmosphere in the room.

West is chattering on about baseball or something. Ethan appears to be listening intently. He turns his attention to Dr. Jackson, but his eyes quickly shift to me as I step out from behind the doctor.

"Abigail!" he cries, beaming. He looks so happy to see me, my emotions grab hold. Tears well in my eyes, and I have to bite my lip to keep myself in check. I am so overjoyed to see him after days away it's hard to maintain control.

I kiss his mouth and squeeze him tightly, burying my face in his neck to give me an extra minute to calm myself. He locks me in a bear hug and murmurs, "I've missed you so much, baby."

So much for not crying. When he finally releases me, I have to swipe away the tears that escaped down my cheeks. I laugh them away as I squeeze his hand. "I missed you, too."

"Good morning, Ethan." Dr. Jackson clears his throat to remind us we aren't the only two in the room. "I'm just going to do a quick exam, take a look at your chart, and then I'll be out of your hair."

I reluctantly let go of his hand and get out of the way of the good doctor, stepping over to West, who has picked up one of Ethan's books and started thumbing through it. I wonder if I should say something about what I heard. I mean, it sounded important—was it something I should know about?

"So, you're feeling better, huh?" West asks before I can formulate my plan of attack.

"Um, yes, definitely." I can't hide my smile. I am more than feeling better.

"Good. Nothing contagious, I hope," he teases taking a step back.

"No, West, nothing contagious." I don't know why I can't stop smiling. Maybe it's that whole I-know-something-you-don't feeling. "So, thanks again for bringing the bag of clothes to him for me. I'm sure he appreciates not having to wear the same clothes all week."

"Not a problem."

For once I feel truly awkward around West. I really want to ask him about the conversation. Dr. Jackson is asking Ethan some questions, so he won't be listening . . . if I could just bring myself to ask. West is thumbing through the book again. He glances up at me. Does he suspect I overheard them? I suck in a deep breath. Nothing to be afraid of, right? Just ask.

"Um—"

"Okay then, Ethan, I'll stop in again later after your treatment," Dr. Jackson says loudly, cutting me off. He nods goodbye to us before striding out of the room.

"Hey, man, I'd better get going," West offers, probably sensing I was about to ask him something he wouldn't want to answer. It can wait. Now, I'm excited to get Ethan alone. I am bursting to tell him our news!

"So, I'll call you later, okay?" West says to Ethan as he walks toward the door.

"Yeah. Thanks, West," his voice holds mountains of meaning. West nods his understanding.

I gaze at Ethan, slightly lightheaded for a moment. Is it nausea or excitement? I am thrilled to be able to see him again, that's for sure.

"I missed you so much, baby!" I squeak, hurrying over to kiss him again.

"Mmm. I missed you, too. It's so dull around here without you."

I lower myself to the edge of his bed and push back his stocking cap a bit so I can kiss his smooth forehead. I place my forehead against his, trying to calm my nerves so I can tell him the news.

"So, what's new? No West Nile virus, huh?"

"No," I say with a smile. "No West Nile."

"So, you're all better?"

"For the most part, yes." Aside from the bouts of nausea and vomiting.

"What does that mean?" He pushes up on my shoulders so he can see my face, a quizzical look in his eyes.

I sit upright and squeeze his hand in both of mine. I look down, almost embarrassed at this ridiculous smile plastered across my face. Here goes nothing. I take a deep breath and fix my gaze on his beautiful blue eyes. I hope the baby has his eyes.

"Ethan, I have not been feeling well . . ."

Just say it.

"Because . . . I'm pregnant."

He stares at me for a long minute, eyes wide, mouth agape. "What? Are you kidding me?"

"I am not kidding. You're going to be a father."

His eyebrows shoot up, then his brow furrows. I can see it registering in his mind. "Are you sure?" he whispers, doubt etched across his face.

"Yes. I peed on two sticks at home last night, and I had lab work done this morning to confirm." It's hard reading his reaction . . . is he happy? Or not?

"Abby, this is . . ." He glances down at my stomach. "Amazing!" He lets out a hooting laugh and pulls me into a bone-crushing embrace.

I giggle at his reaction. Happiness explodes inside of me when I see how happy he is.

"I don't believe this!" He laughs again, releasing me. "How? When?"

"Um, well . . ." I shrug. "I forgot to pick up my pills at the pharmacy with all our trip planning and everything." I dab the wetness from my eyes with my fingers. "And it only takes once, you know."

"Once . . ." He smiles coyly. He knows when. I grin in return, pressing my fingers to my mouth, remembering how we made love stealthily in his hospital bed before his surgery. How we never got caught still amazes me.

"I just can't believe it," he says incredulously as he reaches out to stroke my belly. When he looks up, his eyes are misty, red-rimmed with emotion. He leans forward and rests his other hand on the back of my neck. "I love you," he murmurs as he kisses me, deeply and passionately. He hasn't kissed me like that in a while. My breathing stops as I surrender to his kiss. My pulse quickens and I reach up, caressing his face. In this sweet, sweet moment, we are lost in one another. Gone are the sounds of the hospital. Gone are the worries about his health. It's just me and him. And this new little life we've created.

His lips finally release mine, his chest heaving as he tries to catch his breath. I immediately feel guilty. This has probably been more exertion than he's had in weeks. He gently kisses me twice more, then presses his forehead to mine. My pulse gradually slows, as does my own breathing. The sounds of the hospital slowly creep into my consciousness. The nurses talking in the hall, the paging system calling a doctor to radiology, the beeping of an alarm at the nurses' station. The reality of our situation nags at the back of my mind.

"This is a good thing, right?" I whisper, my throat tight. The fears that seized my mind last night push to the forefront again. What if Ethan doesn't survive to see his child born?

I shake my head to expel those heartbreaking thoughts. I can't allow myself to think that way!

"Hey." He tips up my chin, so my gaze meets his. "Hey. Of course it's a good thing. An amazingly wonderful thing. We're going to have a baby!" He exudes confidence and joy—so much joy—in that statement. I have to believe he is right. I smile in wonder at how he can always have such a positive outlook.

He pulls me into his arms, holds me like he's never letting go. My courage grows, and my attitude shifts. There is no way he's going to miss out on this. I let my mind wander to the day our child is born, Ethan holding my hand and coaching me through it all. A look of pure pride and joy in his eyes when the doctor places the baby in his arms for the first time. Then, as the years go on, I see him pushing our little boy in a swing, playing with tractors in the yard, and teaching him to ride a bike. Playing catch, tossing a football to the young man who looks just like him, blue eyes and all. I smile at the visions.

But what if it's a girl? I don't have time to envision that little life as we are interrupted from our quiet moment.

"Good morning, Ethan! I have your meds here." Tabitha's familiar peppy voice draws me from my reverie. I sit up straight on the edge of the bed as he shifts up against the headboard. His face is positively glowing. He looks healthier than he has in weeks.

"Did you hear the good news, Tabitha?" Ethan's eyes dance as a goofy grin spreads across his face.

She steals a quick glance at me and winks. "What news would that be, sir?"

"I'm gonna be a daddy!"

"No!" she gasps. She is a good little actress. "You are?"

"Yes, ma'am." He can't stop grinning. I am thoroughly enjoying his excitement.

"That's wonderful! Congratulations you two!" she gushes. "I'm so happy for you." She reaches over and pats his hand while she holds out a small white paper cup with several pills in it. "Now take these, and I'll let you get back to celebrating." She winks at me again. "Drink." She hands him a Styrofoam cup of water after he obediently takes his pills. He swallows back the water and hands her the empty cup. "Thank you, sir." She collects her tray and heads for the door. "I'll be around for your lunch order in a bit."

Ethan turns to me, still grinning. "Did you tell Kate?"

"Not yet. I thought I'd run to the store this afternoon and fill her in. I'm sure you need another book or two by now, hmm?"

"Yes, please. How about a parenting book this time? *What to Expect When You're Expecting* or something like that?" he teases.

"I'm sure I can find something good for you."

"How about your mom?"

"What?" I am caught off guard with that question.

"Your mother. When are you going to tell her?"

Is he goading me on purpose? The last person I want to talk to right now is my mother. I am pretty sure she hates babies and children anyway. I've hardly talked to her since . . . well, the last time I can recall talking to her was right after Ethan's surgery. I had called to let her know he'd gotten through it, but he still needed weeks of treatment. She had been all doom and gloom, saying how odds were against him if they thought he needed more treatments after the surgery. She complained about the doctors, whom she didn't even know, and questioned their credentials. But oddly, she'd offered to come and stay with me for a couple weeks since she had some time before the school year started. I had practically yelled "No!" at her after fifteen minutes of listening to her ignorant babble. There is no way I want her around Ethan with her constant negativity.

"Um . . . yeah, I'll call her. Sometime," I say vaguely.

"You know she'll be mad if you wait too long."

"Yeah, I know." I roll my eyes.

I start to feel the familiar nausea creeping up on me. I need something to eat. I glance at the clock on the wall. My hand moves involuntarily to my miniscule baby bump. "Hey, I need to eat something. Do you want me to bring you anything from the cafeteria?"

"You okay?" he asks, concern sweeping across his face.

I nod. "Just morning sickness, I guess. Only it's not just in the morning." I frown. "It helps if I eat as soon as I feel a little nauseous."

"My poor girl." He reaches out for my hand.

"I'll be fine," I quickly reassure him. My cheeks flush as I suddenly feel very guilty. I'm sure my nausea is nothing compared to the sickness he faces after every treatment.

I lean over to plant a chaste kiss on his lips. He grabs my face and holds me there a moment before releasing me. I smile. "I'll be back shortly. Do you want anything?"

"Just you."

My cheeks flush again, this time because of the intensity in his gaze.

"I'm going to call Uncle Geoff and tell him the news," he continues. "Simon's going to freak. He absolutely loves babies. For years, he kept trying to talk Uncle Geoff into adopting with him," Ethan laughs. I can definitely picture Simon doting over a baby.

Thoughts of Ethan, Uncle Geoff, and Simon passing around our little baby carry me all the way to the cafeteria.

"HEY, GIRL!" KATE calls as soon as she sees me.

I walk into a huge hug. "Oh, Kate, I've missed you."

"Back at ya, honey." She releases me and holds me at arm's length. "West says you're better."

"Better is an understatement," I say, barely containing my excitement to share the news. We walk behind the counter and sit on our usual stools.

"You are absolutely giddy, Abby. Look at you!" She eyes me. "Where is this glow coming from?"

"Kate—" I hold my breath for a second, pausing for dramatic effect. "I'm pregnant!"

"*You're what*? You're *pregnant*?"

I nod emphatically.

"Oh, Abby, that's wonderful!" She pulls me into another hug, swaying us from side to side. "What a miracle!"

I hadn't thought of it that way before. Yes, it *is* a miracle. In this turbulent, scary time, we have something so terrific, so amazing—a brand new life—that's come along and lifted us to new heights. A beacon of shining light in the darkness. This miracle will tie Ethan and me together for the rest of our lives. We have created our family.

"What's all the commotion over here?" West demands. "You're scaring the customers."

Kate releases me and waves her hand dismissively. "Calm down, hon. Abby has some fantastic news."

He turns to me with an eyebrow raised. "Oh? Do tell, Miss Abigail."

I swat at him playfully. "What are you, the *National Enquirer*? It's not as juicy as you make it out to be."

"It is, too, Abby. Tell him," Kate insists.

"Well, West, we found out that we are going to have a baby."

"A baby? Are you kidding me? What do you want a baby for?"

"Westley!" Kate swats him this time, landing a hard blow to his upper arm.

"Ow! What was that for?"

"You're an idiot, that's what it's for," she replies sardonically, shaking her head.

I giggle, though I never expected him to have the same reaction as the rest of us. He rarely ever has an "expected" reaction to anything. That is just West.

"Well, don't come to me for babysitting services, that's all I've got to say," he mumbles as he stalks away.

"What a goober." Kate rolls her eyes. "I swear. He's not normal."

"No one could ever accuse West of being normal."

"Yeah, tell me about it. Sometimes I wonder why I'm even attracted to that man," she muses in bewilderment. "Well, I am extremely happy for you. And you can ask me to babysit anytime!"

I COLLAPSE, EXHAUSTED, into the recliner in the corner of Ethan's hospital room. I had a great conversation with Kate. I hadn't realized how much I missed talking with her. I found a couple parenting books for Ethan. I called Emory to let her know about the baby, a conversation that stretched over an hour before we realized the time. I picked up my vitamins from the pharmacy. I called Tabitha's obstetrician to set up an appointment to meet the doctor. Since I had lab work done and prenatal vitamins already, they scheduled me for about four weeks out. They encouraged me to call if I have any questions or concerns in the meantime.

Ethan isn't back from his chemotherapy session yet and will probably be another half an hour or so. I yawn. I could sneak in a quick nap before his return. I let my eyelids surrender to the heaviness and drift off, thoughts of him holding our baby in his arms relaxing me.

I wake sometime later with a start. My neck aches from the angle I slept in the chair. I scan the room as I stretch my neck, remembering I'm at the hospital. My gaze finds Ethan lounging in the bed, smiling at me.

"Have a good rest?"

"I did," I say stretching my arms up and arching my spine. That feels so good. "How long have you been back?"

"About an hour or so. I was enjoying my reading while you were sleeping." He holds up one of the books I bought him, *A Father's Guide*.

I grin. "You could have woken me."

"It's all good. This is some interesting stuff here."

I push up out of the chair and go to see for myself. He scoots over in the bed so I can climb in next to him.

"There are charts for everything in here, like the size of the baby at each week during pregnancy." He flips to the front of the book. "Do you know how many weeks?"

I blush, remembering our tryst again. "I think we want to look at week seven."

"Oh, yes," he murmurs, his blue eyes alight. "So, seven weeks." He runs his finger across the page until it rests on the illustration of a pregnancy at seven weeks. I gasp, shocked at how different it looks from a baby.

"Wow. That's interesting, huh?" Ethan jokes. "It says, 'The tiny embryo has sprouted arms and legs with weblike hand and feet stubs and is starting to form joints. The brain goes through a growth spurt this week. The embryo has a large forehead, and eyes and ears continue to develop. Your baby is about the size of a raspberry or grape.' Aww..."

I stare at the picture. *That's* what's inside me? I scan quickly across the page from weeks eight through twelve. It doesn't take long for it to start looking more like a baby. I look back at the week seven picture.

"Look how tiny it is right now," I say in awe as I point to the tiny speck in the womb of the female body. "That little thing is causing me all this trouble," I say, almost admiringly.

"Amazing, huh?"

I nod, unable to say anything as a rather large lump has formed in my throat. I suppose being on an emotional roller coaster is a part of the deal too for the next however many months.

We spend the better part of an hour looking at each week's development in turn and reading about what the baby can do or feel. There are forty weeks—*forty*! That's a long time to have to wait to meet our tiny little guy or girl.

A knock at the door draws our attention away from the book.

"Are you ready for dinner?" Tabitha asks. For some reason, she looks extremely excited about bringing Ethan his dinner.

"Yes, yes," he says, clearing his throat. And he suddenly seems nervous. He abruptly shuts the book and looks at me for a long moment. "I have a surprise for you." His eyes are gleaming, a sight I haven't seen in a while. My pulse quickens in response, but fear surges as well.

"A surprise?" I ask nervously. His surprises have historically tragic results.

"A celebration dinner."

"Oh. Okay." That shouldn't be too terrible.

"Let's go." He stands slowly, and I can tell he's tired from his chemo.

"Are you sure? We can just eat here, Ethan, if you don't feel well."

"I'm good." His face is set with resolve. "Let's go." He reaches down into the duffel bag and pulls something out, slipping it into his pocket.

I walk around the bed to him, where he takes my hand and leads me out into the hallway. I want to ask him where we're going, but I'm sure that's part of the surprise. I mentally steel myself to prepare for the uncertainty of what the surprise could be. I can't freak out on him like I have in the past. I must be gracious and grateful and mature about it—whatever it is. I mean, it's probably just dinner. Maybe some nice music, maybe a nice table setting. No big deal.

But this is Ethan we're talking about here, I remind myself.

We head down the hallway to a conference room I've walked past many times. I can see through the row of windows that it is dark, but a soft glow radiates.

He opens the door and enters first, stepping to the side to allow me to pass. Then he closes the door securely behind us. As my eyes adjust to the darkness, I see candles on the large oval table, flowers, and two place settings. Beyond that, on the other side of the room, I hear something before I can fully see it. Muffled giggling and whispering. I realize we are not alone, and I squint at the dark mass of people. They are holding . . . glow sticks? Glow sticks held in a formation that reads—

"Will you?" I ask, bewildered. I look at Ethan for some sort of clue.

He reaches into his pocket as he kneels. And suddenly, time slows, suspends. Is this what's happening? I look over to the glowing "WILL U" and back to him. He opens a dark box and holds it up to me. My heart is racing, making me very lightheaded. I stare, wide-eyed, as he reaches out and takes my hand in his. My eyes have adjusted to the dimness; there is no mistaking what's in that box.

Ethan gently, rhythmically rubs his thumb across my knuckles. My right hand flies to my chest to try to keep my heart from pounding out of it.

"Abigail Templeton," he begins, "you are the best thing that has ever happened to me. You were a breath of fresh air the day I met you, and you've been that sustaining breath ever since. A light in my life. And now you've given me such a precious gift." His voice breaks and he swallows, pauses, looks down to regain his composure. I feel tears pooling in my eyes watching this amazing, beautiful man kneeling before me.

"I had hoped to be proposing to you weeks ago, high atop an Irish castle overlooking beautiful cliffs and ocean. But it didn't work out that way . . . and now, I have candles and glow sticks for you." He smiles his radiant smile, and I giggle. "And I cannot wait another day to ask you. Abby, will you marry me?"

I vaguely hear sniffles from across the room, and I find that my own tears are starting to fall. This man, this wonderful man is asking me to marry him, and I'm not afraid. I'm not worried like I used to be at the thought of marriage. It's all I want now—to be married to Ethan, to have his child, to be a happy family. We can do this.

I marvel at what a splendid surprise this has been! A redeeming credit for Famous Ethan Surprises.

I can barely find my voice, but I manage to say, "Yes." A loud round of cheering erupts across the room as he slips the ring on my finger. I reach down to help him to his feet—he's surely tired from the day's excitement added on top of the toll his treatment takes on him. But he has the strength to sweep me into his arms and kiss me breathless.

Suddenly, we're surrounded by nurses and staff congratulating and hugging us. The side lights in the room are raised to create a soft glow that allows us to see everyone.

"What a perfect ending to a perfect day!" Tabitha beams at me.

"Yes! How did you pull this off?" I ask in wonder.

"I had lots of help. And it didn't hurt that you were sleeping while we were planning." She looks knowingly at Ethan.

"Thank you, Tabitha. You did great." He gives her a quick hug.

"Don't mention it." She waves her hand at him, then wipes a tear from her eye. "Now, you two take a seat and enjoy your meal. Everybody out, everybody out," she commands as she shoos people toward the door.

In no time we're alone, gazing at each other across the table.

"You amaze me, Ethan."

"It's you who continually amazes me, my dear."

I blush at his kind words. "How did you pull this all together so quickly?"

"Well, the idea came to me during chemo today. I've had the ring for months, but I missed my chance to propose on our trip when I ended up here. And after the news you gave me this morning, I couldn't wait another day. I had to do it. I want you to be my wife now more than ever. So, I asked Tabitha if she could help, and before I knew it, twenty people were involved," he chuckles. "And I had time to call West while you were sleeping to get the ring here. Which, by the way, I'm sure you'll have to call Kate right away to let her know. You know West can't keep a secret, so she's probably dying to hear the official word."

"Oh, Kate." I smile. I'm sure she's going insane waiting.

"But please, eat. I'm sure you're hungry."

"I am, actually." I inhale the savory scent of fettuccini alfredo, a favorite dish of mine. I know immediately that this food did not come from the hospital cafeteria. Between bites, I notice how the candlelight flickers across the diamonds of my ring. I stare at it, mesmerized. "It's so big. I can't get over it. And so many diamonds."

"You like it?"

"I love it," I breathe.

"Good," he says proudly. "You have no idea how much pressure there is to pick out the right ring."

"Oh, you did, Ethan. It's beautiful."

After a couple more bites, I realize he's not eating. "Are you doing okay? You look tired." I frown. I place my fork on the table and slide my chair out to rise. "We should get you back to bed. It's been a long day."

"I'm fine," he protests, his hand grabbing my arm, preventing me from standing up. "Don't worry about me. You enjoy your food. I'm just going to take it slow." As I reluctantly sit in my chair, eyeing him suspiciously, he releases me and eats a bite of breadstick, no doubt to appease me. He probably has no appetite so soon after his treatment. Or he knows he'll be sick after he eats.

This gigantic elephant in the room keeps stealing my joy. Irritated, I wonder when I'll be allowed to be happy again without threatening dark clouds rumbling over and reminding me that I still have so much to lose.

Chapter Twenty-Three

My Life, My Love, My Everything

It's Sunday afternoon, and I've tried on countless wedding dresses. The first couple hours were fun, admiring all the styles, trying on famous designers' dresses, and having Kate and Emory both here to critique. But I'm having a hard time finding *the* dress. And I know I'm frustrating our attendant, Celeste, because I can't tell her the exact style I want. I'd never given it much thought before now. What I do know is I'll know it when I see it. But how many more dresses will I have to try on until then?

"This one looks fantastic on you, Abby," Emory says.

I size up my reflection in the mirror and turn slightly to view the back. The dress *is* pretty, very form-fitting, but the neckline scoops so low—halfway down my chest, showing way too much cleavage—and that's just not me. The open back exposes most of my skin, dipping dangerously close to my behind.

"Um, I think it's a bit too sexy for a wedding dress." I frown, wondering what Ethan would think about a dress like this. "I feel half-naked."

"Okay, so we can eliminate any dresses with a low neckline and open back, correct?" Celeste chimes in, seemingly happy to get some feedback to narrow down her list. Up to this point, I haven't been able to offer her much other than,

"I don't like this fabric," or, "This dress feels too heavy," or, "This one's not for me."

"Hmm . . ." She taps her index finger on her mouth while she appraises me. "No plunging necklines, no lace, no excessive embellishments. I think I might have one or two in mind. Back to the dressing room," she orders.

"Well, if you don't pick that dress, Abby, I may just get it for my own wedding!" Emory calls after me. I hear her tell Kate, "I'm writing that one down on my list of finalists."

I smile and shake my head as I duck into the dressing room. Sighing, I not-so-patiently wait for Celeste to return with the promised dresses. I knew this would be a challenge when I told her I needed to buy a dress today that required no alterations. Her reply of, "Oh dear. We shall see what we can come up with," left me feeling much less confident than when we started off this morning.

I knew pulling this wedding off in a week's time would be difficult, but Ethan had insisted he didn't want to wait any longer to get married. He said it didn't have to be anything fancy—just me and him and our closest friends. He'd already requested permission to use the hospital chapel before he even proposed!

The joy of the engagement was quickly replaced by worry and a heavy pressure to get everything accomplished in just over a week. I'm tired as it is, surprisingly tired for eight weeks of pregnancy. But this is what Ethan wants, and so I will do everything in my power to give it to him.

It has been a godsend to have Kate and Emory to help. Emory has a wealth of information since she started planning her own wedding the day after she and Dylan got engaged. She knew where to go dress shopping, where to order flowers on short notice, and where to get a cake. We discovered we could get one of the sample cakes from a bakery downtown, though we wouldn't have a say in the flavor or design, which doesn't really bother me. The fewer decisions I have to make the better.

A knock on the dressing room door startles me.

"Abby, I have found two dresses I think you'll love," Celeste sings as I open the door. She helps me out of the current gown and into an antique white satin dress with a fitted bodice and a fluffy skirt, strapless with a sweetheart neckline. The bodice has intricate stitching in a floral pattern. The skirt gathers in waves all the way to the floor, giving it the appearance of cascading fabric. It's beautiful, but I'm rendered breathless with a violent jerk, and I realize Celeste is tightening the ribbons down the back of the dress, yanking and tugging it against my body. I reach out to steady myself against the wall, struggling to breathe while she attacks the dress with fervor.

"Oh, my," I gasp. "This feels more like medieval torture than a wedding dress!"

"Yes, it's difficult to get on," Celeste says breathlessly, still tugging, "but the end result is magnificent."

We'll see about that. Several minutes of that torture and I am quite exhausted.

"Okay," she heaves as she fluffs out the skirt. "Let's go have a look."

I stiffly walk out to present the dress to my friends. I can barely breathe, the unforgiving wires sewn into the bodice digging into my sides. There's no way I can wear this dress for any amount of time.

"Oh my God!" Emory cries as soon as I emerge.

"Look at you," Kate whispers in awe.

I blush. I haven't gotten this kind of reaction with any of the other dresses. I step up to the mirrors and scrutinize my reflection as Celeste busies herself fluffing the skirt around me.

"This particular dress has a short train, as you can see. It can be hooked up in the back after the ceremony, so you are not tripping over it all night."

She steps away for me to get a good view. The dress really is spectacular, fitting my figure perfectly. I love the strapless look. But I'm becoming lightheaded from only being able to take shallow breaths, and I start to wonder if my little baby is getting squished in there. I glance at Celeste in the mirror, her expression hopeful.

"Um . . ." I turn stiffly to face the girls.

"You look so beautiful!" Emory gushes.

I twist my mouth into a half-smile at her compliment. "I'm just not feeling this is it. It's unbelievably tight. And I'm not a huge fan of this." I trace my finger over the sweetheart scoop at the top of the bodice. It's too girlie for me.

"What do you like about the dress?" Celeste prods.

"Well, I love the skirt, the way the fabric gathers and falls all around. And I love the strapless look. If you could find one like this—not so tight, white in color, and less floral going on, I think we'd have a winner." I inhale as deeply as I can, since that much talking with such constraint on my lungs has left me wanting air. The wires jab into my sides, causing me to wince.

"I can work with that," she confirms. "Back to the dressing room, and I will be right there with just the dress." She flits off.

"Can you help me down?" I ask breathlessly. My sides are really starting to hurt.

Kate rushes up to take my arm as I struggle down the three steps to the floor.

"I think I'm squishing the baby!" I whisper.

She giggles. "Oh no! Let me help." She turns me around and, to my relief, unties the ribbons and gently pulls at them, freeing my lungs from the constricting prison.

"Oh, thank you!" I breathe a huge gulp of air.

"We're getting there," she reassures me and gives me a little push toward the dressing room.

"I sure hope so," I mumble. I just really want a nap right now. The Shania Twain song being piped throughout the dress shop does little to get me into the joyous wedding mood.

Celeste meets me at the door to the dressing room, a confident smile on her face.

"Here it is," she sings excitedly. I'm glad she's still into this, and her excitement lifts my spirits a bit higher. *Please, let this be the dress.*

It takes as long to get out of the Medieval Torture Dress as it took to get into it, and Celeste is as breathless with exertion at the disrobing as she was tying me in. I wonder how she has the patience to dress women in wedding dresses all day long. I couldn't do it.

I'm immediately relieved to see the dress she brought has a zippered back and only two eyehooks at the top. Easy entry. I step into the white strapless dress and hug the bodice to me while she zips and hooks the back. I love the way the gathered fabric of the bodice feels. So soft. Happily, I notice the dress is snug but not tight. I can actually breathe.

I gasp as she tugs up on the sides of the bodice forcefully and flares out the skirt. "Shall we take a look?"

I follow her out of the dressing room in anticipation. She was so quick about getting this dress on me I barely had time to really look at it. The gasps tell me all I need to know. Celeste helps me up the steps in front of the mirror.

And I'm awestruck. Speechless, just like my friends sitting on the couch behind me.

The satin bodice of the dress is gathered in uneven horizontal lines. A thin silver belt sparkles at my waist, followed by the long, luscious satin gown that is gathered in all the right places, cascading to the floor. It is elegant yet not overstated. And I love it. Tears spring to my eyes as I realize this is it—this is the one.

Slowly, I spin around so I can see the back. A very short train circles behind. Large sparkling buttons adorn the back of the bodice on the fabric that covers the zipper. Just a little flash. I look back to Kate, who is already dabbing the corners of her eyes with a tissue, and then at Emory with her fingers over her mouth. Still speechless—a rarity for Ems.

Suddenly, my mind scrambles as the lightheadedness from earlier returns, sending the room spinning. So much has happened this week. So much is still ahead next week. My knees feel weak, and I need to sit down.

I stumble toward the couch. Vaguely, I hear Celeste say something, and I feel her hand grasping my arm, helping me down the steps. Kate jumps up and so does Emory, both reaching out to me. A fog overcomes my consciousness as I sink onto the couch. My fingers rest on the soft satin of the dress. I gently stroke it—it is so beautiful. Silent tears begin to fall down my cheeks.

"Abby, hon, what is it? You look beautiful!" Kate dabs my cheeks with a tissue.

Emory looks at me with wide eyes and rubs my shoulder. "You do! You look fantastic! Don't cry."

Why am I crying?

Celeste stands befuddled a few steps behind. Apparently, she's never had a bride-to-be suffer a complete emotional breakdown before. The tears become sobs. Gratefully, I take the tissue Kate has handed me and blow my nose. Seriously, I'm an emotional wreck.

"What is it, Abby?" Kate murmurs as she scoots the dress aside and sits on the couch. She gently rubs my back, which makes me cry harder.

"It's not fair," I choke out. "It's just not!" I shake my head vehemently, feeling a full-scale tantrum coming on, the likes of which I haven't thrown since childhood.

"It's supposed to be—" I inhale sharply "—the happiest—" I inhale again "—day of my—" one more gasp "—life!" I'm blinded by my tears now. "How can I be happy?" I say in disgust. And the anger helps to quell my sobs. "My fiancé is quite possibly dying. And *now*—!" Indignation overtakes me. "Now I'll have to raise our child on my own. Alone!" A fresh wave of tears spills down my cheeks. I can't imagine how many patrons are staring at the bawling girl in the wedding dress. I'm too upset to be embarrassed.

"Hey," Kate murmurs soothingly. "Enough of that talk!" She pulls me tightly to her and strokes my hair. "Ethan is not going anywhere. Now more than ever you've given him reason to fight, to stay with you, to see your baby born. You have to stay positive."

I feel Emory's hand squeezing mine. What would I do without my friends? I would fall into the dark abyss of depression, no doubt. I would curl up into a tiny ball and hide from the emotional trials I face.

"You look so beautiful in this dress, Abby. And Ethan will think the same. You'll see," Emory adds.

I sigh, and my breath hitches as I dab my eyes and wipe my nose again. Their strength lends me strength. I sniff, resolve pushing back at the fear and despair. I can do this. I must do this. It is for Ethan.

And I do love this dress. It makes me feel beautiful—well, before I became a sniveling mess anyway. I pull myself together. It feels good to cry, to get my fears out, but Kate is right, I have to stay positive. For Ethan's sake. For my sake. For our child's sake.

I can't give up on him. How dare I?

"I'm sorry," I sniff and shrug apologetically. "I'm so emotional today. I'm sorry," I say again to an ashen Celeste.

"Oh, honey," she recovers. "Don't worry a bit. So, you like the dress?" she asks timidly.

"I love it," I confirm. I half-heartedly pull at the tag on the side of the bodice. "Three thousand dollars!" I choke. "Are you kidding me?" I cannot believe the dress I absolutely love costs three thousand dollars.

"It's designer, honey," she says as if that should explain it all.

I groan. I can't spend three thousand dollars on a dress while my beloved lies in a hospital room for who knows how many more weeks. For all I know, we may already be broke.

"That's really a very good bargain, Abby, as designer dresses go," Emory tries to reassure me. With all her research, she would know.

"No, that's too much," I say, defeated. I was so hoping to be done dress shopping. I'm exhausted.

"Abby, if Ethan were here, what would he say?" Kate asks. She allows me a moment to ponder the question before she continues. "He'd say you look absolutely astonishing in this dress and you should buy it immediately, wouldn't he?"

I close my eyes, imagining his face when he sees me in this beautiful dress. A slight smile dances across my face.

"Wouldn't he?" she presses.

"Yes, he would," I acquiesce.

"Yes, he would," she repeats matter-of-factly.

"So, this is it?" Emory asks excitedly.

"This is it," I allow.

She lets out a squeal and hugs me so hard I almost start crying again. "Now, for our dresses!" she sings.

WALKING SLOWLY DOWN the aisle in the chapel at Sloan-Kettering, I try to pace myself with Pachelbel's Canon serenely pouring out of every corner. I gaze at my Cutie, my Ethan, standing before me in a black tux, looking beautiful even with his gaunt face, even in his too-thin state. He leans on a black cane for support, one Simon purchased on a trip to England years ago. He sports a blue stocking cap today, with flaps that cover his ears and braided ties that hang down past his shoulders. I smile and try to suppress a giggle. My lighthearted Ethan. The blue brings out the color of his eyes, and I wonder in awe as I slowly make my way toward him how I could be so lucky to find such an amazing, kind, and caring man. He smiles, and my heart soars; I think I see his eyes misting.

I can barely tear my gaze away from him over to Kate and Emory, both smiling at me, looking beautiful in their blue halter dresses. I note how lovely the small white rose bouquets turned out. Nothing too extravagant—just how I like it.

West and Dylan stand at Ethan's side, both looking debonair in their tuxes. West gives me a mischievous wink, which makes my smile pull even further at my cheeks.

I pass by Uncle Geoff and Simon in the small group of people, mostly doctors and nurses who have come to know us well. Uncle Geoff nods his approval as our eyes meet. Simon holds a handkerchief to his face, wiping first one eye and then the other.

Finally, I am standing in front of Ethan, the swell of unspoken words saturating the air between us. And love. So much love. The music crescendos, and he reaches for my hand, which I place in his as I step beside him. Typically, this is the time when a father gives his daughter away, but not in my story. In reality, I'd given myself, my heart and my soul, to Ethan long ago. I steal one more glance at him before I turn my attention to the pastor in front of us. The music ends in perfect timing.

I honestly don't hear much of what the pastor says. I cannot wait until the part where we recite our vows. A tiny bit of me worries I'll forget what I'm supposed to say, what I've been trying to memorize all week long. And then I am center stage. I turn to face Ethan, my gaze lost in his fathomless eyes. I quickly recover, clear my throat.

"Ethan Thomas Lansing," I begin with a tremor in my voice, "you are a light in my life, a constant, calming force pulling me toward happiness unlike anything I've ever known. Your love has saved me, encouraged me to grow, completed my soul in a way I never thought possible. You give me new meaning in this life. In return, I give you my life, my love, my everything. And you will be everything to me. Always. I love you." I manage—with tears threatening—to somehow finish.

I want to throw myself into his arms, but I know it's his turn, so with restraint, I speak to him with my eyes.

"Abigail Elizabeth Templeton, I ask you to open your arms, your heart, your soul, and welcome me into your embrace. I want nothing more than to be your champion, your protector, your lover. I look at you and see definite impossibilities made possible, insurmountable mountains conquered, unbeatable odds crushed. Together, our love transcends all, and I give myself to you unconditionally, knowing that our love *will* transcend all, for all time."

I exhale and cannot find my breath. His words are so beautiful, so moving.

I try to focus on the rest of the ceremony, but I find myself stealing glances at Ethan's face, so tranquil today, and there is something else there, making him glow—happiness? Love? My heart swells at the thought that I am the reason feels this way. Me.

Before I know it, we are exchanging rings. I slide a titanium ring on his finger with an inscription inside that reads, "Abigail loves Ethan forever." He sways slightly on his feet as he takes his weight off the cane supporting him. He must be getting tired from standing so long. He adds a beautiful platinum and diamond band to my already spectacular diamond engagement ring. Our eyes lock in a reverent gaze, and so many unspoken words travel between us. I have never felt closer to him than I do at this very moment. We are one.

"I now pronounce you Ethan and Abigail Lansing," the pastor announces. "You may bring this ceremony to a close with a kiss."

And his lips are on mine in a passionate, grateful, consuming kiss. As I wrap my arms around him, I realize how much thinner he is than he was weeks ago . . . and sadly how fragile he is. I adjust my embrace to one of support.

When we break our kiss, he presses his forehead to mine, continuing to whisper volumes from his blue eyes to mine. I am happier than I have ever been, and yet a fear gnaws at the back of my mind that I could still lose this man whom I have come to cherish and love more than my own being. I break our gaze quickly before the waterworks threaten to spill over.

THE RECEPTION IS wonderful, set up in a large conference room much bigger than the one where he proposed to me. The staff comes in steady procession to wish congratulations. We have our cake, which—even though we had no say in it—turns out to be a delicious vanilla with intricate yellow and blue frosting decorations.

One of the night nurses volunteered to be a DJ for us. The song he chooses for our first dance is a song about how a love like ours is fate not luck. I ask him afterward who sings that song—it's perfect. He tells me it's Christina Perri, then to my surprise, hands me the CD as a gift to us.

Later, as Ethan and I dance slowly, I rest my head on his shoulder, treasuring the splendor of the day.

"Abby, baby, you have made me the happiest man in the world today. I hope you know that." I look up to see his sexy smile beaming at me, the one that makes my heart flutter. I smile in return. What girl doesn't want to hear that?

"Ethan, you have made me just as happy. And you looked so debonair up there in your tux with your sophisticated walking stick." I giggle as I reach up and tug on the hanging braid of his stocking cap.

"But you stole the show—my heart literally stopped when I saw you coming down the aisle in this dress. Breathtaking."

My cheeks flush as I mentally thank Kate for pushing me to buy it. Desired effect achieved.

We kiss for maybe the hundredth time today, but this kiss is very tender, loving, reverent. I stare into his calm blue eyes for a long moment, seeing the same swelling love I feel reflected there. I close my eyes and rest my head on his shoulder once more as we sway to the music. This day couldn't be more perfect.

After a couple more hours, I can tell Ethan is exhausted. Wanting to make me happy, no doubt, he tries to play it off, but I know. So I say I'm tired and ready to get out of my heels. He agrees, and we bid our thanks and good nights to everyone.

In the privacy of his room, we stand at the end of his hospital bed. I loosen his tie for him and slide it through his collar, unbutton his blue vest, and slide it and his jacket off his too-thin shoulders. I unbutton the top of his white linen shirt and kiss the base of his throat, trying to ignore the port taped to his collarbone. I kiss up his neck and his cheek. Place one kiss on his mouth and look questioningly, hopefully into his eyes. I am hornier than ever thanks to my raging hormones, but I know the day's pomp has probably exhausted him beyond any desire.

"I'm sorry, babe. I'm just so tired," he whispers.

"I know. It's okay," I breathe as I kiss him one last time, trying to hide the disappointment in my voice. I would be asking too much of him, and I know it. "Lie down, baby."

He climbs into his hospital bed, and I gently pull off his dress shoes. He has gone through so much today to try to please me—a wedding, a dance. I sigh to myself as I drape the sheet and blanket over him. "You sleep, my angel," I whisper before I kiss his cheek.

"You are the angel. You looked so beautiful today, Abby," he murmurs. "I wish I had the strength to show you how much I love you."

"Soon," I breathe in his ear. "Soon. I love you."

His heavy eyelids droop and close, and I trudge over to the recliner and flop down into it, hugging myself as silent tears stream down my cheeks. I can't even enjoy my wedding night with my husband—how unfair! The overwhelming emotions I felt at the dress shop are once again upon me, forcing me to dwell on the sadness of the reality we're facing: a honeymoon in a hospital. But my anger and sadness subside eventually as my own tiredness creeps in.

Sometime later, I'm startled awake.

"Abby, baby, wake up!" Ethan whispers harshly.

My eyes flutter open, and I turn my gaze in the dim light from the white-tiled ceiling to his face, awake and earnest. He's sitting upright in his bed. I blink twice, trying to ascertain if I'm dreaming.

"Go shut the door," he urges.

What?

I struggle up from the recliner in my puffy wedding dress and do as I'm told. My mind is too foggy to understand what he's requesting.

"Come here, baby."

I walk over to him, still wondering if I'm dreaming.

"Turn around."

I do, and I feel his cool fingers undoing the hooks on the back of my dress. Then the zipper lowers to my waist. My hands instinctively cling to the bodice of my dress. I shudder as his hand caresses my bare skin, from between my shoulder blades to the small of my back. I sigh with delicious longing. As he pushes at the waist of my dress, I let go of my grip on the bodice. I shimmy out and turn to face him.

"C'mere," he murmurs as he reaches out to me. Am I dreaming? Oh, I hope not. It's been too long. I quickly reach up for the curtain at the head of his bed and drag it around to the foot, keeping my eyes locked on my husband's. He smiles wickedly at me.

I clamber onto the bed and sit astride him, gazing longingly into his blue eyes. He gently caresses my cheek with one hand, then pulls me to him with the other. Oh, how I have missed his hands on me! He kisses me so passionately it sets a fire alight throughout my insides. I place my hands on either side of his face and press my body into his. Pushing the stocking cap back on his head, I pepper kisses up his cheek to his forehead. "We don't need this anymore," I tease and toss it behind me.

"Oh, Abby," he breathes. His hands are all over me all at once. "You were so beautiful today. Amazingly beautiful."

"You weren't so bad yourself," I murmur. "You look hot in a tux." I smile against his lips.

"Mrs. Lansing," he says seductively.

"Mr. Lansing," I reply and bite his lower lip provocatively. He groans in response.

"Some honeymoon, huh?" He frowns.

"As long as we're together, it'll be the best honeymoon ever," I whisper in his ear and gently nibble on his earlobe.

"Baby, I love you so much. You're my everything."

"I love you too, Ethan." I pause as I stare deeply into his eyes. My husband. "Always."

And then I slowly remove my strapless bra. His breathing hitches as I toss it to the floor. I lean forward and kiss him gently. I take my time unbuttoning his shirt. This is so rare . . . I'm going to make it last. And we are both going to enjoy this.

Chapter Twenty-Four

I'll Follow You Into the Dark

I WAKE MONDAY morning with a kink in my neck. My body registers the pain before my eyes open. I feel Ethan's steady breathing and grin as I lift my eyelids to see his beautiful face inches from mine. I'm not allowed to sleep in his bed with him, and if a nurse catches us, I'll be in serious trouble. Unless, of course, Tabitha's on duty. I'm sure she wouldn't say anything. It was our wedding night, after all.

I'm thankful I decided to rummage through my bag last night for my sweats. I wouldn't have slept well at all if I had put my dress back on for fear of wrinkling it.

I move my neck ever so slightly to work out the kink. I don't want to wake Ethan yet; he's probably so tired from the exertion of yesterday . . . and last night. I smile thinking about last night. It had been far too long since we'd made love, and it was wonderful.

Watching his face, smooth and peaceful in his deep sleep, I want to reach up and caress his cheek, but I don't dare. I want to pepper kisses all over his face and his shiny head, but I settle instead for imagining I'm doing it. I sigh with a calmness I haven't felt in ages. Ethan is my husband. I am his wife. We are going to have a baby. And he's going to walk out of this hospital cancer-free in mere weeks. I am certain of it. The next time we set foot in a hospital, it will be for the birth of our little one.

I allow my mind to wander again to that day. Ethan, happy and healthy once more, holding up our precious tiny baby. I imagine the love and pride in his eyes as he talks to our little boy or girl, introducing himself and introducing me to tiny blue eyes. He is going to be the most amazing father. I can hardly wait to see that day.

I carefully reach behind me and grab my cell phone off the bedside table. Seven o'clock. I should get up and sneak in a quick shower before the first nurses' round.

I gently untangle myself from Ethan's legs and ease out of bed. I lift up my wedding dress draped across my bag on the chair and pause, admiring the fabric and design one last time. Such a beautiful dress. I can't wait to see the pictures Kate took for us. Reluctantly, I lay the dress back down next to the bag. I rummage through it as quietly and quickly as I can to get to my clothes and makeup bag. Then I dash into the bathroom, stealing one last glimpse at my husband lying peacefully sprawled out on the bed. I note with a tiny giggle that I'll have to get him into some clothes before the nurses start their rounds. At least he has the sheet covering him from his waist to his knees.

Even though I (regrettably) rush through my shower, it's not fast enough. Nausea overtakes me, and I can't seem to shake it. I try thinking of anything else, from what Ethan will say about last night when he wakes up to what new shirts I should bring him this week and what I should eat for breakfast this morning—*oh no!* I shouldn't have thought of food! Suddenly, my stomach is seizing, and before I can shift my thoughts away from eggs and bacon, I'm sick.

Damn morning sickness! I curse as I heave and heave.

I press my forehead against the cool shower wall and turn the water from hot to lukewarm. It takes a moment to regain my strength to stand upright. I make a mental note to add to the list of questions for the OB: *When will the morning sickness end?* There's no way I can handle this much longer.

I finish and dry off as quickly as possible, brushing my teeth twice for good measure. I hastily dress, remembering the box of granola bars on the table. That should hold me over for a bit. My stomach is still churning, and I need something in there to settle it down.

I tiptoe out of the bathroom, check that Ethan is still sleeping, and deposit my clothes and toiletries in my bag. I grab two granola bars, unwrap one, and shove it into my mouth in three bites. I gaze out the window, trying to take my focus off the nausea by watching the traffic on the street.

"Morning, my beautiful wife."

I jump at his voice breaking the silence. I quickly chew the granola in my mouth as I face him. He's staring at me, most of his naked body hanging out of the sheet, with a wicked grin on his face. He is still so handsome, though pale and thin. He's lost some muscle mass, and his IV port by his clavicle glares, unwelcome, at me. The bones of his face are more prominent, and he has dark patches of skin beneath his bright blue eyes. Despite all that, and even though he has no hair, he still looks sexy.

"Morning yourself," I mumble as I put my hand up to my mouth to keep from losing granola out of it, embarrassed to be caught stuffing my face like this. I swallow it down and make my way over to him. "I do like the way that sounds, husband."

He beams up at me. "Wife."

I lean down and kiss him, thankful that the nausea is subsiding so I can focus on him now.

"Breakfast?" He nods at the other granola bar in my hand.

"I wasn't feeling so hot this morning. It helps for me to get something in my stomach."

"I see. Well, I feel more than hot this morning, Mrs. Lansing. Come here."

I settle myself on the bed in his embrace. I just can't get over how giddy I feel to hear him say "wife" and "Mrs. Lansing."

"You were an animal last night," he murmurs into my cheek as he kisses me.

"I was happy last night," I giggle, then sigh. "So happy."

"Me too."

I unwrap my second granola bar, enjoying our quiet moment together. I offer him half; he shakes his head. We sit with his arms around me, his face buried in my neck by my damp hair.

"You smell nice, Mrs. Lansing."

"Thank you, Mr. Lansing. But as much as I love snuggling with you, I think you'd better get some skivvies on before one of the nurses comes in."

"You think we'd shock Tabitha?"

"I do."

"All right then."

I barely finish helping him into his boxers and sweatpants before there's a light rapping and the door swings open. "Good morning, Mr. and Mrs. Lansing!" Tabitha sings in her usual energetic way. "May I be the first today to say—congratulations!"

"Thank you, Tabitha," I say as I begin to pack my wedding dress away in its bag.

"And you looked like a beautiful angel aglow in that dress, Abby. The prettiest bride I've ever seen. Don't you agree, Ethan?" She begins her routine of checking his vitals and writing in his chart.

"Absolutely. The most beautiful bride I've ever laid eyes on."

"Oh, stop!" I wave my hand dismissively. "You have to say that because you're my husband."

He chuckles.

"Oh, I almost forgot," Tabitha says while scribbling on the chart. "Dr. Jackson has requested another MRI today. Wants to check on your noggin."

"An MRI?" I question. "Why?"

"Nothing special, I don't think. Just wants a peek at our progress," she says lightly.

I glance at Ethan, my heart constricting a tiny bit. He shrugs.

"I'll be back to get you in about an hour for that, okay?"

"Yeah, okay," he agrees. I look at him again quizzically. "She said he just wants a peek," he reassures me.

Part of me is glad we'll get to see if all this torture is paying off, while the other part of me is very uneasy. What if it's not good? I shake those thoughts out of my head. *Gotta stay positive—especially now.*

"It'll be fine," Ethan says, sensing my apprehension.

❦

"WELL, UNFORTUNATELY IT'S not what we'd hoped for." Dr. Jackson sets a laptop on the portable table in front of us.

My heart sinks as my world comes crashing down around me. This is exactly what I was dreading. A weight presses on my chest, making it impossible for me to breathe.

On the screen are the now-familiar images of Ethan's gray matter. My ears aren't working right—I can't understand what he's saying. But as he talks, he points to three places in Ethan's brain. I squint and try to focus my eyes. Yes, there are definitely three small masses in there. But maybe these are old scans; maybe he's got them up to show us before and now. I shut out the overriding sound of my own struggled breathing, my pulse pounding in my ears. I need to focus on Dr. Jackson's words, to hear what he's saying.

". . . so, what this means, Ethan, is that the IV chemo is not working as well as we'd hoped. But one thing I notice is that two of the three masses are in almost the exact same spot as two we removed. The third is very close to another previous tumor we removed."

"What does that mean?" he asks. I tear my eyes away from the pictures of his brain and look at his eyes, his mouth. What must he be thinking! But his face gives away none of the fear I feel. His jaw is set, his eyes fierce with determination. He's still in fighter mode. Good. I squeeze his hand.

"It means we need to try a different approach, and I have one in mind that I think will allow us to better target these so-called 'hot beds.' It will require surgery again, not only to remove the tumors, but also to allow strategic placement of tiny wafers in the brain to allow the chemotherapy medication to secrete directly from the wafer into the most vital locations.

"With this technology, the medication works inside the brain. There is no worry that it is not effectively breaching the blood-brain barrier as with intravenous chemo. It's as if you're placing weed killer on your lawn and letting it work slowly to poison the undesired patches."

"Nice analogy," Ethan says dryly. "I've always thought of my brain as a weedy lawn."

I nudge him, shocked he can crack jokes at a time like this.

"Well, it's the same principle." Dr. Jackson shrugs, unaffected. He's probably used to patients acting a whole lot worse toward him when he breaks such bad news. I can imagine yelling and throwing things and beating him on the chest. That's what I'd like to do right now.

"I'm ordering an immediate stop to your IV chemo. We'll give you some time, a couple days or so, before the surgery. We don't want to overload your body with the drug."

"You said before that overloading could damage his liver, right?"

"Yes, that is correct. That's why we will give his body some rest from the intravenous chemo. Then we'll remove the tumors and perform another MRI during surgery as before to ensure we are not missing any other masses. While we have him in surgery, we'll insert several of the wafers and give them some time to take effect. It takes about two to three weeks for them to fully dissolve."

"So are the side effects different for this method?" Ethan asks calmly. How is he not freaking out?

"Yes, there is a risk, of course, of infection since you will have foreign bodies in your brain tissue. But the wafers dissolve as they release the chemo. Other side effects are new or worsening headaches and possible seizures."

"Seizures?" I blurt, eyes wide.

"While not great, the risk is there."

I look at Ethan again, fear grasping hold of me, threatening to make me an emotional wreck. Seizures? And possible liver damage if it's too much chemo? This treatment sounds harsh.

He doesn't return my gaze. His resolve is evident, his jaw flexing while he lets the doctor's words sink in. After a long minute, he speaks. "So there are tumors in there, and they must come out."

"Yes."

"And you believe this option, these . . . wafers will work more effectively to combat the cancer."

"I do."

"What's the prognosis?" His voice is strangely businesslike.

"It is hard to say, Ethan. Yours has been a unique case. You seem to have a very resistant strain of cancer. As I said before, we had hoped to have you in much better shape by now and ready to head home with your wife here in a couple weeks." Dr. Jackson pauses, thoughtful. "The battle against cancer always seems to be better fought when our patients have a strong desire to live, and that you have. And you have family and friends supporting you. We'll try everything we can medically to help you make a full recovery."

Ethan closes his eyes, and I see frustration briefly cross his face, but it's gone as soon as it appears. The steely resolve replaces it. "Let me know when you have the surgery scheduled." There's that weird businesslike tone again.

I want to pull him into my arms, to stroke his back, slide off his stocking cap, and kiss his bald head. To tell him I love him so very much. But an emotional display like that may be what breaks his armor, and I don't want to be responsible for causing his breakdown.

"I will. And we'll have another meeting about this tomorrow. I'm sure you'll think of more questions you'll want to ask." The doctor nods goodbye and leaves, taking the laptop and all my newlywed joy with him.

I feel hollow, too shocked to even feel sad. I really wasn't expecting such bad news. I thought things could only continue on the positive path we've been forging over the past couple weeks. Little did we suspect the danger still lurking in the shadows, waiting until we allowed hope and confidence in our future to fully blossom, then pouncing and entirely obliterating it.

The fear I felt earlier creeps up, little by little. What if this treatment doesn't work? What if Ethan doesn't make it through another surgery? What if—

"Hey, hey." I feel his thumb swipe across my cheek. I didn't realize I was crying. I hastily wipe my cheeks with the back of my hand. I must compose myself. I mustn't be weak in front of him.

"Come here, baby," he soothes as he pulls me into his arms. "It'll be fine. You'll see."

"I'm sorry," I choke, still fighting to gain control of myself. "This pregnancy must be making me overemotional." Blaming the baby on board whacking out my emotions will disguise how truly hopeless I feel.

I quietly scold myself. I need to stop bringing him down—he is fighting for his life.

I sigh. Back into the dark depths of the forest we go.

"WHAT ABOUT JULIA Rose? I think that's pretty."

"Hmm?" I glance up from the book I'm reading, one of Ethan's new father books. I half-heard him as I'm not really paying attention to what I'm reading, just trying to kill time and keep my nerves from getting the best of me before his surgery today. "Julia what?"

"Julia Rose. It has a nice strong yet feminine sound to it. Don't you think?"

"Um, I've never been a big fan of either name, actually."

Ethan appears a little hurt by my unreceptiveness. I soften the blow. "I knew a Julia in high school, and she was a complete snob, so that name's ruined for me."

"But you don't like Rose either?"

"Too *Golden Girls*."

"I see. Well . . . what about Sarah Marie?"

"Too common."

"Jessica Elaine?"

"Definite no."

I let my eyes wander back to the pages in my lap. This name discussion may be an exercise in futility.

But he doesn't give up. "Isabella Katherine."

"Too much of a mouthful. And I'm not naming my child after a character from *Twilight*."

"I thought you liked *Twilight*," he argues.

"I do, but I'm not Twihard enough to name my child Isabella," I say matter-of-factly. End of discussion on that one. "Besides, what if it's a boy?"

A wide smile breaks across his face. "Ethan, Jr., of course."

I smile in return and roll my eyes. "Of course."

"I guess I just picture us having a girl. I want a little girl to spoil. And she'll look like you, follow you around everywhere." Proud Papa shines in his eyes as he imagines our little girl. "What names do you have in mind, my dear?"

"I haven't had much time to think about it honestly. Between the wedding and the news we got on Monday . . ." I don't want to give voice to the news we got on Monday.

"Well, think about it now. What names do you like?" he prods.

"Oh, I don't know—Gabrielle, Sabrina . . . Morgan . . . Jaison for girls—"

"Jason? For a girl?" His brow furrows.

"Yes, Jaison." I frown. "Spelled differently than you're thinking."

The sour look on his face quickly softens. "I like Gabrielle—then you'd be Abby and Gabby. How cute is that?"

"Um, not cute. Okay, no to Gabrielle."

"What about boy names?"

"Tristan . . . or Slade . . ."

"What, is he going to be a fairytale hero?"

"I like those names."

"They're silly."

I shrug, offended. Are we really going to get into an argument over names? Besides, he asked.

Our discussion is brought to a close as Uncle Geoff and Simon join us, followed soon after by Kate and West. I should be happy to see them, but it means we are that much closer to Ethan's surgery. Nervousness flares in my stomach, making me a little nauseous. I grab a couple granola bars as a preventative measure and slide them into my vest pocket.

Too soon the nurses enter and prep Ethan for surgery, cutting the conversation in the room short.

"If you'd like, Mrs. Lansing, you and the family can go ahead up to the surgical waiting room," one of the nurses suggests as she continues her preparations.

I realize in a panic that I'm not ready to leave my husband yet. What if something goes wrong in surgery? What if I never see him again? My throat constricts as my eyes fly wildly around at the faces watching me. They land on Kate, and in that moment, she reads my thoughts. She steps forward quickly and wraps her hands around my arm to steady me, which I appreciate because I feel as though my legs could give out at any second.

"Abby," she says quietly, yet forcefully, drawing my wild eyes to her hazel stare. Her silent strength bores into me. I take deep breaths as I focus on her eyes, gather my borrowed strength, and carefully pull my arm from her grasp. *I'm okay.*

I step to Ethan's bedside and clasp his hand in mine. Looking down at him, it is hard to keep my emotions in check. I swallow back a sob then press my lips together so hard my teeth dig painfully into them.

"Ethan, baby," I sniff.

"Hey, I know," he tries to reassure me. Even now, as he prepares to have his brain cut open again, he's trying to soothe me.

I shake my head—I'm going to say my piece. I inhale a steadying breath.

"You need to know that I love you. That we love you." My hand rests on my belly. "You do this, and you come back to us. We'll be waiting for you, okay?" My voice is barely more than a whisper, full of a myriad of emotions—love, fear, sorrow, the tiniest bit of hope.

"Okay," he confirms.

I lean down and kiss him, first gently, then forcefully, as if it were our last—it must count.

West clears his throat behind me, and I remember there are other people in the room besides us two. I lift my face and gaze into Ethan's sky-blue eyes. My focus blurs as tears prick at the corners.

"I love you more, Abigail Lansing," he says, his voice thick.

"I love you, too." And that's all I can say. I'm about to break down completely, and I don't want to do that in front of him. I turn to Kate, who reaches out for my hand and puts her arm around my shoulder. I watch the nurses finish prepping my husband as we walk out of the room.

"I'll see you soon," he calls after me.

And I can no longer stop it; the tears fall freely down my cheeks. Thankfully, we are already out in the hallway before the dam breaks.

THE WAITING IS unbearable. I think it's even worse this time than the first surgery. Maybe because the hopefulness has dwindled with each setback. I chew my fingernails as I think about how I used to feel so certain we would weather this storm, come through on the other side stronger than before. Even a week ago, if you had asked me what I thought the outcome would be, I would have sworn that Ethan would be a cancer-free survivor walking out of this hospital in a couple more weeks.

But once again, the worst that could possibly happen has happened. And now I sit, a tightly wound ball of nerves, begging God not to take my baby's father from us. Not yet.

I pull my legs up on the chair and rest my forehead on my knees. The nausea has returned. I finished off my granola bars two hours ago, and this baby wants more. But I don't dare leave the waiting room. I can't leave.

I feel Kate's hand rubbing circles on my back. "Are you doing okay, Abby? Do you need anything?"

Yes. My husband. Healthy and walking through that door.

"I'm fine. A little nauseous, that's all," I mumble into my thighs.

"What do you need? Can I get you something to eat or drink? We could go to the cafeteria."

"No," I whisper. "I can't leave."

"Okay. That's okay. I'll bring you something."

I feel her get up and hear her quietly talking with West. I try to concentrate on not getting sick in the middle of the waiting room. I groan quietly and squeeze my legs tighter to me. I feel Simon settle beside me and place a comforting hand on my back. I lift my head and allow it to rest on his shoulder, but I keep my eyes closed, directing all my energy into staying sane and not getting sick.

I'm not sure how much time passes, but eventually Kate and West reenter the waiting room. I open my eyes to see she has a Styrofoam cup and a bag.

"I brought you some warm tea and chicken noodle soup."

"Thank you, Kate," I say gratefully. "It sounds really good actually."

She sits, hands me the tea. West takes his seat across the aisle again.

I sip the tea and feel marginally better. "Do you have crackers for the soup?" I ask hopefully.

"Of course." She readies the soup for me. I'm so lucky to have a friend like her—always looking out for me.

In no time, I have the soup finished. I'm amazed, though I shouldn't be—it happens every time—at how good I feel after eating something.

Uncle Geoff and Simon have attempted to lighten the mood by telling some of their stories, but alas, even those run out.

"How long has it been?" I ask, feeling very tired. It feels like an eternity has passed since nine o'clock.

"Um . . . six hours, I think." West checks his watch.

Six hours. Surely, they should be done soon. Unless . . . unless—

"We'll hear word soon," Kate reassures me and squeezes my shoulder. I nod.

But as the minutes tick on, worry consumes me. What if they couldn't get all the tumors? What if they found more with the MRI? What if he had a stroke? What if his brain couldn't handle another operation? What if—

"Mrs. Lansing?"

A lifeline. I stand and look expectantly at the bearer of news in blue scrubs. She's not Dr. Jackson, but it is news, so I don't really care. "Yes?"

"Your husband's surgery went well. We have removed the tumors and placed the wafers. We found no new tumors. He is in recovery now, and you should be able to see him soon."

I inhale sharply, my heart rejoicing. "Thank you," I whisper. And I can't help the flood of tears that tumbles down my cheeks.

I vaguely feel Kate and Simon and Uncle Geoff hug me. I'm crying at the realization that my husband is still alive. Relief washes through me first, followed by weakness. I am so tired. I slump into my chair and let my head fall against the wall. It has been such a long and stressful day. But as I stare at the ceiling, a gratefulness surfaces, and the tiniest bit of hope blossoms in my heart.

Thank God the surgery was a success.

And my husband is still alive.

I HAD NEVER paid close attention to the baby and children's sections at Food for Thought. I only learned what I had to about the books and authors in case I was asked questions by our patrons. So I am shocked by the sheer volume of baby name books we carry and how thick some of them are! My eyes widen in disbelief as I thumb through the thickest book. I had no idea there were so many possibilities.

The past few days since Ethan's surgery have flown by. It was nice not having to take him to chemotherapy daily with these wafers inserted into his brain. But he seems to have a constant headache since the surgery, and that worries me.

I thought we could take our minds off it and discuss baby names again. Our last conversation was not fruitful at all. In fact, I think we both ended up very frustrated with one another. If we had a book of names, we would have a vast array to consider. Maybe ones we've never even thought of.

"Hey, girl!" I hear Kate's voice calling. I turn around to see her making her way toward me, arms outstretched.

"Kate," I say warmly as we hug.

"How is Ethan?"

"He's okay. Still dealing with headaches, but . . ." I shrug. *He's still alive,* I think.

"Oh, honey, that's too bad. I hope he gets to feeling better soon. How long does it take for those things to work again?"

"They're supposed to dissolve in two to three weeks."

"Hmm . . ." She ponders then abruptly changes her train of thought. "What are you looking at?"

"Baby names," I confess guiltily as I show her the book in my hands.

"Oh! Baby names!" She claps.

"Yes," I laugh. "I thought we needed something to draw our attention to happier things."

"I agree. So, you're headed back to the hospital?"

"Yep. I need to stop home quick and check the mail and grab some clean clothes first."

"Well, call me in the morning, okay? I want to do lunch tomorrow."

I nod. She hugs me once more. I am reminded again of how lucky I am to have a friend like Kate. My rock.

"WHAT? LET ME in there!" I shout. I push with all my might against the male nurse holding me back. I briefly think about pummeling him with the bag of baby name books I'm gripping. It's heavy. It'll serve the purpose.

"Please, Mrs. Lansing, give the doctors some time."

Some time. Some time! *What do you mean some time?!* I want to shout. That's my husband in there, and I deserve to know what's going on!

I was only gone for a couple hours. I just went to the bookstore and stopped at home. How could things have gone so bad so quickly? I don't understand.

My head is spinning. I grasp tightly onto the nurse's arms barring my way—I am suddenly very dizzy. I try to focus my scattered mind. Last week we were getting married and this week . . . ? What is happening?

I can't bear not knowing. It's killing me. I knew he was drained this past week. He'd had a lot to deal with—the wedding, the news of the tumors, the surgery, the headaches. What the hell could be going on in there?

I pull a conversation out of my racing thoughts.

"Other side effects are new or worsening headaches and possible seizures."

Seizures!

Is he having seizures?

No, oh no! My mind swirls and sways. I can no longer focus on the nurse I'm now clutching for dear life. My knees buckle. I feel strong arms enveloping me as I slump to the ground, losing my grip on my bag of baby name books, my head lolling backward.

Chapter Twenty-Five

But I Need You to Stay with Me in the Light

I BEGIN TO stir. A heart monitor keeps monotonous time. A familiar sound for so many weeks. I blink, trying to bring into focus . . . the lights above me.

Where am I? How did I get here? Oh yes, I must have fainted. Because of Ethan—*Ethan!*

My eyes fly open with renewed purpose. I attempt to sit up.

"Mrs. Lansing, please. Rest yourself," a familiar deep voice soothes. I concentrate on the figure standing next to me, bring him into focus. Dr. Jackson?

"What—what's going on?" I ask hoarsely, my throat very dry for some reason.

"Relax, Abby. You've fainted. No doubt a reaction to the stress you've been under these last few weeks."

Stress? My stress is nothing compared to what Ethan's been through, I think, ashamed. I clamp my eyes shut, trying to hold back my tears.

"You haven't been taking very good care of yourself or your baby," he scolds. "You're dehydrated."

What? A new wave of shame washes over me as my hand instinctively hovers over my belly. "Is the baby okay?" I whisper.

"You'll both be fine," he reassures me. "We're giving you additional fluids." He points his pen at the IV next to me before continuing to write on the clipboard in his hands.

Great. Does that mean I'm trapped in this bed and can't see Ethan?

"What happened to Ethan?" I demand.

Dr. Jackson looks thoughtfully at me for a long moment. He lowers himself down onto the edge of the bed and folds his hands over the clipboard in his lap.

"Ethan had a rare, but possible, adverse reaction to the wafers we implanted."

"What does that mean—exactly?" I whisper.

"He had multiple seizures."

"What?" I gasp. "Is he okay?"

Dr. Jackson frowns, and his dark brown eyes look regretful.

"Tell me." I feel my sanity slipping.

"We are prepping him for surgery."

My brow furrows in confusion.

"Abby, Ethan has had several seizures today. He is not responding to the anti-seizure medication. Our only option is to go back in and remove the wafers."

"What? But that was supposed to fix him," I say desperately.

"We were definitely hoping for a better result." Dr. Jackson reaches out, squeezes my hand. He looks defeated. Are we defeated?

"What does this mean?" I know what this means, but I need to hear it.

"This means we have run out of options," he responds softly.

A choked sob escapes my throat. I throw my hands up over my face and feel the IV pull at my wrist.

No. No. *No!*

"I'm sorry." Dr. Jackson comforts me, squeezing my shoulder.

"You were supposed to fix him!" I choke out. My chest shudders as the floodgates open.

"We tried, Abby," he says as softly as before.

I want to yell at him. I want to punch him. But he sits on the side of my bed, looking as defeated as I feel, and all I can do is cry ugly, heavy sobs.

What else can I do?

Dr. Jackson has issued a death sentence for my husband.

GUILT EATS AWAY at me as I lie here while Ethan endures yet another surgery. I am tempted to rip the IV out of my wrist and go to the surgical waiting room that I know so well. But my maternal instincts take over, and I realize I need to take care of the baby first and foremost. I glance up at the hanging bag. Close to halfway empty. I'll be able to join him soon enough. My hand gently strokes my belly. *You and I need to be strong for your daddy. You'll keep me strong, won't you?*

"Abby!"

My eyes flash to the doorway. "Kate!" I rejoice.

"Are you okay?" Concern is etched on her face as she rushes to my bedside.

"I'm fine," I reassure her. "How did you know?"

"Tabitha called. She thought you needed some support, and I couldn't agree more. What you've been through this week!" She squeezes my hand and brushes my hair off my forehead.

"Kate—" I feel the tears building again. "It's bad. It's so bad."

"I know, baby, I know," she whispers, her eyes brimming.

And we cry together.

Sometime later, Tabitha peeks in. "Abby, how are you?" she asks in such an uncharacteristically quiet voice I have to blink a couple times to ascertain that it is her. I'm too tired to speak, and Kate has fallen asleep in the chair next to me.

"Your husband is out of surgery," she says as she checks my IV. "And it looks like you're about done here."

She looks kindly, sympathetically down at me, but I can't make my voice respond. I'm too desolate. Empty after all the crying. I really wouldn't mind if the ground opened and swallowed me whole right now. Except I don't want that for my baby.

I feel a small pull of something—something steeling my resolve and creating an armor around this baby. I may lose my Ethan, but against all odds, I must protect our baby.

Once the saline drip is done, Tabitha returns to check my vitals and remove the IV. "Go to him now," she says, her eyes raw with emotion.

Kate has awakened. She helps me out of bed and walks with me. She opts to sit in the family waiting room while I go in to see my husband, my Ethan.

I pause in the doorway, wanting to cry as soon as I see him lying there, pale and limp. This is not my Ethan.

But it is.

I breathe deeply and pull myself together before I enter. I must be strong for him. He must know I can take care of myself and our baby, no matter what. As I reach his bedside, he stirs.

"Abby," he whispers, his voice groggy.

"Hush. I'm here," I soothe as I sit beside him and hold his hand in mine.

He tries to smile, and his eyes close. He drifts back off to sleep. I sit with him, holding his hand, caressing his cheek for I don't know how long. His head is bandaged yet again. He'll never be the same, never have the same sandy-blond hair falling in waves, without deep scars interrupting its beauty.

I inhale a ragged breath. Who am I kidding? He won't live to have hair again. Dr. Jackson confirmed that. I press my hand to my mouth, trying to keep the grief from overflowing. *I must be strong. I must be strong.* A mantra to keep me sane. I pinch my eyes closed.

My eyelids flutter open as I hear Ethan take a deep breath. He sighs, blinks.

"I'm so tired," he breathes.

"I'm sure you are, baby," I murmur.

"What . . . happened?"

I breathe in deeply—here we go.

"You had seizures, and the anti-seizure medication wasn't helping. They had to take you back into surgery."

"No." He shakes his head feebly.

"They had to remove the wafers."

"No," he continues louder, arguing with me. His hand instinctively reaches up to the bandages on his head.

It's all I can do to keep my composure. "For your safety, they had to."

"I'm so sorry," he chokes, covering his eyes with his hand.

"What are you sorry for?" I ask incredulously.

"I'm sorry I couldn't do better." When he lets his hand drop, I see his tears. It breaks my heart. "For you. For the baby. I wanted to do better."

I wipe my eyes with the back of my hand. "Shh. You did *fine*." I swallow hard, trying to keep it together. I don't know if I can.

"No. I've failed you. I've failed our baby. Oh God, I've failed," his voice cracks.

And I see his armor cracking. He's about to lose it. I see it on his face—a wild, fierce bewilderment.

I have to stop this; I have to help him. All I can think to do is to press my lips on his. I kiss him passionately. I kiss him as if it's our last kiss, a hungry, needy, powerful kiss, and I feel him relax a tiny bit as I continue to dance my lips on his.

I don't know what I will do without his kiss. I must memorize his kiss.

ETHAN IS EXHAUSTED from the trauma he's been through. I leave him to sleep after a bit and go find Kate in the waiting room. I need someone to talk to, to help me sort out the emotions I'm feeling right now.

As I enter the room, I see Uncle Geoff and Simon waiting with her. She must have called them. Normally, I wouldn't want to bother everyone and drag them down to the hospital. My whole life I have faced everything—good, bad, or worse—alone. It's what I'm used to. But I am relieved they are here. I don't think they know how much their strength bolsters me.

Kate jumps up and rushes to give me a hug. "How is he?"

I nod, emotional.

"And how are you, my dear?" Simon asks as he hugs me next.

"I'm okay. I was dehydrated, I guess." I wipe tears from the corners of my eyes before they can escape.

Uncle Geoff puts his arm around my shoulders and squeezes. "Poor thing. You've been through a lot lately. Here, sit." He ushers me to the cushioned chairs and hands me his handkerchief as he sits next to me. I roll the soft linen around between my fingers, trying to concentrate on it so I won't break down in a sobbing fit. I tell them about the day's events, slowly at first, still trying to calm my emotions.

After I finish and have answered as many of their questions as I can, we sit for a while—a silent band comforting one another with our presence. I recognize that I have never felt such comfort and support from a group of people before in my life as I have with Uncle Geoff, Simon, Kate, and West. And there's something else, too—something I can't name, but it fills me and binds me to these souls. I squeeze Kate's hand and gaze into her eyes with recognition and appreciation for all she has done for me, and all I know she would do for me. She closes her eyes, gives me a tiny smile, letting me know she knows—she gets it. I sigh and let my head rest on her shoulder.

Simon begins a story about the amazing places they visited on their trip to Rio de Janeiro several years ago. He wasn't sure if he'd talked about that trip yet, but it was just too beautiful and too spiritual to not share. I relax and listen, trying to focus on his voice and let go of a bit of the stress that's consuming me.

"ABBY," TABITHA STEPS into the waiting room.

I jerk my head up—how long has it been? Is something wrong? But, no, she appears very calm and unexcited.

"Yes?"

"Ethan's awake and asking for you."

"Oh. Good. Can we all go?" I ask, glancing at the faces around me.

"Yes, just try to keep the visit short, okay? He'll need extra rest over the next day or so to recover." The corners of her mouth lift slightly, and she leans forward as I rise, as if she wants to come give me a hug, but she must decide against it and instead turns awkwardly and leads us out of the room.

"Dr. Jackson asked me to monitor you the rest of the day," she says in a low voice as we walk. "Are you feeling okay?"

Mentally, no. Physically, I guess. I'm tired, but I can rest later. I nod.

She scrutinizes my face for a moment, possibly reading my thoughts. "Well, you be sure to let me know if you need anything, all right? And Marybeth will be Ethan's nurse tonight, so you can ask her, too."

"Thanks, Tabitha." I try for appreciative, but I think it just comes out weak.

We file into the room. His eyes brighten at the sight of his family and friends, but the exhaustion keeps it from registering on his face. He's able to talk for a while with everyone. I take up my post beside him, holding his hand, caressing it.

"What did I miss this time?" West's voice resounds above the others as he appears in the doorway.

"It's about time you showed up," Ethan jokes, a bit more conviction in his voice than before. He must be feeling better.

West slaps Ethan's outstretched hand and does some weird handshake they do. West notices, as do the rest of us, that Ethan's strength is just not there. His arm drops onto the bed as soon as the last slap is done. "They told me you were checking out, so I thought I'd better get down here."

Kate's reproving glance reflects my own thoughts. What a terrible thing to say at a time like this.

"I'm not going anywhere, man. But thanks for the concern." Ethan banters jovially. Is he really feeling that much better? I allow myself to relax a little at his humor.

They continue their conversation for a while, both cutting each other down at intervals and laughing about it. I'll never understand how men relate to one another. I look to Kate, who appears equally confused at their bantering.

"Good afternoon, all," Dr. Jackson appears. "You look well, Ethan, after this last surgery."

Dr. Jackson takes West's place at his bedside to do a vitals check.

"I feel okay, Doc. But tell me, how long will it last?" Ethan asks with a cutting edge. I'm surprised at how he speaks to Dr. Jackson. He's never taken an edge like that before.

"As long as we can manage, Ethan," he replies in such a soft tone I can tell he's trying to placate his patient. My heart constricts. He's preparing Ethan—the worst is here.

I slip into a fog as Dr. Jackson finishes his exam. I'm trying to blank out my mind, to numb myself. I can't think about Ethan gradually getting worse as the tumors overcome his brain and cause him unbearable pain. I cannot allow myself to think of what's to come.

I barely recognize that the doctor has finished until I see Uncle Geoff follow him out of the room, and my interest is piqued. I leave Ethan's side and make my way over to the duffel bag on the table near the door. I pretend to search through it for something.

"I can't say. It could be weeks; it could be months. But our treatment options have been exhausted."

"There's nothing else you can do?" Uncle Geoff demands.

"Well, we could continue to open up his skull and remove as many tumors as possible, but his brain won't allow much of that before we do more harm than good. One of these times he won't make it out of surgery."

"It just doesn't seem right," Uncle Geoff argues. "With all of your fancy equipment and treatments—why can't you obtain a better outcome?"

"This cancer is extremely aggressive. And we have no idea what is causing these tumors. They continue to sprout and grow. Treatment of this kind of cancer surpasses our abilities, I'm afraid. The best we can do going forward is make him as comfortable as possible, try to manage the pain." I hear the definitive tone of the doctor's voice and my heart sinks.

Dr. Jackson's lost hope. I look over at Ethan, still trying to joke with West. My poor Ethan. How much longer will we have together?

"LET'S TALK NAMES. We haven't gotten all the way through that book yet." Ethan nods at the baby names book on the table. My eyes follow his gaze. He wants to talk baby names now, at eleven o'clock at night? He was yawning a minute ago but wants to delve into names now?

I sigh as I rise to retrieve the book. I am so tired after the day's events, but I'll humor him. I'll humor him every time until . . . *stop it!* I mentally scold myself. I need to not think like that. I can't.

I return to my spot at his bedside and open to where we left off—the Ls.

"Layne," I offer.

"That's not awful," he responds.

"Okay." I place a checkmark next to it, as I have done for all the other names we've agreed on, which aren't many. I scan through the list. I've made a practice of not even mentioning the names I don't like.

"Lexie."

"That's a pretty name."

"I think so, too." I check it.

"Lily."

"Um . . . not so much."

Okay, no check.

"Lucy."

"What's with all the girl names?" he protests sharply.

"What?" I look up, startled.

"I'm sorry," he apologizes. "Go on."

He seems genuinely irritated. I frown—will he be this upset if we have a girl rather than a boy? I thought he wanted a girl. As I search his face, I notice a sheen of sweat has accumulated on his brow. I reach for a tissue and dab it away. At first, he looks irritably at me, but then his expression softens, and I get a quiet, "Thank you."

"You know what?" he says suddenly.

"What, babe?"

"I think, whether it's a girl or a boy, you should name it Journey."

It stabs me in the chest to hear him say, "You should name it." Does that mean he's giving up on me?

I swallow hard. "Journey, huh?" I try it out.

"Yes. Journey is a name that suits either a boy or a girl. And it signifies what we've been through together—a journey."

I press my fist to my mouth, afraid I may break down right here and now. I struggle to keep hold of myself as I close my eyes and imagine a little Journey toddling toward me with outstretched arms. A Journey who has sandy blond curls and bright blue eyes. When I open them again, a warm tear streaks down my cheek. Hastily, I wipe it away.

"Journey is perfect." I smile at Ethan. A smile full of promise at what our little Journey will be, can become, but a smile with a trace of pain at the recognition Ethan may never see our Journey.

"Like in our favorite Carson Ripley book, remember? Just when you think your journey is over, you realize a new one begins." His voice falters. He squeezes my hand and his gaze drops. He recognizes what I do. A terrible mask of sadness overtakes his face. My heart breaks for him. I can't bear to see him like this. It's so unfair.

"Our journey isn't over, Ethan. It's not," I say matter-of-factly. I reach up and caress his cheek. "You feel warm," I notice, alarmed. I place my wrist on his forehead. "Are you okay? You feel really warm."

"I'm fine. Don't worry about me," he reassures me as he grasps my hand and pulls it down into his.

"Ethan, you're the most important thing to me—how can I not worry?"

"I love you so much. You know that don't you?"

"Of course, Ethan, and I love you. I always will."

"You are going to be such a great mother."

But I'm afraid I won't be. A sudden fear grips me—I have no idea how to be a mother, and I sure as hell don't want to be a cold, heartless, emotionally vacant mother like my own.

"I need you here with me. I need you to help me raise this child. This baby needs both of us." I am pleading. He can't leave us.

"But, Abby, I won't be here," he says regretfully.

"No," I sob.

"Listen to me." He squeezes my hand to draw my eyes to his. His beautiful blue eyes. "Listen to me," he says again softly, urgently. "You will be the *best* mother there ever was. I know this, Abby. I know you. You will love and raise our child to be a true testament to our characters. You will."

As if that was all I needed to hear, his words sink in and fill me with determination. I will rise to the occasion. And now I know what I must do: I must reassure Ethan that I can do this. That I can raise our child into someone who would make him proud.

"I will. I will love Journey to the ends of the earth. Journey will always know how much his father loves him; I'll make sure of that. I have enough love for the both of us."

I lean in and kiss him, a fervent, loving kiss. In the back of my mind, a tiny voice scoffs at me: *How can I raise a child without him? I know nothing about parenting.* But I must overrule the voice. I must be a good parent for Ethan. I will find a way.

"Your lips are even hot, Ethan."

"Why thank you." He smiles, but his eyes are tired.

"No. Really. You shouldn't be this warm." I place my forehead against his. Then I press the call button for the nurses' station.

"HIS TEMP HAS spiked to 104," Marybeth explains. "We'll give him some fever reducer and put a call in to Dr. Jackson."

"What does this mean? What's going on?" I plead for some answers.

"We have to take it one step at a time, dear. Let's give him some meds and see how he responds."

I silently curse Marybeth. Why can't she tell me the truth about what's happening? As I sit next to Ethan, I trace my fingers across his hand. He appears worse than earlier, but maybe it's my imagination. It's been a really long day. So much has happened.

Marybeth returns moments later and gives Ethan pills and some water. She coaxes them down his throat.

"Did you get ahold of the doctor?" I inquire.

"Not yet. We're waiting for him to call back."

I glance at the clock. Almost midnight.

I spend the next hour watching Ethan's face for signs he's worsening, but he appears calm, and his breathing is steady. My eyelids are heavy, but I won't give in to sleep. I need to be sure he's all right. Eventually, when I think he's fallen asleep, I rest my head on the side of his bed, still holding tightly to his hand. Dr. Jackson has yet to materialize. I close my eyes and allow myself a few minutes to rest until the doctor arrives. Then I'll give him a piece of my mind for taking so long when Ethan needs him.

I JERK UPRIGHT. What time is it? I still have Ethan's hand in a vice grip. He's sleeping. I blink a few times to focus my eyes. When my heart rate finally slows, the exhaustion I felt earlier returns. I glance at the clock on the wall. It's 5:30 in the morning. I look at Ethan—he appears to be sleeping peacefully. I barely touch my wrist to his forehead for a moment, then place my hand on his cheek. Not as hot—good. I fold my arms on his bedside and allow myself to drift back to sleep.

I'm roused sometime later by the sound of voices. I look up drowsily to see Tabitha and Dr. Jackson on the other side of Ethan's bed. I glance at him—still sleeping.

"What's going on?" I ask, bracing myself for his response.

"It appears Ethan's fever has returned. We believe he's contracted an infection from the last surgery."

"An infection?" I squeeze my eyes shut trying to make sense of this new information. I open them to glare at the doctor. "What do you mean 'an infection'?"

"Abby, any time we open up the body, there is always a risk. This time, it seems Ethan has contracted just such an infection. We will treat him aggressively with antibiotics, but know this," he cautions, and my heart stops, "with his immune system already so compromised, we may not be able to control it."

What? My mind shrieks. *No!*

I knew we had limited time together. I had begun to accept that. But not this short—not this quick! "How long?" I whisper.

"Not long, I'm afraid," Dr. Jackson apologizes. "If we can't contain the infection, it will only be days."

I clench my jaw and drop my head into my hands. Ethan is still sleeping. He won't know I'm falling apart. Then I feel Tabitha's hand on my back, soothing me. I reach out for her hand. She wraps her arms around me and mercifully lets me sob on her shoulder.

I HAVE CALLED everyone in to say their goodbyes. Ethan awakened midmorning and was able to talk, though he was very tired and a bit confused. He thought they were just there to visit. I had to leave the room to prevent an emotional breakdown. I walked the halls of the hospital for a while, trying to ascertain in my own mind what was happening.

Ethan is ill, very ill. He's getting worse by the hour, not by the week or day like I had expected. This is going way too fast. I am not ready for it. How do I cope with this?

I return to his room as everyone is leaving, filing out with sorrowful faces.

"Abigail," Uncle Geoff says, his voice cracking.

I embrace him, saying nothing. What is there to say? My eyes fill with tears again. As Uncle Geoff releases me, I move to Simon and embrace him for just as long. The tears stream down my cheeks, and I don't try to keep them in. I honestly cannot believe I still have tears to shed with as much crying as I have done over the last week. Simon inhales a ragged breath, and I know he's crying as well.

I move on to Kate and West, who hug me at the same time. Kate whispers reassurances that all will be well. I don't try to argue with her; I just accept her well wishes, and a part of me desperately clings to the same hope—hope that Ethan will somehow turn around and get through this.

Finally, I separate myself from my family and say my goodbyes. I need to get back to Ethan. As I turn to enter his room, I imagine he will be sitting up in his bed, smiling because he's been waiting impatiently for my return.

But the reality of our situation hits me as I see his pale, frail body lying limp, eyes closed, cheeks red with fever. I sigh and take my place in the chair next to his bed. I clasp his hand in mine and watch his face, willing over and over for his eyes to open and meet mine.

I must doze off because I awake with a start when I feel a hand stroking my hair. I lift my face and look up into his eyes. Ethan is awake—groggy, yes, but awake. He has a loopy grin on his face. They must be giving him painkillers as well as antibiotics.

"Hey, baby," he slurs.

"Hey yourself." I try to smile, to make him feel better. I wish they wouldn't have given him the painkillers—will he remember these last moments we have together? But then maybe it's a good thing to allow him to be pain-free with me for a bit longer.

"C'mere, will you please?" He tries to hold out his arms for me.

I climb up into the bed and place my arm across his chest, grabbing his right hand with my left. I gently kiss his forehead and rest my cheek on it. Alarm spikes in me. He's even hotter than before! Damn, these antibiotics aren't working!

He strokes my left arm with his hand as he pulls me close to him. "I love you so much, Mrs. Lansing. You never forget that, okay?"

I swallow hard. "I won't."

"And you be sure to tell our little Journey I love him every day. You will, won't you?"

"I will." I clench my jaw, struggling to keep my emotions in check.

"Good," he slurs and squeezes me to him.

"Ethan, I love you so, so much." My voice cracks. I cannot hold back the tears.

"Aww... I love you more. Always. Always," he murmurs. His eyes are closed, and I wonder how lucid he really is.

I kiss his thin pale lips—once so full and pink—softly, tenderly. He returns my kiss. I pull my hand from his and place it on his cheek. I lift my head up to look into his eyes. His eyelids flutter open, and I am met with his sky-blue eyes, in which I once saw my future. My heart swells at the memory of the first time I saw those beautiful blue eyes. I lean down and kiss his nose, his cheeks, his forehead. I pepper kisses all over his burning face and bandaged head. Lay my cheek on his forehead.

"You were my miracle—you saved me," I whisper, choking back a sob.

"Oh, Abby, no. No. You saved me. Don't you know? I was lost before you. Before your beautiful face showed up in my store and set right all that was wrong in my life. I waited so long for you. And you've fulfilled every hope and dream I ever had. And now you will give me a child." His hand feebly presses against my belly.

My tears flow freely down my cheeks onto his forehead. I want to lift my head so I'm not sobbing all over him, but he holds me so tightly. "Oh, Ethan."

"And I will watch over you two. Forever and ever. I will. Look for me. I'll be there."

"Don't leave me. Don't you leave me!" I beg, kissing his face through my sobs. I kiss his lips again and again. What will I do when I can no longer kiss these lips?

I feel his mouth go slack, and I search his eyes, distressed by how quickly he seems to be drifting away from me. His glassy eyes flutter closed, and he sighs shallowly. My heartrate quickens, and fear stabs my chest—is this it? But he forces his eyes open, tightening them to focus on mine.

"I'll always be here," he whispers. It seems to take enormous effort to raise his hand. He cups my cheek with his burning palm for a moment before it drops to his chest. His eyelids droop closed, robbing me of his beautiful blue gaze. "Always." And then he is silent. He's drifted into unconsciousness.

I curl up next to him, my hand caressing his face on one side, my nose nestled against his cheek on the other as fevered heat radiates off his skin.

My stomach growls angrily at me. I'm so hungry, but I won't leave Ethan. Not while I think he may still feel me with him.

Eventually, Tabitha comes in to check on him. I can tell it's her from the bouncy steps before she enters my view. My focus doesn't stray from Ethan's peaceful face.

"Abby, honey, you need to go eat something."

"No, I'm fine," I argue. I don't even lift my head from the pillow. I can't leave him now. What if he opens his eyes again and I'm not here?

She stands for a long moment, speechless for maybe the first time in her life. I glare up at her to make my point that I am not leaving him and find her concerned eyes searching my face. But she should know she can't help me now. They have failed to save my Ethan. There is nothing else she can do for me.

I see her set her jaw before I turn my gaze to Ethan. I don't even care to wonder what she is about to say to try to change my mind. I just want her to go away.

"Abby, think of the baby."

I cringe. That unexpected phrase hits home. I sit up, anguished. She's right. I know she is. I glance at his motionless body. I can't leave him, though.

"I'll be giving him some IV antibiotics, so you should have time to go eat something. Then you can come right back, okay?"

"Okay," I finally relent. I reluctantly climb out of the hospital bed and stretch out my aching muscles. Tabitha's right—I do need to eat. Ethan would never forgive me if I let anything bad happen to our baby. I would never forgive myself. I wander blindly to the cafeteria.

THE NEXT COUPLE days are a blur of the same thing. I lie in bed with him until I can no longer bear the hunger, then I go to the cafeteria to nourish myself and our baby.

But it doesn't seem to matter if I'm there or not. He never opens his eyes again. Never regains consciousness. Despite the various medications they try, he doesn't come back to me. Despite my kisses and my pleas, he doesn't respond.

It is a very difficult time. I feel his temperature rising each day, and there's nothing I can do to help him. Each nurse who comes in to check his vitals or change his IV bag gives me the same pathetic sorry look I have come to despise. They know. It's hopeless, yet here I cling to him. I don't give up. I stroke his face, talk to him, attempt to coax him back to us. And then his breaths become frighteningly shallow. He struggles with every rise of his chest. I know this is it, and I cling tighter to him, telepathically willing him to stay with us. It's selfish of me—he is suffering so much—but I do it anyway.

When his final breath escapes his lips, I watch his mouth, praying for his lips to part again and his chest to rise, to take in another life-giving breath. I stare so long, concentrating, trying to force what I want to come to fruition. But his lips remain still. His chest doesn't move. I stare so long my vision blurs. I stop breathing myself. Dizziness overcomes me, and I collapse onto his lifeless body.

No! No! My Ethan! Don't leave me, Ethan!

And the floodgates open. I sob for every lost memory we will never have, every anniversary that will go by without him, every birthday Journey will have without him. I am not strong enough for this. This will break me.

I cannot live without Ethan. I cannot.

Chapter Twenty-Six

Echo

"Abigail, people are waiting to see you. Don't be rude to your guests." Her muffled voice pulls me out of my daze.

Honestly, I have been hiding out in here to get away from you, Mother. I want to say it so badly.

The whole afternoon I've suffered a barrage of tactless questions and heartless statements.

"A fine mess you've gotten yourself into now, Abigail, pregnant and alone. Who's going to want that kind of baggage? And you're so young. It's just too bad."

That was before we even left the apartment.

"Do you know if he had life insurance? How are you going to afford to pay all those hospital bills? And you haven't been working . . . not good."

The final straw that sent me escaping to the sanctuary of the upstairs guest bathroom was a question I could not believe the woman uttered.

"Have you thought about adoption? That is your best choice. You surely don't think you can raise a child on your own? And I hope you aren't expecting me to step in and support you two. I am past that stage in my life, Abigail, really."

I walked away from her at that point, burning with fury at her presumptions. I mumbled some excuse to get away before I cursed and screamed at her and made an unwanted scene in front of everyone gathered to celebrate Ethan's life. I felt a very slight tinge of guilt for leaving Emory—who had been holding my hand acting as a protective buffer between us—standing alone next to my mother. This is only the second time Emory has spent any real amount of time with Victoria, whom she knew was emotionally cold and skewed to the point of ignorance at times, but she had no idea how downright insensitive my mother could be. That last spewing of vocal garbage had even left her gaping incredulously.

Thankfully, Emory didn't follow me as I sought out a quiet refuge. I needed time to myself to compose my anger into something that wouldn't launch me straight at Victoria's throat.

It is true I have no idea how I can raise Journey on my own, but one thing is for certain—I will *never* ask that woman for any help raising my child. I wouldn't do that to Journey.

Now, I stare at the bathroom door, my cover blown, knowing my mother will not leave me alone until I have rejoined "my guests." I push off the edge of the bathtub and unlock the door to allow her entrance, quickly stepping back to keep from being hit as she swings it unceremoniously open.

"Why on earth are you hiding out in here? Have I taught you no better manners when you have a house full of guests? You should be downstairs thanking everyone for coming and accepting their condolences. It is the proper way to handle the situation."

I look blankly at her stern face, which registers only concern that I am not "behaving properly" as a hostess. Anger swells anew at having to deal with her on a day that is already so heart-wrenching. And I have my own questions I want to ask, like why is she here? Who told her Ethan had died?

Well, it doesn't matter now—she's here whether I like it or not. And she'll ruin this time of remembering and cherishing Ethan with his friends and family just like she's marred every other important thing in my life. Seriously, whoever told her about this memorial is going to receive a swift kick in the shins.

As I stare at her perfectly coiffed hair and spotless makeup, I realize there is not one ounce of sincere sympathy for me in her features after I lost my whole world three days ago, and it makes me sad. A different kind of sad from the sorrow of losing Ethan—an empty sadness as I wonder if this woman ever really cared for me, if she even has the capability of loving anyone at all.

But what do I say to her now?

"Yes, Mother."

The anger surrenders to the empty sadness, and I no longer want to confront Victoria. I just want to get away from her. It hurts me to look at her. I step past and make my way down to the sitting room.

Uncle Geoff and Simon were so gracious to volunteer their home for the gathering after Ethan's memorial. It was meant to be an intimate celebration of life, so when my mother had called to let me know her flight information, I'd tried to dissuade her from coming. I'd told her the memorial would be small and she'd probably rather not spend the money to come all the way to New York for such a quick service. But for whatever reason, she chose now to be all motherly. She'd insisted she would come and see me through this difficult time, even though she could only afford to stay a couple days—three at the most. *Thank God,* I remember thinking. And unfortunately for me, she's decided she's staying in the spare bedroom at the apartment, so I have absolutely no time away from her while she's here.

I attempt to pull my mind into focus as I step into the sitting room. I feel numb, and I absently wonder how I appear to these people. Is my face sad? Despondent? Unemotional? Oddly, I haven't cried at all today—not during the memorial, not during the barrage of hugs and sympathy from our friends and family. Not even when Emory showed up and pulled me into a sobbing hug.

I'm sad, overwhelmingly sad, but there's a fog creeping slowly around my subconscious. I'm losing my grip on the present. I feel it—I know it's coming. But rather than fight it, I feel myself waiting impatiently for the calming numbness to envelop me, the welcome darkness to subdue all the terrible emotional wreckage I have suffered over the last several weeks. It can't come fast enough . . .

"Abigail, you really should make a point to speak to all your guests. It's proper etiquette," she stresses at my ear as she sinks her fingers into my arm.

"Yes, Mother," I say automatically.

"I'm going to speak with Simon. I must find out how he creates such delicious hors d'oeuvres."

I watch her march over to him, and I silently wish him all the strength to deal with her. I pray she doesn't say anything offensive. My eyes scan the room. Ethan's immediate family is small, but he had several friends he kept in touch with over the years and a few relatives who showed up to express their sympathy. I know two or three of them a little, and I don't know the rest. They're not getting a very good impression of me or of the depth of our love for one another by my interpersonal abilities today. I just cannot do it. I can't put on a mask like my mother and play a part. I have nothing to give these people. Ethan took it all when he left me—us. I circle my hand over my belly, a habitual motion now.

My gaze falls on Kate. She has been watching me; I can tell from the concern in her eyes. Rather than walk over to her, as I normally would for her strength and support, I opt to head through the formal dining room and the solarium, out to the unstifled freedom of the backyard.

I close my eyes, lift my face to the sky, deeply inhale the sundrenched air. But I feel no relief from the fresh air as I had hoped. Just more emptiness. I open my eyes and survey the beautiful gardens Simon so meticulously attends. I wait for Ethan to walk up behind me and place his arm around my waist, to kiss me on the neck as he would so often do. I glance over my shoulder, hoping he may actually be there, walking toward me. Nothing.

Ambling a slow, wide circle around the garden, I take in the vibrant colors of the flowers and the beauty of the sculptures. I know I should be inside, but I can't bring myself to endure the idle talk. I don't want to see the pitying glances and hear, "It's for the best," or, "He won't suffer anymore." That's crap.

Echoes of Ethan are everywhere. My gaze wanders to the pergola at the center of the yard, and my mind drifts to our first visit here together, that wonderful day he introduced me to his family. I remember the confession he made that set my heart singing: "I was afraid I would never get the chance to know this beautiful woman." And that had just been the start of the most perfect day with such a perfect ending. A stab of pain rips through my insides. I can't think of this now.

I turn from the imaginary scene under the pergola and look to the patio beside it where I am besieged by another memory: a warm night in late spring, well over a year ago now, when Uncle Geoff and Simon hosted a small dinner party with several of their friends. We escaped outside for some privacy and somehow ended up dancing to music that was pouring over the fence from the neighbor's house. Very sexy music, I remember: Solomon Burke's "Cry to Me." Ethan swept me into his arms and twirled me around in that suave way he had when he danced. I could never dance that well on my own—only in Ethan's strong arms with his expert guidance. I bite my lip as I feel again how he dipped me so low and kissed me so sensually, trailing his fingers along my neck and my chest, down to my waist, sinking them deliciously into my hip as he held me so tightly. We'd left the party without even saying our goodbyes. It was all we could do to get home before ripping each other's clothes off. In fact, we didn't make it past the kitchen before succumbing to our passion right there on the marble countertop. It feels like yesterday and a lifetime ago all at once.

My throat aches with unshed tears. The pain in my stomach sears up into my chest, burning through my limbs. I shake my head to rid myself of these images, mocking me with their joy and love—two things abruptly absent from my life. I push blackness to the edges of my mind, chasing the images away. I can't handle this right now.

When I open my eyes again, I'm startled to see Kate approaching. "Hey," she calls softly, halfway across the yard already. She quickly closes the gap between us. "How are you doing?"

I shrug and frown.

"Hey . . ." She wraps her arm around my shoulder. "I'm here for you, you know."

I try to force a grin. I exhale loudly.

"So, West says he's really sorry he called your mom."

"*West* called Victoria?"

"Yeah. When he told me, I could have strangled him. I figured you'd rather get through this without her. He'll tell you it's my fault, though. I asked him to help contact family. Sorry," she says sheepishly, searching my eyes as she grimaces.

"Tell him I owe him a solid punch in the arm. Better yet, tell him I'm sending her to stay with you guys," I say sardonically.

"Oh God, no. Please, no. I've only talked with her for maybe ten minutes, and I already see how she could have completely messed up your psyche."

My mouth twists into a sarcastic half-smile. At least my mother is equal opportunity when it comes to unleashing her venom on the world.

"You know, when she found out how long West and I have been together and that we're not engaged, she asked, right in front of West, what the hell was wrong with him. Said men were idiots anyway, and I'd do better to go find a rich Wall Street type and marry for money."

I roll my eyes. My mother, in true form.

"Then she asked if Geoffrey was really gay. Said she had half a mind to go press him to ask her to dinner."

"What?" I gasp, horror-stricken.

"I strongly cautioned her against it."

Actually, I might have rather enjoyed watching my mother make a fool of herself in front of everyone. I allow myself a bit of satisfaction in picturing that scene unfolding.

"But seriously, hon, how are you holding up?" Kate strokes my hair.

I bite my lip and look to the sky, looking for a sign that Ethan is where he said he'd be. "I just wish this day was over already." I sigh. "I can't stand the pitying looks from everyone. It makes me feel so . . . I don't know. But I don't like it."

"Abby, everyone in there cared about Ethan. And they care about you. We all want to help you through this difficult time. Remember that." She squeezes my arms and forces me to look at her.

"Yeah, okay," I finally concede. But the fog rolls around me in waves, pulling me into its safety. In the darkness is a lulling comfort. I welcome it with open arms.

"ABIGAIL, I MUST leave now. I'm sorry I am not able to stay longer," my mother says through my closed bedroom door.

No, you're not, I think to myself.

"Thanks for coming," I call out flatly. I feel the tiniest bit of relief that she is in such a hurry to get back home.

Honestly, I haven't gotten out of bed today. I crawled in, exhausted, last night after the gathering at Uncle Geoff's and have only gotten up once since to go to the bathroom. I don't even know what time it is. The curtains have been pulled since I got home from the hospital, so it's almost pitch black in here. I hug Ethan's pillow closer to me. Sadly, in the several weeks it's been since he last slept in our bed, his scent barely remains.

My stomach growls, but I can't make my body move to get out of bed. I struggle to remember the last time I ate something. I give up trying and drift off to sleep, only to be awakened later by an urpy feeling. I throw the covers back and dash to the bathroom.

After, I crawl into bed, my body tapped out from the exertion.

The next time I lift my eyelids, I'm disoriented about the time of day . . . or night. I realize I need to eat something, and I need to take my vitamins. I stumble over to the light switch and make my way out to the kitchen, using only the bedroom light to navigate. The sparkling city lights shining through the living room windows tell me it's nighttime. There's not even a moon in the sky to shine its light in on me.

I search the cupboards for something to eat. Nothing looks appetizing. Some eggs in the refrigerator—I decide that's as good as it gets. I scramble a couple in the skillet, Ethan's favorite I ♥ NY coffee mug staring at me from its hook beside the coffee maker the entire time. I find a potentially clean fork and eat directly from the pan without tasting, then fumble in my purse for my multivitamins and swallow one down with a glass of water.

After I scrape the leftover eggs in the trash and set the pan in the sink, I pause a moment to gaze around the hollow darkened apartment . . . so quiet, so large and empty. My eyes fall on his green Jets ball cap, his blue stocking cap with the long braids, and his gray Jets stocking cap lined up on the edge of the mahogany table where I left them days ago, next to the bag of his personal effects Tabitha gave me after . . . I just couldn't bring myself to pack these reminders of him away in a drawer somewhere. Gingerly, my fingers trace along the fabric of each one as I walk alongside the table, and I summon the last memories I have of him wearing them.

Another ignored stack of mail sits on the other end of the table. I really should open those. Maybe tomorrow.

I head back to bed.

"HEY, ABBY, BABE. Come on! There's a whole world out here!"

Ethan's voice draws me out of my slumber. I stretch and slowly open my eyes to find him standing in the doorway, leaning against the frame. I smile at his beaming face.

"Come on! Get up! Let's go!"

"No, you come here." I hold out my arms to him but realize he's already left the room. I throw off the sheets and rush out to the living room. It is overwhelmingly bright out here. My hand flies up to shade my eyes, and I search the apartment for him. But my smile quickly falls as I spot his afghan crumpled up on the couch; there is no one here. I squint at the offending sun. It must be afternoon, maybe late afternoon. I shuffle to the kitchen and grab his I ♥ NY mug, fill it with water, and snag a granola bar from the cupboard. As I return to the bedroom, I walk the long way around the couch, scoop up his afghan, and wrap it around my shoulders.

I wake, groggy, in the middle of the night, swathed in the afghan, my arms wrapped around Ethan's pillow. I thought I heard something.

"Abby, come out here and talk to me. I miss you. You sleep too much."

I jolt upright. I swear I hear his voice this time—in the living room. I jump out of bed, hurry out to see him. I will scold him for making me miss him so! Why did he do that to me?

But I rush out to an empty apartment, quiet and black, only New York's twinkling lights shining in the windows. My blood runs cold at the realization that I am still alone. I shudder at the empty darkness moving stealthily in on me.

I remember I should take my vitamins and find something to eat. Then I crawl into my sanctuary. I hug Ethan's pillow to my chest, inhaling deeply, struggling to find his scent somewhere, anywhere, and fall into a fitful sleep.

I NO LONGER know what day it is. I stumble out to the kitchen, my growling stomach getting the best of me. I open the refrigerator—no more eggs. Nothing but ketchup and coffee creamer. And a container of something that is probably two months old. I grab it and toss it into the garbage without even opening it.

I search every cupboard to find very little staring back at me. One can of soup, broth really. I warm it up and devour it. I really need to get some groceries. I grab my prenatal vitamin and water and head over to the window seat. I shade my eyes against the overwhelming brightness.

What day is it? It looks to be midday by the sun, but I don't even remember what month it is—August still, or September? I gaze out at sprawling Central Park and see that the trees are still a deep green. I swallow down my vitamin and chase it with water. I run my hand through my greasy hair; I really need a shower. I take in the New York skyline for another long minute and stare up at the fluffy clouds in the brilliant blue sky. *Ethan, you promised me you'd be here. Are you here?*

But I don't feel him. I only feel alone. I frown, realizing I haven't been sick for a while. Panic-stricken, I wonder if I've managed to kill Journey as well. Why have I not been sick? I haven't been eating much, true. My mind races wildly—have I killed our baby?

My hands fly to my stomach, and I cradle it, worried. What day is it? I go to the table in the foyer and grab my phone from my purse. Fifteen missed calls. My eyes bug at the sight. Five messages.

"Hey, Abby, just checking in. We miss you around the store . . . so, I was wondering if you wanted to have coffee or something—"

Kate. I delete the message.

Someone trying to sell me a timeshare. Delete.

Uncle Geoff inviting me to Sunday brunch—some Sunday, maybe it's already passed, I don't know. I delete it.

"So, ah, Abby . . . I was really wanting to talk to you about something. Can you stop by the store? It's—"

West. Delete. Whatever it is, I can't deal with it now.

The last message confirms my appointment on Monday with the OB. *Crap!* I scribble the time on the wall calendar so I won't forget. I already called once to reschedule. How long ago was that? Must have been a week or two. I focus on the calendar. Today has to be . . . Saturday—no, Sunday. The doctor's office left the message on Friday. Tomorrow is my appointment. I sigh with relief that I'll see the doctor tomorrow and hopefully have some confirmation that Journey is okay in there. I absently wonder when I will feel like there is actually a baby in my belly, aside from the awful morning sickness.

I head to the bathroom, trying not to worry too much about Journey. I mentally assess that I haven't had any pain or bleeding, so I tell myself the baby is fine. I turn on the tub faucet then gaze at my reflection in the mirror. I don't even recognize the person staring back—she's unkempt, thinner than she should be, and despondent with sunken eyes.

"Are you finally getting yourself out of here?"

I snap my head toward the sound of Ethan's voice—but no one is there. I hesitantly return my gaze to my reflection. I should probably be worried that I am hearing voices. I shake my head to clear it and climb into the bathtub.

I linger in the water until my fingers are sufficiently shriveled, then reluctantly pull myself out of the soothing warmth. I wander around the apartment in my robe, my hair swept up in a towel, feeling marginally better. My fingers drag across the laptop on the secretary desk as my eyes fall on the picture collage I gave Ethan at Christmastime of his family and us.

I stare at it forever, letting the faint aching in my chest grow stronger and stronger as I fight my way through the dark fog I have lived in for so long. Ethan would be so disappointed in me, in how I have failed to take basic care of myself and our baby, how I've hidden away from our friends and family. I let a wave of sadness crash over me as I stare into Ethan's smiling blue eyes, and I savor every harsh moment of it. I choke on a sob as I let every emotion I've run away from tear at me from all angles. It's cathartic to push myself through the numbing fog and feel these jagged, prickly emotions. I should never have hidden from them, should have embraced them. The fact that it hurts so damned bad means that the love we shared was so important to me, will be missed so entirely.

Tears stream down my cheeks as I look from the picture of us together to the picture of Ethan's family on vacation. There's a separate sadness that I never had the chance to meet his parents. And they, along with Ethan, will never get to meet Journey. I feel deep regret that Journey will never know the wonderful person his father was.

But there is something I can do, a way I can share Ethan's legacy. I snatch up the laptop and march over to the window seat. I wipe my cheeks with the sleeve of my robe and power up the computer, then look out the window through blurred eyes at the blue and white sky. As I wait for the login screen, I wonder, *Ethan are you out there?* When no sign comes, I focus my attention on the computer, log in, and open a blank document. I stare at the white page in front of me, feeling all sorts of emotions for the first time in a long while and wanting to translate them onto these pages. But I'm not quite sure how.

There's an overwhelming need to communicate to our unborn child who the father he's missing out on was, the love his parents shared, the struggle we endured, the journey we traveled together.

Before I know it, my fingers begin to type, the words flowing out. The emotions crash through me and onto the pages. I am doing what I always wanted to do, what Ethan encouraged me to do: I am writing. My audience is Journey alone. This is what Journey needs to know about Ethan, about me, about us.

Chapter Twenty-Seven

After the Storm

THE SUBWAY RIDE is quick enough, but as it draws closer to my stop, the uneasiness grows. This is the day of reckoning. The day I find out how Journey is. *If* Journey is . . .

I shake my head to dispel the awful thoughts and try to focus on random strangers in the subway car with me. The elderly couple holding their sacks of groceries close to them. Teenagers with headphones wrapped around their heads, bobbing time to a beat no one else hears. A mother with more young children arguing around her than it looks like she can handle. And just like that the train stops and the doors sweep open.

Three city blocks later, I pause a brief moment to look up at the tall glass building looming up to the sky, no color or personality. Through the automatic doors, the lobby looks impersonal as well. Metal sculptures positioned throughout intertwine, trying to appear as a mother holding a baby or a father with a small child on his lap. Very modern, but still sterile-feeling. The muted gray walls add to the coldness. I walk slowly up to reception, wondering if this was the right choice. A voice reminds me that Tabitha personally recommended this place and used these doctors, so I should get over it. I reach the counter and inform the receptionist who I am here to see.

"Third floor, take a left, Sanderson and Robertson." She might as well be gray, like everything else around here, for as bland as she is.

Third floor and to the left. A long wall of glass windows showcase a room full of waiting expectant mothers, a couple of them with strollers, and even a few fathers. I glance to the right, just to be absolutely certain Bland Receptionist gave me the right directions. At first glance, the long wall of glass windows on the other side looks the same. But looking closer, the waiting people that fill that room are older, and the title on the glass door reads Podiatry Physicians & Clinics. Yeah, not the place I want to be.

So left I go. The ball of nerves in the pit of my stomach starts snarling again as I enter the office and check in. The receptionist here says it will be a short wait, but as I scan the room for an open seat, it's clear many of these people have set up residency. I find a vacant chair next to a very expectant mother and overly anxious father and settle in.

"So, today we talk about inducing the baby, right?" the father asks.

"Yes. Zachary's due date was Tuesday, so the doctor feels we should think about helping him along," she replies, sounding a little put out. I'm not sure whether it's due to the overbaked baby or the doctor's suggestion of inducement.

"So, is that bad for the baby?" the father asks.

Or maybe from the continuous questions assaulting her while she waits impatiently.

"No. It isn't bad for the baby. The doctor said it's just like scheduling any kind of appointment. You say, 'We will induce on this day,' and you show up at the hospital and have the baby. It's standard procedure when you go over the due date," she drones like she's answered question one million and one.

"Okay—okay. So, standard procedure, huh?"

"Yes, Tim. Standard procedure," she replies tiredly. "You know, maybe you should just make a list of questions and ask the doctor when we get in there, okay?"

"Yeah. Yeah, okay."

I think he knows he's hit her last nerve because, thankfully, he's quiet after that.

It isn't long before I find myself digging in my backpack for my laptop. I'm not really interested in the whole alien world going on around me—it's too different from what I know. I want the solace I have found in writing.

The words flow out of me now like a tidal wave, rushing and rushing toward the shore. The kind of large wave that is angry and frightening when viewed from afar. I keep waiting for it to break on the rocks, but it just keeps coming, like the shore is retreating farther and farther from the wave, taunting it. The angry wave rushes through my fingers and onto the keys, then leaps into words on the screen. I'm unable to yield time to read what I'm typing as it goes. I merely open up that laptop and the wave comes tumbling and roaring in, healing me tiny piece by tiny piece as it rolls through.

"Abigail Lansing."

It takes a few seconds for me to recognize my new last name. My head jerks up when she says it a second time. A tall nurse wearing scrubs covered in cartoon characters surveys the waiting area expectantly. Of course, she has no idea who she's looking for. I quickly click save and close my laptop.

"Abigail Lansing," she calls once more, a little louder than before, still searching. I half raise my hand while I stand so she will stop calling my name, shove my laptop into my backpack, and hurry over to her.

"Hi. Follow me right through here, please."

I follow her down the long pastel hallway. Cork boards line both sides covered in photos of babies: brand new babies, toddlers, babies with siblings, and even a few photos of graduates in caps and gowns. So many photos.

"Every time you visit, we'll record your weight and check your urine," the nurse explains pleasantly, like it's no big deal to display my pee every time I see her. "Step on the scale, please." She records my weight then walks me down the hall to the bathroom. "Just grab one of those cups and write your first initial and last name on it. Then bring your sample around the corner here and place it on the green tray. Okay?"

I nod.

"I'll be waiting for you here, and I'll take you to an exam room."

I get through that fun and realize even more fun is waiting for me in the exam room. The nurse motions toward the exam table. After vitals and a quick assessment of how I am feeling today, she says, again like it's no big deal, "Dr. K will be with you in a few minutes. Go ahead and disrobe and put on the paper gown, opening to the back. The other napkin you can place across your lap. You can pull the curtain while you change if you feel more comfortable." She tugs on a pale pink curtain hanging from a metal track on the ceiling. "See you in a few."

She must catch the doubtful expression on my face as I stare at the tiny folded-up paper napkins that are supposed to cover me because she smiles and nods encouragingly before heading out the door. What am I getting myself into? I didn't sign up for *this*. Grudgingly, I do as I'm told and strip out of my clothes, hurrying, because how embarrassing will it be if I have my derrière hanging out when the doctor comes strolling in? In my haste, I trip over my pants, and I rip the napkin gown a little on the side as I try to figure out the right way to wear it. Really, these things need instructions on the side or something.

I manage to get my clothes folded on the chair and get myself situated on the table before there is a knock on the door. A second later, the doctor enters, sending a cool breeze through the opening in the back of my gown and making me shudder. I realize in horror that the napkin has no tie to keep it closed! *Nice*.

But the doctor is looking down at my chart while he walks across the room, only looking up once he comes around to my front side. I relax the tiniest bit. He extends his hand. "Doctor Kirby Beckman. You may call me Dr. Beckman, Dr. Kirby, or as most people around here refer to me, Dr. K. You must be Abigail Lansing. Nice to meet you."

"Abby," I offer as I shake his hand. "Yeah, you too." I realize how much I like the sound of my new last name linked with my first name. It makes me smile.

Dr. Beckman—Dr. K—sits in front of me on a round rolling stool and continues to look over my chart. My nerves start to flare again as I wonder what this visit will entail. I focus my attention on his salt-and-pepper hair, cut short and kind of spiky in the front. When he turns his attention to me, I notice his kind green eyes and gentle smile. His cheeks crinkle at the corners of his eyes. He looks athletic and has the posture of a younger man. It is hard to tell his exact age, but his mannerisms and soft voice put me at ease. I figure he's been in this business for quite a few years now.

"Today, Abby, I'm going to ask you some standard questions, just to get to know your history, and give you some information. We'll do a quick exam and go over our future appointments. Does that sound okay?"

"Yes, sure," I agree, nervousness creeping in at the word "exam."

Dr. K goes down the basic list of health questions and family history. Yes, this is my first pregnancy. No, there is no history of Down Syndrome in either family. Yes, I plan to have a normal delivery in a hospital.

Next comes the tough questions.

"When was the first day of your last period?"

Uhhhh . . . time has been a blur for so many weeks, can I even recall? So many things flash in my mind as I try to unravel the tangle back to before . . .

"A lot has happened lately," I say sheepishly. "I'm trying to remember."

"Take your time. No rush," he reassures me.

What is today . . . September 12, right? No, 11. And when did I take the pregnancy test? July . . . 28. No—25. So, the first day of my last period would have been . . . why is it so hard to pull anything concrete out of these past few months? June . . . June . . .

"June 4?" Why am *I* asking *him*?

The doctor gives me a satisfied grin, so I relax a little. He pulls a small cardboard wheel out of the front pocket of his white coat and examines it closely. "June 4 puts us right about . . . March 11 for a due date."

I am stunned that small wheel can tell me my due date with just a little bit of information. March 11 . . . that seems so far away.

"And you should be roughly twelve weeks along now." He smiles again. Such a comforting smile, it draws me in like a child to a favorite uncle. "Are you taking prenatal vitamins?"

"Yes. I have a prescription already."

"Good. Prenatal vitamins are important, especially during early pregnancy. They help the baby develop properly and help your body supply the proper nutrition throughout your pregnancy. Folic acid is especially important, which is in a higher dosage in prenatals. It helps proper brain development." He pauses, regards me thoughtfully, as if trying to decide the best way to word his next question.

"Do you have a support system to help you through your pregnancy?"

I must have a blank look on my face because he rephrases his question.

"What I mean is, do you have a significant other or parent or friend who will be with you during delivery? Sometimes they even like to come along to appointments or ultrasounds."

"I—I haven't really thought that far along yet," I stammer.

His kind eyes show concern.

"What I mean is, it seems like just yesterday we found out we were pregnant. And so much has happened since then. And now he's gone, and I haven't even thought about what I should be doing. I'm—just—starting to function again." My voice breaks, a swell of grief threatening to take over. I bite my lip and stare at my napkin gown. This is so not a place I want to break down, especially not in this silly pink paper napkin!

Dr. K places his hand on my knee and pats it a couple times. I look up to see that his face has softened into a look of condolence, and I fight even harder to settle the sobs that threaten just under the surface.

"I'm sorry," I mutter. "I guess I haven't prepared myself for a life without Ethan yet—for raising our child without him. We just found out I was pregnant before he passed." Again, I have to fight for control of my emotions. "He was so happy when I told him." I smile ruefully, remembering his elation. Even though he looked so ill, he had also never looked happier. I bite my lips into a hard line and decide I should stop while I'm ahead. I wait for the doctor to ask his next question. He watches me thoughtfully for a moment, allowing me my moment of grief. His face is kind, his eyes sincere. I feel a calmness settle over me as my gaze locks with his. I fear he thinks I'm a basket case, but he appears to truly care about what I'm saying. Definitely not the kind of doctor I was expecting. But then, I wasn't expecting to fall apart at the OB either.

"Abby, I'm so sorry for your loss," he speaks in his soft, even voice. "This will be a difficult time for you, there's no doubt about that, with all the hormones and physical changes that will be taking place. I strongly urge you to share this experience with someone, whether it's a family member or a close friend. You will want to share many of these moments. And you will want someone to be there as delivery approaches. You think about that, okay?"

I nod.

Dr. K clears his throat and stands. "Let's have a look." He smiles reassuringly. "I'll have you lie back, and we'll take some measurements." I still feel somewhat apprehensive about this exam thing as I watch him walk to my right side. He presses on my stomach. I flinch, my ticklishness getting the better of me, and try to brace myself. He presses in several more places around my abdomen. Next, he pulls a paper measuring tape from the same pocket the due date wheel came from and measures this way and that.

"Have you been experiencing any abdominal pain or bleeding?"

"No."

"Good." He walks out of my line of sight. I hear a cupboard door open and close and then a drawer. Moments later he returns to my side with a handheld gadget attached to a speaker box with a cord and a tube of something. My nerves get the best of me as I wonder what he's going to do to me now.

"Let's do a sonogram and see if we can't hear a heartbeat today."

Oh. Silly me. Of course, a sonogram.

"This may be a little cold on your stomach, so I apologize in advance," Dr. K says before he squirts gel onto my bare skin. I flinch. He places the handheld part on my stomach and starts dragging the gel around my skin. Several long moments pass, and I glance up at his face. Is it supposed to be doing something? Is he as nervous as I am? His face is calm. He continues to push the gel around. I feel my own heartbeat quicken in worry. And then—

There it is!

An odd rapid pulsing sound, a definite rhythm, crackles through the speaker in the doctor's hand. Wetness pricks my eyes as my breath catches. My hand flies up to my mouth in amazement. The sound grows louder as he carefully positions it a little farther to the left. A tiny gasp escapes my throat when I can finally breathe again, and a rush of pure emotion floods through me. Happiness and awe and excitement . . . and love.

Immediately, I feel a strong love for this baby I can't say I felt before. As I stare at my stomach, I realize it is *real* for the first time. Not just a hope on a stick or a confirmation on lab paperwork. This is proof of life. Proof of the love Ethan and I shared. Proof of the gift Ethan left behind. Journey is alive and well and growing inside me!

When I look up at Dr. K, he is blurry. My eyes are overflowing with a very different kind of tears. He smiles as he hands me a tissue.

"Beautiful sound, isn't it? One hundred thirty beats per minute. A healthy heartbeat, Abby."

He wipes the goo off my stomach and pulls the napkin down over me. I have totally lost all self-consciousness of the two pink napkins that thinly cover my body. He helps me up into a sitting position and places the equipment and gel on the counter before grabbing my chart and making notes. I am amazed at how different I feel—I can't explain it—just from hearing the baby's heartbeat.

"Okay." I'm pulled from my euphoria by Dr. K's voice commanding my attention. He places my chart on the countertop beside him and leans back, folding his arms across his chest. "I'll have the nurse give you an order for bloodwork. Standard procedure. You can go to any lab to have it done. And we'll see you again in four weeks." He smiles his kind smile. "Unless you have any questions for me?"

"Um, no. I don't think so." My mind is happy jelly right now, so no—no questions. Everything feels so surreal, and I can't help smiling. A real smile, for the first time in a long time.

Dr. K nods and heads for the door, turning abruptly as he reaches my side. He places his hand on my arm. "And, Abby, please think about what we talked about for your support system. See you in four weeks." And with that, he's out the door.

A huge weight has been lifted. As I crumple up the pink napkins and get dressed, emotion is running wild through me. I can't seem to put together a string of thoughts to quantify these feelings. How strange . . .

When I float out the glass doors and onto the busy street, all I notice is how the sun is so much brighter than it has been in weeks. I shield my eyes and dig into my purse for my sunglasses. I take off in a random direction, barely noticing the throng of shoppers and commuters milling about me on the sidewalk. As if in a dream, I'm moving forward without my feet touching the ground. A haze surrounds my peripheral vision. I am thoroughly enjoying the heady feeling—not sad for once—but I feel as though I need to pull myself together, to focus.

When my insides finally settle, I pull my backpack around me and reach in the front pocket for my phone. I heft the bag around and lace my arms through the straps.

"Hey, it's Abby. I know. I'm sorry—do I sound strange? Oh, huh . . . well, I really want to see you. Can you meet me tomorrow at Java Web? Yeah, ten o'clock is great. And I really am sorry, I've been horrible. Thanks. I'll see you tomorrow!"

I'll admit, I do *feel* strange. But I like it.

"I HAVE TO say, Abby, hon, I was so happy to hear from you yesterday. And *relieved*. West and I have been worried about you. The way you detached from everyone for so long had us a little scared."

I don't tell Kate, but that's what I do, that's how I cope. I detach from the emotional ties that bind me to anyone. The one person who finally pulled me away from that is gone now, so I reverted to the safe pattern that has gotten me through all these years.

"But look at you," she continues. "You look well."

I shoot her a questioning look across the table.

"Well, you look *better*," she amends.

That I can handle. "I feel better."

We sit at a small table out on the courtyard of Java Web. Kate has an iced coffee, and I am sipping on a caramel latte. Again, it seems like such a bright day in the city. It's as if a veil has been lifted from my eyes, and I'm seeing everything the way it should be—no haze of despair clouding my vision and thoughts.

"I probably shouldn't be drinking this," I muse. "The nurse loaded me down with all kinds of pamphlets and printouts yesterday on what I should eat and not eat, what medications I can take and not take, all about my changing body and emotions. Honestly, I don't know how they expect people to read all that," I complain.

"You've got plenty of time, Abs," she reassures me. "So . . ." Kate leans over the table expectantly. "What did the doctor say? Do you know the due date? Did you hear a heartbeat? Aww . . ." Her face gets all mushy. "You're gonna be a mommy!"

I can't help but smile as I shake my head at her and roll my eyes. "Kate, you're insane!"

"But you love me." She grins impishly.

"But I love you," I agree. "It was... definitely an experience yesterday. Not what I was expecting in so many ways. But better than I was expecting, too. Oh, Kate! When I heard that little heartbeat, it was *amazing*! I can hardly explain it—so emotional." I'm surprised that my eyes mist, remembering the pulsing sound of the tiny heart. She stares at me with that mushy look plastered all over her face like she's looking at the cutest little puppy ever. I sniff, trying to keep my emotions in check. "Um, due date is approximately March 11. I am around twelve weeks along." I rub my habitual circle around my belly.

"Ohhh," Kate melts.

I smile again. She is just ridiculous about this baby stuff!

"And... there's something I want to talk to you about," I start slowly, gauging her reaction. "Dr. K suggested I find a 'support system.'" I add the air quotes to the phrase. "He thinks it will be... beneficial for me—and the baby—to have people around, involved I guess, in the pregnancy and the delivery. Says it's important to have someone to share my emotions and my experience with." I wave my hand dismissively and look out over the busy street. "I don't know. It's silly, really."

"Abby, are you asking me to be your coach?" she asks with an eagerness for which I am not prepared.

"I guess, yeah, you could say that. I know I've been terrible lately, Kate, but you're like a sister to me. It would mean a lot if you would help me through this journey."

"Oh, hush, Abby. You've been coping as best you know how. I'd like to see anybody do better considering all you've been through." She squeezes my hand. "Of course I'll be there for you."

We smile like we're about to embark on a grand adventure. Neither one of us has been through a pregnancy before. This is uncharted territory. And now I have someone to take along on the trip with me. I feel a huge sense of relief and gratefulness for Kate. I should never have worried that her response would be negative. Of course she would be here for me.

She then pulls a gift bag from her huge handbag and sets it on the table in front of her.

"What's all this?" I demand.

As she pulls items out, I can tell she's so pleased with herself, depositing an array on the table in front of me: baby booties in blue and pink; onesies in blue, pink, yellow, and green; onesies with zoo animals and farm animals; burp rags with Noah's ark designs. She explains the latest trends in pacifiers as she shows me. She makes that mushy face again as she shows me the tiny nail clippers with a special guard on them specially designed for baby's tiny fingernails and toenails. She displays an assortment of baby care washes and powders and ointments. Then she reaches into her handbag again and produces catalogs with crib sets and furniture and design ideas for baby's room. I am blown away by it all.

"And last but not least, a journal for you to record your doctor appointments, your weight, your ultrasounds. There's a place to write what the doctor said here, and then you can write your thoughts and feelings over here. Then one day you can share this with the baby. A real keepsake." She has clearly taken great care picking out this particular journal for me. I am touched. She hands it over, awaiting my reaction. But I'm speechless.

My fingertips trace across the gorgeous pastel green tapestry cover with its intricate Noah's ark design. It looks too delicate to be a journal, but as I open it, I see the binding and the pages are very thick. The pages remind me of parchment paper, creamy white with blue lines for writing. There are even pouches inside for mementos or pictures. I smile, thinking about the entries I will write in here, tonight even. I imagine how I will pull this out from time to time as Journey grows older and relive the joys of impending parenthood as I share it.

"It's perfect, Kate. Thank you." I hop up from the table and give her a tight squeeze.

She grins. "There's so much to do and to buy, but we have time yet."

"Yes, we do. Are you doing anything now? We can stop by some stores and look at baby furniture."

"I'd love to come along! Oh—one more thing before I forget." She loads the baby goodies back into the gift bag. "West has been trying to get ahold of you. He has something really important to go over with you."

"I know . . . he's left messages. I feel so bad that I've ignored him," I say apologetically. "Tell him I'll call tonight, okay?"

"Good. I will. Now let's go shopping!"

Chapter Twenty-Eight

Wait. What?

I STARE INTO the store I haven't been able to enter since Ethan's death. Standing out on the sidewalk looking in, it's reminiscent of the first time I came across this place three years ago. But a heaviness weighs on my chest now. And at the same time, an emptiness.

As I gaze through the window, I'm greeted by the familiar sights of Food for Thought. Once a place of comfort, it now somehow feels foreign—the happiness previously enjoyed so far off in the distance. Swallowing hard, I wonder if I will ever feel at home again here without Ethan.

A frantic waving from inside catches my attention. West has spotted me, and he's waving me in. I take a deep breath and look over at the door. Can I go back in there? I just don't know. It doesn't feel right.

But West needs to talk to me. About what, I have no idea, and Kate made me promise to see him this week. I don't understand why, and she wouldn't explain, but here I am . . . planted on the sidewalk in the seasonably cool autumn weather, staring at the door. I look through the glass window, poised to walk away. I'm so afraid of the memories this place holds. West remains, staring at me with his hands on his hips, one eyebrow raised. Knowing him, if I walk away now, he'll come marching out after me and drag me inside.

Resigned to my fate, I sigh heavily. *Dig down deep, Abby. Find your strength.* I close my eyes for a moment and summon the power to move myself forward. One more deep breath and I propel my legs toward the door, pausing one long second with my fingers on the handle before I set my resolve, entering the store with my eyes shut tight.

In my mind, I'm transported to the first day I entered this place. There's Ethan helping a customer, talking in his confident way about a book he recommends. I wait for him to turn and notice me...

"Abby—hi," West says awkwardly.

My eyes flash open and I notice he's hovering weirdly around me, his arms half-raised, as if trying to decide whether to hug me. I shoot him an *Are you sane?* look, then respond, "Hi, West. You... needed to see me?"

"Uh, yeah." He shoves his hands in his pockets and raises his shoulders upward, shifting from foot to foot.

I stare at him, assessing his behavior, waiting for him to explain why I'm here.

"So," he says quickly, "let's, um, head to the breakroom. There're some things I need to go over with you, okay? We should have time before I have to open the store."

"Yeah, whatever." I shrug, still wondering why he's acting so strangely. After a beat, I stride past him toward the breakroom. I don't look to see if he's following me. I keep my eyes forward, focusing on the door ahead. I can't afford to let my gaze wander around here. I can't bear the overwhelming ache I know I'll feel when I realize this place is thriving without Ethan.

As I enter the room, I notice a stack of papers and folders on the table. West walks over to the chair beside the stack and sits down, his hand resting atop it. He clears his throat and motions to the chair across from him. "Um..."

I obediently pull out the chair and sit. Why do I feel like I've walked into an ambush of some sort?

He fidgets in his chair, taps his index finger on the stack of papers, and clears his throat once more. "Abby, I'm just going to apologize in advance for this. If it were up to me, I wouldn't be the one telling you all of this now... but Ethan insisted it happen this way." The mention of his name here, at the store, sends a shockwave through me.

I narrow my stare, trying to understand. Ethan insisted?

Suddenly, my mind is drawn back in time to the morning in the hospital when I overheard their conversation. Something Ethan didn't want me to know yet. No wonder West is so nervous about my reaction. He has to deliver the bad news. "Oh, God," I groan. "Oh no. Don't tell me—there's no life insurance, and we're broke. I knew I shouldn't have trusted him when he told me not to worry. How long until I have to move out of the apartment?"

My stomach knots with the realization that I am back where I was three years ago. Broke and worrying about how to pay all my bills. But a drastically worse feeling grips me knowing I have another life that depends on me now.

"No, Abby. That's not it—"

"What's all this about then, West?" I demand, fear of the unknown making me very edgy. "You know, I overheard you two that day in the hospital. I heard your little secret conversation. I would so much rather have heard all this from him than to have to hear it now, after everything I've been through. I can't—I can't deal with this, too." I drop my fist onto the table, feeling defeated. How much worse can it get?

"Hey, hey—listen to me," he says as he clasps his hand over my fist and looks urgently into my eyes.

Resigned to my fate, I wait for him to say his piece. Then I can leave this damned store and find a hole to crawl into to wallow for a while.

"Abby, it's not like that at all. You have to trust me on this."

Without faltering, I continue to stare at him, making my discontent with their actions well-known in my expression. What could he say that will change my reality?

"I do wish he would have been the one to have this conversation with you because it is a life-changing conversation."

I blink. "What are you talking about, West?"

He inhales deeply and squares his shoulders like he's preparing for something. I wait for the bomb to explode in my face.

"Okay, so this is some pretty heavy stuff, as I've said already, so please prepare yourself . . . and let me explain it all before you freak out on me, okay?"

I finally offer a faint shrug as I realize he's waiting for some sort of assent from me.

"We had a type of insurance on Ethan, and on me, called key man insurance, which basically protects the store if something happens to one of us by paying out cash to help us through the major loss to the business."

I stare in confusion. What does that have to do with me?

He hastily continues. "So, what that means is the store will receive a million dollars from an insurance policy to help us regroup and adjust to the loss of Ethan."

"Okay," I respond when he doesn't say anything else. I'm still confused.

"Okay. So, there are other things I need to discuss with you. Are you up for this?"

"Ah, yeah, I guess." I shake my head though.

"Abby, did Ethan ever tell you how this store came about?"

"Yeah. He told me . . . he said he ran into you one day, and you had this idea for a bookstore that you talked him into."

"Right." He looks at me tentatively. "What else did he say?"

"That's pretty much it. What are you getting at?"

"Well, the bookstore *was* my idea, but I needed an investor to get the idea off the ground. Ethan was my investor."

"What?" Ethan was the investor? He always made it sound like West was the boss around here.

"He put up the cash to get the store going. And in return, he had a seventy percent stake in the business. I'm the manager, if you will, but he was most of the funding behind the deal." He continues as I level him with an unfathomable stare. "Abby, Ethan owned seventy percent of this business. So now you own seventy percent of this business. Do you understand what that means?"

"No," I whisper. Ethan owned most of Food for Thought? And now *I* own most of it? How can I run a business? Especially this business. Especially right now.

"You don't really need to do anything right now," he says, reading my mind. "I know you've been through a lot lately. But you do need to know this. And I do need you to sign some papers as the new co-owner of Food for Thought."

"Sign papers?" I ask, still trying to process this new information.

"I'll walk you through it all, don't worry. And there's some other stuff, too," he continues warily.

I wonder if he senses how out of my depth I feel—and still so bewildered. I mean, what else could there be? A personal submarine Ethan held title to in the harbor? A private island in the Caribbean? Children from a previous marriage? What other bombshells are there?

"I have all Ethan's bank account and investment information in this stack of paperwork here. He made me promise I would go over it all with you. And his personal life insurance policy that lists you as the beneficiary is here as well."

Closing my eyes, I slump back in the chair. This is so much unexpected information. I had no idea when I came to see West today that I would have all of this dropped on me like a ton of bricks. I am a co-owner of a business now? I have to understand his investments?

"So, I need to show you the policy Ethan had in place. You'll sign a couple places and then send it off with a copy of his death certificate. Can you do that?"

"Yeah, I guess," I agree noncommittally.

"He wanted to ensure you were well taken care of in the event anything ever happened to him. He actually took out the policy right after you started living with him. So remember, he has always kept your well-being first and foremost." He pauses so the truth of what he's said has time to sink in. I take comfort in knowing he's right about that.

He continues, "The face value of this policy is five million."

I nearly choke on my tongue.

I DIDN'T GO home right away after my meeting with West. I walked through Central Park for a while. I sat across from Belvedere Castle as Ethan and I had done so many times before. I walked to Strawberry Fields. I walked back.

I have been trying to process everything. I'm a small business owner now. I have a *five million dollar* life insurance benefit headed my way. I live in a paid-for multi-million dollar apartment. The final tally of all Ethan's investments and retirement accounts? Nearly another five million dollars.

I just—I don't understand why he never told me about all this before. What were his reasons for withholding the fact that he was wealthy? He really was.

I think back on all our conversations, and true, he never pointedly talked about money other than reassuring me that I didn't ever need to worry about it. He even told me I didn't have to work if I didn't want to. But there was never any indication he had *so much* money.

Admittedly, I feel a certain amount of relief knowing our home is paid for and I won't have to worry about how I will provide for Journey. But part of me feels betrayed as well. Did he truly believe the money would change me, change our relationship? I just don't understand.

I may never understand. I wish I could talk to him somehow, find out why he kept all this from me. Did he not trust me? Did he think I would think differently of him if I knew how rich he was? Was he that burned by his former fiancée that he couldn't trust women and their true feelings when it came to money? I hope he thought better of me than that.

I shift my thoughts to what this financial security will mean for me and Journey. I never have to work again. I can devote all my time to raising Journey. But would I want to walk away from West and Kate and Food for Thought? They are my family. The store is a huge piece of Ethan's legacy. And that place has been such a large part of my life and my happiness for the past few years. After all the years of working as a necessity, I don't know how I can handle *not* working. It seems so unnatural.

I wander around Central Park until I start to shiver in the cool evening air. I leave not feeling any more confident about the direction of my life than I did when I first arrived late this morning.

Staring blankly at the elevator buttons, I make my slow ascent to the seventy-second floor of the Metropolitan Tower. I unlock the door to the apartment and pause in the foyer to gaze around the large space that I now own. That Journey will soon toddle around in. Time and reality slowly return to me. It is still so unbearably quiet without Ethan here. Pain constricts my heart, and I gasp at the unexpectedness of it. When I finally recover, I toss my keys in a familiar motion onto the side table, then I head over to my laptop and power it on. Time to write again.

Chapter Twenty-Nine

W.T.F.

THE EARLY AUTUMN sun warms my face deliciously as I relax on the window seat. My new favorite place. I often gaze out at the green park below and the blue sky above, watching for signs of Ethan. Occasionally, I feel his presence. Like now, when the warm rays of the sun feel like his palm touching my face. I close my eyes. In this moment, I am content. But as the warmth fades I turn my attention to the book in my lap, the baby book Ethan and I spent so much time looking at right before . . .

I force my mind to focus on the picture of a baby at fifteen weeks. Each week I look at the progression of this life inside me, and each week I am amazed at the miracle of it all. Later this week is my next checkup. I wonder if I will get to hear the baby's heartbeat again. That would be such a treat, like a postcard from the inside: "Hey, Mommy. I'm doing just fine in here."

My gaze drifts over to the journal Kate gave me for the pregnancy. I wrote in it right away after that—about how I found out I was pregnant, about Ethan's reaction, about my first appointment. Pretty basic stuff. I've been spending so much time lately writing on the laptop I haven't even picked up the journal in two, three weeks? I decide it's time to do a little documenting for baby.

As I settle in with the journal, I begin by rereading my previous entries. Basic facts, really. I feel I should be saying more than just height, weight, heartrate, stomach measurements. I want to actually convey my thoughts, feelings, fears—to encompass the true journey from conception to birth. I want to tell the story—to Ethan. I want him to feel like he hasn't missed out on one moment of this event I'm sure he so desperately wishes he could be here for. I scrawl down my next entry:

Ethan,   15 weeks

I felt you with me today. I hope you know how very much I miss you. I'll admit, I've been a little upset with you lately. Ever since West dropped that bomb on me. I still don't understand why you never told me about it all. I will never understand your decision to keep me in the dark. But I forgive you. You must have had your reasons. Maybe you meant for this to be another one of your infamous "surprises"? Maybe not...

I want to tell you—Journey is fifteen weeks along and about four inches long. Can you believe that? Four inches! The lungs are developing and little legs are growing longer. I am so excited because Kate is coming with me to the next checkup this week. She has agreed to be my coach, and I am so relieved knowing she'll be there to get me through.

I cannot wait to hear little Journey's heartbeat again. It's such a beautiful, inspirational sound. I wish you could hear it.

Well, I'm sure you hear it. We miss you. We love you.

♥ A & J

I stare out at the waning sunlight as I close the journal. The warmth of Ethan's presence has faded, and I feel very alone again. I rub my belly, grateful for the reminder that I am not truly alone.

The ring of my phone from across the room startles me. I hop up and dash over to grab it before it goes to voicemail.

"Hello?"

"Abigail, hello."

My mother. Great.

"Hi. What's up?"

"Nothing's up," she responds a bit petulantly. "I haven't heard a word from you since I left, so I felt like I should check in. Although, you do seem to take some sort of joy in knowing you are worrying me."

"Mother, I do not take joy in worrying you. You know that."

"Well, it sure feels like it. You've not called me in weeks."

"I'm sorry. I haven't really been reaching out to people lately," I say flatly. Why am I apologizing to her?

"Are you going to your doctor appointments?" she presses.

"Yes. I have been to one, and I have another appointment later this week, on Friday."

"Good. And the baby is healthy?"

"He's fine." The tone of her voice is leading. She's about to ask me something, but what? "Did you need to talk about something specific, Mother? Because I need to get going if not. I'm meeting Kate for dinner."

Not true, but Victoria doesn't need to know that.

"Oh, well then, by all means, let me cut to the chase. Have you thought any more about the discussion we had previously?"

"Which discussion are you referring to?" I blocked a lot of the conversations my mother and I had during her last stay out of my conscious memory.

"The discussion we had pertaining to adoption. I have a connection here at the school. The guidance counselor's sister and her husband have been trying to adopt for some time now, and she thinks they may be interested in speaking with you."

My immediate confusion fades to recognition as I remember that discussion, or rather the lecture she gave me the day of Ethan's memorial. The recognition rolls into disgust. How could she? Lining up parents for my baby? Is she doing a full-scale screening process as well?

"Mother!" I spit out indignantly when I find my voice. "Are you advertising that I want to give up my baby for adoption?"

"No, of course not. Don't be silly. You think I want all my friends to know the situation my daughter is in? No. I overheard Sally talking about her sister's troubles with adoption, and I approached her privately."

I am floored at the statements assaulting my ears. The *situation* I am in? What, is she *embarrassed* of me? I have an inkling it's not a new feeling for her. The shock of her revelation keeps my true anger from fighting its way out to put her in her place. I'm just too stunned.

"Well, I wish you wouldn't have done that." It's all I can muster.

"Abigail, someone has to get the ball rolling on this before you run out of time. The sooner you obtain a committed couple, the sooner they can start handling medical bills and the like. Have you even made any contacts?"

"No, Mother, I haven't. And I don't plan on it either." How can she speak of Journey like a business deal to close?

"You're not being sensible. It is understandable, considering pregnancy hormones have your mind all out of sorts, but it is time for you to start thinking seriously about the options available to you." She speaks as if lecturing a classroom full of her students, so calmly, so authoritatively.

I am anything but calm now. I am infuriated.

"You need to listen to me because I am only saying this once." I fight to keep my voice even. "I have no intention of giving this baby up for adoption. It's the last reminder I have of Ethan, and I will not let that go. I'm sure it will be difficult, but I plan on raising this child on my own." The conviction of my words gives me the strength I need to stand up to this woman. I will not let her try to manipulate me into doing what she wants as she so often has in the past.

"Oh really?" she taunts. "And just how do you plan on doing that? Have you returned to work? Did he have some life insurance policy to support you? How do you think you can afford to be so selfish?" She has uncharacteristically raised her voice to reprimand me.

In a moment of weakness, I let it out. The thing I never wanted my mother to know. "Because I'm rich now, Mother! I *can* afford to keep this baby and this apartment and my life in New York! I am wealthier than I ever could have imagined! Ethan had an unbelievable life insurance policy, and he owned that bookstore you think is so silly, and he had all kinds of investments. So yeah, I know I can afford to be this selfish." My anger transforms into gloating as I lash back at her. *Take that. I'm wealthy now, the one thing you would kill to be.*

But my smugness quickly dissolves into regret, and a rock forms in my stomach. The other end of the line is dauntingly silent. What gears are turning in her mind? The silence continues, and I begin to wonder if I have really hurt her feelings. Guilt creeps up on me and I bite my lip, unsure what to say next.

Finally, she speaks in a flat, quiet voice. "Well. Do you feel better now that you have yelled at your mother?"

"I'm sorry, Mom. I am." I close my eyes as I inhale deeply, trying to find that conviction I had moments ago. Why am I apologizing again?

"You have played me as quite the fool, haven't you?" Her even tone disarms me. "When were you planning on disclosing this information? After I had several potential adoptive families lined up for you? Do you think I enjoy wasting my time trying to fix your messes? Turns out it wasn't even a mess at all, was it?" A slight edge enters her voice.

"I'm sorry. I only just found out about it." Three weeks constitutes a short time, right? "For some reason, Ethan was tight-lipped about it. He had West go over everything after his death. And actually, I avoided most people for a while, so we just recently discussed it. I'm still trying to process it all myself." I sigh, disappointed that I let my mother get to me so easily . . . and disappointed that I let slip how much money I now have. Money she will now think she deserves a piece of no doubt.

"I see," she says simply.

So now I feel the need to fill the empty space with excuses, with penance, with something. "Thank you, though, for going out of your way to try to help where you thought I needed help."

"Yes. And perhaps next time you'll feel the desire to keep me up to date on the goings-on in your life. I would appreciate that courtesy," she replies coolly.

"Yes, Mother."

"I'll let you go now. I am sure you have more pressing matters to attend to. Goodbye, Abigail."

"Bye." The line goes dead before I even get the word out.

Once again, I feel like a Mack truck has slammed into me after a conversation with my mother. I stare for a long time at the phone in my hand, wondering what repercussions my confession will have.

❦

"WHAT ARE YOU doing out here?" Kate waves me over to the door of Food for Thought as she pokes her head outside.

I haven't been here since my meeting with West weeks ago when my whole world shifted yet again. I've walked past several times, always planning on stopping in but unable to cross the threshold. I'm too afraid of the pain my memories will unleash on me in there. It's a silly fear, I know, but I've dealt with the onslaught of memories at home, at Uncle Geoff's, even in Central Park. I have yet to deal with our memories here, and I'm not up to the heart-wrenching task of facing them.

I drag in a deep breath as I focus on her comforting hazel eyes. She's smiling at me in a confused manner—she doesn't understand my dawdling. I steel myself as I step forward.

"How many times did you walk past? Three? Four? What's up?" She hugs me before she pulls me into the store.

"Five, actually," I confess. When I see her look of consternation, I add, "I know. I know. I'm not normal."

"Abby, don't be ridiculous. You're fine. Let me grab my jacket, and we can go."

She heads to the breakroom, leaving me alone. I look down at my feet.

"Hey, stranger."

I jerk my head up to see Josh has appeared. It's been weeks since I've seen him. "Oh, hey."

"How's it going?" he asks casually.

"Oh, you know. It's going. Kate's coming with me to my ultrasound today."

"Yeah?"

I nod.

"That's cool."

We share an awkward silence. I mean, we got along just fine when we worked together, but I never had a chance to get to know him that well before I stopped working.

"So, Josh . . . I don't think I ever told you this, but thanks. A lot. For helping out here while Ethan was sick . . . and . . ."

"Oh, yeah. No problem, Abby. I'm glad I could help. Really."

Kate finally emerges with her jacket on and purse in hand.

"So, are you planning on coming back any time soon? People miss you around here."

"What?" People miss me?

"Yeah. You've got a few customers who still ask about you. A lot of people really liked Ethan and felt awful about what you two went through. I think they'd like to see how you're back on your feet. And how you're getting fatter," he throws in, a mischievous smile on his face.

I don't know how to respond. He mistakes it for embarrassment.

"I'm sorry. It's none of my business." He blushes. "I just thought you should know that people miss you."

"Oh, no. Yeah, Josh. Thanks. I appreciate it." I give him a little smile. He relaxes and grins in return before he heads over to help a customer.

"Ready?" Kate asks.

"Yes." I turn to her as we head out the door. "People miss me?"

"Of course, people miss you, Abby! They ask about you all the time," she replies like it's a given fact.

"I thought maybe Josh was exaggerating."

"Doubt it. We all miss you at the store. Especially me!" She loops her arm around mine. "When are you coming back?"

I roll my eyes to the sky and exhale loudly. Kate's going to think I'm a lunatic when I tell her why I don't feel comfortable being at the store.

"I know it's got to be tough for you. With Ethan not being here anymore. I don't know if I could handle it if I were in your shoes and something happened to West. But we're your family, Abby. It will do you good to be surrounded by people who care about you. We can help you through this."

I look gratefully at her. She always knows the right things to say. "I know you're right, Kate, and I do appreciate it." I sigh. "I'm just not sure I'm ready to face those memories."

"Well, we're here for you when you are. Don't forget that."

"GOOD MORNING. I'M Rebecca. Are you ready for your ultrasound?" A woman in a colorful baby-rattle-print smock smiles as she enters the room and heads straight for the ultrasound equipment.

"Definitely, I think," I say nervously. I'm excited for sure, but also worried that we may see something wrong with the baby. And then what would I do? Kate squeezes my hand reassuringly.

"A bit nervous too, right?" Rebecca offers. "That's completely normal, believe me. Come on over to the table here and we'll get started."

Normal, huh? Okay, good.

"I need you to lift up your shirt and pull down your pants a bit. Yes, like that." She begins pushing buttons on the screen and keyboard of the equipment. Then she grabs a tube of gel—the same kind the doctor used when he did the sonogram. "I apologize in advance. This may be a bit cold."

I wince as the goo hits my stomach. She uses a wand attached to a cord that connects to the ultrasound equipment to rub the goo around and tilts the screen toward me as she does. The screen jumps from black to gray fuzziness to definitive shapes.

I gasp as my Journey appears on the monitor—I can make out a profile!

"Oh my," Kate murmurs in awe as she comes to my side. I clasp her hand and squeeze it hard in my excitement.

"There's your little one. Good-looking nose and chin there," Rebecca says, pointing to the monitor. "Now, I'll be taking some measurements today. I'll ascertain the baby's due date according to current measurements, and I'll be taking some pictures for you to keep."

"Aww," is all I can say. My heart is soaring at the sight of Ethan's beautiful baby.

"Pretty emotional stuff, huh?" Kate whispers.

I can only nod.

Rebecca shows us the baby's arms and ten fingers, legs and ten toes, and some of the major organs as she measures them.

"Everything looks good. One last thing . . ." She pauses and looks at me. "Do you want to know the sex of the baby?"

"You can tell that?"

"Yes. If we can get him or her to move just right, we should be able to tell."

"Hmm. It's tempting, but no. I don't think I want to know." I turn to Kate. "It'll be like one last surprise from Ethan."

"Are you sure you don't want to know?" she probes. "I do!"

I laugh. "No, Kate. I'm sure."

"Okay, then. Let me get your tummy cleaned off, and you can go." Rebecca wipes my stomach with a cloth, washes her hands, and presents me with four pictures of my little Journey: one profile, one of the heart and stomach, one of a tiny hand and fingers, and a 3D close-up of the baby's face. They are so precious, I melt.

A relaxing calm floods my body knowing Journey is healthy and looks so darn adorable. Now to meet with Dr. K for the checkup. I am on such a high—nothing could bring me down now.

Ethan,   *19 weeks*

Today was so amazing! I got to see Journey, actual images of Journey! Our beautiful little miracle has such tiny perfect fingers and a tiny perfect nose. I saw the heart beating a rhythm and the other organs that are forming right now. And yes, everything is in there that should be. And no, I didn't find out the sex. Kate wanted to know, but like I told her, I'd like to think of it as one last surprise you can give me. Your most successful surprise yet!

Journey is about half a pound in weight and six inches long. Still so tiny but looked so big on the monitor! Heartrate today was 135 bpm. I tell you, the sound of that heartbeat is one of the best sounds you'll ever hear—a miracle in itself.

My tummy is really starting to balloon out. I'm nearly halfway through—can you believe it? Kate has been helping me clothes shop. You know how much I hate to shop. I'm too embarrassed to tell you the size I'm up to now, so don't ask!

Next appointment with Dr. K is in four weeks.

I just really wish you could have been there today. We still miss you. We still love you.

♥ *A & J*

A knock at the door jolts me. I stare from the window seat at the door, wondering who it could be. Kate or West would have called if they were coming over. Same with Uncle Geoff and Simon.

At the second knock, I jump up from my seat and tuck the journal in a drawer of the secretary desk as I make my way to the foyer. I peer through the peephole, and my heart drops. So much for the baby high I have been riding all afternoon. I hesitantly unlock the door and pause with my hand hovering above the doorknob. Against my better judgment, I swing the door open.

Chapter Thirty

Mommie Dearest

"**M**OTHER. HI."

"I know I should have called before I flew out here." She breezes past me well into the foyer, plants her luggage at her feet, and spins around. "But since our last telephone conversation ended with us near argument, I felt it better for me to save any discussion for a face-to-face interaction."

My eyes widen at the volume of luggage she has deposited in the middle of my entryway. I tighten my stare, scan her face for clues as to her motivation for appearing out of thin air. She smiles broadly, which in and of itself frightens me. She appears relaxed, her eyes calm, almost happy. Is she trying to pass this off as a smoothing-over of our recent disagreement?

"Oh. I had no idea you were even considering a visit." I reach for her coat. "Come in, please," I add ironically.

What did she mean by saving any discussion for a face-to-face interaction? I think she must know I'm much braver, much more willing to speak up for myself when there are several states between us than I am when standing in her presence. I motion toward the living room, and I hang up her coat, pausing to collect my bearings before following her.

"Can I get you something to drink? Tea? Water?"

"I am fine, thank you. Come, have a seat. We have much to catch up on." She pats the cushion next to her expectantly. I tentatively make my way over to join her. A nagging thought at the back of my mind warns me to keep my guard up. There's something subtly off-putting about her behavior. Something a little too . . . happy.

The next hour consists of her catching me up on her friends, their book club, her newest hobby of painting with Janice. She keeps the conversation remarkably lighthearted. For my mother. She asks me how my friends, "the perpetually unmarried couple," are doing. I say they're fine. They have been very supportive. She asks me how "the male couple" is doing. I inform her they are on an Alaskan cruise at the moment but have invited me to dinner next Sunday after they return. My mother perks up at this last bit of news.

"Next Sunday, you say?"

"Yes." I nod warily.

"Excellent. It will be wonderful to see them again."

My eyebrows shoot up in surprise. "You'll—be—staying that long?" I try to mask the shock-filled dread in my tone. "Don't you need to get back to work? I thought you were unable to . . . take much time off?"

"True, but I spoke with the principal and the superintendent. I explained to them the difficulties you are facing with losing your husband and expecting your first child. I told them if it was at all possible, I needed to make myself available to help get you through this very tough time. They agreed to give me a leave of absence for as long as necessary."

I am sitting next to an extraterrestrial being. Who is this person that replaced my mother in her own body? After our previous conversation, it makes absolutely no sense.

"Why?" I muster softly.

"Why, of course," she states matter-of-factly, "they know my classroom skills are second-to-none, so they have no problem holding my position while I'm away."

"No—I mean . . . why do you want to be here to help me?" I can't keep the bewilderment from my voice or my expression.

She shares her own look of confusion. "What do you mean, Abigail? Can't I want to help you?"

"No. I mean, yes, of course you can. That's very kind of you, actually. But—in every conversation we've had before, you made it perfectly clear you weren't going out of your way to offer support for this baby. You acted like my pregnancy was causing unwelcome stress in your life. So naturally, I'm surprised at the change of heart."

"Don't be ridiculous. I've never thought of your pregnancy as causing stress in my life. You misunderstood me. I had very legitimate concerns for your welfare without a job or a stable financial situation to carry you through. That is all. Apparently, you've remedied that situation, so there is really nothing for me to worry about. The only stress I ever had was over your well-being."

Wow. She actually sounds sincere. She reaches over and squeezes my hand in hers. I stare down at the unnatural gesture.

"So, I am here as long as you need me. I know this is a scary time for you, having a child alone. I could tell how much it was affecting you when we last spoke. So—don't worry. We will get you through this. You'll see."

I'm torn between doubting my mother and wanting to believe her words. I'll need time to process her actions and comments today, that's for sure. And apparently, I'll get just that. Plenty of time. An indefinite amount of time.

"I'd like to get settled in now," she interrupts my inner dialogue as she rises and collects her luggage. I watch, speechless, as she strides into the guest bedroom as if it has always belonged to her. Instinctively, my hand gravitates to my belly. I wonder if Journey feels the intrusion as well.

My high spirits have effectively crashed with the arrival of our houseguest. "Don't worry, baby, you will get your room back soon enough. We still have plenty of time to get it ready for you." I rub my hand over my tummy as I mull over the implications of my mother's visit. Are her true intentions as transparent as she claims?

I can't help but wonder.

"IT WAS A surprise of Ethan proportions. And he's not even here to blame!" I say, exasperated.

"Why, exactly, is she visiting again—or is it moving in? I thought she was adamant about you giving your baby up for, you know, adoption?" Kate points out.

On a positive note, my mother's constant presence in my apartment has managed to push me to seek refuge elsewhere. I only paused very briefly outside Food for Thought this afternoon before I entered in search of the comforting company of my best friend. I barely registered the pang of sorrow and emptiness I've felt lately when coming to the store. I had no time to allow those emotions a voice—I was too distraught after spending three whole uninterrupted days with Victoria.

"It's funny, Kate. Her whole perspective seems to have shifted. She took an indefinite leave from teaching to help me with the pregnancy—and baby." I shake my head in confusion over my mother's actions. "So honestly, I'm afraid of how long she intends to stay."

"Oh, honey!" She squeezes my hand sympathetically. "You come hang out with us any time you need a break. No worries."

"Thanks. I will, you know." I smile half-heartedly.

I stare out the window at the passersby on the sidewalk, not really paying attention to any of them. My heart feels so heavy today. Even hanging out with Kate has done little to lift my spirits. I think I'm having Ethan withdrawals. I haven't been able to write since my mother arrived. She is everywhere in that apartment. I haven't written in Journey's journal either. I decide to make time tonight, even if I must lock myself in my bedroom to get away from her oppressive presence.

"I just miss him so much. Especially now." I turn my attention to Kate and fight the prickling of tears I feel gathering behind my eyes. "He always tried to be the buffer between my mother and me, always had the right words to say to help me bounce back from her verbal onslaughts."

"Abby, I hate to say this, but you know you need to stand up for yourself—for the baby. If her influence in your life is so toxic, you don't need it around. Set up some boundaries, or you'll never be happy. Journey will sense your unhappiness, and it will affect him or her in turn."

I don't know what to say to Kate's honesty. I know she speaks truth, but I don't know how I could possibly garner enough strength to set boundaries with Victoria, a woman capable of annihilating me with her vicious stare.

"Just think about it. Think about protecting yourself and the baby. I know you. You'll stand up when the time comes. You've got it in you," she assures me.

Maybe so. I'd like to think that with all I've been through I can handle a little dose of my mother. "Little" being the operative word. I sigh. When do things get better for good? I need a great, big, long span of some good times.

I GLANCE NERVOUSLY over at my mother. The cab ride to dinner with Uncle Geoff and Simon has been a silent one so far. The early November chill has me feeling cold this evening. Or maybe it's the iciness she exudes filling the space.

Mother is in her commanding and composed state as usual, blond hair perfectly styled and secured on the left side. No strand out of place. She sits, statuesque, staring straight ahead. I imagine she's mentally congratulating herself on how stylish she looks and how wonderfully she will impress our hosts. She had insisted upon going to a salon I'd never heard of, but she apparently had, to have her hair colored and styled. I've never spent as much on my hair in my life as she did today, and somehow I ended up being the one who paid the bill. Then she thought it would be "fun" to have some mother-daughter shopping time to pick out new dresses for dinner. I was fine with that until about the fourth store when she still hadn't found anything desirable. So she suggested we go to Saks Fifth Avenue—she knew she could find something decent there. And she did, an hour and a half later. I had given up shopping for myself at the second store. It became clear early on that this trip was more about Victoria than about us spending time together. Besides, I had plenty of dresses at home to choose from. Somehow, I paid for her dress and shoes as well, though I'm not really sure how. By then I was just ready to get home. My feet were starting to ache.

"Why are you fidgeting so much, Abigail? Sit still, please," she commands without looking at me.

Because I'm afraid of what you'll say or do to mortify me, I want to say.

Instead, I mutter an apology.

I called Simon when they returned from their trip earlier this week to ask if it was okay for Victoria to come along with me to dinner. Of course, Simon was fine with her coming; I knew he would be. Mostly, I wanted to give them plenty of warning. I clench my jaw just thinking about the things that may come out of her mouth tonight. The cab pulls to an abrupt halt in front of Uncle Geoff's house, and I fumble in my purse for the cab fare. Irritated, I realize my fingers are starting to tremble.

"Well, let's go then," my mother insists, eyebrows raised.

I finally get my wallet out and open and count out the fare plus tip. She's out of the cab and halfway to the house when I hand the money up to the driver. "Thank you," I say as I hurriedly exit. I have to practically run to catch up to her before she hits the top step.

"There you are." She looks at me from the corner of her eye as she rings the bell. She lifts her chin and squares her shoulders. "Pregnancy seems to really be slowing you down, dear."

I frown but say nothing.

When the door swings open, I feel comfort swell inside me at the sight of Simon. It's been too long since I've seen him. He is dressed impeccably as usual, and he beams at me before turning a pleasant smile on my mother.

"How wonderful to see you again, Victoria," he coos with an outstretched hand. "Do come in."

She places her hand in his, glowing at the attention. He pulls her into the grand foyer and turns back to me.

"Abigail, we have missed you, my dear." He holds his hand out in an identical manner but pulls me into a tight embrace. "So good to see you, love," he whispers in my ear.

I tear up, overcome with emotion. I inhale deeply, amazed to feel the nervousness from moments ago dissipating. Simon finally releases me and holds my hand in one of his. With the other, he gestures toward the sitting room.

"Let's catch up, ladies, shall we?"

We enter the ornate sitting room, greeted immediately by Uncle Geoff.

"Good evening, Victoria." He nods to her. "Abby, come here, girl," he demands in his warm, gravelly voice.

I walk into another big, emotional hug. "Uncle Geoff! How was your trip?"

"Just grand," he says as he releases me. "Simon will tell you all about it. Have a seat, ladies. How's the little one?" He pats my growing belly as we make our way to the sofa.

I smile. "All's well."

"Good to hear."

I sigh as I sit with Uncle Geoff on one side and Simon on the other. With my family around me again, I feel at ease, happy.

Mother sits taut across from us in a high-backed leather chair, a cold, proper piece of furniture well-suited to her personality. I smirk at the realization.

Uncle Geoff and Simon have each taken one of my hands in theirs. I notice a frostiness cross my mother's face as she takes in the scene before her. Clearly more affection than her senses can handle.

"Tell me, Victoria, how long are you in New York?" Simon makes small talk.

"As long as my daughter needs me. Her health and welfare are my highest concern right now."

My eyebrows lift a little at the sincerity of her answer.

"Wonderful. Good to know our girl will be well cared for." Simon squeezes my hand as he smiles at me.

"And please, we hope you both will visit often during your stay," Uncle Geoff offers.

"We would love to, Geoffrey. Thank you." My mother flashes him her thousand-watt smile, the one she reserves for people she wants to impress.

Simon rises. "I shall return with drinks. Excuse me." He bows gracefully and exits the room.

As soon as he's gone, my mother turns her full attention to Uncle Geoff. She leans a shoulder forward and drops her head subtly, unleashing a seductive stare from under her eyelashes.

Here we go.

"Abigail tells me you were on an Alaskan cruise. I've always wanted to go on one. You must tell us all about it."

"Yes, we were. A wonderful adventure. I recommend that cruise to anyone looking for beautiful scenery, a closeness to nature, and a relaxing, refreshing experience."

Victoria belts out a ringing laugh. "Oh, that sounds amazing. How were the amenities of the vessel?"

"They were fine. What one would expect." Uncle Geoff smiles at me rather than my mother.

"And dancing? I'll bet you are a marvelous dancer, Geoffrey," Victoria says salaciously. "If I were on a cruise with you, we'd spend all our time dancing."

Uncle Geoff clears his throat before he responds politely, "No doubt."

I shift uncomfortably at the direction she has taken this conversation. She obviously still thinks she can steal his interest.

"Uncle Geoff," I interject, "did you see any whales or dolphins or anything?"

"Yes, actually, we did, my dear. We saw three species of whale and many schools of dolphins. Fascinating creatures, I tell you."

"I imagine. How wonderful to be so close to the wilderness," my mother tries to draw his attention again. Thankfully, Simon reappears with the drinks. He sets the tray on the side table next to my mother. She keeps her gaze trained on Uncle Geoff.

"Lemonade with a personality for Victoria and us gentlemen," he says handing a crystal glass to my mother. She barely glances at him as she thanks him. "And plain, boring lemonade for our Abby and our baby guest."

He winks at me, and I giggle as I take the glass from him. "I love plain, boring lemonade, Simon. You know that."

"I do." He smiles at me as he hands Uncle Geoff a drink and then retrieves his glass from the tray before returning to the sofa with us. Does he notice how my mother is still staring at Uncle Geoff? It appears blatantly obvious to me, and I wish I were closer to her so I could kick her and force her to stop making eyes!

"Uncle Geoff was telling us about your cruise," I say, knowing Simon will begin an elaborate story that will keep my mother from opening her mouth for the next fifteen to twenty minutes. And he does. He pauses only to invite us into the dining room for our meal. Surprisingly, he has wait staff to serve us tonight.

"Letting someone else take the reins today?" I ask, surprised.

"Yes, my dear," he confirms as he places his napkin on his lap. "I wanted to spend as much time as possible with you tonight. I haven't seen you nearly enough lately, and I miss you. So I have, in fact, hired someone else to cook, serve, and clean for me tonight. That's how important you are to us."

A lump forms in my throat. He has never hired help for his dinners before—ever. "I—I don't know what to say, Simon. I'm not worth all that."

"Nonsense, child," he scolds me. "You are worth all of that and more."

"And don't you forget it," Uncle Geoff chimes in.

"Thank you. I appreciate that."

I catch sight of my mother, coolly assessing our interaction. She clearly does not see the value these men have placed on having me in their lives.

"What is on the menu tonight, Simon, if I may?"

"You may, Victoria. Lobster bisque starter, roast duck, seasoned steamed vegetables, mashed sweet potatoes, and Abby's favorite, cheesecake topped with chocolate and caramel for dessert."

I smile at that last.

"Sounds delicious," Mother says approvingly.

On cue, two gentlemen in pressed white button-up coats and black slacks enter carrying trays of lobster bisque and dinner rolls. The smell is heavenly as a bowl is placed in front of me. I panic briefly when I register the lobster. Is that something I can't eat during pregnancy? Ocean shellfish is not good . . . but lobster? I think lobster is okay. I realize everyone is staring at me with my mental dilemma.

"Umm . . . I can't remember if lobster is okay to have during pregnancy," I admit sheepishly.

"Don't be foolish, Abigail. Cooked lobster is fine," Mother responds curtly and raises her spoon to her mouth.

"Oh. Good." Relieved that that question is answered, I begin to eat a little too quickly. I am so hungry.

I sense my mother's disapproving glare after about five spoonfuls. I self-consciously sit upright. Against my stomach's demands, I slowly eat the rest of the bisque, matching my spoonfuls with hers.

Simon, thankfully, shares another story from their Alaskan trip, which takes the attention off me and my poor manners. He tells of how they befriended the captain and spent an afternoon on the bridge. They each even were allowed a turn at the wheel, steering the ship. They spent the rest of the cruise at the captain's table for every meal. The captain's storytelling was allegedly even more fantastic than Simon's, according to Uncle Geoff. I can tell Simon doesn't appreciate that comment, but the hurt expression on his face vanishes when I ask him what his favorite part of the trip was.

"Oh, my dear Abigail, that is easy. My absolute favorite part was watching the magnificent sunsets every night on the ship with Geoffrey. The most beautiful I have ever seen with the best company." He reaches over and squeezes Uncle Geoff's hand.

"Very spectacular, I agree." Uncle Geoff nods as he holds Simon's hand.

"Tell me, Geoffrey, what was your favorite part of the trip?" Victoria's sharp voice cuts through the reverent silence.

Way to interrupt a moment, Mother.

"Well, let's see," he ponders as he finally takes his gaze from Simon's. "I believe my favorite part of the trip was being so close to the icebergs and mountains, being around so many large natural creations. It really puts a person's life into perspective. God has fashioned Himself a wondrous planet here—He truly has. And we are but a small part of that creation."

"That's an interesting perspective," Victoria muses with a hint of irony in her voice.

I have never heard a more deafening silence in this house than at this very moment. We all heard her tone, understand her insinuation. "So, cheesecake? Is that next?" I ask a bit too loudly.

"How do you mean?" Uncle Geoff's eyes narrow almost imperceptibly.

"It's just—I didn't take you for God-fearing gentlemen," she continues, "what with your lifestyle choice."

No. Seriously? Why, Victoria? My wide eyes dart back and forth between Simon and Uncle Geoff's faces. Their once open and warm countenances have been replaced in a split second by guarded, somber façades. If they registered any shock at her comments, it has been well-hidden.

"Mother, that's really inappropriate—"

"It's fine, Abby. Don't worry about it," Uncle Geoff interjects. "We've spent more years than you know defending our relationship." His expression hardens as he turns his gaze upon my mother. "And neither one of us believes that God forsakes us because of our love. We are God-fearing individuals who have our own ways of showing our devotion to that God, and we do not concern ourselves with the judgments of others."

"I make no judgment, Geoffrey. You can be assured of that. I am glad to hear that you are men of faith," Victoria states as if bestowing her own blessing. "It comforts me to know my daughter is surrounded by others who share our belief and trust in God. So many do not nowadays, you know."

I stare, astounded, at the straight B.S. spewing from Victoria's mouth. I have never known my mother to be more than religious for show.

Thankfully, the wait staff enter again, causing a welcome distraction. Simon clears his throat tightly as the cheesecake is served. Uncle Geoff still has his stony eyes locked on my mother, who appears to be basking in the attention she's receiving.

"This looks delicious!" I exclaim a little too excitedly. I blush, embarrassed that I can't tactfully direct the conversation down a new route. And that I am related to an IED like my mother, exploding like a roadside bomb on our unsuspecting dinner, burying shrapnel in all of us.

As I look around at the three quiet people politely eating their dessert, a sadness crushes my chest at the knowledge that my mother has hurt the feelings of two people I deeply care for. Why did I bring her here? I knew it would not end well. I chew on my lip as I drag my fork through my cheesecake, creating designs in it to match the explosion that just rocked this room.

PROMPTLY AFTER THE dessert plates are cleared, we say our goodbyes. I think Simon and Uncle Geoff really do want me to stay longer, but I must get my mother out of here before she causes any more damage. We say our thanks for the wonderful meal, my mother a little too animatedly. She acts as though she's won some victory here tonight.

They escort us to the front door and nod their goodbyes to my mother as she heads out to the waiting cab. I can't leave this way, though. This disaster is all my fault. I rush up and grab them both by the necks and pull them down to me.

"I'm so sorry," I whisper near tears. "I love you both."

"No worries, child," Simon murmurs as he smooths my hair, and I feel minutely better.

"We love you—you know that," Uncle Geoff reassures, rubbing my back. "You cannot control the actions of others, dear Abby. We'll talk again soon."

I release them and wipe the errant tear from my cheek. I smile at my two uncles—my family—before I turn to go.

"You take care of yourself and that little baby," Simon calls as I follow my gloating mother to the cab. I turn one last time to wave goodnight. They wave from the doorway, arms around one another. I fight the urge to run back to the comfort and safety of their home. Reluctantly, I join my mother in the waiting cab.

We ride in silence for several minutes, my mind racing with the reprimands I want to shoot at her. How dare she make my loved ones feel so terrible? How dare she insult them in their own home when they have been nothing but cordial? How dare she ruin the precious little time I have with them—my link to Ethan?

I feel the fury bubbling over, and I have to clench my jaw shut tight to keep from unloading on her right here and now. Instead, I force myself to count streetlights as we pass, keeping my mind from replaying her poor behavior. I will deal with her when we are in the privacy of the apartment, and I can yell at her at the top of my lungs.

"Well, they sure know how to make a houseguest feel unwelcome." Victoria breaks the silence halfway home. "I do not remember them being so uncouth."

My head snaps around to her. If it wasn't so dark, she'd see the flaming glare of equal parts disbelief and anger boring into her. Suddenly, I realize I'm trembling. I could lunge at her right now and relish her surprise as I choke her with my bare hands. She'd never see it coming. "You. Are. Unbelievable." I say through clenched teeth. Yeah, I'm not waiting for the privacy of home.

"I'm sorry?"

"You. You insult them in their own home, and you're surprised when they become *uncouth*?" I spit at her.

"Abigail. Honestly. What has gotten into you?" she questions sharply. Normally, that tone would make me back down. Momentarily, it does.

When I regain my voice, I shake my head. "You don't even see what you've done, do you?"

"I have no idea what you are getting at, Abigail." She turns her face forward, leaving me staring daggers into her still-perfectly-coiffed hair.

"You questioned their faith—you implied they were godless because they are gay. And you don't see how that could have insulted them? Seriously?"

"I was merely making conversation. I can't help it if they were offended by my comments. Conversation is supposed to be a sharing of ideas and an exchange of questions. I had no idea Geoffrey was so sensitive. I will remember that in the future," she says noncommittally.

"Well, I expect you to apologize the next time we see them—if you're even invited."

"Calm down, Abigail. All will be well. Don't get yourself so worked up."

I gape at her in the dark. I cannot believe I came from this woman; she is a foreign being to me. There is no explanation for her behavior that could ever get me to understand her.

My boiling blood cools as I resign myself to the fact that this argument is futile. Victoria is not someone to be reasoned with or convinced of something she chooses not to see or understand. I know this is a battle I have lost, but at least I have fought. This may be the first time I have ever taken a strong stand against my mother in person. And though I was not successful, I feel like I have accomplished something. Made my voice heard, let her know I was unhappy with her. I was forceful with my delivery.

Yes. I gained some valuable ground tonight.

Chapter Thirty-One

Tropical Depression Victoria

Ethan,   23 weeks

Another doctor visit today. It's terrible—I almost cried when I stepped on the scale for the nurse. 140 pounds! 140! I'm barely halfway through my pregnancy, and I already weigh 140. Dr. K even said something about my weight gain (only about a pound of that is baby!). Eating for two has given me the excuse to eat whatever I'm craving. I'll need to be more thoughtful about what I'm giving little Journey. If you were here, you'd keep me in check, wouldn't you? You'd be my Food Czar.

Other than that, everything is good. The baby book says Journey can hear sounds outside the womb now and suggests playing music or singing. We had our first little dance party yesterday. I'll admit, I didn't know what kind of music to play. I started out with classical, then classic rock, country, 90s grunge, a little pop, and ended up at dubstep. It was fun. I think Journey enjoyed it, too. Our little baby is moving around a lot. To see my tummy push out on the side with a tiny bulge and watch it move around *to my front boggles my mind! I love this part the most so far—feeling and seeing our baby move. You would be so amazed.*

On another note, we missed you so much at Thanksgiving dinner. Your very gracious uncle and Simon turned the other cheek to my mother and not only allowed her back into their home, but they were also divine hosts. But it wasn't the same without you. I don't think it will ever be the same without you.

♥A & J

I think about that Thanksgiving dinner, the first time my mother and I had been invited to their home since the Dinner of Disaster. If the situation caused them any grief or annoyance, they never let it show. I think my mother realized she was being given a second chance and she, for the most part, behaved herself. It was awkward to say the least. I could tell she was trying hard to hold her tongue much of the time. I made sure to thank her afterward, which of course confused her. "What are you thanking me for?" she asked. "For behaving," I said simply. She gave a defiant snort and turned her cold gaze out the side window of the cab.

Even though I was among my family all day, and even though Uncle Geoff and Simon were wonderful hosts and served a delicious meal, I still felt an emptiness in my heart. Really, it had started on Wednesday when I recognized the holiday season was upon us—and Ethan was gone. On Thursday, I awakened feeling a bit of sadness hovering around me. I pushed back on it enough to enjoy the time with my family. But Friday was a different story. And then Saturday.

Christmas commercials were all over the television. Every store, every business, every building I went into piped holiday music throughout. I realized I was not ready to face a Christmas without Ethan. Not after he had given me three memorable Christmases in a row.

On top of the sadness, I had Victoria to deal with. Her answer to everything: shopping. I managed to get her out the door without me on Friday and Saturday. All I had to do was give her my debit card and tell her everything was my treat—clothes shopping, present shopping, manicure, spa day, whatever she wanted. She weakly attempted to argue that I should join her, but after one firm "Not today" from me, she rushed out the door. Alone with my thoughts for far too long, I felt the familiar signs of my old depression knocking on my door. I fought against it this time though. I grasped that I couldn't let this negativity affect Journey. It was up to me to shelter and nurture our baby.

So on Sunday, I forced myself to smile—a lot. I set up the Christmas tree. I even played some Frank Sinatra, Dean Martin, and Johnny Mathis. The Christmas Greats. Those songs transported me . . . to when I was young, and my parents were still in love, and the world was still a happy place. My dad would play his old Christmas records like Elvis Presley, Old Blue Eyes, and other artists, and we would decorate the tree together. A real tree. One that filled the house with the smell of pine and pricked my fingers when I wasn't careful placing ornaments on the drying branches.

While decorating the tree (alone—Victoria apparently needed a salon visit that day), I decided that even though Journey wasn't here yet, I wanted to make this a special Christmas. I wanted all our Christmases to be special. Always.

So I stuffed my depression into a shoebox and buried it in the recesses of my closet. I took control of my frame of mind and vowed not to let my emotions get the best of me. And it was working. I even placed a picture of Ethan on the side table by the tree, pretending he was with us as I decorated, that we were doing it together. It had been nice, a bit healing even.

As I remember that day, I shut my eyes tight to freeze that moment in place, and then I gently close the journal and tuck it into my nightstand. Even though my mother isn't here at the moment—out shopping for Christmas presents or something like that—it has become a habit for me to do my journaling in the bedroom behind closed doors in a protective bubble away from her eyes and her questions.

I never write in the apartment anymore, either. It's too cold outside to continue my trips to Central Park. Now, I mostly find a coffee shop or small restaurant with Wi-Fi to set up my laptop. I've even set up my station a few times in the corner table at Food for Thought. It's strange how the store has gradually become a place of comfort. And at times, I even feel inspired by Ethan's passion for the store and the times we spent there, and it translates into more vivid storytelling.

I am both amazed and relieved at how much better I feel when I'm at the store. Relieved because it's a place that had been such a big part of our lives, and my best friends still pour themselves into it. And I really should, at some point, take over Ethan's duties that have fallen on West's shoulders.

Not that he's ever complained. He's too laid back for one, but mostly he just wants his dream to work. He can't imagine doing anything else, and so he will do whatever it takes to keep the store going. I know he's hopeful I'll return someday, the sooner the better. Actually, he's pretty obvious about it. He has "strategic" conversations with Kate while I'm there about the financials or scheduling or marketing ideas. And he often glances my way to see if he's piqued my interest. And truthfully, he has. But up until recently, I couldn't picture myself as a part of the store no matter how much I wanted to. It hurt too badly.

I think my writing and journaling have provided some valuable healing, allowing me to hope and plan for the future again. A future with only memories of Ethan. What better way to keep those memories alive and honor him than to step up and keep his and West's vision alive, help it thrive?

"Abigail? Are you here? Please come help me with these bags."

I frown briefly and sigh before I force my face into the placid mask I've become accustomed to wearing around her. *Never let her see how much she irritates you. It will only give her that much more power.*

"Coming," I call, scooting to the edge of the bed so I can drop my legs over the side and stand. I am becoming uncoordinated with my growing tummy. Simple maneuvers have become something I have to plan. *How will I angle myself to perform this task?* And forget about bending over to pick something up.

I rub my belly as I stand as if to say, *Don't worry, Journey. I don't begrudge you for making my body an uncoordinated mess. Mommy knows you can't help it.*

Remembering that Journey can hear me well now, I say to my tummy, "I love you, you know." A responding movement across my belly tells me the feeling is reciprocated. I grin.

I emerge from the bedroom to see that Victoria has been on a serious shopping spree. She'd mentioned this morning that while Kate and I were at the doctor, she was going use the time to do some Christmas shopping for me. Happy to have her out of my hair so Kate and I could have breakfast, go to my appointment, and generally hang out the rest of the day, I handed over my debit card again. "Maybe I should get you your own card," I'd joked, thinking about the numerous times I've given her mine since she arrived. "You know, that is not a bad idea, Abigail," she replied in a tone I never hear from her: the you-are-absolutely-right tone.

Three of the five bags contain already wrapped and ribbon-adorned packages. I assume the other two contain items she has found for herself. She always manages to come home with several items for herself, no matter the original purpose of the shopping trip. Even a dash out to the coffee shop results in a brief trip somewhere or a sale at a store that caught her eye on the way back. I admit, I'm starting to wonder if Victoria is a shopaholic. I don't know, maybe she's just not accustomed to being able to buy whatever she wants whenever she wants. I'm not accustomed to that either, but my general aversion to the Retail World keeps me out of stores as much as possible.

"Wow, what lovely wrapping paper," I comment as I take two bags of presents over and arrange them around the base of the tree. I pause for a beat, mentally trying to count the number of presents . . . six, eight, eleven, sixteen? We've never had that many presents before, and it's not even December.

"Do you suppose you're about done shopping?" I haven't been out looking for my mother's presents yet, or Kate's, or West's, or anybody's for that matter.

"Possibly. I'd like to get something for Janice and something for Caroline. We exchange gifts every year, you know."

No. I did not know.

"And maybe one or two more small things for the baby, of course."

I nod my head a few times in response. One thing I have noticed: My mother is much more affable lately. I wonder if this is the side her friends and co-workers see. The side she has never before shown me. Even as a child, I remember her exuding a certain standoffish nature toward me. Maybe she just never figured out how to interact with children. But then, I haven't been a child for years. Her behavior modification seems to have coincided with her arrival on my doorstep. And it confuses me. Is she trying to make up for all the years she was an abhorrent parent, for my sake and for her grandchild's? Part of me hopes this is the start of a brand new and improved relationship with her. For Journey's sake.

But part of me is also waiting for the façade to crumble and her true intentions to surface.

Ethan,   *26 weeks*

Christmas is just around the corner! I finally finished my shopping. There's so much stuff out there for babies now. Even though Journey won't be here to open presents, I couldn't resist—I have about five under the tree.

Kate went furniture shopping with me yesterday. We found a gorgeous antique bassinette that will go right next to our bed. And we purchased a crib, stroller, sport stroller, exersaucer, bouncy chair, car seat (I made sure it's lightweight enough for hauling in and out of taxis), and several of the most adorable baby outfits. You know how I am with shopping, but honey, baby shopping is a whole different realm. I could shop for precious tiny baby clothes for days!

The big news about Journey this week is, if he's a boy, his testicles will be dropping! Exciting, huh? The baby is also doing small breathing movements as well. He or she is causing Mommy some back discomfort now, too. As fun as our shopping excursion was yesterday, by the end of it, I was paying for it.

Time to start strategizing furniture placement. Kate and West are stopping by this weekend to help put together the crib and changing table. It will be nice to have the time to hang out away from the store.

By the way, Kate has been photographing Journey growing in my belly and all manner of baby-related shots of us. She says she's going to include the photos in her next art show. After she gets some pictures of Journey out in the world as well. I'm kind of excited to see the final product. What a neat way to document our growing miracle!

♥ *A & J*

SUNDAY AFTERNOON, WE sit on my living room floor, cardboard and plastic packaging, wood and metal pieces, and various tools sprawled about. With the changing table successfully assembled in just under two hours, we've moved on to the baby crib. I assumed, incorrectly, with West being a guy, the assembly of the baby furniture would go quickly. Actually, Kate has turned out to be the most capable one of our group with tools and written instructions.

But we are having a blast anyway. Kate takes the occasional break from assembly to snap photos of West and me trying (unsuccessfully) to be as productive as she has been. He keeps the humor flowing, taking the opportunity to make a funny after my mother makes one comment or another. Like when she emerged from her room about ten minutes ago and looked at West and Kate, saying, "Oh, you *are* still here." To which he replied matter-of-factly, "Yes, Vickie." (He's taken to calling her Vickie, which she absolutely hates and brings me sardonic joy.) "We've moved in, actually. Just putting together our bed now." And although I was dying inside, I didn't dare let my laughter show on my face. Kate snickered but was quickly silenced by my mother's icy gaze as she turned for the kitchen.

Victoria strides into the living room now with bottled water and a fat-free snack cake, and the temperature in the room drops. After fifteen minutes of attempting conversation with us earlier today, which resulted in two sarcastic but hugely funny comments from West at her expense, she haughtily retreated to her bedroom and left us alone to assemble in peace. Apparently, she's ready to unfurl her storm clouds over our sunny day once again.

"Abigail, I would like to attend your next doctor appointment with you."

I wince as I feel the grenade explode in the center of our group, among the wooden spindles, metal brackets, and cardboard pieces.

Recovering, I tread lightly. "Umm. Well . . . actually, Kate usually goes with me to my appointments."

"I'm sure she would be willing to relinquish her position for one appointment. Would you not, Kate?"

She glances from my covertly pleading face to my mother's expectant stare and back to me. I can tell she's torn. She knows I'd really rather not include my mother on any of my appointments (I've told her as much multiple times). But the power of my mother's glare is strong, and Kate is faltering in her conviction to bar my mother from our special time.

"I have been here for weeks now, Abigail, and I feel I should be included in this important time of your pregnancy. I would like to meet the man who will be delivering my grandchild and ensure he is up to the standard I expect."

Well, it's hard to argue with her seemingly good intentions. I stall but can't think of a viable reason she shouldn't be allowed to go, other than I don't want her there. But I'd never say that to her face.

"Yes, Victoria, of course you should go to the appointment. By all means." Kate caves. My eyes narrow as I shoot daggers at her. She gives me the tiniest shrug.

"Then it is settled."

Victoria turns and walks triumphantly to her room, turning to face us as she closes her door. Her eyes are unmistakably gleaming. The click of the latch as the door shuts echoes throughout the quiet apartment.

"What just happened?" West whispers, bewildered.

"Victoria just happened," I mutter, no longer excited about my next checkup on Wednesday.

"I'm so sorry, Abby. I didn't know how to say no to that."

"Don't worry about it, Kate. Really. She's a hard woman to refuse. I guess she's right, though. She should probably go to an appointment, meet the doctor. She did come all this way to help. She'll go to one, and that will be that."

And I resolve to make it so.

"I MUST SAY, I am not impressed with this office," Victoria says as she consults her watch for the third time since we arrived.

"It does go rather slowly sometimes. It's a busy practice. Which is comforting to me, because that means lots of women trust these doctors to bring their babies into the world."

"All the same. They should be more respectful of their patients' time."

"Then it's a good thing we have nowhere else to be, isn't it?" I offer good-naturedly, trying to soften her indignation. The last thing I want is for her to be confrontational with Dr. K. He is wonderful, and I don't want him dropping me as a patient because my mother is a bitch. Whether I've convinced her to be cool or not, she is silent for the remainder of our wait in the exam room.

I exhale with relief when I hear the usual knock on the door as Dr. K announces his arrival. He breezes into the room.

"Abby, so good to see you." He squeezes my arm as he walks past, chart in hand. I smile at his comforting, easy bedside manner. He opens my folder and drops it lightly onto the counter by the sink. He skims the nurse's notes quickly, using his pen as a place-marker. "Urine sample is good . . . blood pressure is good . . . weight is better. Good for you."

He glances up for the first time and catches sight of my mother. "Why, hello. I don't remember Abby mentioning a sister," he compliments as he extends his hand to her.

I cringe. This is her opening to berate the doctor on his subpar practice and her irritation with the blatant disregard for the patients' valuable time. To my extreme shock, she instead replies, "You are too kind, Doctor. Actually, I am Abigail's mother, Victoria. Nice to meet you." She coos as she delicately places her hand in his.

Ohhh . . . this is a development. Victoria finds Dr. K handsome. She is using her "seductive voice," if you could really call it that, reserved for men to whom she is attracted.

"The pleasure is all mine. Please, call me Dr. Kirby or Dr. K." He nods once and thankfully turns his attention back to me, the real reason we are all here today. My mother hovers next to me by the exam table rather than returning to the chair in the corner. "How are you feeling, Abby? Any cramping, bleeding, unexplained pains?"

"Nope. I feel good."

"You feel *well*, dear."

"Well. Right," I murmur, embarrassed to be corrected in front of my doctor.

"I am an English teacher," she explains to Dr. K. "I have a passion for correct grammar."

He nods once again at Victoria but for the most part ignores her statement, which secretly makes me happy.

"Any other issues you'd like to discuss?" he continues.

"No. I have some back pain if I stand for long periods of time, but that's been it."

"I see." He scribbles some notes in my chart. "You can try some nice supportive running shoes or cross trainers when you know you will be on your feet for a while. Stay away from painkillers, though. Try resting on the couch with your feet up as well. That should help with leg and back aches. Now, let's have a look at that baby."

Dr. K proceeds to go through the usual—checks measurements, presses around my abdomen, listens to the heartbeat. Victoria asks question after question. It's almost embarrassing. You'd think she'd never had a child of her own.

"What does the stomach measurement tell you?"

"Can you feel the parts of the baby when you press on the stomach like that?"

"What is a normal heartrate for a baby at this stage?"

"Can you tell the sex of the baby by its heartrate?"

"How many babies have you delivered?"

"What does your wife think about you getting called to the hospital at all hours of the day and night? She must be very understanding."

I shoot her a glare that screams *Silence!* twice, but she has her eyes trained on Dr. K. Not that she would heed my warnings even if she noticed my discontent.

After the sonogram and after Dr. K has wiped the gel from my tummy and helped me into a sitting position, the real barrage of questions begins. She launches into a line of questioning about the final weeks of pregnancy:

"When do we discuss inducing?"

"How far apart do contractions need to be before we go to the hospital?"

"What baby items do you recommend we pack in the hospital bag?"

And on and on. Dr. K patiently answers each and every one of her questions.

But with each of these latter questions, my fear grows incrementally. I can visualize her hijacking my pregnancy, taking control as she always manages to do. It's as though she's planning to be the one in the delivery room with me. She's weaseling her way in—kicking Kate to the curb. By God, I'll not let that happen. I size her up while she asks the last of her questions ("Do you have a place for the delivery coach to stay, if need be, overnight at the hospital?"). Before me is a new threat to the safe, calm, and nurturing ushering of Journey into this world. This threat must be assessed and thwarted. From this moment forward, I must be very vigilant to not let Victoria storm her way into this delivery.

"WHAT AN ENLIGHTENING day today, Abigail. I am glad I went along with you. And Dr. Kirby is very knowledgeable indeed. He answered all of my questions satisfactorily."

I stare silently forward as the taxi speeds along. Normally, I would express concern to a driver using excessive speed. Not today. Today, I can't get home fast enough. I use this time to dissect the appointment, my mother's questions, her demeanor. By the time we arrive at home, I'll know exactly what to interrogate her about. I'll get to the bottom of this and assure her that Kate will be in the delivery room—not Victoria.

As I unlock the door and we enter the apartment, she has an inkling something's up. I haven't spoken to her since we left Dr. K's office.

"Abigail, is there something you would like to say?" she asks as soon as the door closes behind her.

Is there ever.

I toss the keys on the side table in the foyer and spin around to face her, crossing my arms defiantly across my chest. Yet no words come.

"Well?" She squares her shoulders and lifts her chin fractionally, standing four feet in front of me.

"Mother," I start. Then flounder. *Come on, Abby. Come on!* She assesses me coolly. It's as if she knows what I'm about to say, and she's just waiting for me to say it so she can condescend me back into submission. *Come on, Abby.*

"Mother, what *exactly* were you doing today? Why all the questions? Why are you so concerned with the signs of delivery and what we should pack in the hospital bag? You're not thinking you'll be with me in the delivery room, are you?"

"Abigail, listen to yourself."

"Because you won't, Mother. That is reserved for Kate. That is her job alone. Do I make myself clear?"

"Abigail, I am your mother. Watch how you speak to me. And why shouldn't I be allowed to help usher in the life of my grandchild? I have experienced what you will be experiencing before."

"Because I want Kate there. It's already been decided." I punch my fists down at my sides like a disobedient child. I recognize I'm raising my voice, but I'm sorry, she's made me mad! And I am fighting for the needs of my unborn child.

"I suggest you rethink your position," she says with little emotion, in stark contrast to me. "I am already here, in this apartment, in case you do go into labor. I will be the one to accompany you to the hospital. It only makes sense for me to be in the delivery room to assist you. There is no guarantee Kate will even be able to make it to the hospital in time."

"And what if we schedule inducement? She'll have no problem being there for that," I argue.

"Maybe so. But I ask you, why does Kate have more of a claim than I do on the momentous occasion of the entry of my grandchild into the world?"

For the fact that your inflection never changes as you stand here arguing with me for one! As if you don't really care about the actual baby involved in all this. It's merely another argument for you to win. A power play. And for the fact that Kate is more a part of my family than you are! Of course, I say none of this out loud, although I scream it so loud in my head, I'm certain she can hear every word.

"I'm sorry, but this is not up for discussion," I say, trying to control my shaky voice. I am so angry with her right now. I mean, how dare she?

"This discussion is not over," she continues calmly as she walks past, watching me from the corner of her eye as she leaves me alone in the foyer, fuming.

Breathing deeply, I try to recover from the wreckage Tropical Depression Victoria leaves once again in her wake.

"ABBY, I DON'T want to be the wedge between you two."

"My mother is her own wedge."

We sit at the counter of Food for Thought on our usual stools three days after Christmas. The big rush of after-Christmas bargain shoppers has tapered off, so the store is relatively quiet this morning. Kate picked up on the tense vibe between Victoria and me during our Christmas celebration at Uncle Geoff and Simon's. Everyone picked up on it. There's an enormous iceberg between the two of us that refuses to thaw. This is fledgling ground for me, new territory. I have never before stood so openly against my mother for a cause. She doesn't know how to attack and conquer it, but I don't know how to turn the tide fully in my favor either. I don't know what argument to make to put her in her place once and for all.

"I feel horrible, just the same." Kate frowns before she takes a sip of her coffee.

"Kate, please do not waste any time feeling bad that my mother is infantile and dead set on always getting her way. I'm over it." I inhale and exhale a cathartic breath. "I am *so* over it. As you said, it's time for me to stand up for myself. And for Journey. I can't allow her toxicity to overflow into Journey's life.

"The more I think about it, the angrier I get," I continue. "This was the first appointment she went to, and already she's trying to take over. Why? Why is she so worried about being in the delivery room? I think I know why, but I'm not certain."

"Why?" she presses.

"Honestly, I think she has to control this part of my life as well," I say. There may be other motivations—there must be—but I can't put my finger on it. "I just really need you to be the one in the delivery room with me. I need your strength. Promise me you'll be there."

She reaches over and rubs my rounded belly. "You know I'll do anything you ask, Abby. Anything."

A wave of comfort washes over me with Kate's promise.

Chapter Thirty-Two

I Don't Apologize (for Once)

Ethan, 30 weeks

Journey is three pounds and almost sixteen inches long, can you believe it? And s/he can even regulate body temperature now. You're asking what that means, aren't you? Well, it means that s/he has started to lose all that lanugo downy baby hair that's made her/him all fuzzy up until now. Bet you didn't realize our baby was a big fuzz ball, did you?

So, I've read that now is the time to start thinking about banking cord blood. I really wonder what you would say about this. I think we should do it. I mean, it could provide valuable stem cells if Journey would ever—God forbid—contract a cancer. And cancer is a very touchy topic around here. I think it would be wise to reserve the cord blood. Ethan, I couldn't stand to go through what we went through a second time. And I know you would never want us to go through that if we had an option.

It's odd, but I feel an overwhelming presence of you right now. As if you're in this room. With me. I feel you as if you were lying right next to me in *this bed.*

I miss you. I love you. And I'm taking this as a sign that you agree with me on the cord blood.

Do you know how much my heart longs for you?

Tears fill my eyes as I finish the entry with my usual ♥ *A & J*. I do feel him, all around. I hope he can read my words as I've written them and know how much I miss him.

I swallow hard as I close my eyes, reveling in this feeling—this presence. I haven't seen him or heard him as I had in the first couple weeks after he died, but his presence is as strong as if he were actually next to me, his skin grazing along mine, making my hairs stand on end.

I force my eyelids open and stare at the goosebumps forming on my arm.

"I know you're here, Ethan. I love you," I whisper.

The lightest sensation of touch travels up my arm, from my hand to my shoulder. Then it disappears, leaving me aching for more.

I inhale a ragged breath. "No, don't go," I beg. But it's too late. The feeling has vanished. I search the room, hoping I'll catch sight of something to reassure me he hasn't left me again. Finding nothing, I shut my eyes tight and let the tears fall.

A knock on the door startles me.

"Abigail, shall I order dinner, or would you like to go out tonight? I could make reservations."

That has been the extent of our conversations over the past couple weeks—reservations or ordering in, items to add to the grocery list, if I want to join her shopping that day.

I clear my throat. "Um, no. No reservations. Just order whatever you want. I'll eat whatever."

I run my fingers affectionately over the Noah's ark cover of the journal. *I hope you come back and visit Journey as well,* I implore. After I compose myself, I open the drawer of my nightstand and place the journal inside.

Less than an hour later we are seated at opposite ends of the mahogany dining table. She's ordered from one of the most expensive restaurants in a four-block radius again, which is fine; that's not what's upsetting me at the moment. No, the thing that's really bothering me is the fact that she took it upon herself to unpack the fancy china. Ethan's family's china. After our ruined celebratory dinner that night, I'd packed the dishes away in the closet, angry at what his treatment put him through, but still hopeful the time would come when we would unpack the entire box together and display it in the hutch, use it all the time. Every day would have become a celebration worthy of using fancy china.

I glance across the table at her. She had to have dug pretty deep into the closet to find the box. I wonder what else she's snooped around in that she has no right to. Before I get a chance to ask, she says, "This china is lovely, Abigail. I can't fathom why you wouldn't display it in the hutch." She nods her head in its direction.

I pull the corner of my bottom lip into my teeth for a moment, then say, "It's Ethan's family's china. He wanted to keep it safe, and I respected that."

"Well..." She pauses. "I think it's time to place it in its rightful home, wouldn't you agree? China this fine should be admired. I'll see to it tomorrow. You won't need to lift a finger."

"I'm not ready to unpack his china, Mother." I feel my voice rising with my anxiety level.

She looks at me, not understanding. "Don't be silly, Abigail. It's just china."

It's just china. No, it's one more thing that belonged to my husband that you want to have control over. Anger is quelling my anxiety. One more example of how she is trying to take over my life. And it pushes me to have the conversation I've been mulling over the past few days. All these little frustrations she's made me endure. I'm always trying to keep the peace; I'm always trying to give a little grace so we can have a better relationship. It's all to my emotional detriment. And all to my mother's great, great benefit. The thing I've been trying to put my finger on is staring me in the face, and I cannot believe I've missed it until now. An intensifying strength radiates from within me.

"So, Mother," I throw at her, "I received my bank statement yesterday."

She barely pauses to acknowledge my comment before continuing to eat.

"Do you know how much money you have spent on shopping and spas and salons in the past month?" My voice is surprisingly calm and clear.

"I'm sorry, what?" She feigns confusion.

"Do you know. How much. Money of mine. You have spent. In a month?"

"I didn't realize we were keeping track. What is this, Abigail?" She tries to exert dominance in her tone and demeanor. But I won't let her bully me, not anymore.

"Did you realize you spent $31,300 and change in one month, Mother? On yourself alone. Not including Christmas presents or food or necessities." I am amazed at how matter of fact I sound.

"What are you alluding to, Abigail?"

I watch as her features turn to stone and her eyes ice over. It shouldn't surprise me after all these years, but it does stab at my heart. And confirms the suspicions that have been nagging at me for several weeks, unnamed before now.

"Why are you really here, Victoria? Be honest with me. You aren't here for the baby. You never showed up until you knew I had millions. And how joyous for you, that you finally have direct access to money. Lots and lots of money." I pause as I wait for her to deny it, to swear she is here for me, for Journey. To tell me she did not selfishly spend that much of my money—of Ethan's money, of Journey's money—on her own desires. That she isn't worming her way into our lives for the luxury she sees right within her grasp.

"How dare you accuse me of such things," she hisses.

But her eyes dart around as she tries to formulate her defense. I see it transpiring. And my resolve strengthens. Then something else grabs hold of me, a deep sadness tugging at my heart as I lay myself open to allow her to confirm the truth I fear I've always known.

"If I hadn't inherited this apartment and a business and millions of dollars, would you be here today?" I speak these words so softly she may not even hear me. That would explain why she doesn't respond. Twenty-five seconds. I count them. Twenty-five agonizing seconds.

Finally: "Abigail, how could you think that?"

"That's not an answer, Mother," I fire off.

For the first time in my life, I see her scared, like a fox in a hound hunt. Even during the worst of her fights with my drunken father, she never looked scared, only angry or condescending or smug. Her eyes are wild—bewildered. Her hands tremble against the mahogany tabletop. She swallows several times before she brings her gaze to my searing glare.

"How can you fault me for a little bit of splurging? How long have we gone without such niceties in our lives? Don't you think I deserve some reward for the years and years I sacrificed my own life, my own desires for you? I was a single parent, had next to nothing. I didn't deserve to live that way. I deserved so much more. And your father, well . . . you know how worthless your father was to us."

"And yet he managed to be a better person than you are," I offer triumphantly. I will no longer let her defile my father's name. Not now that I know the good he did for so many others. And who knows how great he may have been had he never been ensnared by Victoria all those years ago.

"I am trying to be here for you."

I pick up on the desperation in her voice. I relish the power I now hold over her. "Are you? What if I told you I really wasn't worth millions? What if I told you I was just trying to get you off my back about the whole adoption thing? That I would have to return to work soon after Journey is born to stay in positive cash flow? What then?"

"Well . . ." She is beside herself, truly flustered, trying to make sense of it all. And I love it. "Well, why didn't you say something before? Why did you give me your card every time I went out shopping? Why did you let me live high on your last dollars?"

"Mother, I thought you were here for me and for the baby. Were you not?" I twist the knife.

"I was. I am." She flattens her palms out on the table, appears to be studying her perfectly manicured fingernails. After a long moment, she raises her head, although she doesn't meet my hard stare. Her eyes fall short, focusing on the edge of the table beside me. "Perhaps I should return to my teaching career. It appears you no longer wish for my help."

My eyes, if possible, would shoot red lasers this very moment and obliterate her. *It appears you no longer wish for my help.* Did she really just say that? I never wished for her help, never wanted it!

I feel a strength I have never before experienced around Victoria. I feel . . . a freedom in her presence. It disarms me, and I admit, I'm not sure what to do. Comfort her, tell her it's okay, she can stay as long as she wants, spend as much of my money—Ethan's money—as she wants, apologize for hurting her feelings?

Or make my stand, once and for all, putting her in her place and banishing her from our lives until she learns how to be human, a member of our family?

This is what I say: "I appreciate your help, but I think it is time for you to go back to Iowa. You have overstayed your welcome in Ethan's and my home."

Slowly, painfully so, she pushes her chair away from the table and rises. She marches, shoulders squared, along the mahogany table. Pausing beside me, still staring forward, she says, "You really do not have all the money you alluded to before?"

"I do not," I say simply, watching her expression marginally change from the corner of my eye.

After a pregnant pause, she walks to her room and shuts the door. I slump in my chair at the sound, emotionally exhausted. I push my plate away, having lost my appetite.

Oddly, I am not surprised by Victoria's reaction to my confession (or lie, rather). Disappointed after the weeks we've spent together, but not surprised.

I'm not sure how much time passes, but eventually she emerges from her room. I remain at the dining table, trying to sort out my emotions. I hear the familiar click of the designer high heels she purchased the first week she arrived, hear the rolling of her luggage. She pauses, somewhere behind me.

"I guess I am off then," she says as if it were any normal day and she's leaving to go on a shopping trip or to a salon appointment.

I push up from the table, walking past her to my purse on the small table in the entryway without so much as a glance in her direction. I reach into my purse, pull out my wallet. I scribble on a check, rip it from the checkbook, toss my wallet back into the purse, and fold the check in half. I stride over to my mother.

"Thank you for coming," I say evenly as I hand her the folded check. I swallow and gather all my strength to look her in the face. "I hope, someday, you will learn how to love me for who I am. And I hope you will want to know your grandchild for the sake of knowing him or her . . . not for the promise of money. I hope I have not caused any undue hardship in your teaching career, and I hope you have a safe trip home."

She reaches out, pauses for a split second, then takes the check from my hand as if grasping a teacup rather than a piece of paper. She lifts her chin, her gaze never straying from the door beyond my shoulder. "Thank you for your hospitality."

Walking past me, she sets her bags down to open the door and exits, leaving it wide open as she proudly struts out of the apartment. I watch her go, confused by the emotions swirling around me. After what feels like an eternity, when I'm able to move again, I close the door. Still confused and conflicted, I lean against it, wondering how much time $500,000 will buy us away from the Toxic Ice Queen also known as my mother.

Chapter Thirty-Three

Who's Crashing?

"Abby, this is... I don't even know what to say. This is fantastic!" Kate exclaims. She has finished reading my book, my tribute to Ethan and our life together. "It's poignant. It's beautiful. It's... it's... I don't know how to describe how it made me feel."

"Really? Do you mean it?" Kate is the only person I've let read my final manuscript. It has taken me the better part of five months to get it just right. Such a personal journey, and she is the only person I trust to tell me whether my writing is good or not.

"It's fantastic," she repeats. "How were you able to put all this into writing?"

"It was hard. But I couldn't hold it in—it had to come out. I had to do it." I shrug, like it should make perfect sense why I put our life into a book.

"So, what are you going to do with it?"

I chew on the inside of my mouth. "Well, I was thinking... of sending it out to agencies. But what do you think?" I watch her face to see if her response matches her expression—that way I can tell if she really means what she says.

"I say go for it!" she affirms. "You can't go wrong with this."

"You really think so?"

"I know so. And I sell books for a living, girl. This is a story that needs to be told. You get those queries written, and we'll get them out in the mail."

Ethan,   37 weeks

Only three weeks to go, babe! Are you ready? I think I am! No, I am. We're doing weekly appointments now. And you know what? I'm already two centimeters dilated. Do you believe it? That freaks me out. This baby needs to stay in three more weeks, you know.

So everything was awesome with Dr. K yesterday. He pushed around on my tummy and thinks that the baby is in good position—no breach—which is very good. If he felt a breach, I'd have to go through another ultrasound to figure out the baby's position. It's hard enough to have just the right amount of a "full bladder" at twenty weeks. I can't imagine trying to do that without peeing all over the ultrasound table at thirty-seven or thirty-eight weeks!

And hey, I have something else to tell you. I haven't mentioned it before, but I'm sure you already know. How could you not know? I wrote a book. About me, about us, about our journey together. I sent out queries to agencies. Lots of queries, actually. And amazingly, I got some responses. Mostly negative. Thank you but no thank you. But...guess what? I got requests for the first chapters from three agencies! So, Kate and I are going to the post office to send them off tomorrow.

She thinks my writing is good, just like you thought. How great would it be if I could become the writer you always said I could be?

You always believed in me. I love you for that. Among many other things.

❤ A & J

"HOW EXCITING IS this?"

Kate and I have just dropped the last of three packages of my first four chapters in the mail to agencies. It is an unseasonably warm February day, so we decided to get some fresh air and walked directly to the closest post office to make sure we had the proper packaging and postage. Can't have improper postage getting in the way of my dream, right?

She loops her arm through mine as we head to Food for Thought. We plan to pick up West so we can all go out for a celebratory lunch (Kate's suggestion) to honor me and my endeavor into the world of published writing. I asked her not to make a big deal of it—I haven't even gained representation yet—but of course she refused. This *is* a big deal, she insisted. Most writers never even get past the query stage. That knowledge made me hopeful, so I caved and agreed to a small lunch celebration. Just me, her, and West.

"You know, this really is exciting," I acknowledge. "Is this how you felt when you landed your first art show?"

"Oh, yes. The thrill of your dream coming true, knowing that so many people will get to view your creations. The nervousness that follows, wondering if people will like your work. I remember it all like it was yesterday."

"Well, I am so glad you're here to share this with me, Kate." My eyes flutter and I shake my head slightly. "If only I could get rid of this headache I've had for the past two days. I thought once I was rid of Victoria, the rest of this pregnancy would be stress-free," I chuckle good-naturedly, even though it hurts my head to do so.

"Abby, you don't have to do this lunch if you don't want to," she offers. "We should get you home to rest."

"No, no. It's fine. I *do* want to. I love spending time with you guys. I just wish I didn't have to deal with the aches and swollen cankles. Even my wrists seem to be swelling today. It's awful." I offer up my swollen wrist for Kate to observe. "Ooh, that's weird."

"What? What's weird?" Kate stops us on the sidewalk a few feet from the crosswalk. I feel her arm squeeze around mine.

"Oh, nothing. It's just—well, my eyesight went blurry. That little white walking guy on the sign turned into two and then one and then became a fuzzy mass of white." I feel her grip tighten even more. "Just hang on a second," I try to reassure her. "I'm fine, really, I am." I blink my eyelids a few times, tilt my head, thinking that will solve my vision problems.

"Better?" she asks, concern thick in her voice.

"Umm . . ." A sudden anxiousness overwhelms me. Then the tiredness I felt earlier today comes back in force.

"Abby, are you okay?"

"I just . . . need to sit down for a minute, I think."

Am I okay? Everything is swirling around me. My heart is racing. My ears go closed, and I can no longer hear Kate. Panic washes over me as I look over to her face—she's still next to me, right?

"Abby! Abby!"

I see, rather than hear her yell. Why can't I hear her?

And then I can no longer see her. The sky—blue sky above me with bits of green tree and brown and gray building swirling around the edges. There's Kate's face. Why does it seem like she is above me? Swirling with the sky and the buildings. I need to make her stop swirling. I focus on that. My pulse pounds loudly in my ears; it's all I can hear. And I'm tired. So tired. Maybe I'll just take a nap for a bit. But who's shaking me? Kate?

I give in to the tiredness and close my eyes. I'll rest for a bit, then I'll be fine.

THE SOUND OF screaming sirens awakens me. I force my eyelids open to find I'm in an unfamiliar place. Am I dreaming? There's Kate. I want to ask her why she looks so afraid, but my mouth won't move. And things are still a little blurry.

There is another person above me, with an oxygen mask in their hands. *Stop, I can't talk if you do that.* I want to push the mask away, but my arms won't move.

It's really bright in here, but I don't see any windows. I try to reach out to Kate; I'm so tired. I let my eyes drift closed.

Sometime later, I don't know how long, I force my eyes open. It takes all my strength. Sometimes I hear Kate's voice over the pulsing in my ears. It is so cold; a breeze is blowing over me. Why won't they cover me up? There's the medic over me, replaced by someone in scrubs, pushing the gurney feet first through a set of doors and then another set of doors. There's Kate, beside me. She looks like she's running.

Wait.

Wait!

I reach out for her hand but grasp only air as I watch her get pushed back by someone else in scrubs. *Kate! You have to be here with me!*

For a brief moment, I fear my mother is behind this. As they push me through another set of doors, I expect Victoria to appear on the other side, a triumphant smirk on her face. My eyes dart around, searching. But no, she's not here. I still feel this awful anxiousness. Something is not right. It's hard to keep my eyelids open for any length of time. They wheel me into a room; the room spins as the gurney is swiveled around. *People—I'm already dizzy,* I want to say, but I have this mask over my mouth and nose.

"Abigail? Dr. Beckman is on his way, but we have to get this baby out as soon as possible. Can you hear me?"

My eyes flash open at these words. I try to focus on who they came from. There are so many blue figures flocking around me, moving this way and that. I can't tell who is talking. They said Dr. Beckman . . .

Dr. K? No! It's too soon. Kate could tell them this. *Where is Kate?*

"Kaa . . ." I try under my oxygen mask. "Kaa . . ."

"We're here to help you, Abigail. Don't worry." The woman's voice is a muffled, foreign sound to me.

There is a flutter of blue around me as I'm lifted up and placed on a different hospital bed. Or is it a table? I am jostled about. My head really hurts, more than before, and the pulsing in my ears is overwhelming.

"We need to get your baby out now, Abigail. We're going to sedate you."

What? No! I try to shake my head violently, but it only lolls from side to side. They remove the oxygen mask and replace it with another mask. I struggle to keep my face free. *No! It's too early!*

Despite the adrenaline rushing through my body, my eyelids feel like lead. I try. I try, Journey, but I can no longer keep them open. The faces around me fade into whiteness as I attempt to focus on something—the holes in the ceiling tile above me, the flickering fluorescent light. My heart pounds viciously against my chest. I want to cry, but I'm too tired.

"She's crashing!" I hear, even in my dreamy state with my eyes closed. Who's crashing?

Who's crashing?!

Chapter Thirty-Four

I Love You More. Always.

I SEE MYSELF on the bed before me, pale and limp. A nurse hovers, pushing a rhythm on my chest.

"We've got to keep her going if this baby is going to have any chance." The doctor calls out directives, scalpel in hand, ready to slice into my naked belly. I cannot watch what comes next.

I spin around, and my heart stops. Literally stops.

"Ethan!" I gasp. Tears spring to my eyes.

"Abby, my Abby," he says as he comes toward me, arms wide open.

"Ethan! You *are* here for me!" I fall into his embrace, which feels as glorious as I remember. He wraps his strong arms around me.

"Yes. I am here for you." He nuzzles his face into my hair.

Around the pure joy, fear sneaks in that if I let go, he will disappear. I cling tighter to him. When I feel him pulling away, I grasp onto his arms so he cannot disentangle from me. To my relief, he keeps his hands on my waist.

"I just . . . I can't believe you're here." I hungrily take him in from head to toe. He looks beautiful, his hair at its wavy best, his eyes clear blue and glowing bright, his smile—his smile still takes my breath away. This is the Ethan of my memories, the Ethan I met at the bookstore just a few short years ago.

We kiss. A sweet, longing kiss. His full lips are as delicious as ever. How I have missed this man! I'm vaguely aware of a stray tear trickling down my cheek. As we separate, he frowns at the tear and reaches up to swipe it away with his thumb.

"No. I'm happy. So happy," I assure him.

So many emotions swarm around and through me. I *am* overjoyed to see him, to touch him, to kiss him. I feel desire coursing in my veins, heating my blood. But there's something else . . . a sadness? I search his beautiful eyes, confusion filling my own.

"You have no idea how amazing it is to be able to hold you again," he murmurs.

I give him a *You're kidding me, right?* look.

"Okay, maybe you do," he chuckles. That soft, never-forgotten, heavenly sound of his laughter.

I stare deeply into his blue eyes, recommitting them to my memory. "It's been . . . so hard without you." My throat constricts, but I fight back the emotion. I must tell him how I feel now that I have one more chance to do so. "I feel like you've missed out on the best time of our lives. You should have been there with me at the first appointment when I heard Journey's heartbeat, at the ultrasound when I saw Journey's little hands and feet, when I first felt a kick in my belly—these are all things I wanted to share with you."

"But Abby," Ethan says as he smooths my hair, "I was with you through it all. I will never leave you, could never leave you. And those times—the ones when you say out loud that you feel me with you—those are the absolute best moments. It makes me so happy to know you want to include me in those magic moments. And, by the way, I am so proud that you're writing."

"You were my inspiration," I say simply.

I rest my head on his chest, revel in the safety of his strong arms around me. I inhale the heady scent of my Ethan, the scent I've lost on his pillow and his favorite sweater. "Don't leave me again," I whisper.

"But Abby, you can't come with me," he protests.

"What? No, you can't leave me! I can't handle losing you again, not now that I have you in my arms." I frantically search his eyes, looking for some sign that he's here to stay. But all I see is apology. Sadness. Grief.

"Abby, look." His misty eyes dart from mine, over my shoulder. What has caught his attention?

I hear before I see. A loud wailing sound. Crying. I turn swiftly toward it.

We stand frozen, Ethan's arms wrapped tightly around me, and I lean, overwhelmed, into his chest for support, resting my head against him.

"Just look at that, Abby," he says in awe.

"Our baby," I sob.

And at once I understand the sadness I was feeling before; I recognize its place here. I cannot have them both, my Journey and my Ethan.

We watch as the flurry of blue moves deftly around the room. Some of them take Journey over to wash and swaddle and make sure all is well. I smile as I count ten fingers and ten toes. The others hover over my body, lying lifeless and unnaturally pale.

I feel a sharp pain in my chest, different from before, when I was wheeled into the hospital. It's as though my heart is being ripped in two. I look back over at Journey, such a precious baby . . . boy. A boy!

I triumphantly swivel around to Ethan. "It's a boy!" But the pain in my chest deepens, chokes me, as he steps backward. I cling to his hand, my nails digging in. Where is he going? I panic as I search his face for an answer.

"A boy . . . so precious," he whispers. The pain I feel searing through me is etched all over his face. "I am so happy I got to share this moment with you, Abby. You just remember that I am always with you. Can you do that?" A bittersweet smile curls his lips.

"No, Ethan, don't go. I want to go with you! I need to be with you!" Desperation colors my voice.

"I want nothing more than to take you with me, you must know that. But your place is here. You have to take care of our Journey. It's up to you."

He reaches up, squeezes my shoulder, but he's standing so far away now. I press his hand down on my shoulder, willing him to never loosen his hold.

"You have to decide," he whispers. "It's up to you." The wistfulness in his eyes is mixed with hope, hope that I will make the right decision. "Just know that I love you more. Always."

The pain in my chest burns, bringing fresh tears to my eyes. I look over my shoulder at the beautiful, perfect baby being swaddled in a blanket patterned with colorful rattles and teddy bears. Then I allow my gaze to drift to the lifeless body surrounded by nearly half a dozen nurses and the doctor, trying to put me back together again.

"She's lost a lot of blood."

"Let's get her closed up. Call for O negative. Two pints. Make it three."

"I can't get a pulse."

"Come on, people. Let's give this woman a chance to hold her baby."

Somehow, amongst the confusion, I've lost my grip on Ethan's hand. "Ethan?" I call desperately, but I find that I am drawn to the table before me. I want to see my face on the other side of the nurses, to confirm that it is, in fact, me. I glance quickly behind. I can barely see him now. I call to him again. He's saying something...

The crying of the baby drowns him out.

Our baby.

Our Journey.

Chapter Thirty-Five

Just When You Think Your Journey Is Over . . .

MY EYELIDS FLUTTER before finally squinting open. It takes a few moments for me to focus, to recognize where I am. The white dotted mass above me—the ceiling. And the fluorescent lights I remember seeing last.

I blink. Knowledge slowly dawns. Ethan . . . he's gone. He's left me. But—I'm here. Right?

I slowly lift my hand, stare at it as I force my fingers to splay, wiggle. *Yes, I'm still here.* I feel heavy though, tired, as if I've been run over by a truck. I wince as pain floods my awakened senses. Pain in my abdomen, pain in my heart. My breath hitches in my chest, a tear tumbles down to the pillow. *Oh, Ethan . . .*

It's as though he's been ripped from my grasp all over again. The unfairness tears at my soul. And yet . . . I know something amazing—no, miraculous—has happened here. Ethan was somehow able to be with me during Journey's birth. He was here with me, held me. That was no figment of my imagination. It couldn't have been.

Fear rises up—pushing past the pain, the heartache—as I realize I almost died. But I am comforted by the fact that Ethan came to me when I needed him the most. He held me, protected me, and sent me back to Journey. He got me through this.

I send up silent thanks to him and to God for allowing him to be here for me, for us.

"There she is," a familiar voice draws my attention. I quickly wipe my hand across my face.

"Dr. K." I swallow, but my mouth feels like cottonwood.

"Abby, that was quite a scare you gave us all. But by the time I arrived, Dr. Singh had everything under control. She provided excellent care."

"What—" I swallow hard again, unable to get past this parched feeling. "What happened?"

"You experienced a severe case of preeclampsia, Abby. Basically, high blood pressure. Your body reacted negatively to your pregnancy. It can happen in the latter stages of gestation, or even after the birth of the child. We will monitor you closely to ensure you're back to normal before we discharge you. I imagine you feel much better after delivery, though?"

"Umm . . . yes. I guess I do feel better." I struggle to remember the events that put me in this hospital room. The constant headache, the blurry vision, the nausea, the anxious feeling something bad was going to happen.

"Can you tell me exactly how you were feeling before they brought you in? Do you recall?" Dr. K sits on the edge of my bed. He places his hand on mine. This calms me a bit, as the memories of what happened have made me very uneasy. I try to explain to him what I remember, everything up to the moment they pushed Kate back and sent me through the double doors alone . . .

Kate. Is she still waiting out there to see how I am? Is she holding the baby for me right now? I wonder how much time has passed since they took Journey.

"You have been resting for some time now," Dr. K answers my unspoken question. "Your body has been trying to heal itself."

"How long?"

"You delivered yesterday morning." At my confused stare, he adds, "It's three o'clock in the afternoon."

My eyebrows shoot up in worry. Where is Journey? Who's caring for him? I try to sit up, but the pain in my abdomen sends me weakly back onto the bed.

"Relax, now. Just relax. Everything is fine. Your baby is well cared for. The nursing staff has been watching over him until you are able. So don't worry. The important thing is that you focus on getting yourself better."

I breathe a sigh of relief. "When can I see him?"

"Soon. Let's finish here. Then I'll let the nurses know they can bring him in, all right?"

I nod, finally letting the realization that I am okay—and that Journey is okay—sink in.

"OH MY GOODNESS! You gave me such a scare!" Kate says as she and West enter the birthing suite I was moved to. I glance up from the perfect face of my baby and smile. With Kate and West here, and Journey in my arms, I feel the world is right again. "Geoffrey and Simon are on their way, too. I called them as soon as the doctor told us you'd woken up."

Honestly, I don't know how long I've had Journey in my arms. I can't get enough of his tiny perfect face and his tiny little hands and his tiny button nose. I tear my gaze from my baby to meet Kate's hazel eyes, wide with wonder at the little miracle in my arms. "Thank you, Kate. Meet Journey Ethan Lansing," I announce.

"So precious!" she murmurs, taking one of Journey's hands in her own.

"Oh, now I suppose you want one of those, too!" West rolls his eyes. "Thanks, Abby."

"I'm too enthralled by this little creature to let your remarks bother me today, honey," Kate says sweetly, not taking her eyes off the baby.

"I'm so sorry, Kate," I apologize for my episode yesterday morning and how awful it must have been for her to witness. "I had—"

"Oh, stop! Stop. You are safe now, and the baby is safe. All is well, yes?"

"Yes. I guess it is." I smile up at my friends. I press my finger into Journey's other tiny palm. His hand reflexively closes around it. I watch his tiny lips purse and make a sucking movement.

"I'm just . . . I'm so sorry I couldn't be with you when you needed me. I should have been here with you." West puts his hand on Kate's shoulder. She's about to get all emotional; I see it coming.

"Oh, Kate, no. Don't worry about that. You know we had no control over it. Not with the situation."

I can tell she's not convinced. She feels like she's failed me because she was supposed to be my person. She's biting her lip, her eyes watering.

"Besides," I inhale deeply and exhale slowly, wondering if I should say what I'm about to say, wondering if they'll think I'm crazy. "Besides . . . Ethan was here with me. He got me through it all."

I see shock register on her face and confusion on West's. I glance down at my miracle baby, marveling at his perfection, before I look purposefully into Kate's eyes. "It was meant to be. I believe that. I might have died had he not been there to guide me, to show me what was worth staying for. But really, what we experienced together was amazing. We saw Journey come into the world side by side. He was here with me, and he gently pushed me back."

Neither of my friends seems to know what to say. And if I hadn't experienced it all firsthand, I would probably have the same reaction. But I was there. I lived it.

And I will never be the same.

Kate reaches out and clasps my hand in hers. Her eyes tell me what her mouth cannot: She believes me. Her hand drifts up to Journey's fuzzy, hat-covered head. I smile at her. She smiles through the tears in her eyes.

"Where is that precious little baby?" Simon calls out as he enters the room surrounded by an armful of balloons and a bouquet of flowers, followed closely behind by Uncle Geoff toting several gift bags. My heart sings; my family complete, here now to greet Journey.

I STARE AT the blank notecard on the table in front of me, unsure of what to write. Or if I should write anything at all.

I rest my pen on the table for the third time and pick up the note from Victoria. The one that came with the baby gifts she sent. *I look forward to meeting my precious grandbaby.* That's all it says. And no matter how many times I reread it, I cannot figure out what she's saying between the lines. Because why would Victoria ever write something so simply . . . *nice*? Without calculated pretense?

It is now four weeks past Journey's due date of March 11. I haven't been in contact with Victoria since she left—or rather I kicked her out—in January. The peacefulness around here has been heavenly, and now that Journey is filling the empty spaces with his smiles and his little noises, it's hard to remember the loneliness and darkness that fell like a blanket over our home before, stifling everything that was good, everything that was Ethan. I glance over at Journey sleeping soundly in his pack and play, wearing a blue and green dinosaur shirt with matching bottoms. A gift from Victoria. Actually, one of two gifts from her. The other was a frilly yellow dress, bedazzled with rhinestones. She had no way of knowing whether I had a boy or girl. No way of knowing I'd even had the baby at all . . .

I set her note on the table and lift my pen once more. This may be the single most important communication I ever have with my mother. Of course, I should acknowledge her gifts and offer my thanks. I should let her know who her grandchild is. However, I do not want to encourage, on any level, contact from her.

It's just too soon.

Maybe someday. If I do allow her back into our lives, it will be on my terms. And I will protect Journey from her harshness and her unkindness. I will be vigilant with her words, and at the first sign of anything off-color, that will be it. No more.

I inhale deeply and close my eyes for a moment, visualizing my thoughts into words. This is what I write:

Thank you for the baby clothes. Journey Ethan Lansing was born on February 18, 2012, at 11:04 a.m., weighing in at 5 lbs. 10 oz.

Just enough information, nothing more. I chew on my lip as I consider one more thing. In the end, I go ahead and place it in the card—a picture of Journey I took last week in the very same dinosaur outfit he wears today. She'll see it as a positive sign that I've accepted her gift—for a boy. And that's okay. More than ever before in my life, I know that I hold the power in this relationship. It's not satisfying—it's just good to know finally, for once, that I have the power.

"WELCOME TO FOOD for Thought. I'm Abby. I'll be your server today. What can I get you?"

"Well, I'll take . . . I'll take—" The customer is distracted. I glance down and chuckle silently. "What a precious little thing," she says.

"Yes, isn't he?" I kiss Journey's curly-haired head as he coos at the patron from his baby carrier.

"He is," she confirms. "How old?"

"Four months," I say proudly.

I have—well, Journey and I have been back to work for almost two months now. After my first eight weeks of recovery and Mommy Time with him, I recognized I was still missing something, still craved something.

I realized it was my family, Kate and West, and a connection with people. People who love books as I love them. People I used to associate with regularly. I really did miss the bookstore. So I returned, Journey in tow. And I was relieved we were met with open arms. Not only were Kate and West—and Josh—happy to have us, but regular customers I hadn't seen for months were thrilled I had returned. Some even got a little choked up to see Journey—those who had known Ethan well.

And so we fell into a new routine, Journey and I, of working at Food for Thought either on the floor like today or on marketing or bookkeeping with West in the back.

"So precious," the patron at table seven repeats. "Oh, um . . ." She looks at her book menu, remembering why she's here. "I'll try Ethan's Favorite: *At Journey's End*."

"A Carson Ripley novel. Excellent choice," I offer before I turn and head to the bookshelf to retrieve it.

Yes, we kept Ethan's Favorites on the menu. We still have West's Favorites. And we've added Josh, Kate, and Abby's Favorites as well.

I grin as I pluck the Carson Ripley novel from the shelf that began Ethan's and my love story. It is so hard for me to comprehend just how much has happened since the day he recommended this very book to me. Journey reaches out and grabs at the book with a slobbery hand as I hold it out before us. I giggle and squeeze his hand.

Someday... someday he will be old enough to read the book I've written about his father and mother. And even before then, I may read it aloud to him. I will definitely do that. Over and over again.

We hand off the novel to the woman at table seven and head over to the counter. I need to get the display of Carson Ripley's latest novel up and ready before Kate arrives to critique it—and ultimately rearrange it. But she has the artist's eye, and I don't, so I guess I'll let her rearrange it without begrudging her.

I take Journey from the baby carrier and place him in the playpen behind the counter with his soft toys. I remove the carrier and shove it under the counter next to his diaper bag and listen to him babble at his toys as I unpack and arrange the books.

"Glad to have you back, by the way. So I don't have to deal with Kate's complaining about how I set up the displays," Josh says with a wink as he walks past me toward a customer at the register.

I smile as I acknowledge how glad I am to be back, too. This really is my home. And now it will be Journey's as well. I glance down at him to see he's given in to a nap, suckling his thumb in his mouth.

I carefully place the final book just so, then I hear Kate: "Wait. Wait. Let me have a look at that."

"Hi, Kate," I say as she gives me a hug.

"Hey, hon. You've been busy today." She surveys my display as she rests her arm around my shoulders. "Hmm. Looks pretty good."

"Thanks." I beam. "Hey, did you find out when your show opens?" Her next art show has been in the works for a couple months now. The pictures she took chronicling my pregnancy were a huge hit at the gallery, and they have decided to have a show based around them. She really put together an amazing collection. It will be nice to see another Kate Saunders art show. She's in her element in the gallery, and it has been months since her last show. Guiltily, I worry my issues have not allowed her the time necessary to step away from the bookstore and focus on her passion. She'll swear it's not true, and I do feel a bit of redemption in the fact that it's thanks to my pregnancy that she landed this next show.

"Two weeks! And I cannot wait! You have to be at opening night. Promise you will be there."

"I'm sure I can get a sitter for Journey for the night."

"Oh, no you don't. You *must* bring my little muse along with you. Without him, I would have no show!"

"Without him, you would still have a show, believe me. You would just have a different subject. You have so many ideas, Kate, I know you would have landed another show," I say admiringly.

"You are too kind. But I'm serious about you bringing him. Or have the sitter come along to help. Everyone would love to see the inspiration for my artwork. Mother *and* baby."

As if Journey knows we're talking about him, he awakens, fussing for me. I strap on the baby carrier, lift him up, and tuck him in. He quiets as his attention is taken by Kate's face, smiling and winking at him.

"All right, then. It's a date. Now, not to steal your thunder, but I have something of my own to share." As I bend down to grab my purse below the counter, I catch sight of her reaching out to move some books around on my display.

"Quit that!" I chide.

"Sorry. I'm just—"

She tries to explain herself as she shuffles two more books on the display.

"Quit! It!" I playfully smack at her hands. "I worked hard on this."

"Sorry," she repeats, her eyes still critiquing the books.

"I have," I begin, waving an envelope in front of me, "another response. I haven't opened it yet."

My stomach knots with anticipation. Not just another response. The *last* response. My first response of the three was, "We're not interested at this time." The second and third gave me hope—both agents requested a full copy of my manuscript. But after that submission and weeks of waiting, one of the agents sent me a response similar to the first: "Thank you for your submission. However, we do not feel you are a fit for our group at this time. Blah. Blah. Blah."

Two more weeks had passed, and I was beginning to doubt my writing ability, wondering if I should do another rewrite. Then, just as I'd almost given up hope, I received the final letter yesterday. I held it in my hands. I stared at it on my coffee table for half the evening. I held it some more, hoping to gain insight into its contents without having to open it. Finally, I shoved it into my handbag so I could try to stop obsessing over it. I knew I would have to wait to open it with Kate, for support. And it was time to bathe Journey and have our daily tummy time. So, I had to get my mind off that letter until I could meet up with her. She would open it for me (as she has every time). And she would read it for me, with the appropriate inflection at the words, "Thank you, but no thank you."

Today would be different, however. It has to be. Journey and I already agreed this letter is different when we discussed it over a bowl of his rice cereal this morning. He babbled so optimistically between bites, on and on about anything and everything—pointing to the letter sticking up out of my handbag like he knew exactly what it was. So I know this one is different.

Maybe.

"Kate," I breathe. "This is it." I shake my head and close my eyes tight. I hold the envelope out toward her.

She snatches it from my hand. My eyes fly open.

"Abby," she says as she holds it between her palms in a prayer position. "Are you sure . . . you want me to open this?"

"Yes?" I look at her through one open eyelid. Her eyebrows lift in response, questioning me.

"Yes," I say firmly as I open both eyes and nod. "Yes."

"Okay then."

I'm not sure whose hands are shaking more, mine or hers. Journey starts babbling away and flailing his arms. I grasp his tiny hands in mine and purse my lips on the top of his head. He still smells deliciously of lavender baby soap from last night's bath.

Kate rips open the envelope. She pulls out the letter and reads it silently to herself.

"What? What does it say?" I press. I cannot tell from her expression or her quickly moving lips what it says. It's killing me. I let go of Journey's hands as I realize I may be squeezing them too tightly.

"It says . . ." She raises her hazel eyes slowly from the letter to my anxious stare. "It says, 'Your writing is profound and original. Your story is one that needs to be told. You have real potential. I would like to meet with you to discuss. Please contact my assistant to arrange the details.'"

"Whaaaat?" I screech as I dance on my tiptoes. Kate mirrors my reaction. "I have potential? Call my assistant? Meet with me? *Seriously?*" I stop abruptly. "You're not joking with me, are you?"

"No, Abby. No! They really want to meet with you!" She holds up the letter for me to inspect.

They really do. I hug Journey to me and enjoy this thrill of emotions—happiness, excitement, pride—as they wash over me.

It's happening. It's really happening.

I look up, hoping Ethan is watching us now. Without him, none of this would be possible. Because of him, I may be a writer, I *am* a mother, and I have a loving family surrounding Journey and me to boot, a family I never would have known had it not been for him.

Is my journey over? Certainly not. Has it just begun? No. Does it continue? Every day. And I have never before been so excited to see what each new day brings for my Journey and me.

Epilogue

"'I STARTED OUT in this world alone, scared, unsure about what real love was. I couldn't say that I had ever experienced it. Not until him. Once he entered my life, everything changed. With him, I learned the meaning of true love. I learned the meaning of unconditional. We faced the struggle, the strife, the worst in life, and our love only grew stronger.

"'It was during this time that I gained a true understanding of family. How it's not just about blood. In fact, blood may have nothing to do with it at all. Instead, it has so much more to do with the bond, the feelings of protectiveness, of love, of selflessness in relation to those you consider your family. Those who surround you not only in the easy, joyful times, but in your time of need, who are there to support and love you with no strings attached. Those who tie themselves to you unconditionally, who are there for you no matter what, without passing judgment. That is your family.

"'Ethan became my family, my champion, but he brought a much larger network along with him to show me what I was lacking in my life up to that point. People who were in my corner for no other reason than because I was me. They wanted nothing from me, saddled none of their baggage or expectations on me, loved me unconditionally. For that, I am so grateful. I could not have survived the journey I share with you in the chapters ahead without Ethan and without this family I now call my own: Uncle Geoffrey, Simon, West, and Kate.'"

I look up at that moment and take in the enthralled audience before me. It never ceases to amaze, even after dozens of book readings, how an audience can be captivated by my writing. Journey and I have traveled across the country on my book tour, finishing (fittingly) at our home: Food for Thought. The crowd is full of familiar faces, supportive faces, and family.

I survey the roomful of people to find Kate and West, Uncle Geoff and Simon, and Journey at a table near the back of the audience. The gratitude I feel for that table of people is overwhelming. Who would have ever thought eight years ago, as I fled my suffocating and toxic life in Iowa, that this is where I would end up? Who would have thought that these souls would become my true family, would complete my life in such a magnificent fashion? Certainly not me.

I finish reading my excerpt, then I answer questions from the audience before I head over to sign books. And by the way, who would have thought my signature would ever be asked for in a book, in *my* book? Ethan might have imagined such, but not me.

When the book signing is finally done, I rejoin the table of my family. Journey, now inching closer to a year and a half old, is happily playing with a toy on Uncle Geoff's lap.

"You looked like a natural up there, Abby," Kate says.

"Yes. We are so proud of you, darling. And you look so grown up and professional in your dress suit." Simon reaches out and squeezes my hand.

I grin, relishing the little bit of pride I feel as well. "It feels so good. It really does. I still can't believe people show up to see me, though."

"I can," Uncle Geoff chimes in. "Your story is inspiring, and the way you tell it, eloquent. Ethan is smiling down on you—I'm certain of it."

"Well, he deserves the true credit. Without his confidence and encouragement in my writing, I may not have ever written it. I just wanted the world to know his courage and selflessness as I did. I wanted to share his inspiration amid our struggles and his amazing insight about life."

"And now they do," Kate assures me. "Hearing some of the comments here today, how your story has impacted people . . . they get it."

"What I want to know is," West begins, looking at me with an interrogating eye, "are you going to be a One-Book Wonder? Or will we need to create an Abigail Lansing section here in the store for all your books?"

I laugh, not so much at the question of whether I can write more to match the success of this, but because West has actually hit on a question I've asked myself more than once in the past couple months. Can I follow up the success of a best-selling book? Do I have the real ability? I know Ethan would tell me I do. I'll just have to go for it. I'll never know if I don't try. He taught me that—to push my fears aside and go after what I want, not let anything hold me back.

I shake my finger at West. "Well, sir, I guess I'll have to talk to the management around here to see if they can cope with me not being around much to help. Any insight into what they'll say?"

He crosses his arms and rubs his scruffy chin with his thumb and forefinger, knitting his brow as if contemplating my question.

"I *know* they'll be all for it," Kate announces as she throws a light punch into West's upper arm, knocking his hand out from under his chin.

"Hey! What was that for?" He feigns injury and rubs his shoulder.

"You're such a goober!" She shakes her head as she looks at me. "You have real talent, Abby, and nothing, and *no one*—" she pauses and looks pointedly at West "—should stop you from pursuing your dreams."

"Amen to that," Simon proclaims.

"I am so lucky to have you all in my life. Journey's too." I lift Journey into my arms. He is getting so heavy now; I kiss his wavy, honey-colored curls and stare into his beautiful blue eyes. He is the portrait of his father I had hoped he would be. "You have no idea. I would be so lost without you in our lives. You truly are our family. Thank you . . . for everything."

Uncle Geoff stands and pulls us into a hug. "It is we who are lucky to have you, my dear. Never forget that."

Tears spring to my eyes as everyone takes their turn embracing us: Simon, Kate, even West. Tears of joy, tears of love, tears of thankfulness.

As West and Kate start the process of closing the store later that evening, I leave them and head home with Journey, thinking about the journal entry I will be writing to Ethan tonight. Such a fantastic day I've had with our family. Such an uplifting day. I want to share it all with him.

I gaze up at the deepening blue New York sky above, holding our boy close to my chest. The warm early summer evening is the perfect ending to a perfect day. As Journey lets his tired head rest on my shoulder, I let my mind wander into the future. I picture the many times he and I will make this same walk from Food for Thought to our home over the coming years. I imagine the store will be as important a part of his life as it has been for me. I see him skipping alongside me, his little hand clasping mine. I see him walking next to me, standing taller than my waist. His unruly hair, so much like his father's, blowing in the breeze. I see the time that will come when he'll think he's too old to let Mom hold his hand anymore when we walk. I smile at the image.

I can wait for all those times; I will enjoy every day we have together as we continue *our journey*. What I'm having a hard time waiting for is the day when Journey will be old enough to understand the stories I tell him about his father, to recognize the man his father was. But until that day, I'll keep on talking about Ethan, reading the baby journal to him, showing him Ethan's pictures, and reading our story to him.

And I'll teach him to feel those moments when his father is here with us, showing us he is all around.

I imagine Ethan is here with us now, as I feel his presence. He walks beside me, almost touching my arm. I drop my left hand down to my side and enjoy the feeling of his hand slipping into mine.

"All of this . . . is because of you," I whisper. "And I thank you."

Acknowledgements

First and foremost, thank you to my family and friends who have supported me on this journey. Those of you who encouraged me even when doubts plagued my thoughts and slowed my progress on this path.

Thank you to the beta readers willing to take a chance on reading my work. From my first readers, my mother Linda, sister Dulcie, bestie Kippen, to my readers that recently hopped on board the journey, Amanda J and Susan P, and my daughters Cassidy and Cailie, who are now old enough to read this novel. Your insights and feedback have been tremendous in helping me to craft this story into what it is now.

I would also like to thank my editor, Sarah Purdy, and the group at The Write Place, Inc. I first became acquainted with Sarah when I entered an early version of this story to the 2018 Write Place Book Contest. While it wasn't the right time for *A Journey to My Life* to breathe in the open air, when I felt it was time, I returned to Sarah to help me professionally edit my baby. Her editing skills, knowledge, and guidance through the process of publishing my debut novel have been priceless.

Lastly, I want to thank you, Dear Reader, for taking a chance on this story and embarking on the journey with me. I hope to see you again and again as we share our love of the worlds created through storytelling, the lessons and the hope that can be conveyed through books.

Milton Keynes UK
Ingram Content Group UK Ltd.
UKHW041954291124
451915UK00001B/192